Glittering parties, scandalous liaisons,
passionate encounters…

High-Society
Affairs

They're the talk of the Ton!

The EnigmaticRake
by Anne O'Brien

&

The Lord and the Mystery Lady
by Georgina Devon

Regency

High Society Affairs

Regency

HIGH-SOCIETY AFFAIRS

Anne O'Brien &
Georgina Devon

M&B

M&B™ and M&B™ with the Rose Device
are trademarks of the publisher.
Harlequin Mills & Boon Limited, Eton House,
18-24 Paradise Road, Richmond, Surrey TW9 1SR

First published in Great Britain in 2006 and 2003

REGENCY HIGH-SOCIETY AFFAIRS
© Harlequin Books S.A. 2010

The publisher acknowledges the copyright holders of the individual works as follows:

The Enigmatic Rake © Anne O'Brien 2006
The Lord and the Mystery Lady © Alison J. Hentges 2003

ISBN: 978 0 263 86876 0

052-0110

Printed and bound in Spain
by Litografia Rosés S.A., Barcelona

The Enigmatic Rake

by

Anne O'Brien

Anne O'Brien was born and has lived for most of her life in Yorkshire. There she taught history before deciding to fulfil a lifetime ambition to write romantic historical fiction. She won a number of short story competitions until published for the first time by Mills & Boon. As well as writing, she finds time to enjoy gardening, cooking and watercolour painting. She now lives with her husband in an eighteenth-century cottage in the depths of the Welsh Marches. You can find out about Anne's books and more at her website: www.anneobrien.co.uk

Chapter One

❧

Autumn 1819—Paris

This wing of the vast house was silent, the windows and the rooms behind them unlit with curtains securely drawn, the garden beyond dark and shadowed. Sounds of distant merriment drifted on the mild air, of music, laughter, the hum of a large gathering, but here there was nothing to disturb the midnight stillness. With its towers and turrets, gravelled drive and formal gardens, it was a formidable château on the very edge of Paris, the home of the Comte and Comtesse de Charleroi, where a celebration was being hosted for the forthcoming marriage of the heir. An event of notable interest and comment to the blue and noble blood of the Parisian *beau monde*. But here on a stone-flagged terrace of the west wing, overlooking a rigidly ornamental parterre, the felicitous event played no part in anyone's mind.

The terrace was not as deserted as it might first appear. A dark figure merged into the inky shadow of the house where the twisted stem of a wisteria hugged, then overhung the wall to give protection. Beyond the fact that it was a man, tall and broad-shouldered, a solid outline, no other detail could be ascertained. Dark clothes allowed him to blend with the background and he was careful to keep the pale skin of hands and face from attracting any stray glimmer from a fitful moon. He wished to be neither seen nor identified. He was waiting. Unmoving, breathing silent and shallow. Waiting.

At last a noise. A careless scrape of a footstep on stone. Two figures emerged as darker shapes against the dark surround—one from the corner of the wing of the château, the other on the short rise of steps that led up from the garden to the terrace. An assignation, carefully planned. The hidden watcher tensed, but otherwise remained motionless.

There was nothing of moment in either figure, both as sombrely dressed as the one who waited and watched. They met at the top of the steps. A low-voiced conversation—brief and hurried—took place and something changed hands from both sides. Perhaps a letter and a flat packet. Then one turned and vanished once more into the garden, the black density of a yew hedge soon swallowing him and any possibility of footsteps. The whole scene took less than two minutes. The other made no move to return to the house, but stood in full sight, moonlit, against the terrace's carved balustrade, head lifted as if in anticipation. Or perhaps he too was listening.

The watcher, after a brief moment to assess the quality of the stillness that was once again total, stepped out from concealment to advance cat-like with grace across the terrace. The man turned. This meeting, it would appear, was also not unexpected.

'Well, *monsieur*?' The watcher spoke in soft, low tones.

'I have what you require, my lord.' Hardly more than a whisper.

'The list of names?'

'Yes, my lord.' The gentleman took from his pocket the letter that had only a moment before come into his possession. 'Will you keep the agreement? That my name and identity be deleted from any further investigation into this delicate matter?'

'Of course.' Teeth glinted in the dark in a hard and particularly cynical smile. 'I will keep my word, you may be sure.' The watcher inclined his head in a gesture of some irony as he took a bulky package from his pocket.

'Would you sneer, my lord?' The gentleman, still holding the letter, breathed in with some hauteur. 'Your involvement is not beyond criticism. Blackmail, for whatever purpose, leaves a particularly unpleasant taste in the mouth.'

'True.' The smile again. The glint of an eye. 'But then—*I* do not sell the names of my compatriots to the enemy for money, knowing that it could mean their death, for a mere few thousand francs.'

The gentleman turned his face away, perhaps embarrassed by the justice of the accusation, then surprised his companion when he laughed softly.

'As it happens, neither do I, my lord.'

There was absolutely no warning. No sound, no movement of air. Merely a deeper shadow within shadows, which advanced noiselessly from the shelter of an artistically clipped shrub in a marble urn. Before the watcher could react, a heavy blow was dealt to the side of his head from the butt of a pistol, almost robbing him of his senses. He groaned on a sharp intake of breath, automatically raising his hands in defence. But before he could gather his wits to respond to protect himself further, he found himself forced back against the stone balustrade by a pair of strong hands and the force of a well-muscled body. Next moment he had lost his balance, thrust by a wide shoulder and hard-driven thigh against and over the stonework. His fingers scrabbled to find some purchase in the lichened carvings, but he was falling, helplessly, to land heavily and ig-nominiously into the clipped box edges and fragrant plants of the garden some considerable distance below.

After which all consciousness and all knowledge left him.

In the fashionable quarter of Paris, some days later, in the home of the British Ambassador Sir Charles Stuart and away from the sumptuous reception rooms where visiting dignitaries were entertained and suitably overwhelmed, there was a small anteroom usually set aside for informal or private transactions. This particular interview was to be conducted not by the Ambassador, but by a gentleman who made it his business to remain unknown and unrecognised except by a very few. For the head of British espionage it was good policy to remain anonymous, particularly when it was hoped to discover the names of British politicians attempting to undermine British foreign policy, such as those who would find it politic to bring about the downfall of King Louis XVIII of France and the restored Bourbons. Politicians who might even go so far as to plot the restoration of the deposed Emperor Napoleon Bonaparte—if that ailing exile, imprisoned on the distant island of St Helena, lived long enough to see the day.

There was nothing about the gentleman to draw any attention. Indeed, he worked hard to achieve exactly that, being addressed in his public life as Mr Wycliffe. Neat, slight of figure, no longer young and with a quiet demeanour, he sat behind a desk with a document in his hand, a deep frown between his brows, as the door opened. He looked up, the frown growing heavier at the interruption, then rose to his feet with a quick smile as he saw the identity of his visitor.

'My Lord Faringdon! Come in, my dear man. I had not expected to see you so soon. Come in and take the weight off your feet.'

The gentleman entered slowly, without grace: Lord Joshua Sherbourne Faringdon.

Those closely acquainted with the family would have given the opinion that Lord Joshua was typical of the Faringdon mould. Above average height with dark hair, although prematurely silvered to a gleaming and stunning pewter, and with the fine, distinctive features of all the men of the family. The straight nose and dark brows, the dramatically carved cheekbones and seductive mouth, the aura of power and self-will were all instantly recognisable. Under different circumstances he was acknowledged to be both elegant and graceful. Well-defined muscles would have rippled beneath the expensive cloth of his fashionable garments. But on this occasion as he walked forward into the room it could be seen that he was in considerable discomfort. His exquisitely tailored coat fit more closely than might have been usual, with evidence of heavy padding around chest and one shoulder. Furthermore he walked with a heavy limp, making use of an ebony cane, which was not merely for affectation. He lowered himself to a chair as invited with a grimace and a distinct lack of co-ordination, lips tightly pressed into a thin line.

'How are you, sir? We have been concerned.' Wycliffe resumed his seat behind the desk, eyes narrowed on his visitor.

'I have been better.' Lord Faringdon abandoned his cane on the floor beside him and eased his shoulders with noticeable effort.

'I had not expected you to have left your bed. There was no need. We had been informed of—and accepted—your present inability to continue your mission.'

'Perhaps you see no need, but since you would not come to me, sir, of necessity I must come here.' The tone was not conciliatory. Wycliffe found himself pinned by a hard stare from predatory eyes, more austere grey than friendly blue. 'I need to know your intent.'

Not willing to be cornered into any revealing or sensitive disclosures, Wycliffe deflected the demand. He had spent a lifetime in doing such. 'There is time and enough for that. Joshua...' he lapsed into a more intimate form of address, hoping to placate, although his words were not guaranteed to achieve that end '...you could have been killed.'

'I am aware. It has crossed my mind to wonder why I was not. I could not have defended myself, and one dead English spy must have its attractions to those who would work against us.' Lord Faringdon stretched out his right leg, easing torn ligaments of thigh and knee. 'And although it shames me to admit it, I must consider that I was very neatly set up. I had no notion that I too was watched and my cover undermined.'

'Hmm.' Wycliffe steepled his fingers, elbows resting on the desk, to cast a shrewd glance over one of his most able, if most unlikely, employees. It would never do to underestimate the powers of comprehension of Joshua Faringdon. In the circumstances he owed him some degree of honesty. 'It would seem that the Bonapartists have more skill—and certainly more determination—than perhaps we gave them credit for. They had no intention of handing over the names of those who would work to restore Napoleon and they also escaped with the money that you agreed to exchange for the list. You will not be surprised to learn that Monsieur Blanc—such an obvious name!—' his lips curled in distaste '—who lured you to the Charleroi château, has disappeared from all his known haunts in the city.'

'Very sensible of him.' His lordship winced as he shifted his bruised and battered body in the exceedingly uncomfortable straight-backed chair. 'I have a debt to pay there! But as I said before—where do we go from here?'

Wycliffe pursed his lips. There was no point in skirting the issue. 'The problem is, my lord, that your role and your cover here in Paris may have been compromised, although to what extent we cannot yet guess. Perhaps it would be wise for you to remove yourself from the scene in the short term. It may be that you can no longer pose—as you have done with considerable success—as the careless and unprincipled libertine visiting Paris with an eye merely to his own interests and pleasures.'

'No. I agree.' Lord Joshua thought for a moment. 'I still wonder why they did not kill me when they had the chance.' He rubbed a hand over his face, returning to this one aspect of the night's débâcle as if it had been keeping him awake at night, along with the physical pain, a memento of crashing from the terrace into the shrubbery. 'Someone had sufficient affection for me not to wish to hear of my being discovered as a rotting corpse in a garden. So who do you suppose it was who broke my cover?'

Wycliffe pressed his lips into a thin line of distaste. 'As to that, I could not guess. We have no traitors in our camp. Our security is second to none.'

'Marianne?' His lordship's voice was soft, dangerously so. 'Our security was appallingly suspect when dealing with that lady. You may have conveniently forgotten the details. But I cannot.'

'Marianne is dead!' The slight flush along Wycliffe's cheekbones might have hinted at embarrassment if one did not know him better. Lord Faringdon watched him with a sardonic twist to his mouth. His Majesty's spy master clearly did not wish to prolong any discussion of Marianne, the lady who had once had the honour of being Lord Faringdon's vivaciously attractive wife. 'The most crucial matter, since you are so concerned with our next step, is that your value, in this investigation at least, has been destroyed.'

'So?'

'I think that you should go home.' On firm ground again, Wycliffe relaxed and allowed himself a more generous smile. 'Regain your strength. Pick up the reins of your life in England and let the dust of this particular storm settle. I will contact you when things become clearer here and we may see a way to using your services once more. Besides, if Bonaparte dies—and it is my understanding that his health is poor and declining—our work here will be at an end and we shall simply close down this operation. So, as you can appreciate, there is no reason why you should not return to London until the dust clears.'

'I suppose I could.' Lord Faringdon showed no particular enthusiasm. He made to cross one leg over the other, remembered and came to a halt, fingers digging into the screaming muscles of his hip. 'It is true that I have a motherless daughter who will no longer recognise me if I stay away longer. It is over a year since I last saw her.'

'Well, then. Go and see your family.' Wycliffe leaned forward persuasively.

'Very well. You have more confidence than I that I shall be made welcome. I fear that gossip and speculation has made free with my name. I have it on the best authority that my mother considers my remaining in Paris to be of considerable benefit to the family in general and herself in particular, so that she does not have to make excuses for the scandalous behaviour of the head of the family.' His lips curled to show his teeth, but his eyes were cold and flat, accepting of the situation that he had himself created as a prerequisite for his present occupation. Brows raised in polite enquiry, he looked again at his employer. 'How do you suggest that I explain my physical state—considering that I have been here on a private visit of debauchery and excess, and am now returning with an obviously incapacitating injury?'

'Oh, that's easy to explain.' The main business out of the way since Lord Faringdon had, it would seem, agreed to leave Paris, Wycliffe rose to pour two glasses of port, one of which he carried over to his guest. 'I am sure that you can concoct some tale of a jealous husband who disapproved of your attempts to seduce his young and innocent wife. Disapproved sufficiently to dissuade you with a show of force. As you say, you have a reputation that is not inconsiderable—such a tale will be accepted by all. And if you can see your way to it being spread around the fashionable drawing rooms...'

'Why not?' A jaundiced shrug and a bland expression signified agreement. 'It is not a *résumé* that I would have chosen, but I should have expected no less. I suppose I will have to tolerate the fact that, given my injuries, the jealous husband was able to beat me to within an inch of my life. How ignominious!' His laugh had a brittle edge. 'But who am I to cavil at being branded a ravisher and seducer of innocent—or not so innocent—girls? Government service demands a high price indeed.'

'The cause is great, Joshua.' Wycliffe was not unsympathetic. 'Your efforts will not go unrecognised or unrewarded.'

'I am not looking for a reward. I believe in what we are attempting to achieve. A stable government in France—a democratic monarchy with no repetition of revolution or the overthrow of law and order to unsettle the peace of Europe. I need no reward if we achieve such an outcome.'

'Then let us drink to our success.' Wycliffe raised his glass and the two men drank.

'I shall leave next week,' Lord Joshua stated, his decision made.

'Excellent! I expect that you will play the role with your usual panache. If I might make a suggestion?'

'Well?'

'I suggest that you take the Countess of Wexford with you. She will not be unwilling and will reinforce your cover—your, ah, libertine tendencies. I believe she has more than a *tendre* for you.' Wycliffe's tone was dry as he noted the glitter of suppressed temper in Lord Faringdon's eyes. 'It should give the town tabbies all the ammunition they need to destroy your character and mask any further queries concerning your sudden return or the reason for your incapacity. You can embroider on the situation and your liaison with the fair lady as you see fit. There will certainly be no difficulty in persuading her to accompany you. No one will question your arrival in London.'

'No. But my family might question whether they wish to associate with me! The Countess of Wexford. God help me! A more voracious woman I have never had the misfortune to meet.'

'But Olivia is very beautiful.'

'As well as self-seeking, manipulative and unprincipled. She would like nothing better than to get her claws into me and her fingers on my purse-strings. You have given me a hard path to follow, sir.'

'I have every confidence in you, Joshua.' Wycliffe rose to his feet, intimating the end of the conversation. 'Take Olivia Wexford with you.' It was more command than advice.

Lord Faringdon duly drained his glass and dragged himself to his feet, rescuing his cane, cursing as his limbs had stiffened.

'On second thoughts…' Wycliffe stretched out his hand, his frown deepening again. 'About Marianne. I think that—'

'No.' The white shade around his lordship's lips owed nothing to physical pain. His words and the manner of their delivery were harsh. 'As you intimated so forcefully some few minutes ago, the subject of my wife is not up for discussion, Wycliffe.'

'Even so—'

'As you said, Marianne is dead.'

'Very well.' Wycliffe accepted the finality in the statement, if reluctantly. 'I must wish you a speedy recovery, my lord. I know that you will do everything necessary to protect yourself. The identity of The Chameleon must not be allowed to suffer further revelations.'

Lord Joshua Faringdon left the British Ambassador's home, lingering on the front steps to take a breath of fresh air. The Chameleon! A changeable thing, a creature of caprice, of quicksilver versatility. How fanciful. An identity acquired from those who saw only the glamour, the allure of a life dedicated to espionage. Yet, in reality, how sordid. Of course he could play the role of rake and libertine—had he not done so for years?—but that did not mean that he would enjoy doing so. If he needed to spread the gossip in London before his arrival, his sister Judith could be relied upon to do so. But he most certainly would not dance to Olivia Wexford's avaricious tune or welcome her into his bed. He hoped, fleetingly, that the Prince Regent realised the sacrifices being made by some of his subjects to bolster the traditional monarchies of Europe in his name.

But he doubted it.

Chapter Two

Autumn 1819—London

'Judith, I really must not—indeed, I cannot—live on your kindness any longer!' *Or on your charity!*

Two ladies sat at breakfast in one of the elegant and supremely fashionable town houses in Grosvenor Square. A gentleman, the Earl of Painscastle, hid with deliberate concentration behind a copy of the *Morning Post* and determined to stay there. This was not the first time that such a statement had ruffled the early morning calm. Given the decisiveness in the tone on this occasion, matters were about to come to a head.

The two ladies, one his wife, the other his guest, faced each other across a spread of white linen. Much of an age, their appearance and character were very different, yet within the past months they had become fast friends. The red hair and green eyes of one spoke of a lively and energetic lady, dressed in the latest fashion despite the early hour. The other was of a quieter disposition with fair curls and calm blue eyes, her morning gown neat rather than fashionable. A quiet composure governed her every movement.

'Dear Sarah!' The redhead was in no way disturbed by this

announcement. 'Why ever should you not? I enjoy having your company.' Judith Faringdon, now Countess of Painscastle, poured tea into her china cup with a flamboyant gesture. 'Until you have decided what you will do next, where else should you stay? You are never a burden to us.'

'You have been too kind, Judith. You are my dearest friend— but I would not outstay my welcome. I have finally made some decisions,' replied Mrs Sarah Russell, a youthful widow and mother of a nearly six-year-old son.

'Ah.' Judith took a sip of tea. 'Will you then go back to New York? To Henry and Eleanor and the children?'

'No.'

'Oh.' The Countess frowned a little. 'I was sure that you would and I know that they would make you welcome. In her letters, Eleanor writes that she misses you.'

'I have thought of it,' Sarah acknowledged. 'But I cannot allow myself to be dependent on them either. It was bad enough that Lord Henry had to pay the cost of my passage from New York. It is time that I determined the future for myself and John.'

'So what have you decided? Will you perhaps visit Thea and Nick at Aymestry?'

'No.' Another uncompromising answer.

'They too would be pleased to see you. I know that Thea feels that she owes you much in achieving her present state of sublime happiness.' Judith smiled at her romantic recollection of the recent wedding that the family had celebrated, of the love that had so palpably wrapped around Nicholas and Theodora, soft as velvet, strong as forged metal.

Mrs Sarah Russell sighed. That was the problem. Her friends had nothing but good intentions towards her and her young son, however unlikely it might appear that they would be willing to give any thought to her happiness or comfort. Amazingly, her history had become closely interwoven with that of the Faringdons. Instrumental in aiding and abetting her brother Edward Baxendale to make a fraudulent claim against the Faringdon estate, she knew that she did not deserve any consideration from them. There were no extenuating circumstances, even though she had been driven by her conscience to unmask her brother and his trickery. But they had forgiven her, a knowledge that still had the power to warm her heart. Sarah had severed her connection irrevocably with her brother and had been taken under the collective wing of the Faringdon family.

Sarah had aided Eleanor in her elopement to join Lord Henry, Judith's cousin, in America, and Lord Henry had taken her in and given her a home in New York when she had most needed one. Her decision to return to England had been prompted by the fraught relationship between Lord Nicholas, Henry's younger brother, and Sarah's own unknown sister Theodora, an adventurous lady who had been adopted outside the family and brought up by Sir Hector and Lady Drusilla Wooton-Devereux. Reconciled to Thea, Lord Nicholas had made Sarah welcome at Aymestry Manor, both for her own sake and, of course, as a member of the family when he had married Theodora. Judith—well, Judith and Simon had simply held out the hand of friendship. Thus, Sarah knew that her debt to the Faringdons was immeasurable. She could never repay such kindness and they would never ask it of her. But it was more than time that she stood on her own two feet. For herself and her son. Her pride would allow her to be dependent no longer.

'What will you do, then?'

Sarah drew in a breath, anticipating the opposition that would meet her carefully thought-out statement, but would not be deterred. 'I must find a position, some form of employment. I need an income and a settled home for myself and my son. John is now more than five years. He needs a home. So do I.'

'Sarah! No!' As expected, Judith put down her cup with some force.

'I only have a small pension from the navy since my husband's death.' Sarah laid out her argument as clearly and plainly as she could. It had sounded very well at three o'clock in the morning when sleeplessness had finally forced her to weigh her options. 'I shall receive no further income from my own family, the Baxendales, either now or any time in the future. I made an enemy of Edward, did I not, when I uncovered his nefarious pursuits? So,' she repeated, folding the napkin on her lap with careful precision, 'I need a position of employment and an income.'

'You must not work!' Judith was suitably aghast.

'Why not? Many women in my position, women of good family who have fallen on difficult times, would find no hardship in seeking some form of occupation.'

'But what would you do? Tell her, Simon! It is not suitable that Sarah take employment. Indeed it is not! I cannot imagine what my mama would say if I allowed it. Or your sister Theodora.' Judith stopped and blinked at the prospect. 'Although perhaps I can. Thea has a sharp tongue and an apt turn of phrase. She would be horrified.'

The Earl lowered his paper at last. His eyes spoke of understanding and compassion for the lady's predicament. 'Sarah must do exactly as she wishes, my dear. Whatever it is, we will help. But I do agree, Sarah, with my wife. You must consider carefully before you take up any position that might be unsuitable for you. I understand your concern over your situation.' He hesitated. 'Are you sure that there is not a life for you in New York?'

'No, I will not go back.' On that one point she was adamant. 'But thank you, Simon. I knew that you would understand. I shall remain here in England.'

'And do what?' Judith returned to the crux of the matter.

'I think I could be a governess.' Sarah's lack of experience for any position troubled her, but at least this one, based on her own education and upbringing, held a possibility. 'I have some skills appropriate for the education of a young lady. Or I could be a housekeeper, I expect. Would you give me references, dear Judith?'

'No, I would not! I am not at all in favour and so refuse to aid and abet you in this ridiculous proposal.' The Countess reached across the table to grasp Sarah's restless fingers. 'I will tell you what I think. You should marry again. You are so pretty, Sarah, it would be quite the best answer.'

'Judith…!' Sarah shook her head in frustration but returned the warm clasp. 'I am twenty-five years old with a son. And little to recommend me in the way of good looks. Not like Thea, or Eleanor—both of them so beautiful. I fear that I would never draw all eyes if I stepped on to the dance floor at Almack's as they would. I have no income of my own, no influential connections—nothing to recommend me. Who would consider marriage to me?'

Judith frowned and tapped her thumb nail against her pretty teeth, ignoring much of Sarah's reasoning, selecting the one omission in Sarah's explanation. 'So you are not actually *averse* to remarriage.'

Sarah thought about this. A marriage of convenience? Never. The memory of her husband, John Russell, a captain in the Royal Navy, slowly crystallised in her mind. It was more than five years since he had died at sea in the final year of the Napoleonic Wars, before Waterloo. She was shocked at how unclear his image had become with the passage of time. She had been so young, he some years older, and she had been dazzled by the attention of this grave gentleman in flattering uniform with gold braid. Meeting her at the home of a distant relative in London, he had rescued her from an unsatisfactory home, carried her off and married her in the face of family disapproval. She smiled as she remembered him, a warm, caring man, considerate of his young wife's inexperience and insecurity. It saddened her that she had seen so little of him during their brief marriage—a matter of months— and he had never set eyes on his splendid son, meeting death in a bloody skirmish at sea within weeks of the child's birth.

Had she loved John Russell? Well—yes…if love was a deep affection, a warm, gentle, caring emotion.

Her mind flitted to more recent events where her memory

was stronger, her emotions more recently engaged. Where she had seen a quite different interpretation of love. She had seen the strength of love possible between Henry and Eleanor, a bright, all-consuming passion that could sweep all before it. And more recently the unshakeable bond created from the heartbreaking difficulties between Nicholas and Theodora, where love had finally triumphed against all the odds. Love, it seemed, could be found in many different guises.

So, no, she realised, she could not accept a marriage simply for money or comfort or future security. Her heart must be engaged.

She became aware of Judith awaiting her answer with growing impatience.

'No, I am not averse to marriage,' she replied with a little smile, a ghost of regret. 'But only if I find someone I can love. I will not marry for less.' Catching a flash of interest in the Countess's emerald eyes, she raised her hand, but laughed as she recognised the gleam of a plan being formed. 'And I would be grateful if you did not set yourself to put me in the way of a suitable husband, Judith!'

It was almost, Sarah decided only a half hour later that same morning, as if fate in a coquettish moment had determined to take a hand in the game. Although for better or worse, she was as yet unsure. It was one thing to be adamant that she needed some gainful employment, quite another to secure a position that she would consider suitable for herself and her son. But wily fate, in the guise of Lady Beatrice Faringdon, imposing in puce and ostrich plumes, decreed that her dilemma be settled with almost unseemly speed. Simon had taken himself to Tattersall's, leaving Judith and Sarah to finish their desultory conversation over the breakfast cups, when the door opened to admit Lady Beatrice, Judith's mama. She waved Matthews, the butler, aside when he would have announced her, greeted the ladies and settled herself at the table where she accepted a cup of tea from her daughter.

Lady Beatrice, large and dominant in the small room, had an air of ruffled displeasure about her, causing Judith to eye her askance.

'Well, Mama. This is early for you to be visiting.'

'Well!' The stout lady took a breath and squared her ample shoulders, thus causing her fading red curls and the plumes in her bonnet to shiver. 'There has been a *development*.'

Judith and Sarah exchanged glances, but waited in silence. Not for long.

'It is your brother Joshua. He plans to return to London next week. And not simply a passing visit.' The expression on Lady Beatrice's face could only be described as sour. The return of her firstborn, Joshua Sherbourne Faringdon, to her maternal bosom obviously did not fill her with pleasure.

In comparison, Judith's immediate smile lit her face with delight. 'Sher! Why, that is splendid news. It is so long… But I thought he was fixed in Paris for the duration. Why the sudden change of plan?'

'I do not know. Your brother did not deign to tell me in the letter that I have just received. What he *did* do is issue a list of instructions—as if I had not better things to do with my time.'

'Ah!' Judith understood perfectly. 'And you thought that I would be willing to take them on.'

'Why not? You have a much closer relationship with Joshua than I.' Beneath the chill and patent disapproval there was undeniably the slightest layer of hurt, although Lady Beatrice would have been the first to deny it. 'I have heard not one word from him for over a year and then all he can do is send me a list—as if I were his *secretary*.'

'You have not heard from him, Mama, because you are too critical of him and too ready to listen to scandal.' Judith had inherited her mother's predilection for plain speaking. 'You can hardly blame Sher for keeping his distance. It seems to me that—'

Lady Beatrice lifted her hand to bring a halt to any further discussion of her lack of compassion toward her son. 'I will not discuss your brother's habits and amusements. They are extreme and—' She closed her lips firmly on the subject. 'Suffice it to say they bring no credit to the family. Sometimes I am ashamed to own him.'

Judith sighed. The estrangement was nothing new, with no spirit of compromise or hope of reconciliation on either side. Sher continued to conduct his life with a cavalier disregard for the forms of behaviour that would make him acceptable to the *haut ton*. Lady Beatrice would tally his many sins and see no good in her only son. 'Very well, Mama. Tell me what it is that he wants.'

Lady Beatrice extracted a much-folded sheet of paper from her reticule and viewed it with distaste. 'To open up his town house in Hanover Square,' she read. 'To arrange for *the child* to travel up from the country to join him there. To arrange for some suitable staff—cook, butler and so on—so that all is in readiness for his return—by the end of next week.'

Judith laughed aloud. 'Well, that sounds fairly much in character! Anything else?'

Even Sarah, a silent observer of this conversation since she had neither met Lord Joshua nor had any knowledge of him, smiled. Another Faringdon! It seemed to her a familiar response by the men of the family, to issue orders and expect them to be carried out quickly and effortlessly.

Lady Beatrice had not finished. 'He also states that he needs an *educated and proficient person* to act as housekeeper and also governess to take over the care and education of the child— what *is* her name? I can never remember—something French. Why he could not have insisted on a good *English* name I will never understand! Our family have always had *English* names.'

'Celestine,' Judith provided somewhat absently, her mind already occupied with the project and shutting out her mama's habitual complaints and wilful rejection of the Italian derivation of her own name. 'Very well. I will talk to Simon about arranging for the provision of staff and…'

Sarah's interest in the proceedings, fairly mild until this point, now found a sharp focus. Lord Joshua Faringdon. Judith's brother. Needed a housekeeper and governess for a young girl called Celestine. In London. *An educated and proficient person.* Why not? She managed to remain silent in a blaze of impatience until Lady Beatrice completed her diatribe and took herself off, delighted at having passed the burden of her son's return into Judith's not unwilling lap. Then Sarah fixed her gaze on Judith, who was still perusing the list that her mama had thoughtfully left.

'I can do that.' A strange breathlessness gripped her.

'Hmm?'

'It is exactly the sort of position that I need. Which I can do. Housekeeper and governess.'

Which statement made Judith look up with an instant frown. 'No.'

'Why not?'

'It would be too…too demeaning! You know my opinion on the whole foolish project. But to have my friend in my brother's employ—I will not consider it.'

'I need a position, Judith. It is the ideal opportunity, I do assure you—consider the advantages for me.'

'No!'

'It will enable me to remain in London.' Sarah leaned forward, slender hands spread on the table cloth, urgency in every line of her body.

Judith's silent displeasure was answer enough.

'I shall be able to educate both my son and the child. I shall regain my independence. I shall have a home.'

'I do not think that you should.'

'I do.' Sarah dropped her eyes from her friend's searching glance, her voice low. Unaware, her fingers interlaced and gripped tightly. 'It will also perhaps help me to regain some self-respect.'

'But, Sarah—'

'I owe your family much.' Now, her mind made up, her gaze was direct and steady again. 'Here is the best opportunity I can imagine to pay off that debt, dropped into my hands as if it were a precious gift. How can I possibly turn my back against it? Let me do it, Judith. Don't stand in my way, I beg of you…as my friend.'

As a final argument, Judith had no answer against it, and could only continue to frown her distaste for the development. Yes, she was Sarah's friend, and knew better than most the agonies the lady had suffered as a result of her brother Edward's malicious scheming and her own part in his clever fraud. Perhaps this means of earning forgiveness—although Judith could not see the need for Sarah to be forgiven!—would allow Sarah to achieve some essential peace of mind and put the events of the past finally to rest. Furthermore, Judith had to acknowledge that Sarah Russell could, when challenged, be a lady of considerable determination. It was rare to see her cornflower-blue eyes shine with quite that depth of emotion. Sarah was not to be dissuaded.

So, it seemed that in Sarah's mind the matter was settled. But Judith was not at ease with the outcome.

Wisely, Sarah allowed Judith some space in which to ponder the advantages of her taking up the appointment in Lord Joshua Faringdon's household, holding to the thought that she would soon see the sense of it. Then, when she knew that the Countess of Painscastle had spent some frustrating time in undertaking to engage the required staff for her brother, with limited and haphazard success, she broached the subject again as if the matter were indeed settled.

'Will you tell me about him, Judith? Lord Faringdon? After all, he will be my employer and I would wish to have some knowledge of his requirements.'

Judith tutted—but in reluctant agreement. Finding an expe-

rienced butler and cook at such short notice was proving difficult enough, even without the *educated and proficient person*.
So if Sarah was quite determined…

'Are you indeed sure?'

'Certainly I am. I think that heaven has smiled on me in dropping this chance at my feet. I would be foolish to ignore it.'

The ladies were taking an airing in Judith's barouche.

'I would not put it quite in those words. Neither, I fear, will
you after living under my brother's roof. He can be somewhat—ah, unreliable.'

'Unreliable?' This was not what she had expected, although
Lady Beatrice's unexplained disapproval could not be overlooked. 'I wish that you would tell me about your brother. I do
not think I have ever heard you speak of him. And why your
mama is so…so…'

'So unforgiving,' Judith supplied with a rueful smile. 'Well,
now. He is older than I by a little less than ten years—so we
were never close as children. I admired him—the splendid
older brother, as you might imagine. He had no time for me, of
course—the younger sister still in the nursery—but I wor-
shipped from afar.' She wrinkled her nose a little as she
searched her memories. 'By the time that I had my coming-out
Season, he was no longer living at home. I suppose the truth is
that I do not know him very well, although he was never un-
kind to me as some brothers might be,' she added ingenuously.

'Does he have red hair like you?' Sarah cast a quick glance
at Judith's fiery ringlets.

'No.' She chuckled, reasonably tolerant of her own dramatic
appearance, even though it prevented her from wearing her favourite shade of pink. 'Fortunately for him, Sher is dark like
the rest of them. I was the only one to be afflicted by Mama's
colouring. How unfair life is! But his eyes are grey—sometimes
almost silver—not green like mine. He is outrageously handsome, of course.'

Of course. Sarah knew only too well, claiming close acquaintance with the charm and good looks of both Henry and Nicholas Faringdon.

'And he lives in Paris, I understand.'

'Yes. Mostly. Although he has property in England. Sher married a French lady—before I was myself married—Mademoiselle Marianne de Colville was her name. The marriage was very sudden, so I think it must have been a love match. I only met her twice, once when they were wed, but I remember that she was an arresting lady—not a beauty exactly, but one of those dazzling women who take the eye, with dark hair and dark eyes. Very French, you understand, with a most stylish wardrobe. I remember being highly envious as a young girl, when fashion meant far more to me than it does now…' Judith did not notice Sarah turning her head to survey an approaching landaulet and to hide a smile at this remarkable admission. 'But anyway, she died in Paris more than three years ago now. It was all very sad and sudden—quite tragic—some sort of fever that did not respond to any of the advice given by the doctors. We were all quite taken by surprise—from what we knew of the lady, Marianne had always seemed so full of life. But there… She was buried in France, probably at her family home somewhere in Provence.' Judith lifted her hand in recognition of the occupants of the landaulet. 'I did not know Lady Portinscale was back in town. But where was I…? Sher does not talk about Marianne and her death. I expect that he was stricken by remorse, losing the love of his life. Not that you would guess from the manner in which he has conducted his life since,' she added drily. 'But perhaps I should not have said that.'

Sarah thought about this. Knowing Judith well, there was no need to ask the lady's enigmatic meaning. The Countess would assuredly confide every detail to her friend before they completed the first circuit of Hyde Park. 'Why do you call him Sher?'

'It is a family name—Joshua Sherbourne Faringdon. A childhood thing—Hal and Nick always called him that. I think I got into the habit because Mama disapproved. It was not the thing, she said. But Sher did not object—he always did what he could to annoy her.'

'And so he has a daughter?'

'Yes. Celestine. She must be a little older than John. Perhaps eight years old now.'

'And has lived in the country.'

'Sher sent her to England, even before her mother died, when she was quite a little girl, hardly more than a baby,' Judith explained. 'He has a house at Richmond on the edge of the Park, so the child has grown up there. He thought it better than keeping her in Paris—or even coming to London. She travelled with her nurse. One cannot but pity her, brought up by servants, with no other company and no one to play with. Perhaps I should have brought her to live with us—but that was before the birth of Giles and we set up our own nursery. Celestine would have been just as lonely in Grosvenor Square as in Richmond.'

'Poor child. She will have missed her mother.'

'I suppose. It will be better for her to be in London with a governess. I barely remember her, but on the one occasion Sher brought her to visit us when he was last home it seemed to me that she was a very plain child, silent for the most part and quite timid. As I said, she has not had an enviable life.' Judith slanted a glinting smile at Sarah. 'Perhaps it is a good plan after all—that you take over the care of her.'

Inclined to agree, Sarah sat quietly, piecing together her newly acquired knowledge. Poor child indeed, robbed of both parents. Had her father done anything to keep in touch with her? Sarah decided that, as a prospective employee, it was a question too delicate to ask. For herself, she could not imagine abandoning her own son in quite a different country, to be raised by paid employees who had no personal connection with the child. But, she supposed, that was not for her to question.

'Why does your mama not talk of him?' She returned to the blank spaces in her knowledge. 'As the only son and heir and now head of the family I would have expected her to welcome his return.'

'Not at all!' Judith took a breath. Here it came! Gossip was the spice of life to her. 'Sher has…well, he has a *reputation*. If you had been out and about in polite society, dear Sarah, you would undoubtedly have heard.'

'Oh.' Sarah nodded thoughtfully. Lady Beatrice's caustic words had suggested that such might be the case.

'A string of mistresses. And very expensive.' With little encouragement necessary, Judith now had no compunction in filling in the detail. 'When he was younger, Sher was often in debt and, when Papa was alive, he expected him to bail him out. Gambling, you understand. Horses and cards. He lost a great deal of money playing *vingt-et-un* at one of the gaming hells in Pall Mall. I think it was the cause of some harsh words between him and Papa. Understandable, of course, but words that became unforgivable—on both sides.'

'I see.' Sarah's eyes widened in amazement. She had had no idea.

'And then there was the notorious Grayson affair in London.' Judith leaned confidingly toward her friend, all animation. 'The lady was married! And her family was one of the foremost of the *ton*. I remember nothing of it but I am told that it was all *very embarrassing*. *That* was the occasion on which Sher first went to Paris. Papa sent him there until the gossip died down, refusing to pay any further debts unless he complied and put his life in order. It was the talk of every withdrawing room in town. I think that might have been the final straw for Mama, to hear the whispering come to a halt every time she entered a room. So Mama prefers it when he makes his home in Paris. Although,' Judith confided, finally, 'she had not entirely given up on the thought of his remarriage to reform his wicked ways. Although who would agree to marry him, I cannot imagine. Even though he is very rich, most mamas of hopeful débutantes would not willingly look for the connection.'

'I can well understand,' Sarah agreed in lively horror and some degree of fascination.

'So, you see, Sher acquired the reputation as a rake and something of a ne'er-do-well. I think perhaps he did not deserve it. He was very young.' Judith's pretty lips pursed as she tried for an honest judgement on her brother. 'I am extremely fond of him. But there was also the scandal of the ladies of the chorus at Covent Garden!'

'Really?' Sarah found the recital riveting. 'More than one? I had thought that all Faringdons had an eye to propriety.'

'Not Joshua. He has an eye to every pretty member of the female sex.' Judith sighed. 'I shall say no more! Except to suggest that you might—indeed you might—be advised to reconsider your application for a position in his household.'

Sarah laughed and reassured her, knowing that as housekeeper her path would rarely cross with that of her noble employer. How Lord Joshua Faringdon might choose to live his life would have nothing whatsoever to do with her and have no bearing on her own duties in his establishment. But Judith's artless confidences left her to consider that she was not the only one to have a brother in the form of a skeleton in the family closet. She chewed her bottom lip thoughtfully. And that Faringdon skeleton was now her employer.

Two days later Judith's reluctant acceptance of Sarah Russell's new status had undergone a sea change. On receipt of a letter from Paris, she was indeed prepared to say more, and did so unequivocally on running Sarah to ground in the private garden at the centre of Grosvenor Square where, despite the blustery weather, she threw a ball for John to chase and catch.

'Sarah! I have just received a letter from my brother. I am entirely convinced that you should not take up the position in his house.' The fact that the letter was remarkably frank and detailed had given her only a moment's pause. If she had known how painstakingly Lord Joshua had constructed it, how much time he had spent in plotting the scandalous content, and how much he was prepared to gamble on his flighty sister's inability to remain silent when in possession of a delicious piece of scandal, she would have been astounded. But she did not know any of these things and so jumped to the hoped-for conclusion. Presumably Sher did not care one jot about the comment that he was about to provoke in London. He was entirely without principle and honour, despite his birth and upbringing as a gentleman. As a Faringdon! It all went to prove that Sarah should not find herself in the role of housekeeper in the resulting den of iniquity.

'Why on earth not? What can he have said?' Sarah handed the ball to the nursemaid who accompanied her and joined Judith on one of the wrought-iron seats, which provided some limited degree of comfort and shelter from the wind. The day was too cool for them to sit long.

Judith did not reply directly, but allowed her thoughts on her brother to develop. 'I had thought that with age his lifestyle might be less rackety. After Marianne's death I had thought he was a little sad. And he has a daughter to consider, of course… But it is not so. He is as irresponsible as he ever was.' She frowned down at the closely written sheets that she still clutched in her hand as if she might detect the reason for her brother's outrageous manner by absorption from the paper and ink.

'More scandal?' Sarah enquired.

'Scandal! Sher has written to tell me the reason for his return. I am not surprised that he did not tell Mama!'

Sarah merely tilted her head in enquiry.

'It seems that he has suffered some injury. Caused by the husband of the lady whom he…' she leaned close and whispered *sotto voce* '…the lady whom he was intent on seducing. That gentleman was unfortunate enough to discover Sher and his…his most recent flirt in a secluded anteroom at a reception at the British Embassy where they were… Well, I am sure you can imagine—but the gentleman was irate—there was some violence—and the result is a terrible scandal in Paris. As well as being physically incapacitated, Sher is not being received. So has decided to return to London until another *on dit* takes its place and he will be accepted again.'

'He told you that?' Sarah could not imagine a brother regaling his sister with such salacious detail. Clearly he had.

'Yes. I did think…I wonder why? But perhaps he thought that news would spread and lose nothing in the telling—so he would tell me the truth first.'

'I suppose.' Sarah hid her doubts—could the gossip be worse then the truth?—but decided that perhaps the reason for the detailed letter was irrelevant.

'Furthermore—' anger now flashed in Judith's eyes and her voice began to rise, regardless of the proximity of the nursemaid '—he informs me that he will be bringing with him to London none other than the Countess of Wexford. Would you believe it!'

Sarah remained complacent enough. 'I think I do not know the lady.'

'Of course not. No one of good *ton* would claim to know the Countess of Wexford!' Bristling with disgust, Judith abandoned the letter and snapped her parasol into place as a stray sunbeam slanted across the garden. 'I expect that you will not have crossed her path. She is a lady of considerable presence and…and *questionable morals*. Rumour says that her origins are not what they might be. Merchant class from Dublin.' Judith wrinkled her nose. 'But she is quite lovely, a widow, titled and with enough wealth to take her place in polite society. She is accepted by everyone except the highest sticklers—you can meet her anywhere, but she would never achieve tickets of admission for Almack's. It is generally accepted that she is on the hunt for a lover or a husband. I presume she is Joshua's mistress! And, would you believe, will be living in the house with him in Hanover Square.'

'Oh! She will?' Lord Faringdon's new housekeeper did not

know what she felt about this revelation, but still decided that, in truth, it would have little bearing on her own position.

The Countess of Painscastle thought no such thing. 'Indeed, Sarah, it is not suitable for you to take on the running of that house. I would even go so far as to forbid it!'

'Judith…' Sarah sighed as she watched her son's limitless energy as he dashed about the garden. 'Your care for me over-whelms me—but I really do not see why I should not take the post. If Lord Faringdon takes the Countess of Wexford as his mistress, it will make no difference to my position in organis-ing the smooth running of the house or in my appointment as governess to his daughter. And if your brother does not intend to remain here in London any longer than the brief life of the scandal in Paris—then I do not see the problem. Perhaps he will continue to employ me as governess when he leaves, if he ap-proves my work. Presumably the child will then return to Rich-mond and I could go there with her. My reputation is in no danger, Judith. I see no problem.'

'It will not be a respectable establishment, Sarah! That will be the problem! And although I hate to admit it, my brother ap-pears to have abandoned all honour and principles expected of a gentleman. To have the Countess of Wexford living with him under the same roof. It is quite disgraceful. I am sure that you take my meaning. I hesitate to say this about my own brother, but you may not be *safe* in such a household.'

Sarah did understand, all too clearly, but knew with a low-ering of spirits that her friend's concern was not necessary. In a perverse manner, she almost found herself wishing that it was, that she was sufficiently beautiful and desirable to attract the attentions of a notorious rake. There was never any hope of that—not even when she was a young girl. When she looked in her mirror, she accepted what she saw there. Her fair curls did not have the brightness, her blue eyes lacked intensity, her pale skin would have benefited from a hint of delicate colour. No. Sarah Russell would never take the eye of Lord Joshua Faringdon. So she expressed her sentiments with a wry smile and typical honesty. 'Judith…Lord Faringdon is hardly likely to look at me, now is he? Particularly if an attractive woman such as the Countess is more than willing to accommodate his advances. I am not beautiful. I have no talent or skill beyond the average with which to attract his attention. He will see me as the housekeeper, a servant below stairs. Which is exactly what I shall be. That is if he notices me at all! And if the Countess of Wexford moves on to hunt in other pastures, as you put it, there will always be the ladies of Covent Garden to claim your brother's attention.' She silenced Judith's objections with a little shake of her head. 'His conduct in the house will have no influence on my life whatsoever. He can have any number of mistresses. He can hold *orgies* if he wishes. It is simply that this position is too advantageous for me to reject!'

Chapter Three

Within the week, before she could weaken and change her mind, Sarah saw to the packing up of her few possessions and those of her son, and their transportation over the short distance to Lord Joshua Faringdon's town house in Hanover Square. She herself followed immediately. Hugged and kissed by Judith, they shed a few tears because, although the Countess of Painscastle promised to come and see her friend, and was lavish in invitations that Sarah should bring herself and John to visit in Grosvenor Square any time she wished, both were well aware of the social divide that Sarah was creating by her wilful decision. But go she would. As she stood on the shallow flight of steps leading to the imposing front door, flanked by decorative ironwork, John's hand clasped firmly in hers, she wondered what the future would hold for her here, whether she would ever find the acceptance and depth of happiness that she yearned for. But for now she would settle for satisfaction in her new position and a sense of redemption.

Sarah discovered other members of the new household already in occupation and hard at work. The house, elegant and spacious with well-proportioned rooms and tasteful furnishings, had been closed up for more than a year, furniture shrouded in dust sheets and shutters closed. Newly appointed footmen and maids were already cleaning and organising under the strict eye of Judith's butler Matthews, who had been sent to cast his experienced eye over the proceedings. For the moment, Sarah was pleased to leave the reins in his capable hands.

Sarah first took herself to the kitchen and sculleries to discover and make the acquaintance of the ruler of this little kingdom. Mrs Beddows was a small, thin, nervy woman who had already organised her domain to her exacting standards. Fortunately she appeared not to mind a small boy and sat him down at the scrubbed table, with strict instructions for him not to get under her feet, to drink a glass of milk whilst she cross-examined his mama. After half an hour, Sarah found herself in possession of detailed knowledge of every maid and footman under her authority and decided that she and Mrs Beddows would get along.

Instinct warned her that it would be a different tale with the new butler. Mr Alfred Millington, he informed her within condescending tones and a smooth smile. Former butler at Orford Place to the Marquis and Marchioness of Gainsford. Sarah did not like him. And why was he no longer engaged at Orford Place? Opinionated and superior, conscious of his own elevated status as butler in a gentleman's establishment, he looked down his thin nose at her. And he made it plain that he did not like small boys. Sarah adopted a cool professional smile and determined to try hard to get on with this individual—she did not desire to make enemies unnecessarily—but he would bear watching. The rest of the new servants were still nameless faces. It would all fall into place eventually.

The house gradually began to come to life as dust and covers were removed. Oriental silk curtains and hangings were brushed and washed and fires were lit in cold rooms. It was sparsely furnished as yet, but perhaps his lordship would do something to remedy that if he planned to remain in London for any length of time. Sarah walked round her new responsibility, enjoying the stillness and order that they were creating, at the same time trying to absorb some sense of the absent owner. There was nothing. No personal possessions, no atmosphere of anyone having lived here. Even the paintings on the walls were impersonal, mostly dark rural scenes or lurid representations of Greek myths in heavily ornate frames. The family portraits, although clearly of Faringdons with their dark hair and well-marked brows, were from a distant age when the sitters wore whalebone stays and lace cravats. Even a farthingale was in evidence. Nothing to indicate the character or the preferences of Lord Joshua Faringdon. It was as if he had never lived here and Sarah, standing within the splendour of the polished wood and the leather-bound books in the library, had to admit to a disappointment. Judith's brother interested her, despite his wicked ways. Foolish without doubt but she could not deny it.

The rooms set aside for her own use, high under the eaves, had traditionally been used as nursery and schoolroom, but were surprisingly spacious. A small private sitting room and bedchamber for herself, a smaller room for her son and then the schoolroom. Lacking the elegance and comfort of the family rooms of course, but not unacceptable. Beyond it were two rooms cleaned and prepared for the imminent arrival of Miss Celestine Faringdon. She inspected them all with John in tow.

'Do we live here now, Mama?' He bounced on the bed that would be his own.

'Yes. Will you like it?' She ran a finger along the edge of a small table to check for dust.

He thought for a moment. 'Yes. Mrs Beddows gave me a sugared biscuit. She said that when Lord Faringdon comes there will be horses in the stable and I can go and see them.'

'I expect she is right.' Sarah smiled. Horses were her son's present passion.

'Has the little girl come yet?' John dashed before her into the schoolroom. 'From the country?'

No.' Celestine was expected any day. 'We must try to make

her welcome. She will not know anyone in London. Think what it must be like, if everyone is a stranger.'

Opening a cupboard and finding it empty, shutting it again, John came to stand beside Sarah, suddenly anxious. 'Will you be her mama as well?'

'No.' She ruffled his hair, which made him jump out of reach with a squawk. 'I shall teach her—and you, both of you together. Her papa will soon be here.'

'Where is her mama? Is she still in France?' Sarah raised her brows at this evidence that her son listened in to the conversations around him. He was beginning to grow up. It surprised her that she felt a little sad at the prospect.

'No. Her mama is dead.'

'Like my papa.' John pushed a pile of books neatly together, simple acceptance in his voice.

'Yes. Like your papa.' Sarah felt a sudden rush of loneliness to meld with the sadness. Then took herself to task. This was no good. She would soon be sinking in a fit of melancholia! They now had everything she had dreamed of. A home and a paid position that would allow them to live dependent on no one for charity. She had still to hear what her sister Thea might have to say to this change in her circumstances. As horrified as Judith and far more outspoken, if Sarah knew anything about it. But she did not care. Self-esteem was a very important thing, and, whatever Judith might say to the contrary, the need to make recompense to the family she had almost helped to destroy. The whole episode had left a stain, ugly and hauntingly persistent, on her soul. But now she nodded as she watched John climb on to the window seat to peer down into the Square, laughing excitedly at his height from the ground and the sudden swooping proximity of a flock of sparrows. Yes. She had done the right thing. She held out her hand to John.

'Let us go and look at Celestine's room, and see that it has been made ready for her.'

For better or worse, she was now a housekeeper.

* * *

Meanwhile, in Paris Lord Joshua Faringdon was making his own preparations to transfer his life to London, in the company, as advised by Wycliffe, of the Countess of Wexford. It would have surprised his sister beyond measure to know that her brother found the highly decorative lady to be everything that Judith had described to Sarah. Possessor of a beautiful face, an elegant figure, a range of talents that made her much sought after in some social circles for her undoubted charm, her outer beauty hid a grasping and selfish soul. The smiling lips and glittering eyes, the low provocative voice, were knowing and could be sly. They also masked an utter determination to achieve what would be in the best interests of Olivia Wexford. Her dead husband, Lord Joshua considered, sent to an early grave by a fall from a horse when hunting in the Shires, had had a lucky escape.

But without doubt the lady had her uses. Lord Joshua Faringdon would be seen and condemned by all as an unprincipled dilettante, returning to London in the midst of a scandal of the worst possible kind, in the company of his present mistress. Not only a lady of dubious morals, but one who was prepared to live openly with him under his own roof in Hanover Square. The *ton* could make of that what they would—and he could imagine every whispered aside. But nothing could be better in covering up his underground activities or the true reason for his return. No one would find a need to look beyond the obvious.

At the same time, he realised, as he sat at his desk to put his paperwork in order, he need feel no guilt over the masquerade. Olivia had been highly delighted to be invited to accompany him to London and made no attempt to hide it. The delicacy of his invitation had been lost on her. He might be little less than crippled with his broken ribs and damaged tendons, but Olivia smiled into his eyes and offered her lips for a kiss. Blatantly offered far more than that when he could manage to climb the stairs to her room without the use of a cane, when he was capable of pleasuring her body with finesse and some physical dexterity. She would like nothing better than to be his mistress and would enjoy ruling over his establishment in London, notwithstanding the resulting gossip. She might even hold out for marriage if she thought it worth her while to become Lady Joshua Faringdon. He stopped to think about that, his hands stilled on a pile of documents, a line engraved between his brows. She was without doubt an attractive woman. And he was not averse to a light flirtation when the object of his gallantry was so willing and responsive.

But no. He frowned at his wayward thoughts and continued to shuffle. His experience with the fair sex had not been felicitous and had left him with a sharp and lingering distrust. A woman's professed love was conditional on the depth of a man's purse. Or the value and sparkle of the jewels an unwise man might clasp around her elegant neck. And once she had you in her clutches, her claws would not willingly let go until all blood had been drained, uncomfortably like a leech—his lips twitched in semblance of a smile. Manipulative and untrustworthy. In his mind the image of Marianne was suddenly superimposed over that of Olivia Wexford until he deliberately blinked it away with gritted teeth, smile transformed into a cynical snarl. He would not allow himself to contemplate that episode of marital bliss again. Or willingly repeat it.

No. He would feel no guilt over the fair Olivia's unwitting role in his return to London. She would get as much out of it as he did. But it struck him forcibly that the greater the distance he could keep between the woman and himself on a personal level the better. Not an easy task but an essential one. For, without doubt, Olivia Wexford had an eye to his body and his bed as well as his guineas.

The days passed, but Celestine Faringdon did not arrive in Hanover Square. No matter how many times John might rush into the entrance hall at the sound of a coach or large vehicle in the street, there was no sign and no letter to explain the delay. Sarah contemplated sending to apply to Judith to discover the whereabouts of the little girl, but decided that she should not. She must learn to accept her new position of service—where the actions of her employers and their family were no concern of hers.

The cleaning and polishing of the house was complete at last, flowers arranged in the reception rooms, the pantries and cellars stocked, all in readiness for the imminent arrival. Then there was nothing for the staff to do but wait on the inclinations of their betters.

So that as chance would have it, when a large and fashionably smart coach and four finally arrived to draw up outside the house early on a bright morning, luggage piled high on the roof, no one within was prepared.

'Mama! Mama! She is here. The little girl is here.' John jumped and hopped in excitement by the window flanking the front door. No matter how often Sarah had tried to explain their altered status, or the parts of the house that were out of bound to him—and how difficult that was to a child of nearly six years!—John still saw the new arrival as an object of endless fascination and a possible playmate.

Sarah joined him, grabbing hold of his hand. There was indeed bustle and noise on the pavement. Luggage was being unloaded. But no child emerged from the carriage. She clutched her son's hand harder.

'It is not Celestine. It is Lord Faringdon!'

Why had the man not sent word to warn them? Well, why should he? Swallowing against a sudden brush of panic along her spine, Sarah made a hasty dash to the servants' quarters to gather up and send as many staff as possible to the entrance hall, where they might formally greet their new lord. They lined up just as the front door was flung open by a young and self-conscious footman. Sarah, the last to arrive, took a place at the end of the line, twitching her skirts and cuffs into place, thinking that it really would not do for her to meet her first employer in a state of disorder. Then realised that John was still watching the arrival in a frenzy of excitement. She should have banished him to the kitchens—this was no place for her child—but too late. Quick as a thought, she pulled him to stand beside her.

'Stand still, John.' Sarah managed to smile down at him, as nervous as the youngest scullery maid. 'Don't speak unless you are spoken to. Silent as a little mouse, mind!'

Eyes wide, John nodded and grasped his mother's skirts.

Up the flight of shallow steps and into the entrance hall walked a lady. Tall with a slender, willowy figure, she was immediately the centre of attention. A glorious brunette with dark eyes under dark brows and dark lashes that could only have benefited from the careful use of cosmetics. And with a richly painted mouth that smiled, unlike her eyes, which did not. Rather they looked and assessed and discarded with elegant disdain as if used to better things. She took up a position—posed, Sarah decided—just inside the door as if to draw all eyes to herself. There was no difficulty here.

She was dressed, as Sarah supposed, in the height of Parisian fashion in a delectable shade of lavender. Row after row of ribbon and lace trimmed the hem, the same detail drawing the eye to the pleated yoke above the high waist. The sleeves were long and close fitting into pleated cuffs with little puffed oversleeves. The brim of the satin-straw bonnet was trimmed with similar pleating, the crown with flowers and curling feathers, its long satin ribbons fluttering as the lady glided across the tiled floor in matching satin shoes.

Sarah could not prevent a silent sigh of envy, immediately conscious of her own plain gown fashioned of dark blue silk, high necked, long sleeved, not a hint of decoration. As for the lace cap that she had reluctantly pinned to her rigidly controlled curls...all perfectly suited to her standing, demure and understated and of excellent quality. She had never felt quite so *dowdy* in all her life.

Sarah surveyed the visitor beneath lowered lashes, understanding at once who she must be. The Countess of Wexford, no less. Judith's barbed comments came instantly to life and Sarah could well believe the truth of them. Her ladyship said not a word, not condescending to notice such lowly creatures as servants. Drawing off the softest of kid gloves with casual grace and perhaps a touch of impatience about her lovely mouth and a faint line between her brows, she surveyed the entrance hall, the rise of the staircase to the first floor, the side tables and hall chairs—almost as if she were looking for dust. Definitely impatience, Sarah realised, as the Countess tapped one foot, then swept her luxurious skirts out of the way to move back to the doorway to look out. But she smiled, her petulance swiftly disguised. Lord Faringdon was now here.

For Sarah, Joshua Sherbourne Faringdon was a far more attractive subject for her conjecture. She repressed a nervous smile as he came to a halt in the doorway, the sun at his back, casting his features into shadow but rimming him in gold. What would he say if he knew that she was a close friend of his sister, a less than discreet and loyal sister who had seen it in her way to pass on all manner of interesting information. But Sarah had no intention of allowing him this knowledge and had warned Judith of her desires. To Lord Faringdon, she would simply be Mrs Sarah Russell, his newly appointed—if most inexperienced—housekeeper.

It was immediately obvious as he approached the doorway that Lord Faringdon had suffered a number of recent and far from trivial injuries. He moved with a slow and agonising stiffness, using a cane to help him mount the steps, holding himself as if his ribs and one shoulder flared with pain with every unwise movement. Perhaps there was a tightness, a hint of strain around his mouth. But that, although she recalled in some moral indignation Judith's confidences on the cause of the damage, was not what took Mrs Russell's attention. From the moment that his lordship set foot inside his own hall, when he turned so that the light could fall full on his face, for Sarah the glory of the Countess of Wexford became a matter of irrelevance, as tawdry as pinchbeck beside fine gold.

She recognised the Faringdon features, familiar as they were, immediately. Beautifully carved features, all firm planes and interesting hollows cast into relief by the bright sunlight that shone directly into the room. A thin, imperious nose and firm lips. But here there were arresting differences. Dense black hair she had expected, but not with the lustre of dull silver. And his eyes were neither disturbingly dark gray nor intensely blue. As Judith had so casually informed her, they were light, silver even, devastating as polished metal, clear as cut glass. As piercing as the gaze of a hunting hawk as he cast an eye over his assembled staff. And at this precise moment, Sarah decided, they were full of an intense irritation, although with whom or what she could hardly guess.

For Sarah it was an uncomfortable instant of shock and inner revelation. She took a deep breath as her heart gave one heavy beat, then sighed and tensed against a little flutter of butterfly wings in her stomach, a shiver of longing that spread its warm heat from her breast to the tips of her fingers. A delicate flush mantled her cheeks. Capable, sensible, practical—*unworthy*—Sarah Russell, who asked nothing more in life than forgiveness for the part she had played in her brother's malicious plotting, and the chance to carve out a quiet life for herself and her son. Who wanted never to be dependent on the whim of any man ever again. Sarah Russell, who had lived in the same house with both Henry and Nicholas Faringdon, admiring both, acknowledging the charm of both, but without any danger of losing her common sense where they were concerned—or her heart.

And here, in this one blinding moment, her love for John Russell, although it could never be denied, paled into insignificance as the intoxication of longing swam through Sarah's blood.

Why did it have to happen now? And with this man?

She took herself instantly to task, in typical stern fashion, despite the hectic beat of her pulse at throat and wrist. How foolish she was to allow so immediate a reaction to simply the sight of the man. Of what value was a handsome face if the owner lacked honour and respectability? Of course it was impossible to fall in love so instantly, so completely with someone of whom she had no knowledge, apart from the most damaging of gossip, and who was so far above her as to make the situation patently ridiculous. With a man who had arrived in the intimate company of the Countess of Wexford, who was certainly expecting to take up residence in the house, with no attempt to disguise her relationship with Lord Faringdon. How scandalous indeed! Of course Sarah could not have lost her heart!

But Sarah's silent lecture did not at all seem to have the desired effect.

'Joshua.' The voice of Lady Wexford, although rich and sultry, could slice through flesh and bone. 'At last.' She allowed no recognition of his injuries, placing her hand on his arm in a possessive little gesture that merely confirmed all Sarah's presumptions concerning their relationship. 'If you would dismiss your staff, I can discover if there is a suitable room for myself and my maid. That is, if such has been made ready for me.'

'One moment, Olivia.' A flicker of some emotion in those remarkable eyes—far keener than mere irritation—was quickly banished. Sarah, watching carefully, was not even in the end sure of its existence. But Lord Faringdon turned from the lady and her demands with slow deliberation to make his halting way along the line, speaking one by one to the servants appointed to run his home. Sarah found herself listening to his voice. Soft, low. A masculine edge to trip along her senses. And his words—he found the exact greeting and comment for Mrs Beddows and Millington. Even the maids and footmen. When he smiled his eyes warmed, his face lit with a charm guaranteed to win their loyalty to the last drop of blood. Sarah looked away. It would be difficult for any woman to stand against it.

At last he came to Sarah, at the end of the line, by chance rather than status.

He saw a slight young woman, not overly tall but well proportioned, fine boned with an air of graceful competence. Far younger than he had expected, certainly immature for the position of authority denoted by her formal and severe clothing, the little high-standing ruff of her gown drawing attention to her face. Her fair hair was swept back into a neat twist, but allowing no curls around her face to soften her features. She wore a little lace cap. He gained an impression of a classically oval face, of pale skin, quiet blue eyes, an unexpected fragility. But also a calm composure, again at odds with her youth, as her gaze met his with no shyness on her part. Although… There might have been some momentary flicker of response there that he could not read. But then it was gone—perhaps he was mistaken. But he was not mistaken in noting the soft glow of colour that invaded her cheeks during his lengthy scrutiny.

'So you must be my housekeeper?' he asked at last. A mere process of elimination. He looked at her, cool and assessing. He supposed that Lady Beatrice had known what she was about in appointing so youthful a person.

'Yes, my lord. I am Mrs Russell.' Sarah performed a neat curtsy, no expression other than the polite response of a servant.

'You are younger than I might have expected.'

'I am not inexperienced, my lord. The Countess of Painscastle recommended me personally for the position.' She would make use of her connections if she had to and prayed that he would not see a need to question his sister too closely.

'So this is all Judith's doing. I should have realised.' Absorbing Lady Beatrice's rejection of his initial request for help, his lordship's eyes grew flat and dark. But what other had he expected? He turned his attention back to the fair young woman who was addressing him again in a pleasingly educated voice.

'I am also engaged to undertake the education of your daughter when she is in London, my lord.'

'Ah. Has she arrived?'

'No. We expect her any day. All is in readiness, my lord.' A confident voice, he realised, soft and well modulated. Somehow, it matched her appearance exactly. On first impression he approved his sister's choice.

He would have turned away when his attention was caught by the slightest movement at Sarah's side. He looked down.

'And who are you?'

The small boy moved a foot to the left, out of the shelter of Sarah's skirts, yet still keeping a fold tight in his fist. But he smiled and answered readily, 'I am John.'

'What are you doing here, John?'

'I live here. My lord,' he added at a slight nudge from Mrs Russell.

'Well, now. And why is it that you live in my house?'

'I…' A question beyond him. John glanced up at his mother with sharp anxiety.

'He is my son, my lord.'

And he could immediately see the resemblance in the fair hair and light complexion.

'Is it fitting to have a married person as your housekeeper, Joshua?' The Countess, resenting the intrusion of servants into Lord Faringdon's attention to herself, had come to stand beside him, now looking Sarah over from head to foot with frigid disapproval. 'And with a child? Surely that is not appropriate in a gentleman's household. Besides, children are so noisy.' Her glance at the small boy was one of sharp distaste, barely masked.

Sarah stiffened, recognising an enemy in the supremely self-absorbed, supremely beautiful Countess, but addressed her reply with perfect equanimity to her employer. 'I am a widow, sir, and have been so for five years. Forgive me, my son should not have been here.' She would not apologise or explain further. 'He will not be a nuisance—to yourself or to her ladyship, I do assure you.'

The Countess promptly turned her back, walking leisurely towards the staircase, choosing to signal her displeasure by ignoring the situation as one of no interest to her. 'Has a room been made ready for me?'

'Yes, my lady.'

'Good. Then be so good as to direct my maid Hortense with my luggage. I need to rest. Is this the withdrawing room? Perhaps you will send tea.'

Lady Wexford made her languorous way to the withdrawing room, leaving his lordship to remain for a long moment, looking after her with a distinct frown between his brows and making no effort to hide it. Then, with the slightest of shrugs, which caused him to wince, he handed over coat, hat and gloves to one of the waiting footmen and limped heavily after her.

To leave behind him in the entrance hall a flurry of comment and interest. Lord Faringdon *and* his mistress now in residence! A situation promising much food for gossip below stairs. But for Sarah there was considerable personal conflict. She disliked the Countess of Wexford on sight and knew instinctively that the feeling was reciprocal. Perhaps the lady disliked any woman, even the housekeeper, who took the lord's attention from her for even a moment. Whereas Lord Faringdon... Sarah pressed her palms to her heated cheeks. She could not believe the immediacy of her response to him. How her heart had leapt, her blood warmed, her pulse beat with furious intensity. But it could not be. It was merely an attack of nerves, brought on by her first meeting with her employer. Love without prior knowledge, without a desire to seek it, so blinding and uncomfortable, was merely a foolish romantic dream that had no place in reality, certainly not for a careful woman as she knew herself to be. Nevertheless, Sarah was forced to accept that entirely the best policy was to banish his lordship from her mind and keep her distance. After all, there was nothing surer than that *she* would never hold any place in *his* thoughts.

* * *

Celestine Faringdon followed close on the heels of her father and the Countess of Wexford on the following day, escorted from Richmond by her nurse, Edith Watton, a lady of extreme age who had been nurse to both Joshua and Judith, and who would remain with her young charge in London. Hardly had the two new arrivals set foot inside the house than Sarah was called to the library to be introduced to the girl.

Lord Faringdon was standing by the fireplace, his daughter at his side, and turned to Sarah as she entered.

'Mrs Russell. This is my daughter Celestine.' She could read little from his cool manner, but was aware of some undercurrent in the room. If she had not known better, she would have suspected a plea for help in that commanding stare.

The girl made an instant impression on Sarah of being far older than her eight years, a reserved child who perhaps would not readily give affection or confidences. Celestine was, her new governess decided, a child who had grown up much in the company of adults, who had not been encouraged to laugh or play or forget her dignity as Miss Faringdon. How serious she was! With a surprisingly plain and solemn face, her skin was sallow and her eyes so dark as to be almost black. And unblinkingly direct. Her hair, equally dark, was ruthlessly drawn back into a severe braid. She was tall for her age and a little thin, and pale despite country life where she could have run out of doors. And most notably, in Sarah's quick assessment, was the fact that she did not smile or show any animation, either in her polite greeting to Sarah or her responses to her father.

Not at first glance an attractive girl, yet Sarah thought that one day she would be lovely in a dramatic fashion. Her perfect oval face had excellent bone structure, promising high cheekbones and a straight nose. Her skin had the translucence of rippling stream water, and her hair shone as dark silk. When released from its braid, it might even curl. Now she faced her father in the library, quietly obedient, with nothing to say for herself. She acknowledged Sarah as instructed, but did not raise her eyes above the hem of the lady's skirts.

Lord Faringdon appeared to be somewhat baffled by this small contained person as he attempted to draw her out, in the interest of Mrs Russell getting to know her new pupil. Did you have a pet in Richmond? Do you like to ride? What do you like doing when not at your lessons? Which lessons do you enjoy best? Finally he gave up after a string of monosyllabic and uninformative answers, and addressed his comments instead to Mrs Watton.

'I trust that you will be happy here, Mrs Watton. I owe you much for the care of my daughter. Mrs Russell will be in charge of your comfort here…' Again it seemed that his quick glance at Sarah held almost a hint of desperation. Celestine remained distant and silent as her father outlined his arrangements for her, standing straight and prim, hands folded before her, in a dark dress, ruched and beribboned in a manner far too old and sophisticated for her slight figure.

The uncomfortable episode was brought quickly to an end, and Celestine was sent off with Sarah, who readily imagined the sigh of relief behind her. They climbed the staircase side by side.

'I will show you to your room, Celestine. And the room where we shall take most of the lessons.'

'Yes.'

Sarah opened the door and ushered the child in. 'Here is your room.'

It was a pretty room, light and airy, where efforts had been made to furnish it suitably for a young girl with floral patterns in shades of pale green and primrose and with frivolously frilled curtains on the half-tester bed. Celestine walked round, taking her time, to touch the curtains and the soft cushions on the window seat, to run her fingers along the edge of the little inlaid dressing table. To inspect the paintings on the walls.

'Do you like it?'

'Yes.'

'Perhaps not as comfortable as your room in Richmond.' Sarah had no idea, simply wishing to persuade the girl to talk. 'It will soon look like home when you have your own possessions unpacked.'

'It is very nice.'

'Tomorrow we shall begin your lessons and see what you can do. But today it is enough for you to settle in. It must all seem very new and strange.'

'Of course.'

'Come then, Celestine. I am sure you are hungry after your journey.' Sarah was turning to leave when Celestine at last ventured an opinion. But not one expected by Sarah.

'My father does not want me here, you know. He does not like me.'

Sarah angled her head to watch the girl who still stood before the window, looking out at the vista of sky and clouds, hands clasped behind her back and giving the air of a prisoner in a locked room. Why would the child make such an extravagant claim? She tried to keep her expression and her tone light and calm.

'But why do you say that? Who told you such a thing?'

'He has never wanted me with him before. Neither did my mother.'

Sarah tried to hide her astonishment, a little unnerved by the cool acceptance of the situation, if it were indeed so, the flat statement of what might very well be true, given Sarah's knowledge of this troubled household and the child's solitary upbringing.

'Do you miss your mama?'

'No—not really. She was not often in England. I barely remember her.'

'Did you not live in Paris?'

'When I was a baby. I do not remember. I have visited since then—but not for long.'

'I am sure that your father is very pleased to have you here.'

Sarah tried for a reassurance she did not feel. 'It was his idea that you should join him, after all. And that I should be here to care for you.'

'Perhaps.' Celestine made no further reply, as if the truth were clear enough without any clarification from herself.

'Come and have tea.' Sarah encouraged the girl through a connecting door into the schoolroom and then on to the door into Sarah's sitting room, where a table was laid for tea. As Sarah opened the door John burst through it from the outer corridor, hair tousled, eyes shining, cheeks pink with effort.

'There are even more horses in the stable now, Mama—but not as fine as Lord Faringdon's. And a coach—' He slid to a halt, chest heaving.

The two children sized each other up.

'This is Celestine who has arrived at last. This is my son, John.'

'Hello.' John grinned. 'Why did it take you so long, Cel—Celst…?' He blushed in some confusion, but was in no way embarrassed. 'I cannot say it! I do not know anyone called that.'

Sarah chuckled as she reached to draw her son to a halt at her side. 'I think he finds your name difficult,' she explained to the formal young lady.

'It is French.'

'I know. And very elegant. But John is younger than you and has not met French names before.'

It seemed for a moment as if Celestine might sneer at such childishness, but then said, 'I have never met a boy your age before. How old are you?'

'Nearly six.' John eyed her warily.

'I have had my eighth birthday. I shall soon be nine.' The dark eyes watched, weighing up the boy, coming to a decision. 'I have another name.'

'And what is that?' Sarah asked.

'Elizabeth.'

'We could call you Elizabeth,' Sarah ventured, 'if you did not object.'

Celestine flushed a little, her colourless skin warming to a hint of prettiness. 'I think I would like to be called Beth. No one has ever called me that. Can you call me Beth, John?'

'Of course I can! I have been waiting for you for so long, Beth. I have been lonely here with no one to play with. Are you hungry? I am. Mrs Beddows has made a cake for us. Come and see.'

Sarah watched the outcome with interest. Celestine—Beth!—hesitated, but only for a moment. Then stepped out to take John's hand with all the condescension of her three years' maturity.

'Yes. I am hungry. I would like you to show me the cake.'

They sat down at the table, John explaining that after tea he would show Beth his own room and then…

Sarah allowed a silent sigh of relief as she noted the surprisingly tolerant expression on Beth's face. The way she listened as John prattled on, waving his arms about with typical enthusiasm. The girl took little part in the conversation, but nodded when John looked to her for confirmation of some trivial matter. Well! If Miss Faringdon saw herself in a maternal role toward John, it might just be the means to get this frighteningly composed young lady to settle into the household. As for her relationship with her father—Sarah had no idea. The child felt unloved and unwanted, of which sins Lord Faringdon might very well be guilty for all she knew. One more transgression to lay against his soul if he could be so cruel as to neglect his own child. Yet Sarah found herself hoping that it was not so, for how could she have fallen headlong and ridiculously into love with a man she did not know, one with a contemptuous reputation and who could be so needlessly heartless to his daughter?

But that was a matter for the future, she decided as she allowed the children to leave the table. Enough that today Beth was here and was not averse to her new home.

Chapter Four

In the following days Sarah could convince herself that it would be an easy matter to keep a distance from Lord Faringdon. The only immediate ripple on the tranquillity of her pool was a note from Judith, hoping that Sarah would be able to find the time to visit for tea in Grosvenor Square. Sarah did not comply, but penned a brief apology, citing pressure of work since Lord Faringdon was now in residence. She knew that she had made the friendship well nigh impossible by her stepping across the social divide. It hurt, but she had deliberately made the decision and must not, therefore, dwell on any regrets. Judith would realise and accept—she was not so naïve as to be ignorant or careless of the situation. In private, Sarah shed a few self-pitying tears.

Her energies were soon directed towards other matters, not least diplomatic negotiations between a number of strong-willed and self-important individuals. Lord Faringdon's valet, a severe gentleman, was not given to personal chatter, but would hear nothing wrong of his employer, quick to depress any slighting comment with a stern frown and biting words. The Countess of Wexford's maid, Hortense, was very different—a superior little madam, French, of course, who kept herself to herself, yet demanded the best of everything for herself and for her mistress. Celestine's nurse, Mrs Watton, was a comfortable old body who did not regret in the slightest passing authority over her charge to Sarah. The child took too much after her mother. Not that they had seen a great deal of Marianne Faringdon before her untimely death. But even so! Blood would always out.

The gravest problem for her was the one most unlooked for. Mr Millington, the butler, developed an unexpected and completely inappropriate *tendre* for Sarah and followed her with a gleam in his pale eyes. Nor was he averse to glasses of port in the seclusion of his pantry. Sarah avoided him as much as possible after an embarrassing incident in the wine cellar, when the self-controlled housekeeper made her position very plain in a remarkably austere voice, which destroyed all Mr Millington's pretensions.

The Countess of Wexford was demanding, thoughtless, selfish and patronising. She objected to being woken, but complained when her cup of hot chocolate did not arrive on the instant that she opened her eyes. Hot water was expected to appear at the very moment she required it, earning for one of the maids a sharp and quite unnecessary slap; the same intolerance was applied to the laundering of her beautiful clothes, with never a word of appreciation or a genuine smile.

Her smiles were gifted solely on Lord Joshua, offering a source of much interested gossip and speculation. Not that speculation was needed. Of course she was his mistress. What other reason could there be for a lady to be residing in the house of an unmarried gentleman, and one with such presence and address as his lordship? Fortunately, with his lordship somewhat incapacitated, the Countess was frequently away from the house in Hanover Square.

Lord Joshua proved to be an enigma, spending much time at home, nursing his wounds. The library became his personal domain where he read the *Morning Post*, drank brandy and wrote many letters. Millington proved to be a fount of knowl-

edge for the household. His lordship had few visitors, but the
gentlemen who called at the house did so at unusual times, often
late at night. They never gave their names or left a visiting card.
Quite respectable, dark-suited individuals, as might be expected
from the legal profession, but Millington did not think they were
connected with the law. Lord Joshua also received an inordi-
nate amount of mail, over and above the gilt-edged invitations.

Otherwise his life was very quiet, which did not seem to
Sarah to be at all in keeping with what she imagined the lifestyle of a notorious rake to be. But, of course, he had the com-
panionship of the Countess. Millington swore on his own
authority that his lordship visited her room at night. What man
in his right mind would not, with so glamorous and seductive
a lady living under his roof and casting out lures. Millington
whispered rumours of outrageous orgies and scandalous parties
hosted by his lordship in Paris. Not perfectly sure that she knew
what an orgy entailed, Sarah's suspicions were aroused when,
on entering the morning room, she encountered the couple unawares. She was able to retreat, but not before she saw the
Countess of Wexford brush her hand through his lordship's hair
and reach up to kiss him full on his mouth.

Sarah found herself thinking vengeful thoughts against the
lady, disappointed that Lord Joshua Faringdon could not see the
Countess of Wexford for what she was. At the same time she
admitted, with a blush, that she would like nothing better than
to take the Countess's role in this little scene. Standing in the
scullery, a newly polished silver tureen in her hands, her fingers itched to stroke through that silvered hair. Her lips trembled at the thought of the man's intimate caress. Sarah blinked
at the shattering image, putting down the tureen with unnecessary force and little thought to its value.

When Sarah's cheeks had cooled and she had scolded herself out of her bad temper, her thoughts turned to Lord Joshua's
daughter. So young and yet with a studied and disturbing composure. Beth had already been taught the rudiments of reading

by someone in the household in Richmond. She loved to turn the pages of books, poring over the illustrations, and even more to listen to Sarah read the stories, following the words with her small hands. She was soon close to having read all the suitable books in the schoolroom. On the whole Sarah found that her role of governess was not onerous, particularly as Beth took on the role of an elder sister toward John. She reprimanded him and hugged him in equal measure. John at his most good-natured accepted the attention with equanimity.

Given Beth's blunt statement that she was not wanted, it surprised Sarah that Lord Joshua took it upon himself to visit his daughter every day, although there was little obvious progress in developing a closer relationship. His lordship made every effort, inviting her to ride in the park in the barouche. Beth declined, most politely. He asked if she would care to visit her Aunt Judith. Yes, of course, but first she must finish an exercise for Mrs Russell. Beth rarely raised her eyes from her book, almost as if she feared to make contact with her father. It worried Sarah. How she would have hated if John had reacted so toward his own father. If Lord Joshua wished to learn more about his daughter and was not the careless parent as he had been painted, he was having no success. So, certain of one sure way to the child's heart, Sarah decided to take some action.

She arranged to visit his lordship in the library one morning, knowing that the Countess was from home. He looked up as she knocked and entered.

'Good morning, Mrs Russell.' Although he might be surprised to see his housekeeper seek him out, with innate good manners he pushed himself to his feet and approached.

'Forgive me if I intrude, my lord. May I speak with you about your daughter?' There he stood. An imposing figure, a little withdrawn, but not unwelcoming. Sarah swallowed against her breath, which had for some reason become lodged in her throat.

'Of course. Is there some difficulty? She seems well enough.' He was blandly gracious.

'Not exactly a difficulty, my lord. Your daughter is keen to read and she loves books. Would you be willing to allow her to come and read here in the library when you are at home? She is very careful and will cause no damage. Perhaps after her morning lessons? I thought that she would care to see the plant illustrations and the books with the coloured pictures of animals and birds.' If anything would create a bond between them, this might be the answer. At least it would put them in the same room together. But would he refuse? Would he say that it was her responsibility to entertain and educate his daughter?

'Of course. Let her come.' He would have turned away, the matter as far as he was concerned settled.

'Also,' she added as an apparent afterthought, 'she enjoys stories.'

'Are you suggesting, then, that I should read to her?' The Faringdon brows rose.

'It is not my position to suggest that, sir.'

'No? You are, after all, her governess.' A line marred his brow as his attention was caught by this fair lady who had such an air of insistence about her.

'Beth will enjoy it, sir.'

'Beth?' The brows rose again.

'Forgive me, my lord.' Sarah sighed inwardly. She had forgotten her somewhat high-handed change of the child's name. 'Celestine. It is just that John does not pronounce it well. And she enjoys being called Beth.' He would probably demur, she decided as she awaited his reply. It might be that it was a family name that he would wish to keep.

'I see.' He narrowed his eyes at his housekeeper. Neat and self-effacing, yet supremely competent, as he always saw her. But with a strong managing streak, it would seem. He felt as he came under the gaze of her guileless blue eyes that he had been penned very neatly into a corner, although for what purpose he was unsure. Even to the change of name of his daughter! But if it was acceptable to the child…

'Then Beth it shall be. Let her come here, as I said.'

In considerable relief at this anticlimax, Sarah curtsied and turned to go, leaving Lord Joshua to return to his seat by the window. Without thought, he moved awkwardly so that he took his full weight on his damaged hip, staggered a little, and in so doing brushed against a book on the edge of his desk. It fell to the floor, a minor mishap. Sarah's immediate instinct was to pick it up.

'Leave it.' The order was instant and harsh. 'I am not a cripple.'

Tension, sharp and diamond bright, crackled in the still room.

'I was never under an impression that you were, my lord,' Sarah replied immediately, as if the tone had not startled her. She bent to pick up the book.

'Leave it, I said.'

She straightened, eyes wide on his face. 'But why, my lord? There is no need for you to stoop, to put added pressure on your strained joint. It would be foolish of you to do so.' For a brief moment she saw the raw, unguarded expression in his eyes. A sharp physical pain. But an even sharper humiliation. And she understood without words that such a man would detest his dependence on others. Her instinct, her driving need, was to approach him. To touch, offer comfort, soothe with soft hands and kind words. But she could not. She was a servant and it was not her place. And he was not, she thought, a man to accept such comfort.

Lord Joshua stiffened under the gentle but totally unexpected reprimand. She was looking at him, he realised, as if he were a spoilt child in her care, one who had been ill mannered enough to reject a kind offer. And she was right, of course, he accepted with a disgust as the housekeeper continued to upbraid him with perfect propriety. 'I am employed as your housekeeper to pick up after you, my lord.'

'Yet you will disobey me, Mrs Russell.' Inner fury still vibrated through his body.

'You can, of course, dismiss me if that is your will, sir. For picking up a book.' There was the faintest question, a suggestion of censure in her voice and her composure challenged him. He flushed with a sense of shame, even as her forthright words earned Sarah a sharp glance. But he had seen the stupidity of his rejection of her help, born of lack of patience and clumsy frustration at his inability to move about with the readiness of before, his incarceration within the four walls when used to a life of action and involvement. His behaviour was unpardonable. His manners must disgust. He took a steady breath and tightened his control.

'Forgive me, Mrs Russell. I was not considerate.'

'No. But as my employer you do not have to be so.'

She placed the book back on to the desk and went out, leaving him more than a little astounded at the parting shot. So meek and mild as his housekeeper appeared. Nothing like. The lady had teeth! And a confidence above the norm for a housekeeper of such tender years.

Sarah closed her eyes as the door shut behind her and wondered what she could possibly have been about, what fierce dragon she had unleashed from its cave. Seeing the frustration and impatience, she had appreciated its source and her heart had been touched in that moment of physical weakness. But to tell her employer that he was stupid and illogical—if not in so many words—what had she done?

Yet there were no repercussions other than the child spending time in her father's company, in an undertaking that the little girl could not resist. All those books with their coloured plates and leather bindings with gilt and red tooling. Altogether a neat little plot that Sarah prayed would be beneficial for both.

As it proved to be.

Lord Joshua found his daughter to be not tentative or shy, but painfully reserved with an equally painful desire for approval. She came into the library next day, wished him good morning, chose a book and sat in silence, curled up in a window seat, turning the pages with uncanny deliberation. He looked over at her. What did one say to an eight-year-old child whom one did not know? She seemed content with her own company and yet here was a chance he should not overlook since Mrs Russell had effectively thrown them together. He must make a beginning.

'Celestine…'

'Yes, Papa.'

'Mrs Russell says that in the schoolroom you are called Beth.'

'Yes.'

'Do you prefer it?'

'Yes, Papa.'

'Shall I call you Beth?'

'If you wish it, Papa.' Not exactly enthusiastic, but it was not an outright no.

'Then I will. It is a pretty name.' He smiled at her across the width of the library. And, after a heartbeat, she smiled back.

Which was enough for one day, his lordship decided. Mrs Russell and her stories could wait. They both returned to their silent perusal of the printed word, at least one of them aware that an important bridge had been crossed. Lord Joshua found a smile touch his lips as he watched his daughter and considered the possible tactics of Mrs Sarah Russell.

Lord Joshua met the other child in his establishment in the stables. John withdrew into one of the empty stalls as his lordship came in to inspect the horseflesh. Lord Joshua noted the quick movement and spoke to the silent shadow.

'Do you like horses?'

'Yes, sir.'

'Come here.'

John edged forward. 'My mama says I must not be a nuisance or speak to you unless you speak to me first, sir.'

He laughed 'Does she now? Then come and tell me—where were you born?'

'In London, sir.'

'Have you always lived here?'

'I have been to New York in America. I have—' John would have said more, but then stopped and frowned. 'My mama says that I must not say.'

The child ran off before tempted into further indiscretions.

Which admission Lord Joshua thought was probably a tall story, embroidered by a child's desire for adventure—yet there was something about him and his mother that was beginning to take his interest. He sensed secrets here. And the lad's mother had clearly laid down instructions. What was Mrs Russell? Gently born, of course, presumably fallen on bad times. He wondered idly about the boy's father. Perhaps he should ask Judith when they next met since she had employed the lady.

But of course it was not of very great importance. His mind turned to other matters.

Meanwhile, imperceptibly the Countess of Wexford began to make her presence felt more and more in the household, encroaching on the reins of power. It was not appreciated. Nor was her antipathy to Mrs Russell. Her intense dislike was patently evident, for what reason no one could guess, but which had no effect other than to unite the servants' hall against the Countess in support of the housekeeper. What right did she have to look down her supercilious nose at Mrs Russell? If there should be any criticism levelled against the servants, it should be at the hands of Lord Joshua Faringdon. And he appeared to find no cause for complaint in the running of his household.

It had become customary for Sarah to present herself every morning in the breakfast parlour to discuss the menu and any particular needs for the day. It was unfortunate that within the second week the Countess of Wexford was completing her breakfast alone. Her tight smile on seeing Mrs Russell was not pleasant.

'Ah. Mrs Russell. The menu for another tedious meal.' She

held out an imperious hand for the list. 'Tell me, Mrs Russell. Where were you last employed as housekeeper?'

'I have never been in employment as housekeeper, my lady.' *I have never been employed at all!*

'Never? That would account for it, I suppose.' The sneer was most marked as the lady perused the list. 'So how can you presume to know the needs of a gentleman's establishment such as this?'

'I have had no complaints from Lord Faringdon, my lady.' The perfect housekeeper kept her hands folded, her eyes lowered respectfully, her intense irritation veiled.

A glint of anger in the Countess's eyes was hardly masked. 'Who provided your references for this position?'

Well, there was only one way out of this difficulty. Sarah looked up. 'I was employed for this post by the Countess of Painscastle.' She refused to allow her direct gaze to fall. 'Her ladyship found my abilities highly appropriate. Perhaps you could apply to her if you have some concerns, my lady.'

On which challenging statement, Lord Joshua entered, easily catching the tenor of the exchange. 'There will be no need, Mrs Russell. I am more than satisfied with the arrangement.'

'Thank you, sir.' Sarah found it difficult to keep a stern countenance. She was human enough after all to be tempted into what could only be described as a little crow of triumph. But she suppressed the urge.

'Of course not, Joshua.' The Countess's smile was deceptively sweet as she lifted her face towards his lordship. 'I would imply no other. I merely wondered about Mrs Russell's history.' She patted a chair beside her, an obvious gesture that Lord Joshua had no difficulty in ignoring. 'But another matter, my dear. I would wish to entertain. On Friday. Is there a problem if I arrange a little dinner party?'

'No.' Apart from some surprise at the request, he could think of no suitable reason why not. Other than a disinclination to spend an evening in the company of Olivia's set.

'Then I would like to hold a banquet for some particular friends. A French banquet—something a little out of the ordinary, to impress, you understand.' The curl of her lips in Sarah's direction was lethal in intent. She cast an eye over the light dinner menu for that evening again with delicate disdain. 'Nothing of this nature, of course. So plain and uninteresting, do you not think? Only two main courses and a mean selection of side dishes apart from the dessert. Do you think that our kitchen might be capable of producing something suitably impressive, Mrs Russell?' Sarah's earlier challenge was thus returned in good measure.

'Of course, my lady. A French banquet.' *I will do it if it kills me in the process.* But her heart sank at the prospect.

'I really do think that we should employ a French chef, Joshua. So much more imaginative and exciting.' The Countess sighed heavily and dramatically. 'I suppose that I must leave it in your hands, Mrs Russell, on this occasion. I trust that I shall not be disappointed.'

'We shall make every effort to ensure your satisfaction, my lady.'

Sarah took herself back to the kitchen, seething in anger.

'What on earth is the matter, my dear?' Mrs Beddows replaced a lid on a steaming pan and wiped her hands. 'Is it That Woman again?'

'Yes! Of course it is! Can we produce a French banquet for twelve guests on Friday night?'

'A French banquet?'

'The Countess wishes to test our mettle, Mrs Beddows. And if we are found wanting, she will insist on his lordship appointing a French chef!'

'Does she indeed?' Mrs Beddows bridled, her slight bosom swelling. 'You tell me what we need and I will cook it. We will not have that hoity-toity madam or a foreigner interfering in my kitchen! What do I cook?'

'I have no idea. I have never been to a French banquet.' Sarah thought, tapping her fingers against the heavy dresser with its array of blue porcelain. 'But I know someone who has.'

Thus a series of notes passed rapidly between Sarah, Judith and her mama, Lady Beatrice Faringdon, resulting in a formal manuscript arriving in Hanover Square, inscribed on thick cream vellum, being a copy of the menu for the French banquet served on the fifteenth of January in 1817 by the Prince Regent himself within the splendours of Brighton Pavilion.

Sarah, Millington and Mrs Beddows sat down to dissect it with varying degrees of horror and near-hysterical laughter at the splendour and scale of it.

'We cannot do this, Mrs Russell. Indeed we cannot,' Mrs Beddows finally decided, aghast, slapping her hands down against the table top. 'Four soups, followed by four fish and then—well, I never!—thirty-six entrées, four of them with side dishes—and thirty-six desserts. Not to mention eight patisserie! And look at this. Turbot with lobster sauce, pike with oysters…eel with quenelles, truffles and cock's combs.'

'Roast larks in pastry lined with chicken livers!' continued Millington. 'And truffles mentioned six—no, seven times in all!'

'Such extravagance!' Mrs Beddows shook her head. 'With the best will in the world, we cannot—'

'No, no, Mrs Beddows. Of course we cannot.' Sarah patted her hand consolingly. 'But look. We can follow the same pattern of courses and simply select what we require. We can use some of the same dishes, but not the most extravagant. Alter some of the ingredients if necessary. And if we give them their French title…Millington can be sure to tell the Countess when she asks, as she most assuredly will. And since his lordship has placed no restrictions on our expenditure, then I suggest that money should be no object!'

'Well… If you think so…' A competitive spark had entered the cook's eye.

'I do. We have something to prove here. We will also, I suggest, serve it *à la française*, with the dishes arranged in the middle of the table so that the guests help themselves and then pass them on to their fellow guests. Very fashionable in the greatest houses, I understand, and highly inconvenient for those who wish to sample a dish from the far end of the table, but if that is what her ladyship wishes…' A wicked little smile crossed Sarah's face as she contemplated the possibilities. 'What's more, I shall write out the menu, *à la française*, which will be highly uncomfortable for everyone if they do not recognise the dishes. *Haute cuisine* is what she demanded, so *haute cuisine* is what she will get. Whatever happens, we do not want one of the Countess of Wexford's creatures lording it over this kitchen.'

'Certainly not.' The agreement was unanimous.

So they would do it. The servants' hall declared war. The result was a positive *tour de force*. A French banquet in exemplary fashion, served by Millington and the footmen with style and panache. The guests were impressed beyond measure. Millington, when asked, wielded French phrases as expertly as Mrs Beddows wielded her boning knife. The *turbot à l'Anglaise* (turbot *without* lobster sauce) was mouthwatering, the *noix de veau à la jardinière* (veal with fresh vegetables) exquisite, the *côte de boeuf aux oignons glaces* (roast beef garnished with glazed onions) a perfect dish, the meat cooked to a tender delight. As for the *petits soufflés d'abricots*—one of a handful of memorable desserts—what could one say? Olivia Wexford's guests could not but be impressed.

The results were beyond expectation. Lord Joshua sent his compliments and words of approval to his housekeeper and cook with suave and amused appreciation. Never had he been host to so fine a banquet in his own home. Not a vestige of a grin was allowed to warm his stern features as he recognised Mrs Russell's throwing down of a culinary gauntlet. It had certainly added an element of tension and comment to an otherwise tedious evening. A *frisson* of sheer pleasure.

The servants, flushed with effort and triumph, ate well from the left-overs and probably would do so for days. It was a pleasure to toast the achievements of Mrs Russell and Mrs Beddows in the half-dozen bottles of claret spirited magically from the proceedings in the dining room by a cunning and slick-handed Millington.

The Countess of Wexford was furious, her pleasure in the whole evening spoiled beyond measure, but unable to express her true sentiments in the face of such overwhelming satisfaction, particularly from Lord Joshua. She had lost this battle and had to accept it with a gracious smile and flattering words. Her fingers curled around her fruit knife like a claw.

So the evening ended with food for thought. A delicious pun, Lord Joshua thought, much entertained at having seen the light of battle in the eyes of his intriguing housekeeper. And there was an undoubted gleam in his eyes, a gleam that could be interpreted as pure mischief, as the Countess took herself off to her bed at the first opportunity without a word and a disgruntled flounce. He had not been so amused for many weeks.

There was no further discussion of a French chef.

Chapter Five

Very little communication occurred between the Faringdon households. Lady Beatrice kept silence and her distance, waiting for her son to visit her—which he deliberately chose not to do. Joshua visited his sister once at Painscastle House in Grosvenor Square on his arrival in England to exchange family news and other trivialities, but Judith had not returned the visit, partly because she had no wish to be forced into making polite and edgy conversation with the Countess of Wexford, or even to recognise that lady's existence. More importantly because she did not wish to compromise Sarah's situation in any way. Despite her shallow reputation and frivolous approach to life, Judith understood perfectly the reasons for Sarah's reticence with regard to their friendship. The class division between Countess and housekeeper now yawned between them and Judith had no wish to embarrass her friend. But it concerned her that Sarah had refused all invitations to return to Painscastle House or even to accept a more casual arrangement to walk or ride in Hyde Park. Mrs Russell always had a good excuse, especially now that she had duties to Celestine as well as to the smooth running of Lord Faringdon's establishment. Certainly, Judith might understand—but that did not necessarily mean that she would rest content with the estrangement.

In the end, when Sarah had once more cried off from a stroll in Grosvenor gardens, the Countess of Painscastle took matters into her own hands with high-handed Faringdon initiative. After discreet enquiries of Millington, she took herself to Joshua's house at a time of day when she presumed that both her brother and his *chère amie* would be absent. She stood in the entrance hall to face the new and most supercilious butler, Millington.

'Good morning, Millington. I would wish for a word with Lord Faringdon's housekeeper—on a matter of business.' Although why she should need to give a reason, she knew not.

'Mrs Russell, my lady?' Millington could hardly disguise his interest, which Judith promptly ignored.

'Perhaps I could speak with her in the blue morning room. If you would be so good as to ask her to come?'

'Very well, my lady. Would your ladyship require refreshment?'

'No. All I need is a few moments of Mrs Russell's valuable time.'

A short time later Sarah arrived with a carefully blank expression belied by a surprisingly fierce light in her blue eyes, followed by Millington, to come to a halt in the doorway of the elegant room where Judith was standing before the fireplace, removing her gloves. 'You wished to see me, my lady.'

'Indeed I did, Mrs Russell. There is no need for you to stay, Millington.'

He bowed and departed with ill-concealed disapproval and curiosity, in equal measure.

'Sarah!' Judith dropped all formality along with her gloves and parasol on the side table. Seeing the closed expression on Sarah's face—much as she had expected, of course—she decided to approach the matter head on, immediately on the attack. She wasted no time. 'Why have you not been to see me? And baby Giles? Should I suppose that you no longer wish to acknowledge me as a friend?'

'Judith…' Sarah drew in a breath against the obvious tactics. This would not be a comfortable meeting as she had known from the moment that Millington had delivered the message. If only she could have thought of some reason not to face Judith. But she could not, of course. A housekeeper could not claim the absolute necessity to clean out a fire-grate. 'You know why I have not visited you. You should not have come to see me here. It will only give rise to unpleasant gossip.'

'I told you it was a bad idea from the very beginning! I should never have allowed you to come here.'

Sarah could find nothing to say. Neither could she meet Judith's gaze with its mixture of concern and hurt. But her own resentment died away. All she could do was answer the following catechism.

'Are you well?'

'Yes.'

'And John?'

'He is in good spirits—and enjoying living here, I think.'

'How is Celestine?'

'She seems to have settled in.'

'Are you content?'

'Yes.' Sarah risked a glance. 'I must thank you. I know you do not like it, but it was for the best.'

'Sarah! Next you will be addressing me as *my lady*! In fact, you did just that when you came into the room!' Judith almost hissed in annoyance. Except that sympathy for Sarah's plight threatened to bring tears to her sharp and watchful eyes. She surveyed the folded hands, the deliberately quiet demeanour. The lack of any smile or sparkle in Sarah's face. The plain gown and rigidly confined hair, the lace cap. All in all, the epitome of a competent housekeeper or governess! 'You must not cut yourself off, you know. I am your friend.'

'But it is not appropriate for me to be a close friend of the Countess of Painscastle. Indeed it is not, as you are well aware.'

And Judith was aware, but that did not make her retreat.

'Nonsense. I shall inform Thea and insist that she come to see you and take you in hand if you continue to distance yourself in this manner!'

Which brought a smile to Sarah's lips. Indeed, she laughed at her friend's outrageous threat. 'I thought you would already have done so.' Which had the effect of spurring Judith into action. On impulse, oblivious to convention, she covered the expanse of opulent carpet between them to fold Sarah in a warm embrace and kiss her cheek.

'Dear Sarah. You do not know your own worth—that is the problem. You must not allow the past to weigh on you so much.' Judith kissed her again with another quick hug. 'I have missed you.'

Only to become aware of the opening of the door into the morning room. And there, of course, stood Lord Joshua Faringdon, dark brows raised in total astonishment at seeing his sister warmly embracing his cool and icily reserved housekeeper. He looked from one to the other. They returned the look, green eyes quite defiant, blue ones with obvious discomfort, perhaps even shame. His mind worked furiously. He could think of nothing appropriate to the occasion to say.

'Forgive me, ladies.' He resorted to the banal. Executed a respectable bow, despite the discomfort. 'It would appear that my presence is decidedly *de trop*. Judith—I shall be in the library— if you would care to see me before you leave.' He turned his back, quietly closing the door behind him, leaving the two ladies to look at each other.

'I shall have to tell him, Sarah.'

Sarah set her shoulders. It had to happen some time, she supposed. 'As you will.'

And then I shall see if Lord Faringdon truly wishes to employ Sarah Baxendale under his roof!

'Well?'

'Well what, dear Sher?' Judith cast herself down into a

chair. Her brother remained seated behind the massive Chippendale desk, if not in comfort, at least where the sharp agony in his knee and thigh was most bearable. He folded his arms on the polished surface and regarded his sister with an accusatory stare.

'Don't play the innocent with me, Judith. I was aware, I believe, that you had recommended Mrs Russell for the post here. I certainly did not think to find you on such close terms—intimate even—with the lady. So tell me. Who is she?'

Could she bluff and keep Sarah's cover? Judith had her doubts. She tried an ingenuous smile. 'I have known Sarah Russell for some years.'

'Come on, Ju! Perhaps you have. But you do not normally embrace your housekeeper with such obvious affection. I have wondered about her... Who is she?'

Judith sighed. But what did it matter? She would tell her brother the truth. If he did not wish to employ her—all well and good, even if Sarah would not see it in quite that light. It would rescue the lady from a situation that was, in her own eyes, unpalatable.

'She is Sarah Russell. But her name was Baxendale. She is Thea's sister.' Judith awaited the explosion. She was not to be disappointed.

'What?'

'Theodora—who married Nicholas—when you were still in France.'

'I know very well who Theodora is!'

'Thea was brought up by Sir Hector and Lady Drusilla Wooton-Devereux. But she and Sarah are sisters.'

'So with such a family behind her, what in the devil's name is she doing as my housekeeper?'

'She needed a position and an income—against my advice, I must tell you.'

'I see.' He tapped the papers in front of him into a neat pile with short, sharp gestures. 'Why did you not tell me of this?'

'You would not have approved. Even less than I. Sarah

threatened to take a position elsewhere if not this one. She can be very determined. So I said nothing.'

He thought for a moment.

'I thought she came from some genteel family who had perhaps born a child out of wedlock and been cast off by her family.'

'No—nothing of that nature. She is indeed a widow. Her husband has been dead some five or six years now. A naval captain, killed in action.'

'Wait a minute!' Lord Faringdon fixed his sister with a fierce stare. 'Baxendale. Baxendale, did you say? Edward Baxendale? Surely that was the name of the man who laid a claim against the Faringdon estates in the name of his sister—or his wife, as it turned out. I was in Paris so did not know the full gist of it, but I am aware that it rattled Lady Beatrice. She wrote to inform me of it, without one word of censure in the whole letter of my own errant behaviour, which was a miracle in itself. So—was that the name?'

'Yes—yes, it was. Sarah is sister to Sir Edward Baxendale.' Accepting the inevitability of it, she sat back in her chair and prepared to be communicative. Sarah would not approve, but her brother, as she knew, could be like a terrier with a rat. 'It seems that I must tell you the whole story.'

'I think you must.' Joshua pushed to his feet, to limp across to the sideboard to pour two glasses of claret, handing one to Judith. 'This may take some time.'

'Yes. It is quite complicated.' So she took a strengthening sip and told him. How Edward Baxendale had devised and executed a plot to present his own wife Octavia, masquerading as his sister, as the legitimate wife of Henry and Nicholas Faringdon's eldest brother Thomas, who had died in a tragic accident. Thus Octavia would have a claim on the Faringdon estate and her child, Thomas's son as she claimed, would be the Marquis of Burford. And how Sarah, under severe pressure from her brother, had allowed her son to be used in the charade as the son of Octavia and Thomas Faringdon and had herself taken on the role of nursemaid to the child. Such detail of which Joshua had been unaware.

'And so,' Judith concluded, 'Sarah turned evidence, told Henry and Nick of the deceit, confessed her own part in it and broke all connection with her brother. Henry and Eleanor gave her refuge and—well, the rest you know. She was most cruelly treated by her brother, although she will never admit to it. She had no money of her own and the captain's pension was very small. Edward threatened to turn her and her child from the door unless she agreed to his scheme. So she did—until she could stand the lies and deceit no more. The Faringdons took her to their collective heart. But Sarah has never forgiven herself for allowing her child to be used in the impersonation or for inflicting so much pain on Eleanor. So there you have it. The secrets and shadows in Sarah's life. She believes that she has a debt to pay to our family and must make restitution.' She fixed her brother with an unusually steady gaze, as if he might disagree. 'She had been a good friend to Thea and Nick in their tumultuous love affair. I should tell you, Sher, I love her dearly and will not have her hurt.'

Joshua said no more throughout the unfolding of events, but his lips were pressed in a firm line when his sister rose to leave some hour later. Judith knew that he was not pleased. But of what troubled him most about the situation, she was unsure.

'What the devil do you mean by this, Mrs Russell?'

Sarah had been summoned to the library. She knew it must be. And now she stood before her employer and, although his face was devoid of temper, he was finding it difficult to hide his true feelings. Probably, Sarah decided, outrage at having a Baxendale foisted on him without his knowledge. His grey eyes were dark and stormy now as they swept over her. Fierce, commanding. True Faringdon eyes. There was little point in pretending to misunderstand his furious—although patently unanswerable—question, but she had no intention of showing weakness or allowing herself to be bullied. Had she not promised herself that the days when she had bowed before a stronger will were all in the past?

'Are you dissatisfied with my work, my lord?' She folded her hands as Judith had seen them earlier, praying for composure. Her eyes, steady enough, met and held those of Lord Faringdon.

'Of course I am not dissatisfied! How should I be?'

'Then have I perhaps not fulfilled your wishes towards your daughter, sir?'

His lordship almost ground his teeth. He certainly dragged himself to his feet. He might have to lean heavily on his cane as he made his way across to the fireplace but he would be damned if he would conduct this interview sitting down. 'Your work— or the quality of it, ma'am—is not the matter at issue here.'

'Then I fail to understand your displeasure, my lord. If I have fulfilled the terms of my engagement as a member of your staff, I do not see the reason for your obvious disapproval.' She marvelled at the steadiness of her voice, her ability to stand before him without flinching. She had often flinched when Edward had taken her to task. Had been reduced to tears on more than one explosive occasion. But that had been weakness. Now she was fighting for her independence. For the security and comfort of her son. Pride stiffened her backbone.

Lord Faringdon saw it, but was not to be deterred. 'You are here as my housekeeper and my daughter's governess under false pretences, madam.'

'Hardly that, sir. My name is my own. I have made no attempt to hide my situation.' *Well, not very much.* 'I was appointed by your sister with your agreement. I have worked in your house for any number of weeks without difficulty or any cause for criticism.'

'And Judith was in collusion with you, as you are very well aware!'

There was no possible answer to this. Sarah remained silent, waiting for the blow when he would surely dismiss her.

'Why are you my housekeeper, Mrs Russell?'

'I fail to see the reasoning behind that question, sir.'

'The *reasoning*, as you put it, is that it is completely inappropriate.' He would have paced the floor if he could. He was tempted to fling his cane into the fire-grate. 'The daughter of a baronet? Your birth is as good as mine and yet you have put yourself in a position of servitude.' He fumed. 'Sister to my cousin's *wife*. Close friend of my own sister—and, God help me!—my mother. You have actually lived with Judith and Simon… And with Hal and Eleanor in New York. And yet you say that you do not see why I should object?'

But why *did* he object so much? He looked her over with narrowed eyes. There was courage there, and an apparent fragility that had surprised a need in him to offer protection. He had been touched by her history as recounted by Judith. And astounded by the strength she had shown in asserting her independence. But was that all? Whatever stirred his blood to anger, it hardly mattered, did it? Quite simply, Mrs Russell should not be employed in his household.

'I do not like it,' he stated as if that settled everything. 'It is not right.'

For Sarah, it settled nothing. 'I can no longer live on the charity of those who have been kind enough to show me friendship. I need the money and the position, sir.'

'Never!'

'What do you know of such things? You have never been in the position of having to find the means to feed and clothe your child.' A hint of desperation, even of futile anger, crept into her voice until she brought it under control with the faintest sigh. 'What should you know of such needs, my lord?'

'No, I have not been in such a position,' he snapped, as if that too might be her fault. He frowned at her. 'Who was your husband?'

'A naval officer who was killed in the last year of the war. I have a small pension only.'

'And your family?' A slight flush brushed his cheekbones as he remembered the background of her troubled history and the antagonism of her estranged brother. He watched as the delicate colour fled from her cheeks, leaving her paper white, her eyes stark with distress.

'I presume that Judith has informed you of my family, my lord.' She would say no more.

'I refuse to allow the situation to continue, madam.'

'Then you must dismiss me, sir.' She hesitated one moment and then asked the pertinent question. 'Is it my birth you cavil at, Lord Faringdon—or my name?'

Ah! So there it was, he thought. Mrs Russell would have to live with her brother's sins and her own involvement in them for the rest of her life. 'No, it is not your name.' He made an effort to gentle his voice. 'That has no bearing. I find that I *cannot* find the words to explain to Nicholas's wife why her sister is working below stairs in my house!'

'I can understand if it is my name,' she persisted. 'Faringdons have every reason not to love those who bear the name of Baxendale.'

'Nonsense! It is simply inappropriate, given your connection to my close family, that I should employ you.'

'Then I hope you will give me references, my lord.' She dropped a neat curtsy. 'It would be difficult for me to obtain another position if I were dismissed without a recommendation, particularly after only a few weeks in your employment.'

Without waiting for permission to end the interview, before distress could overwhelm her tenuous composure, Sarah turned her back and stalked from the room, leaving Lord Faringdon with his mind in turmoil.

As Sarah swept through the doorway, Olivia was coming in, dressed as if she had just entered the house. She looked after the housekeeper, who had signally failed to acknowledge or even recognise her presence beyond the, briefest, curtest inclination of the head.

'A most unpleasant, pert woman,' she drawled, lips curving unpleasantly. 'Take my advice, Joshua. You had far better dismiss her and appoint someone more suitable to a gentleman's household.'

Which was exactly what Lord Faringdon had thought he should do—but for far different reasons.

The days passed, for Sarah, with tense anxiety in the air. She continued with her duties, efficient and outwardly calm as ever, yet waiting for her final dismissal as Lord Faringdon had threatened.

Yet it did not come.

Judith sent a letter of abject apology for being instrumental in revealing her friend's true identity to Joshua. She never should have visited. She never should have told Joshua. But it was done and Judith hoped that her brother had the sense to leave things as they were if that is what Sarah wanted.

Sarah read the letter, silently accepting her friend's apology. It would have happened eventually, she supposed. There was no point in dwelling on it or wishing for what could not be.

But she would continue to fulfil her duties so that Lord Faringdon should never have the excuse, whatever her family history, that she had failed to run his London home in a manner suitable to the establishment of a gentleman. If he dismissed her, it would be on his own unjustifiable whim. He must never be able to fault her application, particularly her responsibilities to the two children who were benefiting from regular lessons and regular routine. Beth continued to thrive and learn, to mother John, who regarded her with innocent worship in his blue eyes, even tolerating her sometimes sharp comments and quaintly adult remarks.

With the onset of a period of better weather, Sarah released the children after lunch to play in the railed gardens of Hanover Square. Something Beth had to learn to do, to laugh and to run as a child. Sarah doubted that the little girl had ever played in her life.

So the days were full for Sarah. She went to her bed at night in a state of utter weariness that allowed her to sleep without dreams. Which was a blessing indeed, she admitted as she rose early to secure her pale curls into a plain and serviceable knot beneath her lace cap and don her severe gown. Anything was a blessing that helped keep her mind from dwelling on the one man who caused her heart to flutter wildly and her breath to catch in her throat. Perhaps it would be better if she were dismissed, she thought in a moment of low spirit. Would it not be better if she no longer had to see him—every day unless she could deviously arrange it otherwise—and did not have to school her reactions to him to one of polite competence and self-effacement. Then there would be no possibility of his ever guessing…

But of course, she admitted, as she buttoned her unadorned bodice, reflected in the glass, he would never see her in the role of *lover*—she hissed at her reflection, at her immodest visions—or ever see her as anything other than housekeeper. Then she swept her image a mocking curtsy. Certainly not when he had the Countess of Wexford to amuse him and warm his bed.

Sarah flushed at her thoughts. She had no intention of sharing Lord Faringdon's bed. How could she allow her mind to drift into such fantasies? Ridiculous! She was nothing to Lord Faringdon and nor did she wish to be. With firm steps she made her way down to the kitchen before her heart could betray her further.

She did, however, notice that he watched her.

Because Joshua had been left in a critical state of indecision, as he had stated, how could he explain to Nicholas and Theodora if he continued to employ Thea's sister in a menial position in his household? But if he dismissed her, he was damnably sure that she would simply take a position elsewhere—and perhaps not a very suitable one. He knew of the

fate of both housekeeper and governess in some households—
neglected, imposed on, treated with such lack of respect as to
be an insult. He could not accept that for Sarah Russell. But he
recognised determination when he saw it. She would take up
any position that enabled her to walk her own path and care for
her son.

Nor was there any way in which he could make life easier for
her under his own roof without being inappropriately obvious.

He did what he could, but quickly discovered that if she suspected any degree of preferential treatment on his part, she retaliated. He saw her with the children taking the air in Hyde
Park, noting that she looked chilled to the bone in a velvet spencer not at all suited to the suddenly changeable weather. Without thought beyond her comfort, he arranged for a warm coat,
styled very much in the fashion of a gentleman's greatcoat with
little epaulettes, discreet frogging on the front and in a flattering deep blue velvet, to be delivered to her room with a note
explaining his desire that she should not die of cold when taking his daughter for exercise in the Park. The coat was returned
with an equally polite note. Mrs Russell thanked his lordship,
but had no need of such a garment. She had her own coat and
a voluminous cape for cold weather if he was at all concerned.
Lord Joshua Faringdon swore at the intransigence of women,
but could hardly force her to wear it!

He tried again. When he discovered her intention to visit Judith on a particularly damp afternoon, taking John with her, he
ordered the barouche to be available for her at the front door.
Sarah stared at it in disbelief and ordered its immediate return to
the stables. They would walk. The exercise would do them good.

All he could do was what Mrs Russell could have arranged
for herself. Which gave him no satisfaction whatsoever. He insisted through Millington that fires be lit in the lady's rooms
and the schoolroom, with hot meals for herself and the children,
both at lunch time and in the evening. A ready supply of paper
and pencils and books and free access to his library. She need

never ask for anything. But, of course, infuriating woman that she was, she never did.

For her life below stairs, she would have to fend for herself, but even here he was tempted into gallant and high-handed decisions to remove some of the burden from the lady's slight shoulders. He need not have bothered, he realised with gritted teeth. He was soon left under no illusions when he went too far. After much thought, he arranged for Mrs Russell's responsibilities to be shared by other members of the staff to allow her a full day of leisure every week rather than the usual afternoon at the end of every fortnight. Within less than an hour he found himself facing a highly displeased Mrs Russell in the breakfast parlour. Her voice never rose beyond its usual cool, light timbre, but the emotion that she brought with her into the room was inflammatory.

'I find, to my amazement, that I have been relieved of all my duties for today.' A pause. 'My lord,' she added.

'Correct.' He could not read her face, so tried for the noncommittal.

'I am due to only half a day every fortnight.'

'Today you are at liberty, Mrs Russell.'

'I do not need it. It is unfair on your staff who have to take on my work. And who will teach the children?'

He had not thought of that. 'The children can spend some time with me.' *God help me!* 'Surely you can find things to do with a whole day at your disposal?'

'That is not the point at issue, my lord.'

'As your employer, it is in my power to decide when and how you work.'

'I am your housekeeper and your governess.' Her eyes flashed like sapphires in a candle flame. Flashed with temper. He could now read her face perfectly. 'My terms of employment were agreed with the Countess of Painscastle before you took up residence. I need nothing but the terms on which I first came here. I shall take the afternoon on Wednesday as arranged. My lord!'

Without waiting for a reply, she dropped a curtsy, picked up his empty plate from the table, turned on her heel and left him to enjoy his cooling cup of coffee.

Behaving just like any other servant in the house! Damn the woman! But, by God, she had been magnificent. And astonishingly beautiful when she allowed her fury to break its bonds.

Lord Joshua Faringdon, used to ordering matters to suit himself, might not have felt quite so dissatisfied with events if he had known the lady's reactions to his chivalry. In a moment of idiocy before returning the splendid coat laid out for her, she had buried her face in the blue velvet—before dropping the soft fabric as if it burned her hands. It was lovely. She could not allow it. Must not. But it hurt to throw his gestures back in his face—such as dismissing the barouche when he had been so thoughtful. But then, she did not know what his motives might be.

Neither, to be fair, did his lordship.

But one thing he could do over which she had no jurisdiction. The time had come. The Countess of Wexford, he decided, had long outstayed her welcome. Wycliffe had been instrumental in her presence to strengthen his cover as a dilettante. He had seen the value of that on his return to London when gossip over his immoral ways had run rife, but enough was enough. Nor, suddenly, for some inexplicable reason did he wish to appear quite so unprincipled and lacking in moral decency. He could no longer tolerate her attentions, her clear designs on his time and his interest. Certainly he did not appreciate her heavily patronising manner toward Mrs Russell, a manner that had been allowed full expression since the incident of the French banquet.

It was more than time that their paths parted.

He needed an opportunity to suggest that the lady leave. And if one did not present itself, then he would have to end the situation as carefully and discreetly as possible.

The former did not arise, so he was driven with some distaste to the latter, after making some thoughtful preparations.

* * *

'I have seen so little of you, my lord.' Olivia Wexford entered his library on the following evening, where he was sitting with a glass of brandy and a recent edition of the *Gentleman's Magazine*. A provocative swing of expensively gowned hips advertised her deliberate intent. The neckline of the emerald silk was cut low on her bosom and, unless he was very much mistaken, her lovely face was enhanced by the use of cosmetics. Her mouth, deliciously red, settled in an inviting pout, her heavy perfume invaded his senses. His lordship felt a sudden urge to retreat in disorder, but stiffened his resolve.

'Forgive me, Olivia. I have not been the best of company.' He called on the excuse of his damaged hip and knee, with silent apologies to the deity who had granted him the facility to heal quickly and well. 'My leg. The pain, you understand. Sometimes it is almost too great to bear.' He managed to move surprisingly quickly from his chair, even without the use of his cane, to avoid an inevitable kiss as the lady approached. 'Perhaps I can offer you a glass of brandy?'

'No. I suspected that you were in some discomfort.' Her intense expression was not quite critical of his lack of attention to her. She followed him to where he had lifted the decanter to refill his own glass. Oh, God! 'But perhaps now that you are able to walk more easily, and without your cane...' She smoothed a hand delicately down his arm, looking up into his face with wide and lustrous eyes. 'Perhaps you would be willing to escort me to the opera? It would be good for you to see friends again, I think. And afterwards a light supper where you could spend time with me, of course. Alone.'

'I would be delighted to oblige, Olivia. But I regret not this evening. I have another engagement.' He cast about in his mind, only to come up with the obvious. 'At Brooks's.' The only place he could be safe.

'Ah!' The faintest of lines was drawn between her sleek brows, but then she smiled. It reminded him of a raptor's hungry interest in its prey. 'I have received an invitation to join a weekend party at the country home of Lord and Lady Melville in Berkshire. So gracious of them. I think it would be excellent for your spirits if you accompanied me, Joshua.'

'Olivia—there is something I would say.' He put down the glass of brandy. 'But first, I have a gift for you—a mark of my esteem. And gratitude.' How clumsy it sounded. He winced inwardly as he moved to open a drawer in the desk, to remove a flat packet. Held it out.

The Countess took it, without any sign of pleasure, and lifted the lid on the velvet-lined case.

'How lovely.' Her eyes were flat and cold. She did not touch the sparkling gems, but merely tilted the box so that their facets would catch the light. She angled her head, watching the expensive glitter, then looked at him. 'Could this be in the way of a farewell present? Somehow, in my experience, diamond necklaces always seem to figure at the end of a relationship.'

'I think, yes. I fear that you are bored, my dear Olivia. I have been no help to you in recent weeks, although I shall be eternally grateful for your company. In my convalescence.'

Thick lashes hid her thoughts. She fixed a smile that looked almost genuine. 'But you are recovering now, Joshua. We could still pass some pleasant times together. I think that you are not unaware of my attractions.' She reached over to touch his hand.

'No. My mind is made up.' He tried to be gentle even as he withdrew his hand. 'This is the end for us, Olivia. Much as I admire you.'

'But I have not thanked you sufficiently for your hospitality.' The raptor's talons sank deeper. He could not escape as she tightened her hold on his arm and touched her lips to his. All he could do was to remain still, cool and unresponsive to her invitation. Not quite a rejection—that would be too much like a slap in the face—but his reluctance was plain.

Olivia straightened, allowed her hand to drop away, her face controlled, but her smile had vanished and there was now an edge to her voice.

'I see that you are determined. Will you tell me why?'

'No reason that would be an insult to you, my dear. But time passes. And I need to make some changes in my life.'

'And I have no place in them.'

He could find nothing to say.

'Is there someone else in your life? Have you taken another mistress?'

'No.'

Her smile was brief and bitter. 'How demeaning to be overthrown for no one else.' She turned her back to walk toward the door, pride stamped on every controlled movement. And a simmering rage. 'Is there nothing I can say to change your mind?'

'No.' A brush of sympathy touched his senses before it was ruthlessly checked. 'You deserve better than I can give you.'

The Countess of Wexford picked up the necklace from where she had placed it on the desk. She would not reject the gift, however angry, however humiliated she might be. 'You have been a disappointment to me, Joshua.'

'I must live with it.' The thought came into his mind that Sarah Russell would not have snatched up the necklace to take with her. Sarah Russell refused anything he offered!

'Yes. you must. I hope that you do not live to regret it, my dear Joshua.'

She did not look at him again but left the room, leaving the door open behind her, all grace and cold fury. The diamonds had glittered, stark and blue as the coldest of ice, but never as frigid as the face and heart of Olivia Wexford.

Lord Joshua retrieved the brandy and drank. It was over. And easier than perhaps he deserved, for he and Wycliffe had made use of the woman. Her eager compliance did not make his own part in the masquerade any more comfortable. At least his injuries had given him every excuse to keep him from her bed and for that he must be grateful indeed.

Chapter Six

◇◇◇◇◇◇◇

The contentious issue of his continuing employment of Mrs Sarah Russell was resolved in Lord Faringdon's mind in a quite unexpected manner—indeed one of mind-shattering discovery—one sun-filled afternoon in the following week. He rode into Hanover Square a little after three o'clock. It was the first time that he attempted to get into a saddle since the disastrous and humiliating culmination of his assignment in Paris. The short ride around Hyde Park, one circuit only, had been without doubt excruciating, but it was immensely satisfying that his strength and agility were at last returning. Shoulders and ribs were already more comfortable, allowing him to stretch and turn without immediate and painful repercussions. His knee and thigh might still scream from the demands put on damaged tendons and joints, but there was room for optimism. Thank God he had at last been able to dispense with the cane.

As he rode toward the front steps of his house, his mind occupied with far from pleasant thoughts, shouts and laughter caught his attention from the garden beyond the iron railings. He drew rein. Turned his head to watch. Then simply sat and stared in amazement.

A game was in progress. Not a game that he recognised, but one which involved considerable noise and a lot of running and hiding, with a ball and a hoop. And also, it appeared, involved much enjoyment. He immediately recognised the participants and could not prevent his lips from lifting in appreciation of the scene. Most of the laughter came from John, untidy and red-faced, who whooped and shrieked as if pursued by a band of cut-throat robbers, wielding a hoop to the danger of any who might come too near. But there was his daughter, Miss Celestine Faringdon, no less, hitching up her petticoats and chasing the boy, to wrest the hoop from him with a cry of triumph. Her dark eyes sparkled and she laughed aloud. When she caught John she grasped and hugged him, planting a kiss on his cheek, which caused him to squirm and shriek even more, and his daughter howl with laughter. He had never seen his daughter so…so *happy!* Abandoned was perhaps the appropriate word, he thought. There was bright colour in her cheeks and stains on her skirts from where she had come to grief in the grass. Now she ran across the garden with John in noisy pursuit.

But the shock doubled, for the supervision of this madness was in the hands of one of the younger maids and Mrs Sarah Russell. And they were joining in. He found that he could not take his eyes from the solemn young woman who ordered and organised his life with intense reserve and so rarely smiled. It was a revelation indeed.

Sarah Russell was flushed. She was involved. She ran after the children, catching them, taking her own turn with hoop and ball. She laughed, completely unselfconscious, unaware of the picture she made. *She is no older than a girl!* he thought. She looked radiant, as if all the responsibilities and tensions of her life had been lifted for this short time. Even more, she looked exceptionally, stunningly pretty with pink cheeks and sparkling eyes. The vitality, the sheer…well, *loveliness* of the lady struck him a blow to his chest. His hands tightened on the reins: he could not take his eyes from her.

He would like nothing better, he realised in that one moment of recognition, than to make it possible for her to be so joyful all the time. That was how she was meant to be. If he had ever met Theodora, he would have recognised the same outgoing nature and love of life—now that Sarah had been able to forget her present burdens and her past sins. When she shrieked—then covered her mouth in youthful and delicious embarrassment—as Beth caught her skirts, he smiled. He could not resist.

She had dispensed with the lace cap and her hair had loosened from its neat arrangement, to drift in soft, fair curls around her face. Why had he not realised that she was so pretty when he saw her every day?

The game was apparently over, the players weary but ecstatic. They trooped back across the road in the direction of the house, to halt when they saw their unexpected audience. They came to stand beside him.

John put out a tentative hand to stroke as much as he could reach of the satin shoulder of the bay gelding. Beth smiled up at her father with such openness that it filled him with warmth. This was how his daughter should be. And he cursed his former neglect, however essential it had become to keep her safe in Richmond, away from Paris and its dangers, the threats attached to his own actions in the service of the Crown.

'You are riding again, Papa.'

'So it seems. And you are out of breath.'

'I won.' Beth crowed with a smug satisfaction. 'But John is very good. I am older, of course,' she explained in all seriousness.

'So you are.' Lord Faringdon's eyes moved on to rest on Sarah, who flushed even more at being discovered in so ruffled and unseemly a state. It took much effort to resist the urge to straighten her skirts and push back a wayward curl. But she would not.

'We had finished the lessons for the day, my lord.' Why did she feel the need to explain her actions? She set her teeth. 'The afternoon was so mild…'

'There is no need to explain, Mrs Russell. I could see that the game—whatever it was—was much enjoyed—by all.'

Her colour now became a deep rose. 'I must go in. If you will excuse me, my lord…'

'Of course.'

Transferring the reins to one hand, he swung down from the horse in one fluid movement. And forgot the need for care—until the bright pain lanced from foot to knee to thigh, a red-hot branding. His knee had stiffened during the ride and was reluctant to bear his weight as he landed on the hard surface of the pavement. Momentarily staggering with a hiss of pain, leaning against his mount to keep his balance, he dropped his gloves and riding whip.

The reaction around him was immediate. If his jaw had not been braced against the raw agony and lack of circulation in his leg, he might have laughed at the manner in which his house-keeper and the children instantly leapt to his aid. What price a rep-utation as a dangerous and unprincipled rake? They came to his rescue as if he were a damsel in distress, Andromeda facing her dragon. Beth collected gloves and whip from the dust of the pave-ment, wiping them against her skirts. John caught the loose reins to hold the gelding steady as far as a five-year-old could as Lord Faringdon leaned his weight against it. And Sarah Russell—well, she stretched out both hands to grasp his forearms, to hold him upright with her light strength, without a moment's hesitation.

The reaction between Joshua and Sarah with the touch of hand on arm was instantaneous and elemental. His eyes snapped to hers. She was looking at him with just such a star-tled expression as he knew was on his own face. It lasted only the length of a heartbeat, both caught in the net of awareness. Then he straightened. She snatched her hands away. And, to all intents, the moment had passed.

'See how well I am looked after. And how useless I am.' The little grooves around his mouth deepened at the self-mockery. Yet he was aware of nothing other than the memory of her hands grasping his sleeves, as if the flesh beneath were scorched by her touch.

'You are stronger every day, Papa. You no longer use the ebony stick.' Beth clutched the gloves and whip to her flat bosom.

'You are very good for my self-esteem, Beth.' The mockery was still there, but gentler. And although his reply was for his daughter, his eyes were still fixed on Sarah's.

'I must go in.' Mrs Russell took a step away from him in clear retreat.

'Of course.' He managed the slightest of bows. 'I have to thank you, Mrs Russell.'

'I have done nothing to earn your thanks, my lord.'

'I think you have. In many ways.' An enigmatic reply, which did nothing to still Sarah's heightened emotions.

Lord Joshua Faringdon, as he made his way slowly from stable to house, was left thinking, beyond question, that he knew one means of improving his housekeeper's life. He could suddenly think of no better solution. The clarity of the plan all but took his breath away.

Later that same evening the blinding moment of revelation—but a revelation of quite what he was still unsure—continued to trouble his lordship. He sat in the library, staring blindly at the untouched glass of port. Was he having second thoughts? Undoubtedly. Even third thoughts, he decided. He did not wish to marry. Had no intention of ever marrying again. Had no belief in the strength or lasting quality of love. Would seriously have denied its very existence if pressed closely. Certainly there had been no evidence of its overwhelming power in his relationship with women.

So why the hell should it have come into his mind with the force of a lightning bolt that marriage to Sarah Russell was an outcome to be desired and pursued? There must be other, simpler, more predictable solutions to her—and his—predicament. And there was no certainty that she would actually be tempted to accept his offer. No suggestion in her manner that she felt anything toward him other than a mild tolerance. Except for that

one moment that very afternoon—a slap of physical awareness
such as he had never before experienced. The reaction in her
own eyes as they had flown to his, held there, he could not say.
Yet the image of her in the garden, laughing and joyous, came
clear and unbidden into his mind. Once there, he could not
shake it loose. Of course he did not love her. So why he should
even consider to entangle himself in marriage he had no idea.

But he cared about her. Felt a strong urge—if he were feeling poetic, he thought with a quick grin—to stand as shield between her own slight figure and all the slings and arrows that
the world might unleash against her. To see and hear her laugh
and smile every day. To laugh and smile at him, with him.

He drank the port in disgust. He must truly be going out of
his mind. His thoughts on this problem were neither sensible
nor logical. And yet he was still gripped by a terrible conviction that marriage was the right step to take.

There again, his mind coming full circle and still as unde-
cided as ever, if he did pursue this objective, would Sarah Russell agree? Knowing what he did of the lady, he had grave
room to doubt it.

'You wished to speak with me, my lord. And I have brought
the menu for this evening if you would wish to approve it.'

Lord Faringdon stood with his back to Sarah, studying the
view from the window, his thoughts engaged elsewhere. Nor did
he immediately turn as she announced her presence. Which
gave her the opportunity to study the firm set of his shoulders,
the confident tilt of his head with its magnificent fall of hair. And
it gave her an even greater sense of unease. Of foreboding.

'Mrs Russell. Yes, indeed. If you would care to sit.' He
turned at last and indicated a chair beside his desk.

So it had come at last. Dismissal, with or without references. Sarah chose not to sit, but continued to stand before him,
chin raised, as he approached. She had done no wrong. If he
chose to dispense with her services, there was nothing she

could do to change his mind. She would not think, she would definitely not think of that one moment when she had touched him, when the connection between them had raced through her blood with all the force of a summer flood. When their eyes had locked with such intensity, something vital holding them suspended in time. No. No good could come from dwelling on that.

'Let us try for some honesty here.' His words surprised her and his voice had an edge. 'You have, as you are aware, presented me with a problem. I do not wish to employ you, for reasons that are plain to us both. But I know that if I terminate your employment here you will immediately seek another position elsewhere, perhaps not to your benefit or your comfort. Or even your peace of mind.'

She waited, brows raised, heart beating insistently in her throat. There was nothing she could add to his assessment of the situation. Nor could she guess where this was leading. His face was stern as if he had come at last to a difficult decision and was not now to be deterred.

'I have thought about it all at some length. I feel a responsibility toward you because of the family connection through Theodora. I have a proposition to make.' He paused as he swept her from head to foot with eyes that expressed all his exasperation with females who refused to take good advice. 'I wish you would sit down, Mrs Russell.'

'I would rather stand, my lord.'

'I am aware. But you might consider my parlous state of health. If you stand, then so must I—as a gentleman.' She could not mistake the sneer.

'Forgive me. It was not my intention to be insensitive.' Colour warmed her cheeks as she took the offered seat. It was so easy for him to put her in the wrong! What sort of proposition would he possibly make that did not include her dismissal? On a sudden thought her blood ran from heated to ice in her veins. Her throat dried. She could only think of one proposition. And now that the Countess of Wexford was no longer in residence…

Unaware of this shocking line of thought, Lord Faringdon continued.

'I have seen how you have settled here in so short a time. I have seen how my daughter has taken to you. She has begun to blossom, begun to behave like a little girl rather than a matron of advanced years. And your own son too is content, I think. I believe it is important for everyone that you remain here in my household.'

It seemed more and more likely to Sarah, with every word that he uttered, that she was about to receive an offer that would humiliate her beyond bearing. She discovered that she was holding her breath and her fingers closed, white-knuckled, on the arms of the chair. She forced herself to breathe again.

'So I would ask you…' He rose to his feet and walked forward toward her. Without the cane, she could see the return of grace and well-muscled ease. He reached out and took her hand, which still clutched, albeit wrinkled, the list of dishes for the evening meal, and unlatched it from the chair.

'No. You must not…' She snatched away her hand into her lap, taking him aback.

Lord Joshua frowned. 'What must I not?'

'You must not make such a proposition. I would remain as your housekeeper and governess to your daughter. Never anything else.'

'What proposition?'

'And if you do make it, it will make it impossible for me to stay under your roof in any event. Please do not, my lord. I beg of you…'

'Do not what…?' His frown darkened as the light dawned.

'I will not be your mistress, my lord,' Sarah whispered. 'How would you think it?'

'Mrs Russell!' He fisted his hands on his hips, more in frustration than anger. Oh, God! So much for reputations. When he had tried to deal with the whole matter with some sensitivity. 'Is that what you thought I would offer you?'

'Why…yes. What other could you possibly offer me?'

He took her hand again, both of them, in fact, removing the list to discard it on the floor, and drew her to her feet. This time he held on when she tugged. 'Mrs Russell—it would be the greatest discourtesy imaginable to you to suggest such a thing. It was not my intention to offer to take you under my protection. Your opinion of me is not very high, is it?' *And nor of yourself. How can you have so little notion of the light in which I see you? Of the respect in which I hold you?*

'But… You must explain more clearly, my lord, for I find myself at a loss. If you do not want me as your mistress—and, indeed, I find it difficult to understand why you would!— then what?'

'I realise that you could believe me capable of inflicting so monumental an insult on your good name.' He made no attempt to hide the bitter self-disgust. 'But it was not my intention to do so. Mrs Russell…' He might as well get it over with and allow her the pleasure of refusing him. How could any woman of integrity be persuaded to accept the offer of marriage from a man with so damaged a reputation? But he would try, beyond hope, to paint himself in a better light. Suddenly it had become very important that he remove her from her self-imposed role below stairs and restore her to the ranks of society into which she had been born. And something more, which he barely understood, could certainly not acknowledge, drove him on. But whatever the compulsion, he knew that it was underpinned by an overwhelming need to protect Sarah Russell. So he would offer her marriage, even though she would undoubtedly fling the gesture back in his face.

'Mrs Russell. Will you do me the honour of accepting my hand in marriage?'

Shock drove the colour from her cheeks, even from her lips. Her hands stiffened within his grasp and her lips parted on a little cry of sheer disbelief. Much as he had expected!

'You cannot!'

'Why can I not?'

'You do not know me. You do not love me. You could marry anyone of your acquaintance.' Sarah sought through her tumbling thoughts for all the reasons why his words must be false. 'You do not want me. Why, in heaven's name, would you wish to marry me? I am your housekeeper.'

Sarah Russell! Have you no thought of your own value in the eyes of any man?

'You seem to have an entire list of reasons why I should not. Let me tell you of the advantages for me as I see them. I think I would get an excellent bargain.'

'What could I possibly offer you?'

'If we are to be purely practical, then—the running of my establishments. No trivial matter, as I have a house in Richmond and an estate in Yorkshire. A mother to my child, whom I think you already have some affection for. The removal of one serious cause of conflict—only one of many, I acknowledge—that would stand for ever between myself and my own parent and sister if I continued to employ you as my housekeeper. Also—' But he bit back on further revelations. What other could he say, when he was so unsure himself? He smiled down into her anxious face. 'Enough! I have a care for your happiness. I think that marriages have been made with far less to recommend them.'

'I cannot allow you to even consider it, my lord.' She would have clutched her hands in dismay except that he still had them in his possession, so her fingers tightened around his. 'I do not want charity. I refused it from your sister. I left New York because it would have been too easy to accept it from Lord Henry and Eleanor. I will not take it from you!'

'I expect Henry in New York found you just as difficult to deal with as I do! I wonder how he coped with your uncomfortable desire for independence! Listen to me. Will you at least think about it? I have no intention of offering you charity, as you put it. There are considerable advantages for myself and for you in such a match. I can offer you comfort, respectability'—he winced inwardly—'a home for yourself and your son with no more fears for the future. Will you at least consider it?'

He would have raised her captive hands to his lips, but she tugged them free at last, to rub her damp palms down the skirts of her gown. She shook her head, took a step in retreat.

Which Lord Faringdon accepted and made a little bow. 'Mrs Russell—you owe me that at least you will think about my offer, as my employee. I would ask you not to reject it out of hand. I think that would be…fair.'

She heard the hint of a plea in his voice and for that moment, her treacherous heart picking up its beat, she could not doubt the sincerity in his outrageous offer. Of course she must consider it. Even if she could do nothing other than refuse it. Because, however much her heart, in its secret depths, might desire such an outcome, her common sense told her that it could never be. But since he had appealed to her sense of justice—with a certain low cunning—she must comply. She acknowledged the inclination of his head with a graceful curtsy. 'Very well, my lord. I agree that your proposition demands my consideration. I will think about it. I will give my answer tomorrow.'

Abandoning the suddenly irrelevant list of courses and their appropriate side dishes on the floor, she almost fled from the room.

Leaving his lordship with the thought that, although he had pressured her into not refusing his offer out of hand, he still had no confidence that she would accept. And that perhaps he had done too well in creating a reputation for himself, which no honourable woman would willingly take on. Remembering the shock—the outrage—at his offer and her readiness to believe that he would humiliate her by taking her as his mistress, he suffered an unaccustomed sense of hurt, but firmed his lips against it. It was his own fault and he must live with the consequences.

It was no surprise at all to Sarah that she spent a sleepless night. Disbelief refused to let her rest. A proposal of marriage. Lord

Faringdon's *wife*! She might as well have wished for the moon. As a lady of neat and fairly predictable habits she sat in her room before a dying fire with a pen and paper and prepared to compose two lists, absorbing the quietness around her. Aware of her son sleeping next door. And Beth in her own room. All was comfort and luxury. Warmth and security. Yet nameless anxieties and indecision gnawed at her mind, troubled her heart. What would it be like to put herself into Joshua Faringdon's power? To give him the rights of a husband over her, to allow him to take her to his bed? Sarah shivered a little despite the warmth of the fire. It was unimaginable.

She put pen to paper to write in her careful flowing script.

Why I should not even contemplate marriage to Lord Faringdon.

1. It would be accepting an offer of charity.

She had told Judith that she would make her own way in the world. And promised herself that she would never again be dependent on the whims or desires of any man. She nodded agreement with her first point.

2. He has an undesirable reputation as a rake. It would not be a respectable marriage.

Well, that was certainly true. She had seen him with the Countess of Wexford in a situation that gave credence to all rumours about their relationship. Living in the same house together, they had flouted all convention. Then there were the opera dancers. Not that she had seen any, of course. As for what had occurred in Paris… No, Sarah decided, she was far too conventional to consider such a liaison with a man who had cast aside the honour of a gentleman.

3. What is Lord Faringdon's reason for his proposal?

She had no idea and it worried her. As she had said to his face, he could marry anyone he chose. A mama of a hopeful débutante might consider overlooking his disreputable past if he was willing to bestow his wealth and his title on her daughter. So why should he want to marry *her*? She was *five-and-*

twenty years old and a widow with a son. She frowned at her list. She did not want to be in the hands of a man who might use her for his own ends—a legacy of Edward's treatment of her. She should undoubtedly refuse Lord Faringdon's offer. She wrote again.

4. I have nothing of my own to bring to this marriage.

Her mind repeated her written words. She would bring nothing of her own to the marriage. No money, property or connection. No beauty or superior intelligence. No dramatic traits of character as did her sister Theodora. She did not care to admit it, but honesty forced her to do so. She appeared to be a very dull—a very ordinary—person, which once again caused her to nibble the end of her pen with unease—until she threw it down in disgust. Only to pick it up to add one final flourish.

5. He does not love me.

That was not a matter on which she cared to dwell.

These were very strong arguments, Sarah was forced to agree. So she would refuse Lord Faringdon's kind but inexplicable offer. Which decision caused her to pick up her ill-treated pen once more and a clean sheet of paper.

Why I should accept the offer and become Lady Joshua Faringdon.

A lot of thought was required here. It was not a list as easily begun as the previous one. But at last she began.

1. Security.

For herself and for her son. She would never again have to worry over the future and whether she would have the means to put a roof over John's head or clothes on his back. And there would be so many advantages for him. John would be able to have a horse of his own and— She stopped her mind dwelling on such material trivialities to return to the matter in hand.

2. Beth.

She would have the continued care of Beth, which she would enjoy as a mother, not merely a governess. She would enjoy a daughter.

3. I can renew my friendship with Judith and Simon.

That would be good. And she would not have Thea bearing down on her, demanding to know what she was about. Sarah smiled. She would have liked to talk to Thea about this whole unbelievable situation.

Then pursed her lips. She had told Judith that she would only marry again for love. For nothing less. With a sharp inhalation she rubbed ink from her fingers. Then, before she could change her mind, she wrote:

4. I love him.

As she closed her eyes against her admission, written there for all to see, the image came into her mind, startlingly clear. The sharp planes and angles of his face, the beauty of his eyes, which silvered when he smiled and they caught the light, the dense metallic pewter of his hair. The elegance of his figure, even though he still struggled with pain and discomfort. How very splendid he was. How he caused her breath to shorten and her mouth to dry—foolish woman that she was! And there was also his kindness to her and to John. And that extra quality, which drew her emotions inexorably to him, however much against her will. So what if he was a heartless rake and a libertine? He had never been heartless in his dealings with her. What if he could never love her? She could love him and live with him as his wife. She could certainly keep him out of the talons of avaricious women such as Olivia Wexford. His title and his wealth meant nothing to her. But the chance to be his wife, to be near him, meant everything.

Sarah sat and simply looked at the two lists, one beside the other, measuring and discarding. It was the matter of her dependence—or lack of it—that was the thing, she decided. And the Countess of Wexford, of course. She would be foolish to deny that! She bared her teeth in a fair imitation of a snarl as she recalled the lady's smug complacence when she placed her slender fingers on Joshua's wrist, demanding all his attention, to the exclusion of all else. But perhaps there were ways around such obstacles if she really wished… A little smile curved her lips, a bubble of excitement erupted in her blood. She hugged herself. Perhaps after all… Then rose to her feet to consign both lists to the flames, watching as they disintegrated into ash.

Next day Mrs Russell duly requested an interview with Lord Faringdon and wasted no time.

'I have thought of your proposal, my lord. I made a list.'

'A list? I see.' Or perhaps he didn't. What an unexpectedly fascinating woman she was. 'And your decision?'

'I will accept. I will marry you if that is your wish.'

Lord Joshua tightened his muscles against the sudden and unexpected surge of satisfaction at her words. He had not, in all honesty, thought it a possible outcome.

'But I would make a suggestion,' his housekeeper continued before he could reply.

'Ah…' Now what on earth…?

'I think we should consider a contract before we make our final decision.'

'Well, if you wish it…' He tried not to allow the puzzlement to appear on his face, in his voice. 'Do you not trust me to deal with you fairly as my wife? Of course there will be a legal contract, a binding settlement to ensure the future of yourself and John.'

'No—I did not mean that… I know that you will do everything that is right in way of a settlement. I meant something in the way of a more *personal* contract—what we expect from each other and from our marriage to each other—if you take my meaning,' It was suddenly very difficult to explain. She looked at him with anxiety, praying for understanding.

Lord Faringdon experienced a sharp tug of amusement, but he would not dare to laugh while faced with this most serious lady. 'If that is what you wish,' he agreed, a little warily. 'But why?'

'You may not wish to marry me when you see what I would hope for.'

'I see.' Again he didn't, but he would allow her to have her own way.

'Then I will write a list of…of my terms—and you should do likewise—of what you wish from me as your wife.' Colour rose to tint her cheeks deliciously, instantly captivating him.

'And if our two lists are acceptable?' His expression remained remarkably solemn. 'Compatible?'

'Then I will accept your kind offer, my lord.'

It was hardly a romantic basis for a marriage, but he inclined his head in stern agreement. *He would not smile!* 'Thank you, Mrs Russell. And how long do you envisage for this writing of compatible lists?'

'I would like a week in which to consider it, my lord. If that is to your liking.'

'Very well. You shall have a week to decide on my fitness to be your husband.'

Ignoring this deliberate provocation, suspecting his amusement at her expense, Sarah immediately turned to go, the business completed, but he stopped her, his voice gentle yet still commanding. 'Will you allow me to do one thing, madam? To seal our agreement?'

'Of course, sir.'

'I would like to kiss your fingers.' Her lips, he decided, with some degree of disappointment, were clearly beyond bounds here.

'Why…yes…if you wish it, sir.'

Never had he approached so reluctant a lady. But nothing deterred, he bowed with due and solemn courtesy before her and, when she placed her hand in his, he raised it to his lips in the most formal of gestures. Her skin was cool and soft beneath the warmth of his mouth. 'You are very practical, Mrs Russell. It would not do to embark on a liaison that stood little chance of success. I shall pray for compatibility.'

'Yes, my lord.' *He was laughing at her!* Her brows twitched together in suspicion.

He really would have to stop her inclination to use such formality—but perhaps not yet. 'Perhaps we shall deal well together, madam.' He took the opportunity to capture her other hand, to kiss those fingers as well.

'It would be my wish, my lord. I would not desire you to be dissatisfied with the results of your most generous offer.' The colour deepened with her reply. If she had but realised, he thought, it was a very sad little comment on her experience of life. He found himself reluctant to release her hands after all.

But Sarah drew away. 'If you will excuse me, sir, Beth will be waiting for me for her lesson.'

'And what is it to be today?' He tried to lighten the tension between them.

'French, my lord.'

'Of course. Then I should say *"Merci et au revoir, Madame Russell".*'

At some time during the following week Lord Faringdon sat down at his desk with a sheet of blank paper before him. For some inexplicable female reason, Sarah Russell wanted a contract between them. He supposed that he must give it some thought before the eleventh hour. What on earth would she expect from him? She had said that they should write what they hoped for from the match.

Be practical! *That* was what she would expect. Mrs Russell was a very practical lady. With his black brows drawn into a forbidding line, his lordship selected a pen and without a heading to the sheet wrote for a minute in forceful black script.

To undertake and oversee the running of my houses in London, Richmond and Yorkshire. Also my rented property in Paris.

He looked at it. That was good. Then:

To care for and be a mother to my daughter Celestine.

Fine! He had spoken to her about these two issues after all. Now what? He could think of nothing more and, in a similar frustrated fashion to that experienced by his beleaguered housekeeper, threw down the pen with disgust. It read like the dry and formal words of a lawyer rather than the tender desires of a prospective husband! Lord Faringdon poured a glass of port and sipped it, contemplating the blank space on the page, selecting and discarding ideas. *To allay some of the scandal in my life by providing me with a new bride?* A flippant comment, he decided, and an empty hope. Marriage would not necessarily still wagging tongues. So no point in adding it. *To warm my bed at night?* As his wife, she would, of course. He had no intention of entering into a marriage that was in name only. So why include it?

He looked at the sheet, an accusatory stare. A poor attempt, but he could do no better. He finished the port and abandoned the attempt with a sigh of relief. After all, he still had two more days before he must enter into negotiations with Mrs Russell. Perhaps he would think of something before then.

One week from their previous discussion they met as arranged, for Lord Faringdon at an unacceptably early hour in the morning. Mrs Russell presented herself in the library, all business, to discuss the matter of the proposed personal contract. He would not guess at the rapid flutter of her pulse beneath the discreetly high neck of her gown.

'Well, Mrs Russell. Our contract.' He glanced down at the sheet of paper tucked beneath the blotter on his desk, the content of which had given him so much difficulty. There was little to be seen to reflect all the mental effort. He had added nothing since his original attempt.

'Yes, my lord.' Sarah unfolded the sheet that she carried.

His lordship stared at it with horror. Even from a distance he could see that the single sheet was covered from top to bottom with her neat writing. And numbered points, no less, unless he was much mistaken. There must be at least eight or nine there! What on earth had the woman found to write about? He cast another surreptitious glance down at his own, hoping that it was out of sight of the lady who clearly required much from him. Two sentences only! His brain scrambled furiously as he grew aware of the silence that was beginning to stretch between them. Would she be insulted if he had only two requests or hopes from their proposed marriage? Of course she would!

When he raised his eyes again to the lady, who waited so patiently for his reply, he thought he detected a hint of uncertainty in her clear gaze. She would surely think that he was about to renege on his offer. He must put her mind at rest. So he coughed to hide the astonished amusement that had threatened to rob him of words and managed a smile.

'Forgive me, Mrs Russell. I need another few hours—for so momentous an event, you understand. Perhaps you would take tea with me this afternoon—as a guest, of course—and we can discuss the issues.'

'Very well. This afternoon, my lord. At three o'clock would be acceptable.'

She left the room, taking her list with her.

Lord Faringdon sat down at his desk and retrieved the paltry document from beneath the blotter. He picked up a pen and gave his mind to some serious thought! A desperate remedy was required—and quickly.

He allowed his mind to drift over what he knew of Mrs Russell. A quiet composed lady it would seem on first impression. Yet not so. Under the surface—who knew what tides and eddies surged? She was not unattractive, he acknowledged. If she would relax, smile a little more, and if she had time and money to consider her wardrobe and indulge herself a little, he believed that she would be more than passably pretty. Too often she was pale and strained. Life had not been kind to her.

Then there was the problem that she was self-effacing in the extreme. Would willingly fade into the Chinese wallpaper if she could rather than draw attention to herself. And yet she was competent and effective when dealing with areas under her jurisdiction. He could not fault her administration of his house or her authority over his staff.

He tapped the pen against the surface of the desk as he considered the crux of the matter as he saw it. She was totally lacking in self-worth, unaware of her own attractiveness and her own merits. Knowing of her background from Judith, the manner in which her brother had bribed and manipulated her until she had found herself involved in a despicable pretence, he understood that she suffered from a severe attack of guilt. And so suspected that she felt herself unworthy of love or affection. Yet she had been married. His lordship found himself contemplating the unknown Captain John Russell who had, it would appear, won Sarah's heart and trust. A difficult task, it would seem—if not impossible! She was quick to withdraw from all attempts at personal contact. From any moves to show friendship or warmth. Yet Judith found her a good friend and had much affection for her.

And if Theodora was her sister… So much energy and confidence there if Judith were to be believed. There must be hidden depths indeed locked in Sarah's neat figure. And perhaps he had seen them to a small extent. He recalled the delight of the French banquet, the Countess of Wexford firmly thwarted and put in her place. There was humour there, too, despite her frequently solemn exterior. And her joy in the garden with Beth and her son. Energy and innocent pleasure, a total joy in the foolish activities—until she became aware of his watching her. If he could give her that freedom and opportunity to enjoy and blossom… Well! He could soon fix that! A personal contract, she had said. Very well. He would add some very personal demands to his list.

With a sardonic twist to his lips, Lord Faringdon wrote for several minutes without pause, covering the rest of the sheet and part way down a second. Then threw down his pen with a laugh.

Mrs Russell might find that she had met her match. And if she would, might just enjoy the result!

Once again, at three o'clock precisely, Sarah had presented herself in Lord Faringdon's library. She had been ushered to a chair, had measured out the tea, poured the fragrant liquid, and had immediately put down the fragile painted china without tasting. Now she watched him and waited, with her heart in her mouth and her hopes for her future in his lordship's beautiful hands. Or, almost her hopes. She could hardly include in her list her yearning that one day he might love her, as she loved him, unconditionally and based on nothing but an unreasoning desire. She watched him as he read down the single sheet. As his brows arched at one point, then immediately drew together into a heavy frown, she swallowed. No need to be nervous, she chided, and blushed at some of the thoughts she had allowed herself to include. He could only refuse, after all, and she would have lost nothing. Except that she would be obliged to terminate her employment here and find another position. It would be too uncomfortable to continue. She waited as he read to the end, palms damp with nerves. Then sighed as he returned to the beginning and reread it, wishing not for the first time that she could read his face.

Fortunately, she could not.

Typical Sarah, he thought. *Careful and thoughtful and…and prim.* He hid his enjoyment of the situation. How right he had been in his assessment of her character. And he had every intention of destroying the demure sobriety that could frequently rob her of joy and pleasure. He would take the weight of care from her shoulders and allow her to blossom without restraint. She did not know that she needed liberating, of course, and would probably resist at every step, so his campaign must necessarily be devious. Her marriage terms touched not only his sense of the ridiculous but also his compassion.

Freedom to run his establishments and appoint servants to her own liking. He would expect that. But had there been some problem here of which he knew nothing? He had been unaware of any difficulties in Hanover Place. Whatever she desired on this matter, she could have her way.

A comfortable financial settlement for herself and her son to cushion the child's future. Well, that would be confirmed in the legal settlement, of course. And would be far more than comfortable, but there was no need to worry her with details of amounts and jointures.

Freedom to decide on the upbringing and education of John. Both acceptable and anticipated. As she would concern herself over the nurturing of Beth. He had no qualms on that issue. And had every intention of doing his best for the boy.

Her own wishes to be considered. Ah! Not to be coerced or dictated to or forced into actions against her will. His heart went out to her as she sat across from him silently awaiting his decision, even though he restrained himself from glancing in her direction. He knew exactly where that came from—and damned the unknown Edward Baxendale for his bitter legacy. In future, Sarah should have all the freedom she desired.

His brows rose in amazement, then snapped into a dark frown as he read on. No inappropriate orgies, entertainments, opera dancers or actresses in the house when she herself was present. Orgies? In God's name, what had she heard? Surely not Judith! Then, with a wry curl of his lips, he once more had to accept the far-reaching tendrils of gossip and innuendo surrounding his life in Paris and could not complain.

He shrugged and read on to the final lines. A comment that touched his heart. *I do not expect to be introduced to or be called upon to meet or acknowledge your mistress. I do not expect to have to receive her in my home.* The Countess of Wexford, of course! *I accept your freedom to take a mistress, given the pure convenience of our marriage, but I trust your sensitivity on this matter. I do not wish to have to acknowledge her.*

How tragic. That Sarah should consider herself so undesirable and unworthy of love that he would continue to keep a mistress. His reputation again stood him in no good stead. He was gripped with a need to remove all such doubts from her mind. And make her feel loved and desirable.

He placed the paper on the desk where his own cup of tea also remained untasted. Without a word, unsmiling, giving no hint of his feelings, he handed her his own greatly revised script. And watched with deceptively stern features as she sat and read.

When she had finished she raised her head, her face registering a curious mixture of bafflement and pleasure, colour tinting her cheeks. 'Well... You are very generous, sir. I do not see the necessity. The personal allowance...it is far too large for my needs...'

He knew that she would argue the issues at hand, but had no intention of retreating. 'When did a woman ever have enough money to spend on herself? Judith never does, if what she says is true. You will need pin money to keep you in fripperies and such.'

'But so much... And here...' She pointed at the page. 'That I should be willing to receive gifts from you...' She shook her head.

'Because I know that if I do not make it a prerequisite of marriage, you will decline. I wish to give you gifts and I wish you to enjoy them without feeling a need to refuse.'

'I hope that I would not be so ungracious!' More than a little ruffled now. 'And you desire that I should become fashionable and elegant.' He almost laughed aloud at the sudden anxiety on her face.

'Of course,' he replied with due solemnity. 'I expect Lady Faringdon to present herself in nothing but the height of fashion. As my wife I will expect you to go about in society.'

'But I do not know how—'

'Sarah!' He clenched his fists against a need to take hold of her shoulders and either kiss her or shake her into compliance. 'Speak to Judith. Or Theodora. Your sister's taste must, I am certain, be beyond question. And I think your colouring is the same as hers. Take her advice.'

'I suppose.' Sarah consulted the firm handwriting again. 'You seem to think that I will gain no enjoyment from this match.' Did he almost detect a flounce of temper there as she looked up? It delighted him. So he twitched the pages from her hand and read aloud: 'I expect you to enjoy—and you will notice that I have *underscored* the word many times—the benefits of my wealth and consequence.' He fixed her with a purposeful eye. 'I would wish you to be happy, Sarah.'

'And you would expect me to accompany you to Paris.' There was the faintest suggestion of panic there.

'Of course. We will employ a governess for Beth and John. As my wife, that is no longer your direct concern—except that I know you will wish to be involved. But I shall expect you to spend time with me.'

'Oh.' *My wife.* Wings of delicious terror fluttered in her belly.

'So, Mrs Russell. Can we live amicably together, do you suppose? To the advantage of both?'

'But you have said nothing in reply to my list.' She regarded him with sudden suspicion.

'I do not need to. I comply.'

'Are you sure?'

'Mrs Russell. Will you do me the honour of becoming my wife?'

'I—'

'If it truly worries you, I promise that there will never be orgies in this house—or any of my establishments. Whether when you are in residence or when you are not. If I change my mind and decide to host some tasteless extravaganza, I shall demand that you organise a French banquet worthy of the Prince Regent. Does that satisfy you?'

Sarah could not help but laugh. 'I should not have written that, should I?'

'No.' The laughter died a little from his eyes. 'You should not believe all rumours, particularly those to my detriment'— *even if I deliberately fostered them.* 'But still I promise that I will not.'

'Then—if you wish it—I will agree to marry you.' A shy smile touched her lips at last.

'Thank you. I might tell you that I have never fought so difficult a battle in all my life. Waterloo was nothing to this. Wellington did not know the half of it.'

She had the grace to blush. 'I did not mean to be difficult.'

'No. I am sure you did not. Since we are in agreement and since you have agreed to my terms, it is my desire that you wear this.'

From the drawer of his desk he produced an old silk pouch. Untying the strings, he extracted a circle of gold. 'It was in my mind to give you a diamond necklace to mark our betrothal, but I have it on the best authority that such tawdry gems can only signal the end of a relationship.' His voice was dry, but his smile was gentle and he shook his head at her questioning look. 'No matter. Give me your hand.' When she obeyed, he pushed the ring on to her finger 'Not a bad fit—a little large, but it can be remedied. It suits you very well.'

'It is beautiful.' It all but took her breath away. Never had she possessed anything so precious or so skilfully made. No one had ever given her jewellery before.

'It is old and has not been worn by ladies of the family for some generations, but it is pretty and I thought it would complement your beautiful eyes. As my affianced wife I would like you to wear it. If it would please you, dear Sarah,' he added on a thought, mindful of her fear of domestic dictates and the return of the velvet coat. His teeth glinted in an understanding smile.

'It would please me. I can think of no lady who could refuse so splendid a gift.' She moved her fingers, a little purr in her throat as the hoop of sapphires and pearls sparkled and glimmered in the light.

He sighed in some relief. He still could not quite believe that she had accepted him. Or understand why it should matter quite so much.

'Thank you, Sarah.' With a formal bow, he lifted her hand and kissed the ring where it encircled her finger, a potent symbol of their agreement and union. Then turned her hand to press his lips to her soft palm, a symbol of his own sense of achievement, had the lady but known it. 'We will fix a date for our marriage. And soon.'

'As you wish, my lord.' As Sarah made to leave the room, her cheeks decidedly pink, she came to a halt and looked back.

'What will you do with the—with our contracts, my lord?'

'Put them in the desk drawer for safekeeping,' was his prompt reply as if he had anticipated the question. 'And to find them easily if we wish to refer to them at any given moment.' His expression remained bland. 'If you decide that I am not keeping to my side of the bargain, Mrs Russell.'

Sarah laughed. 'No. I do not anticipate that will ever be necessary.'

'No? Well—I should warn you.' There was mischief here now. 'It is my intention to add a codicil. That since we have agreed to tie the knot, you will henceforth address me as Joshua.'

Sarah tilted her chin, her eyes glittering as brightly as the sapphires that bound her finger. 'And I will do so, now that we are in agreement. Joshua.' And left the room. Leaving Lord Faringdon to consider the pleasure of watching Sarah Russell—Sarah Faringdon!—open herself to her courageous heart and a playful humour.

Chapter Seven

Lord Nicholas Faringdon and his wife Theodora travelled without delay from Aymestry Manor in Herefordshire when the news of the impending nuptials reached them via Judith's astonished and information-laden letter. Theodora hardly stayed to set foot within the imposing portals of Faringdon House in Grosvenor Square before descending on the other Faringdon residence in Hanover Square and demanding from the overawed Millington that she wished to see Mrs Russell immediately.

'Sarah! Why did you not tell me? I had no idea.'

'Well! Neither did I.' Sarah served tea in her own sitting room to this dearest of sisters who, brought up as their own child by Sir Hector and Lady Drusilla Wooton-Devereux, had come into her life less than a year ago. They would not immediately be recognised as sisters, she thought as she cast an eye over the stylish creation that Theodora wore with such panache. Their fair colouring was the same, but Sarah knew that she must appear a pale imitation indeed beside this glowing and burnished beauty. Not to mention the confident sophistication with which Thea conducted herself, having been raised and introduced to the *beau monde* in the courts of Europe. Yet however much she might envy her sister her self-assurance and ability to take hold of life, Sarah loved her dearly and valued her advice. She smiled, her body relaxed for the first time in days as she lifted her tea cup to her lips. 'I am so very pleased to see you, Thea. I have felt in need of some support.'

'Well, of course. Dearest Sarah.' The deep sapphire of Thea's eyes shone with love and concern. 'I have never met Joshua Faringdon. He was still in Paris when Nicholas and I were wed, of course. All I know is that he is a widower with a young child. But I have heard Judith speak of him. And Lady Beatrice *refuses* to do so. I have to say, he does not sound quite the thing, Sarah. I think he has a…an *unfortunate reputation*. As Judith put it. And Nicholas is being particularly close-lipped.'

'I know,' Sarah replied with remarkable complacence. 'But…I do not think his reputation can be quite accurate. He has never behaved in a less than principled manner towards me.'

'You only met him a matter of weeks ago! You do not know him.' Thea could not understand how her careful sister could be so untroubled by the rumours of her intended husband's libertine propensities.

'True. Or not very well, at any event. And yet I cannot believe he is as lacking in good *ton* as the gossips make out. I know that Judith loves him dearly, in spite of everything. And he…Lord Faringdon…is very caring of his daughter. And to me he has been very kind.'

'*Kind?* Sarah…I cannot like it,' Thea persisted. 'I would not wish you to be hurt. If it is simply a matter of finding a home for yourself and John, you could live with us. John would love to be at Aymestry. You know that you would always be welcome.'

'No.' Sarah blinked at the force of her own denial. 'Forgive me, Thea. How rude that sounded! You see, I am perfectly capable of earning my own living. And…I find that I wish to marry Lord Joshua.'

'Of course you are capable. I would not imply… Sarah— are you sure? Of marriage?'

'Yes.'

'Do you like him?'

For the length of a heartbeat Sarah was silent. Then: 'I love him,' she replied with pure and shining simplicity. 'I barely know him, yet I know that I shall love him until the day I die. From the first moment that I set eyes on him when he entered the hallway here in this house. It is as uncomplicated as that.'

'Oh.' Thea frowned her concern. 'Does he know?'

'Of course not.' Sarah's eyes held her sister's in sudden distress. 'And you must not say. He must never know.'

'Do I then understand that his emotions are not similarly engaged?' Thea's frown deepened.

'No, I think not. Indeed, I am sure that they are not.' Relaxing again with a little smile, she took Thea's offered hand, accepting the warmth and not a little sympathy. 'He is, I think, driven by an affection. Beyond kindness, I think—but not love. I would never expect that. And he has, I think, a well-developed sense of chivalry to rescue me from invisible dragons!'

'Sarah—are you quite certain that this is the path which you wish to take?'

'I am.' There was conviction in her soft voice and a wry acceptance. 'But I am not sure that Lord Faringdon is. I cannot think why he would want to marry *me* when he could have his pick of the beautiful débutantes of the Season!'

Neither could Thea, given his lordship's reputation for escorting stunning and expensive females to the opera, as Judith had informed her in glorious detail. But she could hardly say that to Sarah, could she?

Nicholas ran his cousin to ground at Brooks's and sat with him over a decanter of port.

'Nick. I did not know you were in town so soon. I wonder why! Will you join me in a hand of whist?'

Lord Nicholas laughed as he poured the ruby liquid into two glasses and picked up the cards. 'You know very well why! Thea insisted. We had a letter from Judith, of course. She waxed eloquent of your doings, Sher.' They sat at ease, choosing and discarding the cards, the family likeness very evident in their height and build and striking Faringdon features, although, unlike his cousin, Nicholas's hair was dark as a crow's wing without any hint of silver.

'Ah.' Joshua's brows rose. 'Then all is clear.'

'Indeed. And will be even clearer when you have met my wife.' Joshua grinned. 'A strong-willed lady, I am led to understand.'

'She can be.' Nicholas drank, fully satisfied with his domestic situation after his fraught courtship and marriage with the outrageous but entirely intoxicating débutante, Theodora Wooton-Devereux. 'So. Marriage, is it?'

'Yes.'

'I can recommend it.' Nicholas angled a sharp glance at Joshua's impassive face.

'I have tried it before,' Joshua reminded him gently.

'I know.' Nicholas hid his concerns. 'I hope that this is a more propitious marriage.' Then, unconsciously mimicking his wife: 'Sher—are you sure?'

'Yes. But I am not sure that the bride is.' Lord Joshua abandoned his cards face down on the table, eyed the dark intensity of his port with a crease between his brows.

'You know, Sher...' Nicholas leaned forward to make his point, although unsure of his true intentions '...I have come to know Sarah very well. On the surface there is little similarity between Sarah and Theodora, as you will see for yourself. But beneath her gentle exterior Sarah has a spine of such strength, you could never imagine it. She can be truly intimidating, with a strong sense of justice, as I found to my cost when I was caught up in a web of intrigue and deceit with Theodora. I am not sure what I wish to say here—except that she is not as fragile as she might seem.'

'Oh?'

Nick shook his head. 'No.' He remembered Sarah taking him to task over his heartless treatment of Theodora when he had unjustly, cruelly, accused her of a harsh betrayal. 'All I mean to say is that it does not do to underestimate her. But perhaps you know that already.'

'I do.' The lines on Joshua's face smoothed out. 'Although I do not yet know her well, the lady has surprised me on more than one occasion.'

Nicholas nodded his satisfaction. 'So let us drink to your future happiness.'

They raised their glasses and did so.

Meanwhile Thea and Judith took Sarah under their combined elegant and sophisticated wing and carried her off to one of the most fashionable modistes in Bond Street.

'I need you to tell me what to wear for the occasion.' Sarah could not quench the very feminine ripple of pleasurable anticipation at the prospect as Judith's barouche collected her from Hanover Square. She had never in her life worn stylish clothing, having neither the money nor the opportunity. And now she was faced with a necessity! As she informed her interested audience of two, 'My lord—Joshua—insists that I be fashionable and stylish. That I spend a considerable amount of his money—and enjoy it. And I must accept gifts from him without argument. And I agreed.'

Which the ladies thought a strange statement for the bride to make but, beyond a quick glance between them, declined to comment.

'We shall be delighted to help.' Judith could think of no better manner in which to spend a morning. 'It is to be so soon.'

'And I am so nervous,' Sarah admitted. 'I am not sure why. It is not as though I have never been married before.'

Judith hugged her in quick understanding. 'Sher will never neglect or hurt you, you know,' she advised. 'He was always the kindest of brothers when I was growing up and a considerable nuisance.'

'I know, but I suddenly think I should never have agreed to it.' Apprehension washed over her again in a chilling wave, as it seemed to do with unnerving frequency as the day of her wedding grew ever closer.

'You deserve your good fortune.'

'Well—as to that…' She took a deep breath, her fingers clasping in white-knuckled tension. 'What if Lord Faringdon begins to have second thoughts when he remembers—'

'Sarah!' stated Judith sternly. 'You have long paid your debts to this family. Accept what Sher is prepared to give you. He never does anything that he does not wish to do, you can be very sure of that. Enjoy it.'

'Very well.' She visibly forced her pre-wedding nerves to settle, relieved beyond words that his lordship had found a need to visit Richmond for a few days and so would be away from home until the day before the wedding.

'Have you written to tell Eleanor and Hal?' Thea asked to distract the bride's mind from any further fears for her future marriage.

'Yes, indeed. I wrote this week.' It seemed to have the desired effect as Sarah's face brightened. 'I think they will be surprised. They do not even know that I have met Joshua, thinking he would still be in Paris.'

'But they will be delighted, I am sure.'

Sarah nodded. 'They have always wished me well.'

'We had a letter—last month, I think it was,' Judith informed her companions. 'One of Nell's lengthy epistles. Has Nicholas heard anything more since then, Thea?'

'No. Tell me that they are very happy.'

Judith laughed. 'Ecstatically—according to Nell. The baby is growing—Nell says that he has a will of iron exactly like his father when he is thwarted. But he is a delight—the baby and Hal, I suppose.' Judith chuckled. 'Hal is making money and a name for himself in local politics. Tom is more like a Faringdon every day. He will be a year or two older than John, I expect.' She turned to look at Sarah, only to see a flicker of unease in those quiet blue eyes.

'Yes. He will be eight years old now. I envy Hal and Eleanor— their love and commitment and happiness together.' Which caused Judith and Thea to realise that they had not distracted Sarah's mind from her problems at all.

'Here is Madame Stephanie's,' Judith said with some relief as the carriage pulled up.

Sarah smiled and set her mind to please her friends and solve the vexed question of clothing. 'So what do I wear? Nothing of your choosing, Thea! You would have me decked out in emerald and cream stripes, which would swamp me entirely. You can carry it off, but I could not.'

'Of course not.' Thea laughed as she smoothed the skirts of the stunning gown that she wore to magnificent effect. 'Not you at all. Now, let us think…'

The result of their lengthy visit to Madame Stephanie's was highly satisfying and in the way of a transformation. Sarah finally paraded before them in a high-waisted gown of delicate *eau de nil* with slender fitted sleeves and discreet ruffles around hem and low neckline. The watered silk shimmered in the light as she moved, as insubstantial as shadows under water. A velvet spencer was added in case the important day, so late in the year, was inclement. Gloves, kid sandals, and the ladies pronounced themselves delighted with the new bride. Finally a lace parasol, faintly ridiculous in November, but entirely necessary to a lady's wardrobe, which Judith insisted on buying for her as an impromptu wedding present, along with a matching silk reticule and a satin straw bonnet with silk ribbons and flowers in the same hue. It was supremely elegant. Youthful but with a touch of maturity, exactly suited to a young widow. Festive enough for a quiet wedding and an informal wedding breakfast.

Perfect in every sense, Thea decided as she watched her sister, delighted for her happiness, but not without a hint foreboding. And hoped that Lord Joshua Faringdon might be more than a little surprised when he set eyes on the lady whom he had known only in the plain and formal garb of his housekeeper, solemn and withdrawn, rather than the laughing lady who posed before her reflection with grace and charm, her eyes shining with innocent pleasure in her new gown. There was so much in the way of love and generosity about Sarah for him to discover. Theodora smiled with perhaps a gentle malice towards the absent gentleman and silently wished her sister well.

Madame Stephanie nodded her approval with gushing compliments, seeing the future opportunities for dressing the new Lady Joshua Faringdon.

Judith clapped her hands in delight. 'Poor Sher. He has taken on a beauty and does not realise it. It will do him good!'

Sarah simply shook her head and blushed. But glanced at herself in the mirror with something like shock.

'The neckline of the dress sits well on you,' Thea observed as they prepared to depart. 'I think I will give you a string of pearls to wear with it.'

'I had some,' Sarah admitted, a trifle wistfully. 'From our mother—the only jewellery she had left for me to inherit. But I had to sell them. I needed the money, you see, when John, my husband, died…' She turned her face away to hide the flush of embarrassment. 'I did not mean to tell you that.'

'Oh, Sarah. I don't think I ever realised how difficult things must have been for you. I am so sorry.'

'On occasion they were.' Sarah turned back with the sweetest of smiles. 'But not today. Today I have forgotten the dark times.' Her quick smile illuminated her whole face as she squeezed Thea's hand, and Thea prayed silently that the tranquillity and happiness, so absent from Sarah's life, would now enfold her for eternity.

Although Sarah might have been entirely caught up in preparations for her marriage, she was determined not to neglect her responsibilities as housekeeper and governess since she had not as yet been replaced in either role. It was not in her nature to do so—nor to sit at ease; since Joshua was still absent in Richmond, it gave her thoughts something to occupy them. But not enough. At any time during the day—or night—she found herself thinking of what he might be doing and when he might return. Was he missing her, even a little, or did he never give her a passing thought beyond that of an obligation to which he was now tied through some quixotic impulse and which he was coming to regret? She hissed her frustrations and looked round for something else to do. So, the next day, after a particularly tedious lesson—even to her mind—in the use of globes with John and Beth, she decide to investigate the attics. The top floor of the house in Hanover Square was a place, like all attics as far as Sarah was concerned, of dust and cobwebs and stored treasures that had long outlived their usefulness.

'Just look at all this!' She stood with her hands on her hips, daunted by the extent of abandoned relics of a past life in the house.

'It's exciting.' Eyes round, John could hardly restrain his joy. 'Like Aladdin's cave in the stories. Or buried treasure.'

Beth twitched her skirts from the dust with superior distaste, but was secretly enthralled. 'Can we look in the boxes?'

John was already opening and closing them, declaring it better than lessons. 'It's just like exploring an unknown country, as Captain Cook did. As I will do when I am old enough to have my own ship. I shall discover a new country. Perhaps more than one.' He pulled out an elderly stuffed bird, probably an owl, its feathers moulting on the floor. 'Which country did this come from?'

'England, I think. Nothing too exciting.' His mama smiled. Today it was ships and exploration rather than horses.

She regarded the jumbled piles of unwanted items with a sudden decision not to embark on such a project until she really had nothing better to do. Pieces of furniture, some heavy and carved, some spindly and gilded, but all long out of fashion. A box of unframed water colours of pastoral scenes by some eighteenth-century Faringdon lady—no talent here, Sarah judged, so no wonder they had been allowed to moulder in the attic. There were boxes of clothes, dry and dusty and lavender scented, with a hint of moth, which allowed Beth, to her delight, to dress up and parade in some outmoded creation in heavy damask with whalebone stays and a heavy train.

'Look at me!' Beth swept the floor, sending up clouds of dust. 'Am I not a lady?'

Sarah chuckled. 'You are indeed a fine lady.'

Beth fastened a spray of egret feathers in her hair, albeit lopsided. 'I think I am like Grandmama Beatrice. She often wears feathers and is very grand.'

'So she does. Take care with those backless slippers.'

'I can walk perfectly well in them.' Laughing, she swept an ungainly curtsy.

John entertained himself with cries of glee in a chest of discarded toys, lining up a row of broken long-faded lead soldiers. 'Perhaps I will be a soldier instead. Or a pirate. Can I be a pirate, Mama?'

'We'll see.' Now was not the moment to discuss so lawless an occupation. Meanwhile, Sarah inspected the rest. A firescreen, a birdcage with a broken door, frayed and worn bedhangings, packets of letters and old documents—all the detritus of life over the years—no, she certainly did not have the energy to clear it all out. Besides, as Lady Faringdon, she would have every excuse not to roll up her sleeves and tackle it herself.

Stacked against the far wall were paintings, some of them of houses and parkland. One was of the estate in Richmond, from the name inscribed in the frame, one might have been the Faringdon country house at Burford under its discoloured varnish, the rest she did not recognise. And portraits. One of Lady Beatrice, probably in the early days of her marriage, which brought a glint of amusement to Sarah's eyes. She understood exactly why that lady had banished it to the dust and darkness. The artist had no flair and had captured no flattering features in the sitter. One pair of matching portraits showed Joshua and Judith as children. Very attractive, with Judith looking positively angelic and Joshua vastly superior. The rest, as far as she could tell, were old, of people she did not recognise, with Faringdon colouring and features, but with the stiff formality and dress of the past two centuries.

Finally, a group of smaller portraits came to hand, which she turned over with little interest. Family again. Until coming upon a small portrait, life size, but head and shoulders only, which caught her attention. From the neckline of the gown, low across the generous bosom, and the styling of the hair into high-crowned ringlets, it would seem to be of recent origin. Perhaps even in the last decade. A striking lady, young, but not a girl, and not a Faringdon. A dark brunette with distinctly slanted brows and high cheekbones, not a classic beauty, but arresting. And with a tantalising smile on her full mouth and a flirtatious sparkle in her dark eyes, as if she would beckon and beguile. A charming representation. Sarah gained the impression that the artist had caught the lady's expression to perfection.

So who was this?

Beth had staggered dangerously to her shoulder in a pair of high-heeled damask slippers, to investigate what she was doing.

'Do you recognise any of these portraits, Beth?' Sarah spread them on the floor and against the wall. 'Or this lady?' She held up the portrait to the branch of candles that they had brought with them.

'That is Grandmama.' Beth pointed at the disapproving image of Lady Beatrice as it leaned against the wall. Then shook her head, showing no interest in the rest, before returning to her less-than-stately pursuits.

Leaving Sarah to collect them together again and re-stack them against the wall. Was this lady perhaps Joshua's wife, Marianne? Beth's French mother. Sarah regarded the painted face with narrowed eyes, searching for any similarity. Beth might be too young to remember and recognise her. She would have been barely five years old when the lady died, and if she had rarely seen her… But if so, why would her portrait have been discarded here? Unless Joshua had indeed been heart-broken over her death as Judith had suggested, not able to bear the sight of her beloved features. Understandable, yet Sarah felt a tug of jealously that he should have been able to feel such affection for the enchanting Marianne. Certainly he never spoke of her, which might indicate a blighted passion and a damaged heart, and Sarah knew that she did not have the courage to initiate a conversation on the subject of Marianne Faringdon. She prepared to tuck the portrait away. If only Joshua might one day feel such overwhelming emotion toward *her*. But Sarah shook her head at her foolishness. How could she ever compare with this attractive lady in her husband's affections?

Or—another thought suddenly struck, a painful dart to her heart—perhaps it was not Marianne at all, but the portrait of a mistress, discarded here when the affair ended. Again, not a thought she wished to pursue.

Or more likely, Sarah decided with a firm determination to reclaim her common sense, it was a lady with no close connection whatsoever to the family. In which case there was no reason for Sarah to feel such a lowering of her spirits. She sighed, rose from her knees, to brush her cobwebbed hands down her skirts in resignation. Whatever the possibilities, it was not her concern.

She turned the lady's demanding and flirtatious gaze to the wall, to set about persuading a pair of extremely dusty children to leave so miraculous a source of unexpected delights.

Pictures in attics proved to be only one cause of disquiet for Sarah. And not the most unsettling. During her continuing over-seeing of the house, she found herself in the rooms occupied until late by the Countess of Wexford. They had been thoroughly cleaned and set to rights on that lady's departure. Sarah, critically, looked around. The maids, she was forced to acknowledge, had done an excellent job, probably rejoicing in being able to sweep all remnants of that demanding lady from their existence. But then she saw that there on the bed lay a pair of gloves, in the softest of pale grey kid, undoubtedly of French manufacture. Overlooked and forgotten probably, in a drawer, when Hortense packed her mistress's belongings so rapidly. Perhaps the maid who had cleaned the rooms had found them and forgotten to bring them downstairs.

Sarah picked them up. Smoothed her fingers over their fine surface, lifted them to take in the scent that clung to them. The perfume immediately assailed her senses, heavy and sultry, highly reminiscent of the Countess's presence. For Sarah it brought the image of the Countess forcefully into her mind— beautiful, stylish, sophisticated—as if she had just polished a magic lamp and a genie had emerged to stand before her. Sarah frowned.

'I do not need *you* to continue to haunt this house! You are not welcome here!' Then, realising that she was speaking to empty air, she laughed softly. But she replaced the gloves and left them where she had found them. She did not wish to think about the Countess of Wexford, or her previous status in this house with regard to Lord Joshua Faringdon. It left her feeling edgy and not a little unhappy. What on earth was Lord Joshua doing, to offer marriage to Sarah Russell when he could have Olivia Wexford as his mistress?

So that by the time Joshua returned from Richmond, it was to discover that his intended bride was in a difficult and skittish mood. After greeting him formally, as his housekeeper, she made herself scarce below stairs, and then was impossible to pin down. Lord Joshua had no intention of treading on Mrs Beddows's preserve in the kitchen to find her. What a ridiculous situation this was when he could not separate his wife from the housekeeper, when she had found a bare two minutes to welcome him home as if she were still in his employ and then taken herself off to God knows where! He felt his temper building. He had spent his time at Richmond between the tedium of necessary estate business and contemplating his forthcoming nuptials with some bemusement. He was not sure how he had got himself to this point of asking Sarah Russell to marry him. Surely marriage was not the only way to solve the lady's problems. But he had, for better or worse. His lordship gritted his teeth. And now he wanted to see her and speak with her again. If he could just find her.

He ran her to ground in the formal dining room overlooking the Square where she was in process of replacing the ornate branched silver candlesticks. They had been newly polished and Sarah was engaged in repositioning them on the dining table and the sideboards. For a moment she was unaware of his standing in the doorway, giving him the opportunity to simply look at her. This woman, still little more than a stranger, to whom he had offered marriage. The first impression to deal him a flat-handed blow was that she looked different. Charmingly different. And being well versed in the niceties of female fashion, Lord Joshua immediately knew why. This was the influence of Judith and Thea, if he were not much mistaken. His lips curved in an indulgent smile. They had obviously taken his bride in hand with splendid results. Nothing outrageous or overstated for her delicate role between housekeeper and Lady Faringdon, but an elegant high-waisted gown in a clear summer blue, which he knew immediately would match and enhance her eyes. The sleeves were long and sleek to draw attention to her slender hands. The hem was ruffled and ribbon-trimmed, deliciously feminine. And her hair. It was caught up in frivolous ringlets that fell to her shoulder in the palest of gleaming gold silk, little curls fanning onto her cheeks. He had never thought of Sarah as being frivolous and found himself outrageously moved by the cool, calm elegance of the lady, the quiet dignity with which she completed so menial a task. With the sun angling through the window to gild her with its warm radiance, she was quite lovely. What had he expected from the lady who would be Lady Joshua Faringdon? Just this, he decided, but it still took him by surprise.

He stepped forward and she looked up, then swiftly back down to her task of placing the candlesticks with a nicety of judgement. What he had seen fleetingly in her eyes worried him. She was not at ease. But then, why did that not surprise him either?

'Sarah.' He walked toward her, a little hum of anger in his blood, replacing the sudden pleasure, whether at her or himself he had no very clear idea. But his nearness had the desired effect of forcing her to look up.

'Yes, my lord.'

'*Joshua.*' They were making no progress here. He stifled a sigh and kept a firm hand on any further sharp comment.

'Yes. Of course.' She looked at him, eyes wide, assessing, for some female reason that would doubtless be impossible for a mere male to determine.

'What is it? What is wrong?' He felt the frown begin between his brows, but could not prevent it.

Sarah saw it too. 'Nothing is wrong—exactly.'

'Then if it is nothing exactly, perhaps you could abandon my silver and give your attention to me for a moment. I think I am more important.' Nor could he prevent the edge in his voice.

It raised the faintest of smiles from his bride as she recognised the arrogant response, which ruffled him still further. So he leaned forward, took the candlestick from her fingers, placed it on the table with less care than might be expected for the highly polished rosewood surface and kept a grip of her hands when she automatically stepped back.

'Don't step away.'

'I didn't… I wasn't…' She was watching him, he realised, as a mouse would watch the approach of a large and hungry cat, wondering if she was about to become a tasty meal or could make a bolt for safety. The humour of it struck home at last and his face relaxed into a smile. The strange ill temper drained away to leave a sensation of lightness and relief.

'I have missed you. Sarah.' He kept his voice steady, willing her to respond.

'I have been busy.'

'So I see. You no longer look like the housekeeper I left behind.'

Her face was instantly flushed with deepest rose. 'I have only—that is, I bought some clothes.'

'Again, as I see. Definitely not my severe housekeeper!'

'I did not think that you would mind if I spent some money—'

'As I do not. Did I not tell you to be extravagant?' There was still no warmth here, no acceptance of their new relationship. He would try again. Perhaps he should not have left her alone at this critical time before their marriage.

'The colour is most becoming. And your hair—very elegant.' He lifted a hand to stroke one finger round an errant curl. Her light perfume touched his senses. 'All in all, my dear Sarah, I believe you are quite the thing.'

Sarah merely shook her head, misery clouding her eyes.

'What is it, Sarah? Whatever it is cannot be so bad that you flinch from telling me. I am not an ogre.'

'I know. I would never suggest…' Well, she would say it. 'I cannot think why you would wish to marry me.' Sarah found herself speaking her fears against every intention.

'Why should I not?'

'I am not beautiful or elegant or sophisticated—or any of the things you would look for in your wife.'

'Why do you say that? I find you to be everything I wish for. At this moment you look perfectly lovely. Why should you deny yourself?'

'How can I believe you?' The memory of the gloves returned in bright focus. 'I know that I cannot possibly measure up to the glamour of the Countess of Wexford.'

'I do not wish to marry the Countess of Wexford.' Here was dangerous ground.

'No. But I still do not understand why you should wish to marry *me*.' All Sarah's self-doubts and insecurities rolled back to swamp her.

'Then I will show you.' He drew her closer, releasing her hands to run his hands the length of her arms, smooth and slow, to her shoulders. 'Look up.' What he saw in her face, trepidation, nerves, a little fear, persuaded him of the need to be considerate with her, but he would kiss her. So he did. The first intimate demand he had ever made on her. A kiss that began as a simple touch of mouth against mouth. Until his response to her astounded him. Taken aback by the utter sweetness of her, hunger lunged as a wild beast and gripped him. And heat struck him as a fist to the gut when her mouth opened under the demand of his. Her light perfume filled his head and his loins, seductively sweet. Instinctively he tightened his hold and deepened the kiss, changing the angle of his head to take her lips as he wished. His body would not allow him to refuse the gift she offered so innocently as she moved closer within his arms and let him mould her soft curves to his firmly muscled frame.

Joshua lifted his head and took a breath. Well. He had not expected so basic a response to her. Sarah might claim to have no skills to attract, but her effect on him was undoubtable. Eyes wide, her lips parted, she looked up at him, as much shocked as he. He had, of course, to kiss her again. Thoroughly, needily, absorbing the warmth and softness of her body against his.

Sarah could not recognise, could not accept, the sheer glory of it. Every nerve in her body jumped in immediate answer to his demand, the thrill of his mouth on hers. Every inch of her skin so sensitive from that one kiss, so that when he claimed her mouth again she had no qualms about surrender. Her lips parted to accept the imperious invasion of his tongue, her arms crept around his neck, her fingers locking against and through his soft, dense hair. Had she not desired exactly this? When he pressed her closer yet so that she might be aware of his need, she did not resist but exulted in it. She could feel the hunger in him and allowed it to dissipate her own insecurity.

Did he truly want her in that way?

Joshua released her, held her a distance away from him, knowing his own vulnerability. His dining room was no place to satisfy so raw a hunger with his housekeeper, no matter how great the temptation. He took a step back, but not before he smoothed his thumb along her lips—so tempting to take them again—in a tender caress.

'As I said, I had missed you, dear Sarah.' He bit down on the urgency that swam in his blood. 'I just did not realise how much.'

The marriage of Lord Joshua Faringdon and Mrs Sarah Russell, celebrated by special licence in St George's Church, Hanover Square, followed by a breakfast at the home of the happy couple, was an occasion for a positive fusillade of good wishes and advice and warnings from all sides. It was, the groom decided, since most of the barbed comments were fired in his direction, a most exhausting occasion. The bride was composed and charmingly pretty in pale silk. The groom austerely dramatic in a deep blue superfine coat, highly polished Hessians, his cravat superbly tied by the hand of a master. The bride was suitably fragile and slender, the groom stood straight and tall at her side. He would not limp to his own marriage.

'Be happy,' Theodora whispered to her sister with a congratulatory kiss. 'The Faringdon men are magnificent.'

'I know it,' Sarah replied with a quick hug, unable to believe that this splendid man, head bent in serious and probably unwelcome conversation with Lady Beatrice, was now her husband.

* * *

Since Nicholas had already expressed his concerns to Joshua, he said no more than, 'I wish you well. We have a habit of marrying Baxendale women, do we not? You have a lovely bride, Sher.'

'So I have.' Joshua turned to watch her, the obvious pride in his face causing Nicholas to smile.

Theodora found much more to say to Lord Joshua. She pinned him with her direct regard, but was not unfriendly. Joshua seized the opportunity.

'Theodora. Rumours, may I say, were not false.'

'Rumours?' She eyed him suspiciously.

'That Nick has found himself a prize. A jewel of great price.'

'Are you trying to charm me?'

'Of course.'

'Ha!' But, allowing herself to be charmed by this extremely handsome man—only second to her own darling Nicholas—she touched a hand to his wrist as her lips curved and her eyes twinkled. 'Be kind to Sarah.'

'Well—it was my intention to beat her soundly every night until she obeyed my every whim!'

'That is not what I meant, as you very well know!' She had the grace to laugh and ask forgiveness. 'Can I tell you? Perhaps I should not, but Sarah… Well, she carries a—'

Joshua put out a hand to stop her. 'You are a good friend, Thea, but there is no need. Judith has told me of Sarah's life and the…the difficulties she encountered.' Thea could not but admire his sensitive discretion. 'I know the truth of it. I hope that I can win my lady's trust.'

Thea decided to take a risk. 'And her love?'

He thought for a moment, eyeing his cousin's beautiful wife. And with a steady gaze, chose not to dissemble. 'It would be my wish.' If his answer surprised him, he hid it well.

The reply was certainly one that robbed Thea of any light-hearted repartee. Before she could think of a suitable answer,

Nicholas stepped up to take her arm. 'Thea. Don't harass the poor man. Come and talk to Aunt Beatrice, who is most concerned about your state of health! As ever. Try to be tactful.'

Which gave Judith the opportunity to descend on her brother. 'I am delighted,' she announced with a kiss to his cheek. 'But don't break her heart. I will never forgive you if you do. She is my dear friend. And there is John to consider.'

'I shall, my dear Judith, do all that is necessary.'

By which time Lord Joshua Faringdon was feeling besieged and in need of a fortifying brandy.

Lady Beatrice, still unbending but at least present for the occasion in deep purple satin, had nothing but smiles and good wishes for Sarah.

'I presume that you know what you are about, my dear. It pleases me to have you as one of the family, now that all the past unpleasantness is over.'

Which surprised the bride, who had always regarded the imposing Dowager with not a little trepidation.

To Joshua she was less complimentary but, as he admitted to himself, at least in communication again. Perhaps he had discovered a way to redeem himself in her eyes.

'Congratulations, Joshua.' She raised the lorgnette, bringing back to his lordship uncomfortable memories of the misdemeanours of his childhood. But the Dowager was inclined to be generous. 'The best decision you have made for years. A far more suitable bride than that French person whom we rarely met. Not that I would have wished Marianne's death, of course, but Sarah is *English*. A perfect outcome, I must tell you, for that poor neglected motherless child of yours.'

And that, Joshua decided with a non-committal reply, was the best that he could expect.

* * *

The motherless child, anything but neglected, eyes sparkling with excitement over her new dress with its pink ribbons, was present with John's hand clasped in hers to ensure his good behaviour. John was completely overawed by the whole proceedings and the sudden inexplicable smartness of his mama.

Olivia Wexford was not invited.

One shadowy figure, unknown to any of those present in the church, watched and noted and wrote a concise but highly specific report of the marriage of Lord Joshua Faringdon to Mrs Sarah Russell, late of Whitchurch and New York, and had it hand-delivered to an unobtrusive address in the City.

At last Joshua managed a private conversation with his bride.

'Well, my lady? Are you satisfied?'

'Oh, yes.' For once the new Lady Faringdon answered without hesitation, straight from the heart, without thought or pretence. 'I think it must be the happiest day of my life.'

Joshua was entranced.

'Then it is my wish to give you many more such days. Why do you suppose that my family presume that I will bring you nothing but pain and heartbreak?'

Sarah tried to hide her amusement, having seen Lady Beatrice's censorious expression when in conversation with her son, but failed. 'I cannot understand where they got that idea!'

He laughed. 'You are very loyal. I think we shall deal well together.'

'As do I.'

'And if I do not, you can wave the contract under my nose at the breakfast table.'

'As I will, my lord, without doubt.'

'Joshua.'

Sarah laughed in response, unable to repress the bubbles that positively glittered through her veins as if she had drunk more

than a single glass of champagne at her wedding breakfast.
'Yes, Joshua.'

'Why did I not realise that my housekeeper was so beautiful?'

'It is the dress.' Suddenly sober again, as if she would deny
the evidence of his own eyes. 'It is all Thea's and Judith's
doing.'

'No. It is definitely you.' *Because today you are happy.* It
made his heart turn over. 'Thea is a remarkable woman. But so,
I believe, are you.'

Sarah flushed under his gaze, a comforting warmth stealing
around her heart. She had never been called remarkable in her life.

Joshua bent his head to kiss her hand and then her cheek,
where the skin was satin-smooth, and then her lips. They were
warm and soft and trembled a little under the easy pressure of
his own. But she did not pull away. And when he lifted his head
she smiled up into his face with unclouded joy.

It stopped his breath. If the occasion had not been so public, he would have claimed her lips again, in a sudden heat of
desire that no longer took him completely by surprise. It was
so easy to be seduced by her sweetness.

Whilst for Sarah, his kiss painted a gloss of crystal-bright
happiness over her whole world. She loved him. And perhaps
he did not find her totally unattractive.

And those who saw them together wished them well and noticed his care of her.

The deed was done. She had married him. Sarah sat at her
dressing table. Her maid—she had a maid now and a sumptuous bedchamber—had left her after folding away her wedding
finery. Now she sat in a dream of cream silk and lace, more delicate than any garment she had ever owned.

She sat quietly, her hands clasped loosely on her lap, and
thought back to her first wedding night. A long time ago now.
And tried to call to mind the first time that she had stepped into
the arms of her husband John as his wife. How sad, she thought,

a little melancholy that she could remember so little. It was difficult to bring his precise features to mind now beyond a fair complexion and eyes of a deeper blue than her own, although there were echoes of his face in their son, in the angle of his jaw, the line of his nose, the flat planes becoming clearer as he lost the chubby contours of babyhood.

As for intimate relations, they were even more hazy and indistinct. There had been so few. A short time together after the wedding—of necessity, dependent on shore leave and the prosecution of the war. Then war and John's untimely death had robbed her of his comforting presence. She remembered more than anything that he had been kind to her. Understanding and careful of her shyness and innocence. He had never hurt her. But, if honest, she could recall little pleasure of a physical nature except for the warmth of curling into his arms. The safety and comfort. Had that been love? Sarah supposed it had.

Then her fingers entwined in her lap with a fierce grip. If it was love, it was nothing in comparison with her feelings for this man whose name she now bore and whose ring encircled her finger as a mark of his possession. A ripple of heat shot down her spine to centre in her loins and her mouth was suddenly dry. She had no previous experience of this emotion. Or the sensations that overwhelmed her when his mouth claimed hers.

Sarah looked at her reflection in the glass and began to take the pins from her hair. The soft waves and curls, released in a cloud of perfume, drifted to her shoulders. She suddenly looked so much younger, so unsophisticated without her fashionable garments. What would her lord expect from her? If he hoped for the experience and knowledge of the Countess of Wexford, he would be severely disappointed. She had little experience and no knowledge of how to bring pleasure to a man. Nerves shivered in her belly. What if he did not like her? What if he did not desire her physically? A flush stained her cheeks and she turned her eyes from her reflection. There was nothing in her contract—or his—to cover that embarrassing eventuality.

What did she have to offer to an experienced man of the world compared with Olivia? Her eyes flew once again to her image before her, eyes wide, lips a little tremulous. Or an opera dancer. She had neither the face nor the figure to entice a man. Insipid was the word that came to mind. And perhaps the cream lace did nothing for her colouring. How lowering it was. Her confidence, built up through the day through the power of good wishes and kind words, drained away along with her finery.

What had she done?

Joshua opened the door quietly from his dressing room to see her sitting there.

As a doe facing the hunters, was his first thought. Apprehension was winding her nerves into tight coils, although he could see that she tried to hide it. The gentle blue of her eyes, the pale fragility of her skin, both were enhanced by the flattering candlelight, giving her a glow comparable with his pearls, which banded her finger. Not the hard glitter of a diamond or an emerald, to be sure, but definitely the deep glimmer of a pearl or an opal. She had unpinned her hair, was his second thought. He had never seen her with her hair down. It curled around her face in little drifts of pale gold, lay on her breast in a shimmer of softness. It increased her vulnerability, as if she had handed over control of her life with her ordered and restrained ringlets. The thought moved him, but cast him into a quandary of indecision. How much did she remember of her previous wedding night, her previous marriage? What had been her experience there, and what would she expect from him? He could, of course, simply consummate the legality of their marriage, take her physically as his wife and get it over with. A bleak prospect indeed. Perhaps that is all she required from him. But, as he watched her, he thought not, felt that she deserved more consideration at his hands. There should be pleasure in this relationship for her. And for himself.

'Sarah.'

Her nerves jumped a little. She dropped her comb onto the floor. It almost made him smile, except that she pushed herself to her feet and took a nervous step back. It determined his next move.

'Talk to me.' He held out his hand.

'Talk?' She was horrified to hear the uncontrolled squeak in her voice. Any remaining confidence evaporated entirely as she became aware of the man standing before her. The man to whom she now belonged. Impossibly handsome, clad in a rich satin dressing gown. She swallowed as her heart tripped and she found herself frozen to the spot.

'Yes, Sarah. Talk.' He smiled. 'Did you expect me to pull you to the floor and ravish you?'

'I do not know.' Still she could not move.

'I will not do that. I promise you.' She continued to ignore his outstretched hand.

'No. It is a marriage of convenience, after all.'

'You think I do not find you attractive.'

'I do not know that either. But there is no reason that you should. I have looked in my mirror and I am not blind.'

This would go nowhere. Nothing he could say would persuade her otherwise. So he must show her. But first he must overcome her reserve.

'Come and sit.' He reached to take hold of her wrist and led her to a chair beside the fireplace where the fire still burned with comforting warmth and pushed her to sit. He took a chair opposite. Far enough away not to intimidate, near enough to get her used to the idea of intimacy. 'Tell me about your first marriage. Your husband. Your life before I knew you.' A safe topic, he thought, that would allow her to select and discard at her own discretion, and speak without self-consciousness.

So Sarah found herself doing exactly as he intended, her nerves gradually dissipating, her voice becoming soft and relaxed. Her hands rested easily against the cream lace of her lap. She was able to smile and meet his eyes as her memories unfolded.

And he listened. To a picture of youth, inexperience, an escape from a troubled home, a brief but affectionate relationship with a man who was kind and loving. Joshua felt the sharp spur of jealousy as she spoke wistfully of Captain Russell, but this drained away when she told of her sad loss and then loneliness with a child and no security. She told him of her journey to New York, her life with Eleanor and Henry, her return and her first meeting with Theodora and the deep friendship that had grown between her and Judith. But all in a broad sweep. She filled in little detail, made light of much that must have caused her concern and unhappiness, and, most telling of all, made no mention of her brother Edward. As if she had cut him out of her life, out of her very existence, which was by all accounts true. But also out of her mind, which Joshua knew was not so.

He experienced a surge of pity for the young woman who sat before him, but he would never tell her that. His instinct to protect her and give her all the contentment she had lacked in her life grew stronger than ever.

'Were you happy here as my housekeeper?' he eventually asked with a smile as her ramblings came to a halt.

'Why, yes.' She found herself amused by his question and allowed it to show. 'Except for my employer, a difficult gentleman, who sometimes was arbitrary in his decisions.'

He laughed. 'Only sometimes?' Delicate colour had returned to her cheeks, animation to her face. It pleased him that she could smile without reserve. And made the decision at last.

'Come to bed, my wife. You have talked enough for one night.' He rose to his feet.

Sarah mirrored his actions. 'You have told me nothing of yourself. Whilst I have so little to tell, but have burdened you with all my past history. I feel like Scheherazade and her stories to fill a thousand and one nights.'

'Fortunately you do not have to tell a new tale every night and your life is not at stake, dependent on my enjoyment. Besides, the beautiful Scheherazade enchanted her royal master, did she not?' He touched her cheek with light fingers, savouring the silken texture of her skin. 'I shall enjoy you, my own Scheherazade. And I swear that I will do all in my life to make you happy.' Easy words to say, he realised, easy vows to make, but it was suddenly important that he keep that promise.

He led her to the bed. Blew out the candles, knowing instinctively that she would want the reassurance of the dark. Ever practical, Sarah drew back the fragrant linen and removed her own lace négligé. A prosaic little action, he thought, a calm acceptance of the situation as she turned to face him. Without a word he stooped to lift her, to place her against the soft pillows. Cushioned by the near dark, illuminated only be the warm glow from the dying fire, he could sense nothing but a composed acquiescence. She had married him and so would come to his bed. No fear, no denial, but neither was there any anticipation. She would give her body to him because it was a legal necessity and therefore he would require it.

It became for him a matter of some urgency to change that.

He slid out of his heavy robe and joined her, to do nothing more than put an arm around her and pull her close until her head rested against his shoulder, her body against his side. She did so, willingly enough, turning into him, allowing her hand to rest against the hard expanse of his chest. Of course she was not innocent of intimate relationships between man and woman. Not ignorant of the physical act or the pleasure to be experienced in a marriage bed. Yet Joshua Faringdon was aware of a distinct unease. His lips curled in a gentle self-mockery in the anonymity of the darkness because, for once in his life, he was uncertain how to proceed with this reserved but compliant woman whom he had made his wife. He let the problem drift and unravel in his mind as Sarah softened against him, her hair curling against his skin, the lingering perfume filling his senses.

They did not know each other well. That was the problem. They had not come together out of love or even lust, but from the binding of a legal document. But why should he feel this sense of disquiet? It was her fragility of spirit, he decided, her willingness to take herself to task when she believed her actions to be wanting, her inability to believe that he should need to possess her, to desire her for herself. So he must persuade her of her desirability, that she was capable of giving him pleasure, just as she was deserving of accepting it from him. So he would give her gentleness. Kindness. A soft awakening to what he could bring her.

So this was the task he set himself when he turned to her at last, angled his body so that he might look down at her. His kisses were whisper soft, his touch light and undemanding as he began his progress over the contours of her face with his lips. The delicate line of forehead and jaw, the softness of temple and the little hollow beneath her ear. The flutter of her pulse at the base of her throat. And he explored her lips. There had been few kisses between them in their brief association. Now he had the time to claim and explore, his tongue brushing along the edge of her lips, increasing the pressure of his mouth just a little so that hers would part to allow him to seek and enjoy. She sighed, complied, her breath fragrant against his face.

'Tell me if I do anything that you do not like, that you do not wish for,' he murmured against the delectable curve of her throat where the pulse had begun to beat more strongly. He did not think he had ever said that to any woman, presuming that he could seduce through skill and finesse. But Sarah was different. 'You have to accept nothing at my hands that does not bring you pleasure.'

'I like your kisses,' she whispered against his chest. 'They make me feel warm. As if I had drunk two glasses of champagne.'

'Good.' A soft laugh against her hair at her artless admission.

So with this tacit permission, his deft fingers unfastened the ribbons to push the cream confection from her shoulders, absorbing as he did so, his hands brushing over her skin, the fact that she was warm beneath his touch and not as unrelaxed as he had feared. So far so good. Then with hands and lips he set himself to discover more fully this woman whom he had so wilfully taken as his wife, to lure her unquiet mind into tranquil pathways, allowing her to enjoy all that he could bring to her. Delighted by the feminine curves beneath his fingers, he was enticed to touch and caress, following the delicate swell and hollow of breast and waist and thigh, from soft skin to softer yet. Until she shivered against him, and turned in his arms to offer what he might wish to take.

Of course she knew what would be required of her. He wanted her, was hard and ready for her. What man would not respond so strongly with so deliciously feminine a partner? He pulled her close, holding her firmly so that she might know the strength of his hunger.

He lifted himself above her, yet careful to take his weight on his forearms to hold back from crushing her. Her response was immediate as her thighs parted quite naturally to hold him, to allow him access. It was no difficulty at all for him to enter her, slowly, pushing gently as she opened for him. Keeping a firm hold on the instinctive desire to drive on and possess her, to fill her completely, even though there was no pain of virginity to overcome. Although Sarah stiffened at first, the smallest resistance to his invasion in so intimate a fashion, she sighed and arched a little against him, lifting her hips in the timeless feminine response. A gesture of acceptance and invitation that he was quick to recognise, and she lifted her arms to close around him, to hold him fast. A supremely innocent gesture that effectively destroyed all his self-control. So he thrust deep. Again and again, conscious of the slick heat of her, her body more than willing to receive him, even if her mind remained aloof and watchful. When his urge to complete the matter could not be withstood, she moved with him, arching her hips against him, all soft compliance and acceptance. Until he climaxed, chest heaving, muscles taut with strain.

A perfectly satisfactory completion of their new relationship. And yet… And yet what? As he held himself still, deep within the impossibly soft heat of her, he knew that Sarah had not come to her own fulfilment. Suspected that she had never been close, hedged round by reserve and restraint, afraid to abandon her self-control, which, in her eyes, would make her vulnerable to him. So he felt a wave of disappointment coat his own satisfaction. She had not been unwilling—indeed, she had been wonderfully soft and pliant—but neither had she shown any true enjoyment, giving him no intimation of whether she had experienced any pleasure in their intimacy or not. She had not told him that she didn't, but neither had he gained any sense of her complete involvement in the act. He had taken her body, but she had been a passive onlooker, willing but uncommitted, with no indication of her own thoughts or feelings But then, as he turned his face against her throat to breathe in her perfume, he was left to wonder if Sarah ever would.

Withdrawing from her, he moved to lie beside her and pulled her close beside him again.

'Well?' he murmured the word against her hair when she still made no sign, no comment. What the hell should he say to a woman who was so quiescent?

Sarah promptly stiffened in his arms, as if to be asked her opinion of so momentous an event would frighten her to death.

Joshua sighed. Could his pride and his masculinity take it, he thought, on a touch of humour? 'Was it too bad?' he asked, the humour clear in his voice, hoping to lull her into a warm response.

Sarah did not notice, but answered the question rather than the intent. 'Not at all.' Her voice was tight and strained. As if he had asked her opinion of a visit to the theatre to watch a particularly bad play and she did not wish to hurt his feelings. 'I enjoyed it. You were very kind. I hope you found me satisfactory.' It was so bleak a statement it touched his heart. He could think of nothing to say that would make any sense. It had been a long day and it was clear that the lady was not receptive of reasoned thought, only strained emotions. With time, he hoped, it would improve between them. So he resorted to kissing her again, a long and lingering kiss, full of tenderness that would make no further demands on her. Had she not admitted that she enjoyed his kisses?

'You gave me great pleasure, lady. Can you sleep now?'

'Yes.'

He positioned her head more comfortably in the curve of his shoulder and kept his arms firmly around her. Why did he get the strongest feeling that she would escape if given the chance?

'Joshua?'

'Mmm?'

'Will you stay with me?' There was the faintest suggestion of surprise here as if she expected him to retire to his own room. Perhaps she did. Indeed, if she were honest, perhaps she wished it. Again he was conscious of a ripple of disillusion, but if she would not be completely honest, he would.

'It is my intention. But only if you wish me to do so. If you wish for time alone, I will give you that seclusion.'

There was a silence. She was thinking about it and he had no idea what she would say.

'Sarah?'

'I would like you to stay with me.'

'Then it will be my pleasure.' The relief in his heart seemed to him totally out of keeping with her simply stated desire. He tucked the covers around her, around both of them. 'Go to sleep, my dear girl. There is nothing to worry you now.'

But Sarah did not sleep. Without doubt she was weary, but her mind could not rest. It played over and over the events of the past hour. Causing her to flinch at her naïveté and lack of confidence. At her lack of suitable words to say to him, when he had been so tender, so considerate of her. What could she possibly say to him? That he had awakened emotions and sensations of which she had never been aware, wonderful sensations that drove a flush to her cheeks? She could not tell him that, could not admit to such lack of knowledge. So why had she not been able to give as freely as he had given her? She did not know the answer to that. And yet Joshua had made her feel cherished, wanted, desired. How skilled he had been. Just the thought of the power of his clever hands roused shivers along her flesh. All she could do was hope that he had been satisfied with her poor efforts. The dread spectre of the Countess of Wexford returned once more to the edge of her mind, to stand beside the bed with a disdainful lift to her perfect brows. She could never be like the Countess—confident, experienced, knowing—no matter how long she lived, no matter how tolerant her lord could continue to be. Sarah sighed against his chest. He had been honourable enough to pretend that she had been everything he had wanted. She must try harder to achieve that so that he would not turn from her in dissatisfaction.

Because if she had known before that she had loved him, it was now engraved in her heart, for all time, in letters of pure gold.

Lord Joshua held her, aware of her wakefulness, guessing at the swirling pattern of thoughts that refused to permit her mind to sink into sleep. But he said nothing, allowing her the pretence, conscious only of her softness against him. It seemed that for tonight he must be satisfied with her willingness to rest in his arms and was relieved when at last exhaustion claimed her and her breathing settled. She slid into sleep with a little sigh. It would not be an easy marriage, he realised. She was too tense, too nervous, too much embattled by fears and past influences. But they had made a start and it would improve. He smiled at the direction of his thoughts. He would like nothing better than that she could find it in her to come to him with joy and pleasure, with confidence, to find fulfilment in his arms.

The thought remained with him, one of hope, as he, too, drifted into unconsciousness.

Chapter Eight

⁓⁓⁓⁓⁓

Rather than a more conventional honeymoon, perhaps in the Italian Lakes or on the romantic shores of the Adriatic, Lord and Lady Joshua Faringdon took themselves, the children and their household to the attractive estate on the edge of Richmond. After the flurry of activity to prepare for the wedding, by the bride at least, the rural tranquillity was a blessing, and an opportunity for the new family to become better acquainted. And not merely the bride and groom. Sarah would have been particularly interested in a private conversation between Lord Joshua Faringdon and Master John Russell when she was not present. She might have blushed at her son's blunt style, but she would not have been surprised and would certainly not have been displeased at the outcome.

'Sir.' Joshua looked up to see the boy standing just inside the open library door one morning, the opportunity still there for flight if his courage failed him. 'Sir… Will you now be my father?'

Ah. He should have expected this—but perhaps not quite so soon. John, it seemed, was as expedient as his mother. Joshua held out his hand to encourage the child to approach. 'No. Your father is Captain John Russell, for whom you are named.' And waited.

'Yes.' John nodded. 'He was a hero and died in a battle. Mama told me. He sailed a ship all by himself.'

'He did.'

'He was very brave, but he died.' A thoughtful pause as John leaned against the polished desk, rubbing the edge with none-too-clean fingers. 'Does Mama like you?'

'I hope so.' Joshua fought against the irresistible ripple of laughter that threatened his composure. 'She likes me enough to live with me.'

Which was accepted with a nonchalant shrug. 'Will we always live here, sir?'

'Some of the time.' A catechism, no less! Much like Lady Beatrice, he decided, so he was well practised in fielding questions. But where was this leading?

'Where else? Shall I like it?'

'In London, which you know. I have an estate in Yorkshire that I think you will like. And perhaps one day you will come with me to Paris.'

'Can I ride a horse in Yorkshire?' Paris as yet had no such attraction. 'I used to in New York. I was very good!'

Considering his age, Joshua doubted it, but recognised the ambition and had no intention of shattering dreams. He kept his face solemn despite the gleam in his eyes. 'Of course. And here too. We can ride in the Park.'

'I like horses more than ships,' the boy confided. 'I was sick when we sailed here. Will Beth be my sister?'

The change of subject did not throw his lordship. 'Yes. Does that worry you?'

'No.' John glanced at his lordship under fair brows, assessing. 'She likes her own way.'

'I expect she does. Women often do. They enjoy managing.' Joshua leaned his arms on the desk, angled his head, still waiting.

John frowned, accepting but not quite understanding. 'I can almost run as fast as she can.' Then: 'What do I call you?'

So this was it. There was a lot of Sarah in this splendid child.

Not just his colouring, but his squared shoulders and determined stance. And his courage. The unknown Captain Russell should be very proud of his son, as should his mama. Perhaps one day... But there was a serious matter to be settled here.

'Can I suggest...' Joshua's reply was gentle, full of understanding of the child's insecurities. 'Captain Russell is your father and for now you will keep his name. But you could call me Papa, as Beth does. That might be easier. Do you think?'

John thought. 'Yes, sir. Papa. I can do that.' His face was lit by a sudden disarming grin. 'I'm glad I asked. I must go now. Mama says I still have to have lessons.'

He ran to the door in some relief.

'John...'

'Yes...Papa?'

'Ah...it does not matter.' He did not know what he wished to say after all. 'This afternoon we will ride in the park.'

'Yes!' And left.

Which was a pretty good outcome for a morning's work.

When Sarah heard her son address Joshua as Papa for the first time that very afternoon, her head whipped round, a range of expressions on her face. If her life had depended on it, she could not have explained her emotions in that one moment. Her lord saw and understood.

'It was his choice,' Joshua explained when the children were out of earshot. 'He knows that John Russell is his father. But it is simpler for him this way. We came to a...an understanding. At present he likes horses better than ships, so I am an attractive prospect as the owner of an extensive stable.' A smile—a little wry—touched his face. 'Unless you object, of course.'

'No. No—how could I?' A flame of heat warmed her heart for this man who could take her and her son with such ease. Perhaps one day they would have children of their own. It was by no means an unpleasant prospect. Sarah turned back to watch her son, who was longingly and impatiently clinging to the head of a lively pony, hoping to hide the sudden heat in her cheeks.

Beth quickly came to her own understanding with Sarah. A pragmatic child as ever, she decided that she would address Sarah as Mama and did so in her solemn fashion from the very beginning.

The relaxed days in Richmond also gave Lord and Lady Faringdon time and space in which to discover each other. Sarah learnt that although her husband might appear stern, sometimes austere and given to moments of deep distraction, he was blessed with an appreciation of the ridiculous and a quick infectious grin. He was a man who liked matters arranged to his own way of thinking, but could be sensitive and thoughtful of her needs too. It was a shock to have her desires preempted, her wishes attended to, sometimes before she had even voiced them. How could she not love a man so stunningly attractive, so graciously disposed towards her? Sometimes he surprised her by his impulsive actions. He was very *Faringdon*, she decided as she observed Joshua ordering their removal from London to Richmond. There were traits of both Henry and Nicholas here, particularly his impatience when thwarted. But those two gentlemen had never made her heart race, brought a blush to her cheeks or a tingle to the surface of her skin at the very thought of the man's touch. Even the slightest brush of his hand on her arm was enough to stir a heat in her belly. A response to him that she became very adept at masking.

When he came to her at night, Lord Joshua continued to be careful of her. Gentle at all times. He made no demands on her with which she might be uncomfortable. A man of honour in all things, she thought, no matter the scandals that surrounded his name. Perversely, she felt just a touch of disappointment. What would it be like if her lord felt real passion for her—to love her, to possess her with such intensity, such lack of control as to rob her of her will and her choice? She thought she might like it. Then blushed an even deeper hue. And had to accept that she lacked the confidence or knowledge to do anything about it.

But of course she did not expect her lord to be carried away, his control destroyed, in the heat of an overwhelming passion, did she?

Joshua at first found his wife shy. But then, perhaps not shy. It was just that she was not at ease with him yet. He had learnt very quickly that she needed encouragement to relax and be herself. She thought too much about what people might think of her, if they would approve of her, if they would be critical of her actions and opinions. She had a gentle humour, a tendency to chuckle before she became aware and stopped herself. But her quiet blue eyes would still dance. Patient, generous with her time, she lavished love openly on the children, Beth as well as John, determined that they should never lack for affection. Joshua watched her with a sharp prick of guilt for it seemed that Sarah knew his daughter better than he did. For herself, she needed to know that she was wanted, appreciated. When he came to her bed, a freedom within their relationship that he could not resist, she responded to his needs readily enough. But here, too, there was a reserve that made him hold back, prevented him from making too many demands on her. It pleased him that she slept easily in his arms.

Whatever the difficulties, they found a rapport in the days together. And a startling moment of illumination for both of them.

It became customary on mild days to ride in the expanse of Richmond Park, Lord Joshua with the two children. Sarah did not accompany them, but one afternoon, on her son's insistence, went to the stables to admire his prowess. Joshua handed his horse to a groom and walked toward her, a welcoming smile.

'Will you join us?'

'No.' Sarah shook her head, but he caught a glimpse of what he interpreted as regret.

On a thought he asked, 'Can you ride?' He had never considered that she could not, merely that it was not to her taste. Theodora rode, so he had presumed that her sister did also.

'No. Our horses were sold.'

Of course. He had not thought of that. A childhood blighted by lack of resources, a profligate father and a feckless mother. Horseflesh would be the first luxury to be sold. He saw the faint colour in her face at the admission, but did not embarrass her with further comment.

'Do you wish to? I can teach you.'

Sarah hesitated, finding herself struggling between a sharp desire to achieve that skill for herself, yet not wishing to put the burden of her inexperience on to anyone. Certainly not on to Joshua, who probably had his hands full with her son's enthusiastic efforts. She must not be demanding of his time more than she already was. So: 'No, but thank you for your kind offer. You go on. You will enjoy the air. I shall take a turn in the garden.'

He would have allowed her to turn away, to deny her interest, but her voice held so wistful a note. He realised in that moment that Sarah had lived her whole life at the whim of others, doing what would please them, never putting her own wishes forward. So much unlike his own life, where the desires of the Faringdon heir were paramount. Well, he would change all that. Today, she would be given the desires of her heart.

'Sarah.' He stretched out his hand to grasp hers, to stop her making a retreat. 'Would you truly wish to ride?'

'Not an animal such as that.' She laughed, retreating into light humour, effectively hiding any personal inclination with consummate skill. She had been doing it for years, Lord Joshua decided. And he had only just come to realise it. He watched her as with a shake of her head she indicated her lord's dark bay stallion, which was in process of pawing up the turf.

'Sarah…' He allowed just a hint of impatience to creep in. She heard it. 'I might.' To agree was to escape.

'Go and find something to wear.' Definitely a command.

'But I—'

'We will wait for you.'

In a mild panic, Sarah cast an eye over to where the children were growing impatient.

'Go on, Scheherazade.' Joshua clasped her shoulders, turned her round and gave her a gentle but definite push in the direction of the house.

Sarah stalked off. She never stalked—but on this occasion she felt like it, ordered about as if she were a servant. Scheherazade indeed! The thought brought a shocked giggle to her throat, unsure of which emotion took precedence. Terrible nerves at the coming ordeal, disapproval of being ordered to ride whether she wished to or not or…or delight that she might actually, at last, learn to ride a horse.

Within the half hour Lady Faringdon marched back again into the stableyard, clad in plain skirt and close-fitting jacket, accompanied by an obvious cloud of indignation and an invisible but strong bout of nerves.

'I don't at all know of the wisdom of this…' The frown between her brows was directed at her lord. Until her attention was caught by a movement in the stable doorway. 'Oh…'

'Mama. This is Jewel.' A groom beside him to hold her head, John held the end of the reins of a little mare, so pale grey as to be almost white. Soft and gentle, perfectly proportioned, a lady's riding horse with side saddle. Exactly like a painted palfrey, all neat lines and elegantly curving neck, glowing in the winter sunshine as if from a gilded medieval illustration.

'She'll look after you.' Joshua could only smile at his wife's obvious enchantment with the little animal. If any mare in his stable could entice a reluctant lady to risk the dangers of a first ride, it was The Jewel. And, he knew as he watched her, his wife was just as enchanting as the mare. 'This is one of Nick's breeding from Aymestry. She is a gentle little animal, as comfortable a ride as a feather bed. You need have no concerns of her running off with you. She will go to sleep on her feet if you let her.'

'Well!' Sarah was speechless. She stroked the satin coat and almost purred as the mare turned dark, long-lashed eyes on her. 'You are so very pretty.' The mare promptly sighed and leaned her shoulder against her. Sarah fell instantly in love. Now she had two objects of unreserved love in her life other than her son, she realised. And both of them Faringdon.

'Come then, my lady.' Lord Joshua gave her no time to renege, lifted her into the saddle, helped her hook her knee in place with brisk efficiency, held her as she arranged her skirt in graceful folds. 'The Jewel will do nothing that you do not ask of her.' He enfolded her hands in his, gave them a light pressure. And made her a promise. 'And I will not allow any harm to come to you.' He swung up onto the back of the well-mannered bay and was rewarded by a smile that illuminated his wife's face with such joy and beauty that it took his breath away.

So they rode in the Park. As a family, Sarah thought, a family of her own. As she had always longed to do. Nothing could have given her greater pleasure. She was nervous, but The Jewel was as precious as her name, as placid, as careful of her rider's comfort, as had been promised. Sarah could not believe the level of happiness that threatened to overflow and reduce her to emotional tears. She swiped at the dampness on her lashes before anyone could see. The shame and terrors of the past receded into distant impenetrable mist whilst at the centre of her existence was Joshua Faringdon, her world, her universe, filling her heart with love.

The pleasure for Lord Joshua Faringdon was quite simply to see his wife's delight. The colour, delicate rose, in her face. To hear her laugh when she succeeded in mastering the mare's slow trot without loss of dignity. He felt the splendour of it as a blow to his gut, a heavy thud of admiration and also of arousal. The desire to draw her close and caress her, mouth to mouth, soft curves to hard planes, her sweet breath mingling with his.

He blinked against the image. And set himself to ignore it. Of course it pleased him to give his wife pleasure. What man could not be moved by the sight of so attractive a lady basking in a new-found confidence and praise from those around her. Any man would feel a need to touch and hold her. It was nothing more complicated than that.

All in all, it was a most satisfactory sojourn at Richmond for everyone. There was only one matter to catch Sarah's notice and gave her cause for speculation. She found herself remembering Millington's comments on the anonymous individuals who visited Joshua in London. And the deluge of correspondence to come through the door. The visitors and correspondence followed them to Richmond.

'Who was that?' Sarah asked one evening, crossing the path of an unknown gentleman who bowed and wished her good night as he made his way to the front door.

'My lawyer.' Joshua's reply came without hesitation.

'Is he connected with Mr Hoskins?' Sarah was acquainted with Hoskins, the Faringdon family's man of legal affairs.

'Ah. Yes. A new member of the firm.'

'Is there a problem?'

'Why, no.' Joshua smiled at his wife and held out his hand in welcome. 'I have an interest in purchasing some land, which he is dealing with. That is all.'

With which Sarah had to be content. Of course he would have business interests. What gentleman of considerable fortune would not?

The Faringdon family returned and took up residence in Hanover Square.

One of Sarah's first dilemmas was the continuing position of Millington in the household. She remembered his depredations in the wine cellar and her own distressing encounter with him of a more personal nature. With her lord's permission to dismiss and choose the servants as she saw fit, it would be a matter of common sense to appoint a new butler. But now that she could, she did not at all know that she wished to do so. As she thought about it, the little smile that curved her lips grew, recalling with a degree of affection his part in the French banquet and the subsequent celebration in the servants' hall. Millington had risen to her support, a positive champion, with aplomb, unquestionable arrogance and an impressive French accent, overseeing the serving of the meal with supercilious hauteur. Not to mention the appearance of the bottles of claret in which they had toasted the defeat of the Countess of Wexford. So Millington remained as butler in the Faringdon household, but with strict instructions as to the amount of port he might consume in any one week.

Within the first week of their return, Lady Joshua Faringdon found herself in receipt of an invitation to pay a morning visit on the Countess of Painscastle in Grosvenor Square. Presenting herself at the appropriate time, she was far from surprised to find Theodora already sitting comfortably with Judith, both awaiting the bride's appearance. Both were sipping glasses of madeira, both looked up as she entered. Sarah immediately realised that she had been the topic under discussion and with quick understanding set herself to repel any questions of an intimate nature.

She need not have bothered. There was no hope of her holding out with dignity under the scrutiny of two determined ladies.

They rose to greet her, sat her down, presented her with a glass of madeira and proceeded to quiz her on her state of health, her enjoyment of the wedding, her appreciation of the house in Richmond and, of course, her new relationship with Lord Joshua Faringdon.

'So how is the bride?' Thea surveyed her critically over the rim of her glass.

'Very well, Thea. As you see.' She winced at the prim note in her voice, but determined to give nothing more away.

'Are you enjoying being a married lady again?'

'Yes, indeed. Most enjoyable.'

'I expect your stay in Richmond gave you the opportunity to get to know Joshua better.'

'Why, yes.'

'Does Joshua please you?' There was just a hint of impatience in Thea now. Perhaps the clue was the slight tapping of her foot against the Aubusson carpet.

'Of course.' Sarah gripped the stem of her glass rather more firmly and took a fortifying sip.

'Sarah!' Thea sighed. 'Is he virile?'

'Theodora!' Judith cast her a look no more horrified than Sarah's.

'What?' The lady's brows rose in perfect astonishment. 'We want to know, do we not? And if I do not ask Sarah outright, she will never tell us!'

'He is my brother!' Judith explained. 'It does not seem to me suitable to be discussing such matters of Sher's...of his... Well! You know what I mean!'

'Well, I can discuss it. You are suddenly very mealy-mouthed, Ju.' Thea turned back to her sister with a laugh and a sparkle in her delphinium-blue eyes. 'Sarah. Did Joshua make you happy?'

The tell-tale colour began to creep up the bride's throat from the fashionable ruched neckline of her morning gown. 'Yes. He gave me The Jewel for my own.'

'That is not what I meant, as you very well know.'

'I know,' Sarah admitted, but her smile was now mischievous. 'Are you not going to say?'

'No.'

'You look very happy.'

'I am.'

'Does he give you pleasure? Is he a good lover?'

'Oh, yes.' By now Sarah's cheeks were as pink as a June rose. 'Oh, yes!'

They laughed. For indeed there could be no doubting it. Thea and Judith clucked in a maternal fashion, Judith pouring more glasses of madeira so that they might toast the bride. Because Sarah Faringdon positively glowed. And her friends were more delighted for her than they would ever have admitted.

It became necessary later within that week for the object of their intense discussion also to pay a morning visit on his sister, fortunately for his dignity knowing nothing of the previous conversation. The visit to Richmond had been more pleasurable than he could have imagined, for a surprising number of reasons, not least his attraction to Sarah herself, his increasing desire to make her happy. So when a thought came into his mind, one that he could not resolve, he decided to pay a visit on Judith.

'Sher. At last. I am delighted to see you.' Judith kissed his cheek. 'How well you look. And completely healed, I see. No cane and no limp. Country life has been good for you.'

'I am very well.' He grinned at her obvious ploy, but shook his head before kissing her cheek.

'I have seen Sarah. She said she enjoyed Richmond. She certainly looks in the pink of health.' The lady's sly smile was also ignored.

'I need your advice, Ju. I wish to buy Sarah a wedding gift.' Judith laughed. 'So?'

'I have no idea what. She can be very… Well, I was hoping for some help. You probably know her the best of any of us.'

'Joshua!' Judith blinked at this ingenuous admission, but was immediately caught up in the project, although not without a sharp dig. 'And I thought you knew women so well.'

'But not Sarah, it seems.'

'There is always jewellery, of course.'

'No. That is not what I want.' Joshua frowned a little. He knew instinctively that his wife would have difficulty in accepting precious stones. 'Besides, she will have the Faringdon jewels that Lady Beatrice has promised to hand over.'

'Mmm. If Mama will part with them. Let me see… You pay for her clothes anyway…'

'Of course.'

Judith thought for a moment, eyes narrowed, contemplating the young woman whom she had indeed come to know well. 'I know exactly what Sarah would like. It is easily done, but will take some organisation. Let me talk to you about this.'

It took a week to put the plan into operation. It demanded some organisation, as Judith had intimated, some surreptitious furniture moving in Hanover Square, some expenditure on Joshua's part, the compliance and secrecy of the Faringdon servants and, finally, a need for Judith and Thea to arrange to remove Sarah from her home for a whole day. Sarah suspected nothing underhand when the morning visit to Thea became a light luncheon, then a drive around Hyde Park and finally a visit to a number of establishments in Bond Street with her sister and Judith. She arrived home in the growing dusk of late afternoon, pleasantly weary, changed her clothes, spent some time with Beth and John, who appeared to be particularly excitable, and at last went to search out the whereabouts of Lord Joshua, whom she had not set eyes on since leaving the breakfast table. For some reason she found him awaiting her in the entrance hall.

She smiled as she descended the stairs. He could not but smile back as he waited and watched her. She had no idea how lovely she was, he realised, or how her looks and her demeanour had unfurled as a rose with the warmth of the morning sun since her marriage. He could not help but experience a degree of purely masculine pride at the thought. Her skin was flawless, her eyes shining, enhanced by the favourite viola-blue of her gown. Her neat figure could not but attract attention as she conducted herself with confidence and a charming simplicity. Her fair curls gleamed softly in the light, held in place by rosettes of satin ribbon to match her gown. She had banished the lace cap—he had *insisted* that she banish the cap! Now she appeared as she was, a young matron of wealth, style and the gentlest degree of sophistication. That was Sarah.

'Sarah.' He took her hand, would have kissed her fingers, but could not resist drawing her closer to press his mouth to hers, a lingering pressure, a memory of more heated kisses, despite the possibility of their privacy being broached. It did not matter. She was his wife and he... What exactly? He did not know, except that he was coming to care for her...although *care* suddenly seemed too mild a word to describe the manner in which his pulse picked up its beat when he set eyes on her. Or even thought about her. But he deliberately banished from his mind the uncertainty of his exact emotions. Because here in the following few minutes a greater uncertainty was in the process of unfolding. Would the lady appreciate what he had done?

'Joshua.' She coloured, a delicate brush of rose, but let him hold her a little longer. Why not? It was the stuff of dreams after all, to see him standing there, all Faringdon magnificence, waiting for her, waiting to take her into his arms, to claim her lips with his own. What woman would not dream of that? She sighed softly and looked up at him. 'Were you waiting for me?' Just a little breathless as she noted the fiery heat in his eyes.

'I was. It was in my mind that I would like to give you something. A wedding gift.'

'Is it a diamond necklace? A parting gift?' Her nose wrinkled deliciously. But was it humour or concern here?

He did not smile. In fact, his expression became quite severe. 'Are you dissatisfied with me as a husband after a mere few weeks, ma'am?'

'No.'

'Well, neither am I with you as my wife. So, no, it is not a diamond necklace. Although, if you find a desire to sparkle and impress at a ball or soirée, there is at least one in the Faringdon collection.'

'I might.' She chuckled as he tucked her hand companionably through his arm to lead her back up the stairs in the direction from which she had just come. 'Where are we going?'

'Wait and see.'

Sarah knew the house well. Had she not been responsible for its cleaning and furbishment? So when he led her to the rarely-used parlour on the first floor with its view over the square and its garden she looked up, a quizzical expression. Her lord refused to respond, but opened the door and ushered her in before him. Then stood back to test the waters.

Sarah walked forward to stand in the centre of the room. Then turned slowly in a full circle. Of course, she knew this room as well as any of the others. The wall paper was still the Chinese silk, a little worn but deliciously festooned with pale pink and blue cranes and chrysanthemums on a silver background. The tall windows let in what was left of the evening light, to warm the pale marble of the Grecian fireplace. All of this she knew. But as for the rest, it was all quite different and effectively robbed her of speech. The curtains and swags that had suffered from age and faded over the years from the heat of the sun had been replaced with splendid new drapes of cream and silver silk damask. All the dust sheets had been removed from the furniture—and that too had changed. Her eyes flew to her lord's in astonishment.

'Do you like it?' He stepped forward to light a branch of candles at her side, the soft flames adding a further layer of charm to the little room.

Sarah's mouth opened, but she could find nothing to say.

'It is yours.' Joshua found a need to explain. 'Thea would call it a boudoir. It is a wedding gift to you. I...er...took advice...' A moment of horror suddenly silenced him. 'From Judith,' he added quickly, in case she should think it might be Olivia Wexford.

Sarah laughed softly in appreciation, then turned again to survey the full magnificence of the gift. Small and decorative pieces of furniture suitable for a lady's sitting room or boudoir had been collected from various rooms in the house, with the notable addition of some new pieces. Walnut, rosewood, all light and well polished, inlaid with various and decorative woods, they seduced her senses and beckoned her to enter and claim it as her own. Two bergère chairs with gilded sides and cushioned seats to match the drapes stood on either side of the fireplace to accommodate any guests Sarah might wish to entertain, between them a sofa with scrolled ends, upholstered in cream silk, perfect for a lady to take her ease. A side table rested beside the wall next to a beautiful writing desk with a tambour top, which had been shrouded in a dust sheet, unused, in the morning room when Sarah had first come to the house. On the walls were two of her own framed paintings of rural scenes, last seen in the schoolroom. A small bookcase stood beside the fireplace—she had never seen that before—with some favourite novels in marbled covers—which hinted at Thea's influence. She saw an inlaid work table for her silks and embroideries, nothing like the old battered box she used in the schoolroom. All tastefully enhanced by a satinwood firescreen, a gilt-edged mirror above the fireplace, silver candlesticks, an extravagantly pale carpet and—oh, wonders!—a pianoforte beneath the window, of rosewood and satinwood inlay, its ivory notes gleaming softly and simply demanding to be played.

'Well?'

Sarah walked to the pianoforte to stroke a few notes. They sounded soft and clear in the still room.

'Sarah.' Her silence was unnerving. 'Will you put me out of my misery? I remember you once returned something so trivial as a coat that you thought I should not have given you. What will you do if this does not please you?'

'Does not please me? How could it not?' Now she turned to him. The smile on her face stopped his words. And the tears that coursed silently down her cheeks.

'Sarah!' His arms opened wide and she simply walked into them, to lay her forehead against his shoulder and weep. 'Don't weep, Scheherazade. We shall both be drowned. I will take it all back if that is your wish.' But he knew there was no danger of that. He had seen the pure joy in her face. Everything was good. His heart clenched hard in a foolish beat of triumph as he pressed his lips against her hair.

'No one has ever shown me such kindness. It is beyond anything I could imagine.' She wiped away the tears with unsteady fingers. 'I love it.' She risked a glance at his face. 'I suspect you had help here.'

'Indeed I did!' He waved his arm to encompass the room. 'This is beyond me. But you have some good friends. And your children love you. The flowers are from Beth.' They bloomed, waxy hellebores, in a little crystal vase on the side table.

'It is beautiful. All of it. And the pianoforte… I cannot express how I feel. You have no idea how happy it has made me.'

And that, of course, was all that he desired to hear.

It put Sarah, being Sarah, into something of a difficulty.

A room of her own. A boudoir. How extravagant in the extreme. But it pricked her conscience. What could she possibly give Joshua in return? It behoved her to give him some symbol of her gratitude and—well—her love. But she could hardly spend his own money on a gift for him. It needed some serious thought. And eventually some skilful application of her talents. The result was a small package wrapped in silk, left on Joshua's desk in the library with his name inscribed on a single sheet of paper.

Where Joshua duly found it. And that was so like Sarah, he thought, his smile a little sad. That she should leave it for him rather than present it personally, rather than risk his displeasure or disappointment. His constant dream was that one day she would find the courage to stand before him and speak her mind—and damn the consequences. Perhaps one day she would. But not yet. He unwrapped the silk to extract a small portrait, little more than a miniature, painted in water-colour on ivory. An image of a young girl, head and shoulders only, with dark eyes and dark hair released and allowed to curl onto her cheeks, ribbons in her hair. The edging of her dress, a soft blue, just visible, brought colour to her cheeks. She had a smile on her lips and looked out at him confidently.

Beth, of course.

And, more importantly, Sarah's work.

It was a good likeness, painted with a free hand to give a sense of youth and energy. The Beth he was coming to know, in fact, rather than the stiff, formal child who had arrived so short a time ago. The frame, too, was of Sarah's making, silk embroidered with tiny flowers stretched and pinned over a wooden frame. A pretty thing, guaranteed to please. It still lay before him on the desk when Beth came into the library to se-lect a book. She came to stand beside him to look at what took his attention.

'That is me,' she stated with delightful self-importance.

His teeth glinted in a smile. 'It looks like you. And very pretty.'

She preened just a little and moved closer so that he was able to draw her into the circle of his arm. Beth leaned against him and touched his hand where it held the portrait. 'Mama painted it.' It still gave him a little jolt of pleasure to hear the word on his daughter's lips. 'It is good, isn't it?'

'Yes. She is very talented.'

'Do you like it?' Beth had the persistence of the young.

'Yes.' He touched the painted face gently with his fingertips. 'I shall keep it here on my desk, perhaps, so that I can see it when you are not curled on that window seat. What do you think?'

Beth nodded, perfectly satisfied with the arrangement. 'Mama is painting another of John. It will take her a long time.'

'Why is that?'

'He does not sit still. It sometimes makes Mama quite cross. She says John will be all of one and twenty before it is complete.'

Joshua grinned. 'I can well imagine.'

* * *

Later in the day, he found Sarah on her way to the kitchen to speak on some domestic matter with Mrs Beddows.

'Sarah…' She came toward him with a light step, a smile.

'Thank you, my lady. Your style, as always, is excellent.' Joshua knew from the quick flush of colour in his wife's face that he did not need to say more. He smoothed his knuckles over her cheek, soft and intimate, before lowering his head to kiss the corner of her mouth. Sarah returned the caress and then escaped before her inner delight overcame her.

So it would appear that some warm and blossoming depth of closeness and understanding would bless the marriage of Lord Joshua Faringdon and his new bride. But it was equally apparent to the two individuals concerned that this rapport was not to be replicated when his lordship came to his lady's bed, something that Lord Joshua continued to be by no means averse to doing. But by this time Joshua was being forced to keep command of his patience. He had always considered himself to be a patient man, and one who was perfectly ready to indulge the whims of a pretty woman. But in these circumstances, with his own wife, he found himself completely at a loss.

They were making no progress. His wife was willing, welcoming. She never refused him intimacy. She accepted his kisses, his caresses, the demands of his body with perfect equanimity. But it ended there. She had effectively built a wall between them based on restraint and reserve and an inability—or at least a refusal—to communicate on the matter. She said what he would wish to hear, thanked him most politely when he asked if she was content. Reacted as he would wish her to react. But she never allowed her own control to slip for one moment. Never encouraged, never initiated. Never allowed him to take her over the slippery edge of delight to her own fulfilment. Never indicated what her own pleasure or preference might be.

It was, he decided, like making love to a lovely doll. She resisted any attempt to leave the candles burning as if she could only consent to his touch when her face and her responses were cloaked in darkness. She did not have a dislike of him, of that he was certain. Nor did she dislike his advances. But he was the one to take the initiative. He was the one to take his pleasure. As for hoping that she would talk about it... Well, he had had no success there. She smiled and complied with his every demand, but gave nothing of herself. He did not know what to do. If he were honest, he was aware of a creeping hint of despair as the weeks passed and Sarah grew no more responsive.

And Sarah? She yearned for her lord's touch, his heated kisses, the slick heat of his body against hers. The sheer weight of him when he crushed her to the soft mattress in ultimate possession. But she could go no further than that. She feared any adverse reaction to her clumsy attempts to respond to his love making: his pity, his disapproval, his dissatisfaction, even his condemnation. How would she exist if he were to find her wanting, turned away to take his satisfaction elsewhere? And she feared even more to reveal her love for him, her delight in his arms, her desire to allow him to push those amazing sensations further, so that she might lose herself in the splendour of being held and caressed by him. So what was left for her if it were necessary to mask her emotions? A calm and restrained acceptance. When her heart yearned for more.

It was very strange, Sarah thought when they had been returned to Hanover Square a little over two weeks, considering her new lifestyle, which demanded that she now participate in the social world with balls and soirées and breakfasts, but she had the distinct impression that someone was watching her. That since they had taken up residence in London again, she was actually being followed. It crept up on her as the days passed. And Sarah could not deny it, however much she might argue against the sense of it, but she felt the force of invisible eyes focused on her. A presence that did not wish her well. The sensation touched her skin with a faint shiver of fear.

Considering that she was surrounded by people, she lectured herself, it was a ridiculous presumption. Her new family, the servants with whom she had once worked. The *ton* who noted the return of the Faringdons with interest and idle speculation at the sudden marriage. But still Sarah felt the brush of more than interested eyes when she took the children into the gardens in the Square, when she visited Hookham's Lending Library, when she gazed in the windows in Bond Street or walked to Grosvenor Square to visit Judith or Thea. Even in the crowds of Hyde Park at the fashionable hour when Joshua drove her round in his curricle.

The tingle of being spied upon would not go away.

Foolish! She was quickly impatient with herself. Of course it could not be so. Yet she was still uneasy and sought for reasons why it might be, why someone might have an interest in her. There was certainly one possibility that came to mind with a terrible clarity. Was it Edward? Sir Edward Baxendale, her brother, who lived in genteel, resentful and bitter poverty and had proved his willingness to take any action, however disreputable, to increase the funds at his disposal. Now that she had married a man in possession of a fortune, Edward might see an opportunity to make new demands on her. If that were so, she could not possibly tell Joshua of her suspicions. She would do nothing to resurrect old memories.

But if it were Edward, why did he need to have her followed? Why not simply write and demand money, a brother's begging letter to his wealthy sister? It just did not make sense.

So it was all in her imagination. And she saw no need whatsoever to tell Joshua of her fears.

Until one afternoon when they were returning to Hanover Square with Beth and John in their landau, taking advantage of the mild sunshine after a week of rain. As they drew up before the steps, Sarah quickly turned her head, her attention caught by the smallest of movements. Was that a shadow of a man within the darker shadows of the trees and ornamental bushes behind the iron railings? Did he draw back to merge with the deeply dappled light as they came to a halt?

'What is it?' Joshua asked, aware of the sudden stiffening of her spine, her fixed gaze.

'Nothing really. Just a…' Her eyes continued to search the gardens.

'Tell me.' Was that the slightest edge to his voice?

'I just had the sensation that someone was watching me…us.' Her glance back again over her shoulder toward the garden could not but betray her anxiety. 'Do you think it could be so?'

'No.' His hesitation was so slight as to be indiscernible. He smiled briefly, touched her hand fleetingly. 'Just chance—there is nothing to hurt you here. Put it out of your mind, my dear.' Joshua deliberately smoothed the crease from between his brows, intent on preserving an untroubled exterior. So Sarah was being followed, was she? There was only one man who might be involved in such an activity towards himself and his family. He would think about it and its implications when alone; they did not immediately spring to mind. But he would take steps to stop it if it became necessary.

'Of course. How foolish I am.' Sarah returned his smile in apology. Besides, she was wary of saying more for fear of sharp-eyed, sharp-eared Beth picking up the conversation. And Joshua, in truth, probably had the right of it.

The moment passed.

But as Sarah and Beth climbed the stairs together, Joshua having taken John with him to oversee the stabling of the horses, the little girl leaned close.

'I saw him too, Mama. A man in a dark coat.' Then ran on ahead.

Which consolidated all Sarah's fears.

* * *

And then the rumours started.

Gently at first. Softly. Whispered in withdrawing rooms throughout fashionable London.

Then more loudly, insistently. Behind fans, sly hands, turned heads. In Hyde Park. At Almack's. At private parties. Wherever the *ton* met. Eyes glinting in greedy interest, a delectable scandal to enliven the most tedious of gatherings. No one knew whence the information came, but everyone was prepared to discuss and speculate and claim that, of course, they knew it to be true beyond doubt. They had always known that there was room for suspicion when *that* name was spoken…

The details of the scandal were fairly complete from the very beginning. But embroidered with possibilities as the days passed. Until the nasty little rumours came perforce to the ears of Judith and Lady Beatrice, as such rumours must, when they attended a select little soirée at the home of one who might have been considered a friend. She was quick to acquaint them with the details. Horrified, Lady Beatrice Faringdon and the Countess of Painscastle held a council of war in Grosvenor Square on the following morning to compare notes and discuss their response. Considering the dangerous aspect of the content, and their close connection with the main target, the scandal could not be ignored.

The first Lady Joshua Faringdon, those in the know stated, a French lady of considerable charm and elegance, was dead. Nothing new or of moment here. Had died some years previously in France. But not of some virulent and fatal disease as all had been led to understand. Would you believe it? She had been *murdered*.

But who had committed the foul deed?

Well, who, of course? Did it need to be spelled out?

It had been heard on very good, but unnamed, authority that the lady was involved in a passionate love affair with an aristocrat at the Bourbon Court where she had been murdered in a fit of uncontrolled fury by her jealous husband. Lord Joshua

Faringdon. A pistol shot to the heart, no less. Her husband had then summarily disposed of her body, leaving everyone in England to believe that she had sickened, been buried and grieved over in France.

'I don't believe it!' stated Judith unequivocally after discussing the outrageous suggestion with her mama. For once the tea-cups sat neglected between them, the elegant little plate of macaroons abandoned.

'No. Of course not.' The far-from-doting mama might believe much of her son but not murder. 'It is impossible to even contemplate so disgraceful a possibility.'

'But where would such a rumour begin?'

'I have no idea.' Lady Beatrice fixed her daughter with an expression of deep concern. 'And you must admit, Judith, there are some difficult areas here for the family.'

'What? Surely, Mama, you will give no weight to this terrible accusation? You might suspect Sher of being too thoughtless with the family name and we know for a fact that he has had any number of mistresses under his protection—there is no need to frown at me! Everyone knows it—but *murder*!'

'Of course not, Judith! Try not to be foolish. But think. A sudden disease to strike down a healthy young woman. We were not there. Have we ever seen the grave? No, we have not. Does Joshua ever talk about it? No, he does not. The whole affair gives me an uneasy feeling.'

'Sher would never murder his wife. He would not murder anyone! I will accept no truth in it.'

'Neither will I. But I wish your brother would not play his cards quite so close to his chest!' Lady Beatrice could envisage her next meeting with some of her fashionable associates over a glass of ratafia and did not enjoy the prospect. 'It is difficult to know what to say when one is as much in the dark as the town tabbies.'

'A ridiculous suggestion!' was the only opinion given by Nicholas when he and Theodora called at the Painscastle residence and were drawn into the discussion. 'You cannot possibly give it any credence.'

'Will you talk to Sher?' Theodora asked of Judith. 'It would seem to be the obvious next step.'

'Not willingly,' Judith admitted. 'You could talk to him, Nick! But there is one person who must be told, if she has not heard it already.'

'Sarah, of course.' Thea's mind ran along the same lines. Her lips curled in grim humour. 'Better that she hear it from us that her husband is a murderer than from deliberate malice on the grapevine.'

So Thea and Judith immediately took themselves in the barouche to Hanover Square, where Sarah welcomed them with delight, no notion of their intent. Until she saw their concerned eyes, their obvious discomfort. And listened aghast to the lurid picture laid out before her. They spared her no details. She must know what was being said.

Murder!

Sarah would have denied that such damning and unjustifiable gossip was being spread through the fashionable haunts of London. But once knowing, she quickly became aware of the widespread comment. The hushed voices as she came into the room when paying an afternoon visit. The covert glances. Everyone seemed to be discussing Lord Joshua Faringdon's implication in a deed as foul as any she could envisage. And as completely unbelievable. Of course she did not believe it. Dismissed the whole thing as nothing but malicious mischief-making. But why? And who had seen fit to plant the seeds?

And then, as is the nature of such things, it brushed her consciousness again that she was without doubt being followed. Joshua might have denied it unequivocally, but she knew in her heart that it was true. Were the two events connected? Her mind immediately began to consider and weave the possibilities. Joshua might deny the existence of the shadow, but she was certain that it existed. The worries stayed with her and gnawed at her peace of mind. Who could possibly be expected to enjoy peace of mind and the unexpected delights of a new marriage when secretive eyes followed her, when her husband was accused of dispatching his first wife and hiding her body?

Well, there was only one solution to this. She would ask Joshua to tell her the truth.

She accosted him on his return from Brooks's.

'Sarah…' He took her hand, would have saluted her cheek, but was brought to a halt by something in her demeanour. If he was surprised by the reserve in her response to him, he did not show it.

'I need to speak with you.' He saw her lips set in a firm line, little lines of strain—signs of concern that had now been absent for some little time—between her brows.

'Of course.' He led her into the library. Closed the door. Turned to face her.

'What is it that disturbs you? Do you still see phantom followers?' He tried for a light response to the tension that swirled around her.

'Yes. And so does Beth.' His brows rose, but before he could find suitable words, she continued. 'But that is not it…' She might as well ask outright. 'Joshua—have you heard the rumours?'

'Rumours?' The epitome of innocence. She could not deny his lack of comprehension. Or could she? She suspected that Lord Faringdon's ability to dissemble was supreme.

'Obviously not. Perhaps the gentlemen at Brooks's are less inclined to gossip than their wives. Or more discreet when their members are present. Thea and Judith warned me—and then I saw it, felt it, *heard it* for myself. The hush from those present when I walked into the withdrawing room, when I took tea with Lady Stoke. The conversation came to a remarkably abrupt end.'

A cold fear inched its way down his spine. So she had heard. Well, of course she had. Had he expected her to live in blissful ignorance when the whole town was talking? Yet he kept his composure. 'What conversation?'

'About you. And your first wife. About Marianne.'

He preserved all outward calm, his face bland, his gaze level. 'And so, according to Thea and Judith, what are the gossip-mongers saying?' He knew exactly what they were saying, in every salacious detail. But he must do all in his power to reassure.

Sarah kept her voice calm, as if discussing a matter of no moment that could easily be remedied. As if her heart were not thudding against her ribs. 'They…they are saying that Marianne did not die a natural death. That you were responsible.' Her fingers gripped the edge of a gilded bergère chair at her side. 'That you murdered her, from jealousy over her taking a lover.'

'And do you believe it?' A hint of frost over the calm now.

'No. Of course not. It is beyond belief.' She lifted her hand, almost in a plea. 'But I find it very uncomfortable to have the *ton* discussing my husband's so-called crimes.'

'Sarah—'

'I don't believe it,' she repeated in a firm voice. And indeed she did not. But she would continue. 'I should tell you that, whatever your denials, I *am* being followed.'

'I see.' He strode to the window, then whirled round to face her, fighting to keep a firm hand on the reins of temper as all his control came close to obliteration by a wave of sheer anger. At himself. At fate. At the perpetrator of the vicious scandal. He coated the fire in ice. 'And you think that I am having you followed, to discover if you too have a lover, with the intent of murdering you also.'

'I think no such thing!' Never had she seen his self-control so compromised, but she stood her ground. 'And, no, I do not have a lover as you must know, so there would be little point to it. I would merely wish to know who would start so cruel a story if there is no truth in it. Do you know?'

*Oh, yes. I know very well who will have created this partic-
ular pattern of pain and disgrace, to hurt both of us, to carve a
rift between us that can never be mended. And I am so tightly
woven into a web of deceit that I cannot tell you of it. Or extricate myself without untold repercussions. Oh, yes. I know without doubt who is responsible, driven by revenge and bitter hatred.*

He walked toward her. Slowly and with deliberation. Until
he stood close, his eyes searching her face. Whatever he saw
there, he lifted his hand to touch her cheek with light fingers,
the tender gesture at odds with the passion in his eyes. A passion that would burn and destroy if he allowed it.

'I will never cause you harm, Sarah. I will never willingly
hurt you. Do you believe that? I find that it is important to me
that you do.'

'Yes.' Caught up in the moment, she closed her hand around
his wrist. 'I do.' His blood throbbed beneath her hand, echoing
the beat of her own pulse.

'The rumours. I cannot say—simply ask that you trust me,
even when it seems too hard to do so.' He bent his head to touch
her mouth with his, a mere brush of lips over lips, then suddenly fierce and demanding. He could not tell her the truth, but
neither would he deliberately lie. He framed her face with his
hands. 'As for the shadows that follow you, they must not be
allowed to disturb you. Neither can I tell you of them, but I will
take steps to stop them.'

'Can you do that?'

'I think it is possible.'

'Will you not tell me who?'

'No.' He rubbed the pad of his thumb over her soft bottom
lip. 'It is best that you do not know. I know that is no answer—
but I can give no other.'

'Tell me the truth, Joshua.' She held his gaze, more demand
than plea.

But he shook his head. 'It is not in my power to do so at
this time.'

And with that she had to be content. But never content! Secrets, secrets! Sarah could do nothing but accept her lord's word when all her instincts shrieked within her head to demand that he tell her the truth. Could do nothing but accept his kiss when once again he claimed her mouth, now with a deliberate tenderness. But her thoughts remained in turmoil. She had lived her life with lies and deceits. Now even her marriage was prey to them.

For Joshua, the only certainty was that he must not speak, no matter how forcefully his heart urged him to do so. Because to speak of the past and his relationship with Marianne would reveal a whole host of lies and untruths, enough to swamp their fragile relationship beyond hope. And mayhap put others in danger of their lives. All he could do was call on Sarah's intrinsic fairness and loyalty, wrapping her round in soft trappings of consideration and care. Until, despite the nagging suspicions, she should never contemplate his involvement in so wicked an act as murder. With all his skill and finesse, he hoped that he would have the power to seduce her into giving him her trust. His hands clasped her shoulders, to draw her firmly against him. Bending, he pressed his lips against the soft, almost transparent skin at her temple and, as he felt her shiver beneath his hands, a bright flare of desire surged through him, to carry her off to his room and show her that he was not beyond redemption.

At the thought he lifted his head to smile down into her face—and froze as he caught the ghost of an emotion in her eyes, before she swiftly veiled it from him with her downswept lashes. Distrust, fear, despair? He could not guess. Even more, he dare not ask. And suddenly the notion of seduction, of submerging her misgivings beneath the pleasures of her body and his, drained from him. He could not. Not when she was being hurt through his own actions, his own inability to be honest. It would be a betrayal of everything he had hoped to offer to her in their marriage. A wicked destruction of her contentment and her peace of mind. What a cruel outcome it would be if his self-ish actions wilfully led Sarah to give him her utmost trust. Per-haps even caused her to fall in love with him. Would that not make the hurt and pain the greater, when she finally learned the truth about his life, past and present? Because he had no doubt that it would be impossible for him to keep the truth from her for ever. How much less painful if he let her go now. Stepped back from her. It would make her unhappy. She would see it as a bitter rejection, all the more cruel since Sarah would find it difficult to accept rejection in so personal a matter. But at least it would not tear her emotions to shreds, bright silk rent by the sharpest of blades, as might happen if he allowed her to grow too close to him, to expect too much from him.

Joshua knew what he must do. He must distance himself from her so that the hurt should not be compounded. Until his own loyalties were no longer an issue to divide them. If that could ever be.

So Joshua's fingers tightened on Sarah's shoulders, but not to draw her close, rather to push her away. The smile died from his lips. He let his hands fall away. Stepped back. And again and again until the width of the room separated them. Despite the intense longing, it would be so wrong. And perhaps, after all, Sarah was only playing the role of obedient wife. How lit-tle he still knew of her. Did she hate and despise him for bring-ing this dark spectre of death and murder into her life, despite her protestations of belief and trust? So he must reject her, for both their sakes. He drank the bitter lees of the cup, of self-con-demnation and contempt for his lack of choice.

'Forgive me…'

'Joshua…' Disbelieving, Sarah held out her hands, aware of nothing but the distance that had suddenly opened between them and the cold weight of fear within her breast.

'I have matters to attend to.' Tall and straight, her lord con-tinued to face her, face shuttered and cold, refusing to acknowl-edge her plea, resisting every need to close the space and enfold her once again into his arms. Better that she hate him, heap blame on his head, than that he take her to his bed with such issues between them.

'Please.' Soft, little more than a murmur, her voice reached him. 'Don't leave me like this. Do I mean so little to you?' Never during their short marriage had she been so outspoken of her feelings, so uncertain of his response.

'I must.' He fought the temptation to rake his fingers in desolation through his hair, fought against the pain in his heart. How difficult it was to turn her away. But he would do it to protect her from further anguish. 'Don't look so tragic, my dear. Scandals always die a death when the next one surfaces to replace it. You will soon become used to the taint of scandal, now that your name is coupled with mine.'

The bitterness in his words scorched her. 'No. I will not accept that.'

'You were aware when you took my name that it was a tarnished commodity.' He heard his cruel words, wincing at their power to hurt. But to fuel her anger would lessen her pain.

'How can you do this? I do not believe it…'

'You have no choice, my lady.' He bowed his head, a curt cold gesture, and left her standing alone in the room.

Sarah was left to contemplate the cold ashes of the day, one thought following rapidly on the heels of the former. He had rejected her, with cruel barbs and harsh words. And why? What had he seen in her face to make him walk away? Whatever it was, he had misread it, for she trusted him with her life. One moment to hold and kiss her, passion firing his caresses, the next to walk away with such sneering disdain. Her fragile confidence, which had begun to blossom under his caring attentions, all but shattered. But she would not. She would not sink beneath spiteful gossip or bow to those who would destroy her happiness. She might not know the reason for his behaviour toward her, but of one fact she had total conviction—Joshua Faringdon was not capable of cold-blooded murder. It was not possible that she could have judged him so wrongly and given her heart to a man capable of such evil.

She allowed her mind to play over the tension-filled confrontation. When she had told him of the whispered accusations against him, a hard cold rage had touched his face. So much anger, yet not, she thought, directed at her. He knew more than he was saying, admitted it even, but she could not imagine what it could be.

Sarah walked to look out of the window at the darkening sky, watching the rain spatter on the glass and the trees bend before the icy wind. It exactly matched her mood, she thought as she wrapped her arms around herself for comfort. How was it possible that she could simply trust and love Joshua, accepting his silence, when he stood accused of murder? It was not reciprocated. She brushed tears from her lashes with the back of an impatient hand. He never talked of love to her. She did not expect that, accepted that he did not love her. But there were shadows all around them—so dark and impenetrable. Layer on layer, they invaded her mind. He was often absent, for lengthy periods in the day and without explanation. Letters were delivered to the house by elusive individuals who left no name or visiting card. It would seem that he had another life quite separate from her. Well, that should not surprise her. Of course he had business dealings of which she knew nothing. But what was it that he was not telling her? Did he not respect her enough to trust her with the truth, whatever it might be? Her mind returned again and again to that one concern. The fears would not leave her.

And she was being followed!

Sarah retreated from the drear outlook to sit on the little stool before her dressing table, her heart sore. She rarely wept—it did no good, solved no difficulties—but she wept long into the night for the man who now appeared, through his own choice, to be as far distant from her as the stars that shone with such icy indifference.

* * *

But when Sarah rose from her bed the following morning, it was to a new inner strength, a new resolution. She would not accept his rejection. She would destroy the distance of his making. If trust was to be an issue between them, she would show that it was not lacking from her side.

Her lord was in no better frame of mind. Joshua was left to contemplate the fact that his relationship with Sarah, still so new and untried, had been put in jeopardy by the impossibility of laying all before her. How could a marriage survive and bloom on lies and deceit? In truth he could not take her to his bed. Not with the weight of guilt on him. The rumours, as clearly intended, would blacken his name even more with the Polite World, from rake to murderer in one discreetly whispered *on dit*. Why should Sarah believe any good of him? He found himself confronted by a growing need to tell her the truth, to strip his soul bare and to appear a man of integrity and principle in her eyes. Little chance of that! Morosely he studied the blank sheet of paper on the desk before him.

Why should it matter what she believed? Why should it matter to him if he simply covered his tracks with a few well-chosen lies to prevent her from questioning him further?

Because you are falling in love with her, you fool. You need her to believe in you, see the best in you. As simple...and as complicated as that.

The little voice spoke insistently to take him completely by surprise. He recalled her standing there, offering her lips, the warmth and shelter of her arms, Sarah who rarely offered anything of her own volition, whilst he deliberately, coldly, distanced himself from her, holding her at arm's length. Love? It was not so, of course. He cared for her, felt a strong urge to protect her. Without doubt desired her physically. But love? He would never in his life love another woman. Marianne had taught him that much. To allow one's heart to be held by the slender, elegant fingers of a beautiful woman—of any woman—was inarguably a recipe for pain and disillusion. No—he did not love Sarah. He *would* not love her.

Even though he regretted his callous treatment of her from the bottom of his heart.

Having disposed of that little problem to his liking, Lord Faringdon was still faced with the prospect of the damaging rumours destroying any hope of a calm and satisfactory marriage. He doubted that anything could be done to smooth over the immediate damage. It was simply a matter of riding out the storm, taking his own advice, which he had so cavalierly flung at his unsuspecting wife. A subtle flash of colour tinted his cheekbones at the memory. He was not proud of that moment.

There was, however, one conversation that he was determined to have, and as soon as might be. Anger returned in good measure, causing him to place his pen carefully on the desk before he snapped it in two. He knew where these rumours had begun. He would wager his best hunter on it. And he knew damn well who was responsible for Sarah being shadowed. He could most certainly put a stop to that. Picking up the pen again, he scrawled a few terse lines. Between them, Olivia Wexford and Wycliffe were threatening to undermine Sarah's new-found happiness and contentment and create a bottomless abyss between them. He could not tolerate that. He could do that quite well enough on his own, it seemed! His lips curled at his own clumsy attempts to spare her further pain, where he had signally failed. But Wycliffe was resident in England for a few months, his sources suggested. It was time for Lord Faringdon to have some plain words with this elusive gentleman.

Sarah rose early, dressed, drank her chocolate in an abstracted manner and listened unashamedly at the door of her lord's dressing room. He, too, was up betimes. Perhaps he, too, had not slept well. She paced her bedchamber for half an hour until she heard his valet leave the room and walk past her own door. She walked through the dressing room, knocked briskly on the door of her husband's room and entered without waiting for a reply. Then she stood and watched her husband, dispassionately, she hoped.

Joshua looked up from the diamond pin that he was about to secure in his cravat. Still in his shirtsleeves, a little pale, heavy eyed, he was still outrageously attractive and Sarah's heart performed its usual breath-stopping leap of awareness. But she gave no indication of her emotion or of the residual ache caused by his cold retreat from her. She hoped that he had slept as badly as she. He deserved it. She was, she realised, not dispassionate at all.

'Sarah—'

'I have something to say.'

Lord Joshua made no move toward her, but shrugged into his coat. For once he could not meet her eyes, which held the bright light of imminent conflict.

'When Eleanor felt most under threat from the Baxendale scandal,' she spoke of it without a tremor, 'when my brother seemed likely to succeed and the *haut ton* turned against her, when she was not invited to the homes of those whom she would have once called friends, do you know what she did?' Sarah did not wait for an answer. Not that her lord was capable of giving one. 'She went to the opera at Covent Garden. She insisted that Henry take her, to show the world that she believed in her own innocence and she did not care that others would question the legality of her marriage to your cousin Thomas. She sat there throughout the whole performance, with every lorgnette raised in her direction. She smiled, she flirted a little, she conversed. And hid from the world how much she suffered. Henry sat beside her, to shield her and support her with his presence because he could do no other. I admire them more than I can say.'

Sarah stopped to draw breath, then continued.

'We should do the same. You claim your innocence. Then we

should show a united front against those who would disbelieve. There is an Exhibition today at the Royal Academy. I forget whose paintings. It is not important. We should attend. With Thea and Nicholas. And Judith and Simon too, if they will come. And I will stand with you because it is the only thing I can do to show the world that I do not believe what is being said.'

'Sarah…' He was for the moment speechless, astounded at her courage to embark on so public a display. Swamped with guilt that she should choose to have anything to do with him after the events of the previous day. 'I do not know what to say…'

'You do not have to say anything. I will arrange it with Thea. If you would be pleased to escort me, at seven-thirty, I think.'

Without waiting for another word or a response from her lord, Sarah turned on her heel, closing the door behind her with a very positive click. And made sure that for the rest of the day she was so busy that should anyone—should Lord Joshua Faringdon—desire communication of any nature with her she would be quite unobtainable.

The Faringdon party attended the Exhibition in strength. Lord Joshua Faringdon discovered that, despite the strength of the temptation, he dare not cry off. The involvement of the little party and knowledge of the paintings was to be fairly minimal, but that was not the object of the exercise. They displayed considerable if not amazing interest in the hanging. The joint subjects of murder and Marianne were understood by all to be taboo. A brief but detailed conversation between the three ladies ensured that all rose superbly to the occasion. Thea and Judith both instructed their husbands on the purpose of this unprecedented outing, which neither gentleman would have chosen over a quiet evening with cards and brandy at Brooks's.

They talked, smiled, admired, sampled the refreshments. Whatever they felt, they hid behind gracious exteriors. There was a need for Faringdon family unity, which they all recognised and supported. They surrounded their notorious black sheep with firm support and unquestioning loyalty.

A very public statement of trust.

Sarah cast off all her misgivings, her reserve, her lack of confidence, her dislike of attention. Not once did she turn away from interested glances, not once did she fail to meet a speculative eye. Bright, lively, engaging, she stood beside Joshua and dared anyone to believe him capable of violent death. When he offered his arm to lead her round the exhibits, she laid her hand there with perfect composure, smiling up into his face with great charm. What it cost her to put on this performance, her lord had no idea. She bowed, nodded, conversed with acquaintances, flirted a little with her painted fan when Simon engaged her in conversation, as if there was no problem on this earth to trouble her. She had dressed with particular care in—for Sarah—an eye-catching gown in a deep rose pink silk overlaid with silver lace, a pretty string of diamonds and opals clasped around her neck with drop earrings to match. Her naturally pale cheeks benefited from skilfully applied Liquid Bloom of Roses; it required no application of Olympian Dew to bring a sparkle to her eyes. Lady Joshua Faringdon, in her quiet way, had declared war.

No one would accuse her husband of murder and think that she gave it any serious consideration. No one would divide them, whoever it might be who had first dropped the poisonous words into the willing ear of the Polite World. And her family would support her. She felt a warmth spread around her heart as she watched them: Thea, using all her lively charm and diplomatic experience of foreign receptions, Judith calling on her wide acquaintance. The gentlemen relaxed and talked horses and sport when they could escape their wives' eagle eye. Whatever the outcome of this night, Sarah knew that she had made the right decision.

No one could question or intimidate the united Faringdons. With a little crow of success, Sarah wished that Eleanor and Henry were present to appreciate the outcome of her plotting.

* * *

They returned home, exhausted from the constant strain to remain cheerful, but Sarah was content. She had done all that she could. Not least to show her husband, who had tried to distance himself from her because he could not speak the truth, that she would not accept his decision. She would stand at his side whether he wished it or not.

The trial of the evening at the Exhibition left Lord Joshua Faringdon feeling utterly wretched. He had gone along with it because he could think of no good reason not to. Sarah's determination, her refusal to discuss it, had carried him along, a leaf in the current of a millstream. And now he was swamped with shame. His gentle Sarah had walked into the lion's den for him. Such faith, such strength. She had stood by him in glory and splendour to face the gossips. His intention had been to step back from her, to allow her to believe the scandal if she wished, to hate him if she wished. To build a barrier between her and the deceit that was his to bear. To replace any suffering she might feel with contempt, because he simply did not deserve her sympathy. He could not use her innocence and her loyalty in his own interests. But Sarah, with astonishing strength of will, had torn his plan to rags, by standing beside him before the interested eyes of the Polite World.

How had it all become so complicated?

The simplicity of it was that he could not remain apart from her. He did not wish to remain apart. He felt the meanest worm in the face of such loyalty. He must put some of it right with her—she deserved no less.

So Joshua knocked on her door and waited for a reply. Sarah had gone straight to her bedchamber without any attempt at conversation, which was signal enough that he would have to be willing to make amends.

She answered, he entered. She was sitting at her dressing table.

'I thought you would go on to one of your clubs with Nicholas.' She did not look at him, but kept her hands busy.

Took off her jewels and replaced them in their case. Began to take the pins from her hair.

'No.'

'I think we made a point tonight.' She continued to place the pins in a cut-glass bowl. 'I think that Eleanor would have been proud of me.'

'Sarah—'

'There is no need to say anything. I know that you cannot. But we have done what we can.'

She stood to move across the room to find a home in a little bow-fronted cabinet for her gloves and fan. But now he strode forward to take her wrist in a light clasp and pull her to a halt. Yet still she did not turn toward him. Nevertheless he would say what he had to say and try to bridge the yawning chasm.

'You do not realise the debt I owe you tonight, Sarah. I think no man could ask more of his wife than that she stand at his side when any remaining honour attached to his name is destroyed. Yet you did exactly that. With such grace and dignity as I have never seen. I don't know whether you believe me or trust me, but you made so public a gesture in my support…' With firmer pressure, he turned her toward him. 'I need to ask your forgiveness. I treated you abominably.'

'I know you did. I suppose you had your reasons, even if I can neither understand nor accept them.' She would not make it easy for him. Her eyes were accusing. 'It would help if you told me the truth, but we have been through all that, have we not?'

'Sarah…' Never had he seen such a chill in her eyes, so stern a line to her lips. And it hurt to know that he deserved it, and far more.

'I know. You cannot. Let us leave it at that.' She made to pull away, but he dare not allow it. He took her hands in his so that he could face her squarely.

'Then let me say this. I admire you, Sarah. My respect for you is beyond measure. Never more so than this night. Your bravery, your strength, your willingness to put yourself on the line for me. I tried to push you away. To keep the scandal from hurting you more. I find that I cannot do that.'

Sarah waited. Admired, respected, he had said.

Loved? Ah, no.

'I need you tonight, Sarah.' He hesitated, so unusual in this dynamic man. 'I will not force my presence on you if it is distasteful. And in God's name it must be. I would ask for your tolerance, Sarah, until I can put matters right between us.'

'Will it ever be possible?'

'Yes. I promise you.'

She watched, waited, thought of the weight of his words. Read the sincerity in his eyes, which gleamed true silver tonight. Sincerity, yes, but also a terrible uncertainty, which smote at her senses. A vulnerability that had shaken him to the core. It shocked her to see the rare emotion race across his face with vivid intensity. Her heart stuttered. However foolish, however naïve it might be, she trusted him. And would trust him whatever the world might say against him. She allowed her lips to soften, her cold face to warm into a smile. And allowed her woman's heart to dictate her response. She could not refuse him if he had a need of her.

She opened her arms at her sides, almost a gesture of submission. Or was it invitation. For if she trusted him to have committed no evil act, she must surely trust him with the safekeeping of her body and her clamouring emotions. It was time that she had the courage to respond to his love making, to claim her own needs. It was more than time. She forced herself to continue to hold his gaze

'Then come.' Her voice was soft, full of feminine allure. 'If you want me tonight I will not deny you, but it is necessary for you to play the role of lady's maid. You would not imagine the intricacy of buttons and ribbons.' Then he caught the gleam in her eye and was able to breathe more easily. 'But perhaps you are intimately acquainted with them. If so, it will on this occasion be to my advantage.'

Sarah's deliberate humour sliced through the wall of tension between them so that he could step forward with a soft laugh and apply himself to the task. He was, she was forced to admit as she watched his bent head, remarkably skilled. Tiny buttons, delicate ribbons, they posed no problem for his clever fingers. Gown, petticoats, shoes, stockings, all quickly dealt with to give her no room for embarrassment, to be disposed carefully over the daybed. Until she stood in her chemise. He made to blow out the candles, as he thought she would wish, but Sarah had made her decision and now she stretched out a hand.

'No. Leave one burning.'

'Are you sure? If you are more comfortable without…'

Nerves touched her skin with delicate tremors. 'No. Leave it. That is what I want tonight.'

So. A new Sarah, he realised. One who had thrown down the gauntlet in public and exerted her will this night. And one, it would appear, intent on continuing to surprise him. So he complied. She would have turned from him to walk to the bed, a chilly little action in itself if of no real moment, but this night he would not allow it. To turn from him, if only for a matter of seconds, was going beyond what he desired for himself, desired for her. He stepped after her and before she could slide between the sheets he took her arm in a gentle hold, drawing her around to face him.

Fingers brushed over her cheekbone and down, to the fine curve of her throat, then to cup the back of her neck beneath her hair. 'You are a woman of many facets, Sarah. And a woman of outstanding valour tonight. If you will trust me with your reputation, don't hold yourself back from me now. Let me show you what can exist between a man and a woman, without shyness, without restraint, without self-consciousness. Don't retreat from me but let me pleasure you,' he added as her lashes fluttered over her eyes in a moment's insecurity as she felt the beginning of a deep blush at his seductive words.

The lashes lifted, the gaze now direct and steady, more than he could ever have desired when she had hidden her dreams from him. Sarah lifted her hands to place them flat against his chest and spoke, as he was quick to recognise, from her heart. 'Very well. Show me the delights that can exist between a man and a woman. For my experience is shallow and my confidence low. So show me. But do not condemn me, I beg of you, if you find me less than skilful.' And that was as honest as he could ever hope for.

'Sarah. You still do not realise. I could never find you wanting. All I ask is that you will respond as your heart dictates.'

'I promise.'

With a swift movement he loosened the chemise to let it drop to the floor, stepping back so that he might see her in the soft candlelight. It lit her slender, graceful figure in warm tones and deep shadow, first gilding her hair to rim her head and shoulders in pure gold, then the flame flickering to highlight curves, deepen shadows, hinting at dark and glorious secrets that slapped at his senses. It was difficult in that moment to remember that she was not a young girl, but a woman who had married and borne a child. Had he ever told her how beautiful she was during the act of love? He should have done so. She needed to be told.

'You are beautiful, Sarah.' His body tightened to his discomfort in immediate response. Even more when her lips curved in a smile of quivering nerves. Then, because he sensed her considered denial of his words, he covered the space between them and effectively silenced her by framing her face in his hands and taking her mouth with his own.

'You are beautiful,' he repeated against her lips before allowing the hunger to rule and heat the kiss, winding his fingers into the silk of her hair. And Sarah—her reaction was everything he could have hoped for, stretching his command over his response to her to near-snapping point. She moulded her deliciously naked body against his, stretching her arms to clasp around his neck, the sigh of pleasure deep in her throat as she encouraged him to deepen the kiss and allowed his tongue to take possession.

So that necessity soon dictated that he push her away, breathing compromised, but staying only to divest himself of his own clothes before he would tumble her on to the pillows. Sarah watched him with growing anticipation. The glimmer of his white shirt, the dark satin of his evening clothes, all discarded. Until he stood naked before her, back-lit by the moon, which had risen to shine through the windows, outdoing the single candle whose light was now superfluous in the silvered brightness. The shadows were stark, the contours ice-edged. He stood and let her look her fill. Only reacting when she drew in a sharp breath.

'What is it?' A sudden concern.

But she shook her head. She would not tell him that he was beautiful, far more beautiful that she. But she raised her hand, palm up, held it out as in an offering, even though entirely shocked by her own behaviour. She felt, she decided, like Scheherazade as he sometimes called her, a seductive nymph of paradise, awaiting her lover in some exotic harem from tales of Arabian Nights. Out of character it most certainly was, but this night she felt she could play any part demanded of her. Had she not played a role all evening before the eyes of those who would spurn and condemn? This role would be no more difficult, and to her ultimate delight and satisfaction.

So Sarah waited for her lord to join her, her heart beating so loudly that she was sure he must hear it, but aware only of his magnificent body. And welcomed him when he pushed her back, slid beside her and took her into his arms.

His habitual tenderness, his consideration for her, were still discernible, must always be so, but this night his control was threatened beneath a fierce blooming of raw passion that took him by surprise. Or perhaps it did not, because Sarah, his reserved and distant Sarah, stoked the flames in his body with terrible, miraculous skill. This was the woman he had dreamed of, this the true Sarah, desire smouldering, hidden under the soft and fragile exterior. This was the lover who touched him with slender fingers, returned his kisses eagerly, along his shoulders, the expanse of his chest. Discovering with sure instinct where his pulses leapt with desire, throbbed in desperate need.

And Sarah trembled at her own temerity. Where had this courage come from? *Don't dissemble. Don't freeze with fear.* The thoughts ran through her head. *Touch him. He will not reject you, did he not promise? This is Joshua, whom you love to the marrow of your bones. Have you not always dreamed of touching him, longed to feel the strength of him beneath your palms? So firm, so hard, so powerful. So thoughtful a lover.*

With deliberate intent at her own urging, her hands drifted over his shoulders and chest, to waist and flat belly. Outlining the powerful flow of muscled thighs. And, with an intake of breath—oh courage! oh glory!—she curled her fingers around his strong erection.

Joshua groaned, turned his face into her hair, his blood engulfed with fire at the unexpected from this reticent lady. His breath shuddered in his lungs as he clung to sanity. Or were the shudders from Sarah? He could no longer separate the two.

'Shall I stop?' she whispered against his throat, instantly unsure.

'No. No.' He suppressed another groan. 'I can think of no better way to die.'

'Are you thinking of death?' The tremor of a laugh shivered against his flesh.

'Never death!'

So she stroked with a gurgle of delight and a thrill at his immediate response beneath her hand. But now he carried Sarah with him, for her into unchartered territory. And she joined him, answered every demand, returned every caress. How hot his skin, how demanding his hands and mouth, how incredible that she should feel like this. Then she forgot to think any more, aware only of the ripples of intense sensation that he awoke and stirred into flame everywhere he touched. Aware only of her own need to offer and give, to arch and entwine as he took over every sense in her body. Confidence swam through her veins like the most intoxicating of red wine. Until the heat scorched her, wrecked her breathing, blinded her to everything but this room, this bed, this man.

Whilst her lord used every vestige of self-control to force himself to be gentle. Force himself to move slowly, carefully. His instinct was to possess, to ravish, now when the hunger surged though his blood. Ravish as he had once promised that he would not. So he set himself to hold back, to entice and persuade, but it was a difficult task indeed when faced with her complete surrender, her generous response, her deliberate provocation.

Be patient. Give her time. Let her come to you. Let her dictate the pace.

But he burned and the needs that crawled through him became almost too great to deny. Yet he would pleasure her, raise her to such heights that she could not resist, could not deny her own needs. With assurance and skill of hands and mouth, lips and tongue, he waged his campaign with fierce dedication. No, Sarah was not mildly compliant tonight. He doubted, in one moment of heart-stopping clarity, that she would ever be so again.

Joshua pressed his lips in open-mouthed caress along the shallow valley between her breasts, diverted with sly ease to tease her nipples. Refusing to halt when she drew in her breath and stiffened beneath the onslaught of his mouth. Pushed on the assault when she sighed his name against his throat and melted in his arms. Lovely. Impossibly lovely. Soft as silk. A little murmur of delight when his fingers brushed low, lower yet to touch, slide and discover, taking for his own her most intimate secrets. Her thighs parted willingly, hips arched now in blatant invitation. Hot and wet, satin-soft, compromising his banked desire. When she pressed against the heel of his hand in convulsive response, his control came close to destruction.

Yet still, as he knew she would, she resisted the demands of her own body, afraid of the flames which grew and leapt and threatened to consume.

'Do you trust me?' He stilled his hand.

'Yes.' The merest sigh.

'Then don't think. Just feel. Let your mind go.'

Aware that the pressure was building within her from the shivers that ran along her limbs in his embrace, the thud of her heart beneath his lips, he harnessed all his own needs to capture her mouth in a kiss of blazing desire, pushing her to the very edge, to give her that ultimate release. Until she struggled against his body and would have pushed him away in a sudden moment of panic and fear of the unknown.

'No.' He gentled his hold, but would not retreat. 'Take what I can give you.'

He drove her on, ruthless now with determination to give her that intimate experience of her own body, until she cried out, sharp, shocked. He crushed his lips to hers to swallow her cries as she shivered uncontrollably against him, clung to him with gasps of astonished pleasure. Exactly as he had hoped. And triumph swamped his veins in a floodtide, as she quivered from the aftershock, face buried against his chest.

'Look at me.'

Sarah saw herself in his eyes, dark with passion, unfathomable as the waters of a bottomless lake, as he wiped the spangle of tears from her cheeks, tears that she had not been aware of shedding. 'I want to see you when I slip inside you. And you to see me. There is no danger here for you, darling Sarah.' He watched her, at that moment completely enslaved, yet unaware of the endearment.

'Yes.' As was she. She raised a hand that trembled to his lips.

'Now.' It was so simple a word, and all the invitation he needed.

'It must be so. For you are too alluring to resist any longer.'

With sure and elegant strength he moved to pin her body with his own and thrust hard and deep. Held himself there to prolong the pleasure for her, for himself. So intimate an invasion that enclosed him, filled her, overturning the mind of both except for their joy in each other. Slick skin against slick skin, her legs entangled with his, his body owning hers. She watched him, eyes caught and held, emotions naked to his gaze. For a moment he thought that she might have more than an affection for him. Then the fleeting shadow was gone. Hunger and desire, potent and dark, swept over him as Sarah bit her lip to prevent her expressing her love in words that might still return to haunt her. But now she could show him in other ways. So he began to move within her and she mirrored the thrust with innate delight. Until he pushed them both to that precipitate edge. To fly and fall, taking her with him, feeling her shudder again as his own control shattered.

'What was that?' Still pinned beneath him, Sarah could only glory in his power and weight. It seemed to her that any sensible thoughts she might have were still scattered through the heavens, as her limbs were heavy with splendidly overwhelming exhaustion. It was outside anything in her experience. She did not think that her heart would ever again settle into its old pattern.

Joshua raised his head, lifted his weight on his arm, brushed back the fall of hair from her face so that he could kiss her lips with exquisite tenderness. A tenderness that made her heart tremble.

'A miracle, I think. A miracle.'

'Yes. So I think.' And after a little pause: 'I do not know what came over me, Joshua.'

'Thank God for it.' She caught the glint of his smile in the moon's brightness. The candle had long since burned out. And she sighed in an unexpected and strangely moving happiness.

Joshua felt her smile against his shoulder, and his heart rejoiced. She trusted him. He could ask for nothing more. Because, as he slid into sleep with her, it mattered more than anything other in his previously selfish and wilful life that she did.

* * *

'My Lord Faringdon. I did not expect to see you here.' Wycliffe rose from his seat in his unremarkable office in the City, his face set in deep lines of disapproval. Nothing in the austere surroundings, in the inconspicuous building off Fleet Street, would point to the importance of this man to national security.

Lord Faringdon was not in a mood to be impressed by the standing of his host or his efforts to remain invisible. 'I am sure you did not.' He bowed with controlled grace.

'Perhaps it would have been better, my lord, if you had not sought to draw attention to yourself or to me.'

'So you might think, sir. On this occasion, I do not.'

If Wycliffe was critical, his lordship was icily correct.

'You look in the best of health again, my lord. I trust your bones have knit well.' For a compassionate enquiry, it was delivered in a distinctly unfriendly tone.

'Yes.'

'If I might be permitted to say—' the two men still faced each other, standing, across Wycliffe's desk '—you should not have found it necessary to make contact with me other than by discreet channels. You must be well aware of this, my lord.' Wycliffe's lips thinned with displeasure.

'I understand you perfectly, sir.' Joshua's jaw was rigid with suppressed anger. 'In fact, I wrote you a letter—but decided to come in person, so that I might express myself more effectively. And be assured that you did not simply consign my complaint to your fire-grate and continue to issue instructions against the well-being of my wife.'

'So it is a matter of some importance?' Wycliffe's voice rose sufficiently as to make it just a question. His hard eyes expressed no acceptance, but they failed to intimidate.

'I find it so. My wife is being followed by an individual who looks suspiciously like Felton. I wager that it is your doing. Felton was always a favoured employee of yours in such surveillance work.'

'Of course. Felton is very good.' There was no guilt here.

'May I ask why?' Lord Faringdon remained remarkably calm when faced with this clear admission of Wycliffe's involvement.

'We were not informed of your intention to marry again.'

'I was not aware that I must inform you on a matter of so intimate a nature.'

'Of course you should have informed us. Your previous marriage was a disaster of the first order.' There was an edge to Wycliffe's patience. 'We learned a hard lesson with Marianne de Colville. It could have destroyed our whole espionage network, here and in France. It was pure chance that one of her letters was intercepted before any further damage could be inflicted. I would not wish for history to repeat itself with the lady who is now Lady Faringdon. It surprises me, my lord, that you need to ask or question the matter of my…my concern.'

'Damnation, Wycliffe! Of course I need to—' He drew in a breath. 'Sarah is not Marianne. She is nothing *like* Marianne! There is no similarity in the situation.'

'Perhaps not—on the surface. But how well do you know the lady? Do you trust her—absolutely and implicitly? It is my understanding that you have not had a long acquaintance. She has lived in New York. Why did she suddenly return to England? Have you ever considered that she might be in the pay of some foreign interest and saw marriage to you as the perfect entrée into government circles? America is not totally disinterested in European events.'

'What? Sarah a spy?' Joshua laughed in harsh incredulity. 'It takes my breath away that you should even consider it. How can you suggest something so patently ridiculous?'

'Mrs Russell…Lady Faringdon…spent some considerable time in New York. You cannot possibly know what her contacts were there.'

'My wife went to New York to accompany Eleanor, widow of my cousin Thomas. She remained there with her and my cousin Henry.' There was now a dangerous calm in Lord Faringdon's reply.

'And your cousin, Henry Faringdon, my lord, is well known to have republican leanings. He would have no reason to love the British monarchy—or any attempt on our part to support the democratic monarchies in Europe. He is not above suspicion.'

Joshua's brows snapped together, all pretence at equanimity abandoned. 'My cousin might respect republican views, but Henry is hardly likely to be involved in a plot.'

Wycliffe made no reply, but cynicism deepened the lines engraved around his mouth.

'My wife,' Lord Joshua continued, 'is sister to Theodora Wooton-Devereux. Daughter of Sir Hector, who has been British Ambassador to Paris as well as Constantinople and any variety of such places. At present he is in St Petersburg. You must have some acquaintance with him. Hardly the background for an enemy spy.'

Wycliffe was implacable. 'But your wife was not brought up with her sister, was she? The Wooton-Devereux interest would have no influence whatsoever on your wife's sympathies.'

'You have been very busy, sir.' Joshua suddenly found it very difficult to prevent his hands from curling into fists, and making use of them against this man who could so calmly accuse his wife of such devious plotting. He gripped hard on the reins of temper. 'You are remarkably well informed of me and my family.'

'It pays to be so.'

'I find, sir, that I resent it more than I could have believed possible. It is insulting to a lady of supreme honesty and integrity. If you knew my wife, we would not be having this conversation.'

But Wycliffe remained unmoved in the face of such anger. 'There are no guarantees in this profession, my lord, as you are aware.'

'My wife is no spy.' All Joshua could do was resort to denial of a situation so outrageous as to be unthinkable.

'It is not beyond the realms of possibility! Sit down, my lord. Sit down.' Wycliffe waved towards a chair as he himself took his seat behind his desk. 'Nothing is to be gained by us facing each other in this manner.'

Joshua sat, but was in no way mollified. 'What right do you have to set one of your minions to follow my wife whenever she sets foot outside the house, and to loiter outside my London address?'

'I have every right, as you well know if you will consider the matter calmly. My duty is to British security. You are, have been and will be again an important link within my information network. Your recent marriage was very—ah, precipitous—and the lady is unknown to us. Given your connections to myself, you should not have entered into this marriage without my knowledge.'

The air between them remained positively charged with hostility. It was clearly a stand-off. Lord Faringdon continued to fix his employer with a narrowed stare as he diverted to the other problematic issue. 'I suppose you have not heard the rumours. Unless Felton has also seen fit to feed you the vicious content of London gossip.'

A bland look was the only response he got.

'A nasty little rumour. Started, I wager, by Olivia Wexford out of a fit of pique when I dispensed with her…her services, shall we say. Another one of your ideas, to disguise the reason for my return to England and paint my character a particular shade of grey, if not midnight black! Another one of your plottings that has landed me in serious difficulties. Olivia threatened to get even.' His laugh was without humour. 'She is a lady of considerable, although dubious, talent. I can safely say that she has achieved her ambition.'

'I know little of such matters. I do not move in the same exalted circles as you, my lord.' Wycliffe watched his noble employee with keen eyes. They were beginning to walk on dangerous waters here.

'Don't tell me that you have no knowledge of the accusations—I would not believe it! Your ear is always close to the ground. Olivia has confided to the Polite World that I murdered Marianne in a crime of passion. The whole town is discussing the methods I might have used before consigning her body to some secret grave in the forests around Versailles. My wife now looks at me askance—she thinks that I am having her followed with the prime motive of having her done away with.'

Barely visible, Wycliffe's whole body had stiffened. 'You will not comment publicly on such matters. I do not want the Marianne affair to be discussed.'

'No. I will not.' The reply was sharp, immediate. 'But the accusations do not sit well with me.'

'The rumours are not our problem.' Wycliffe shrugged. 'They will soon die a death when a new scandal breaks.'

'Perhaps. But you are not blameless in the whole unfortunate episode.'

Wycliffe hesitated. 'Your marriage to Marianne was a terrible mistake.' It was the only admission that Mr Wycliffe would make.

'That may be so, but why should I have to continue to pay the price?'

Wycliffe swept the papers on his desk together with a wide gesture of impatience at the direction of the whole conversation. He tried for a softer approach, unwilling to antagonise one of his most gifted informants any further than he had already achieved. He would try for a deflection. 'Do you want my advice, Joshua?'

'Advice, is it? Or a demand?' There was no softening here.

'Whichever way you wish to see it! You are fit again. Go back to Paris for us. We need information.'

'So you wish to make use of my talents again. You amaze me. I thought my cover had been effectively infiltrated and I was of no further value in that area. That The Chameleon had outlived his usefulness.' The arrogance should have warned Wycliffe that his lordship was not to be won over.

'Perhaps—but I think you still have much to offer. You have innumerable valuable contacts in Paris and at the Bourbon Court. You will be made welcome, invited everywhere. It will not be difficult for you to listen and report back. We need you, Joshua. I never foresee a time when The Chameleon has no value to my plans.' The gentleman leaned forward, all persuasion. 'We could be facing a major crisis here.'

'Listen to what? Still the plot to restore Napoleon—unless he dies first?' Lord Faringdon's lip curled. 'I cannot see there is much of a realistic threat there. The Emperor was fading by the day, as I last heard. The Bonapartists will have to accept failure without any intervention from us.'

'I agree. But we have received warning, the merest whisper, of a planned assassination. Against whom we are unsure. Or when. Or even the perpetrators. Yet the whispers continue. If it is against one of the royal family, it would not be in our interests. Think of the upheaval if it was a success, encouraging all the dissonant groups to rise against the Bourbons. Their popularity is on shaky ground as it is and they are hardly blessed with a handful of heirs to secure the throne into the future. After Louis XVIII, his brother Charles and his nephew, the Bourbon line stops. An assassination could be highly damaging to stability in France. We need to know more, Joshua. And prevent it coming to fruition, of course.'

'I see.'

'We need information that you would be in the perfect position to obtain with an entrée to all the best houses.' A sly smile coloured Wycliffe's face. 'It could also be in your own interests, my lord.'

A raised brow.

'If you go to Paris, you will escape all the gossip here. When you return,' Wycliffe snapped his fingers, 'it will all have dissipated and the *haut ton* will have forgotten Marianne.'

'And my wife? What are your plans for her?'

'Leave her in London. We will continue our surveillance of

her until we are certain that she is uninvolved—or until we have proof that she is in the pay of others.'

'And if I object?'

'Where government security and policies are concerned you have no right to object. You do not know Sarah Russell. You do not know that you can trust her. We need you and your expertise in Paris.'

He did not like Wycliffe's reply, but was forced to acknowledge the truth of the man's assessment of French politics. Even as he damned the man's callous disregard for any matter other than national security.

'And the Countess of Wexford?' he asked. 'What are your plans for her?'

'She is not your concern. Forget her. Will you go to Paris?'

'I will consider it.'

'Do so quickly, my lord. It is approaching the time of Carnival in Paris. When all the world and his wife celebrates.' Wycliffe sniffed in distaste of such excess and the openings it provided for those who would destroy the restored government. 'What better opportunity to carry out a *coup d'état* against the royal family when no one is prepared to consider anything other than his own pleasure?'

Lord Joshua Faringdon made no response, but slammed out of the room, no more satisfied with the situation than when he had entered the premises half an hour previously.

'Going somewhere?' Lord Nicholas Faringdon refused the services of Millington and announced himself in Hanover Square that same afternoon. He found Joshua in the library, folding documents into a well-worn leather case.

'To Paris.' Joshua barely looked up, but Nicholas could see the hard-held temper on his face, in every line of his body. Every movement was an essay in simmering fury. A brief, authoritative note from Wycliffe had followed hard on his earlier visit to and conversation with that gentleman, delivered by hand. Lord Faringdon was expected in Paris within the week and should make contact with Sir Charles Stuart, British Ambassador to the Bourbon Court. Further instructions would follow. Thus Lord Faringdon was not in a mellow frame of mind.

'Oh.' In no way put out, intimately acquainted with his cousin's moods, Nicholas helped himself to a glass of brandy and cast himself into a chair to await repercussions. 'A sudden decision?'

'Yes.'

Nicholas crossed one booted leg over the other, a study in patience. 'Is this in the way of a rout by overwhelming odds?' he enquired, knowing that the outcome might be similar to that of applying a match to a trail of gunpowder.

'No.'

'So?'

'If you must know—' the leather satchel was flung onto the desk with little vestige of control '—it is a tactical retreat before superior forces.'

Silence.

Until Joshua faced his cousin, hands fisted on hips. 'What is your next question? Are you perhaps going to ask me if I murdered my wife?' he snarled. 'You have been remarkably restrained with regard to the fraught topic of Marianne.' It had been a long and frustrating day. He had not enjoyed the confrontation with Wycliffe or its outcome.

'I have, haven't I? But it was not my intent. Not unless I wanted a sharp left to the jaw.' Nicholas raised his brows, waited a heartbeat. 'But since you broached the issue… Did you? The gossips sound very sure.'

'No. I did not.' Joshua's face was cold and bleak, in contrast to his eyes, which blazed with molten fire.

'So where did the tale arise?'

'A slighted woman, is my guess.' He flung himself into a chair and picked up the glass that Nicholas had thoughtfully poured for him.

'Ah. The Countess of Wexford? I thought as much. Beware a woman scorned, particularly one as self-seeking as the fair Countess. I doubt that she enjoyed being evicted from her role in this household.'

'She had no role in this household.'

'Well…I expect that she wished she had.' Nicholas grinned in appreciation. 'The lady has certainly sharpened her claws and is now intent on sinking them into your tender flesh. The scandal has taken the town by storm.'

'As I know to my cost!' Joshua put down the glass with a force that threatened the perfection of the faceted crystal. 'But I am innocent of this, Nick. I did *not* murder my wife! Marianne…she is…was…!' Aware of Wycliffe's warning and the crevasse opening before the unwary, Joshua bit down on any further incriminating words.

Nicholas choked on his brandy.

'She's what? I thought she was dead.'

'Nothing! She is.'

'Sher…perhaps you need to tell me just what is going on. Of course you did not murder your wife. No one with any sense believes that you did. But something is afoot. What is it?'

Joshua gritted his teeth, the muscles of his jaw hardening. 'That, Nick, is the whole problem. I must keep a still tongue in my head.'

'Does Sarah know?'

'No, she does not.'

'Will you take her to Paris with you?'

Oh, God! 'Yes…no. I haven't decided. It is none of your affair!'

'I just thought…'

'What did you just think?' Joshua glared at him.

'That it would be better for Sarah if you took her with you.'

Joshua sighed. Of course he should take her with him. She would be devastated if he left her in London. He knew enough of Sarah's state of mind to know that she would see it as a personal slight. But there was her safety to consider if death and violence were to be the order of the day in Paris.

'It might,' he said quietly, 'be in the interest of Sarah's safety if I left her here.'

Nicholas placed his glass carefully on the desk before raising keen eyes to pin his cousin down. 'Sher—you can tell me to go to the devil, of course, but—are you involved in government work—something conspiratorial, perhaps—which necessitates your silence? Something which is not without its dangers?'

'Why do you say that?' The silver eyes narrowed with suspicion, but did not waver.

'No reason. It is just that—'

'You have a fertile imagination.' Joshua was increasingly aware of a compulsion to unburden himself to his cousin. To lay before him the whole intricate web of plots and devious scheming that could undermine the peace achieved after Waterloo. To admit to the identity of The Chameleon. And knew he must not. He closed his eyes momentarily against it.

'Perhaps I have. So you have no intention of unburdening yourself.' It was as if Nicholas had sensed the internal battle, impulse waging war against necessity.

'No.'

'Very well. If that is what you truly wish.' Nicholas pushed himself to his feet. 'I cannot force you. But remember, if you ever need a sympathetic ear…'

'Forgive me, Nick.' Joshua also stood forcing his muscles to relax, managing a wry smile. 'It is not my intention to appear churlish.'

'But you do!'

'All I can say is that the decision to unburden myself—as you put it so aptly—is not mine to make.'

Nicholas began to make his way to the door. Then, on a thought, looked back. 'Do I surmise that your…er…*colourful* reputation is not as dire as you would have us believe? That it has all been a disguise for some undercover project?'

'Surmise what you will.' Nicholas could read nothing in Joshua's expression. 'But don't discuss such an idea with Thea. Because she will surely talk to Sarah. And then where shall we all be!'

'What an interesting life you lead, Sher!' Now Nicholas laughed. 'I never could accept that you were such a black sheep in the family as you would have us believe.'

'Ha! I fear that my *interesting life*, as you put it, is about to call in its debts.' For a moment Joshua hesitated, wondering if he were about to make a mistake, but was encouraged by the understanding smile on his cousin's face. 'You could do one thing for me.'

'And that is?'

'Come to Paris with me. I have the strangest feeling that I might just need your support.'

'Will the Countess of Wexford be there?'

'Highly likely. Now that she has done all the damage she can in London.'

'Wouldn't miss it for the world. Thea will love it. She is not unacquainted with the city. Sir Hector was ambassador there for some months.'

'I did not mean that Thea should… But of course she would accompany you.' Joshua looked dubious at the prospect.

'What—me go Paris with you—and leave Thea at home?' Nicholas laughed aloud. 'Have your wits entirely gone begging, man? When did any fashionable woman refuse a chance to go to Paris?'

'Forgive me, Nick—I seem to have said that more than once this afternoon!' Joshua bared his teeth in a passable smile and now, for the first time, there was some warmth there. 'How crass of me! Perhaps both you and your formidable wife can give my fast-disintegrating reputation some much-needed support.'

That same night Joshua had intended to dine early at home before escorting Sarah to the theatre at Covent Garden. To hell with the gossips! And the devil take Wycliffe with his insinu-ations concerning Sarah's loyalties! He would not turn and run from public gaze. Had they not flung down a challenge at the Exhibition and survived the ordeal? But at the eleventh hour he could not face running the gauntlet of the tiers of boxes with their avid eyes and raised lorgnettes, pretending ignorance of the knowing looks and speculation on his relationship with Marianne. The discussion of his sins both in general and in wicked particular. His respect for Eleanor and Henry, who had done exactly that, multiplied. But he guessed, rightly, that Sarah would find no enjoyment in the performance if *they* were pro-viding the audience with more entertainment than the actors on the stage.

Wycliffe's lack of sympathy and insistence that it was Joshua's duty to return to Paris had seriously ruffled the Far-ingdon feathers.

So Lord and Lady Faringdon dined *à deux* at home with a reasonable show of unity, finding enough food for conversation to carry them through the various dishes in the first and second courses. Perhaps with no real appetite, but with no serious con-flict, or even a need to discuss the little matter of murder. Sarah was perfectly willing to follow her lord's lead. What would be the value in their discussing so contentious an issue when there was nothing further to be said, when Joshua was as tight-lipped as one of the oysters on her plate? Until, that is, they reached the dessert, a marvellous confection of peaches in heavy syrup and spun sugar.

Lord Joshua found that he had no appetite; he did not pick up his spoon.

'Sarah—I find a need to go to Paris.'

'Oh.' Her eyes immediately flew from her plate to his face, her enjoyment of the sweetness effectively destroyed by that one short statement. 'When?'

'In two days.'

If he saw a flicker of disappointment, a deepening of the little lines of concern that marked the fair skin beside her eyes when she was troubled, he thought he might have been mistaken. Or perhaps not. He was now intimately acquainted with Sarah's ability to hide her thoughts.

'Some business that has come up.' *I know it is a lame excuse, but it is the best I can do.*

'Of course.' *What business? Has the Countess of Wexford gone back to Paris? Surely he has not arranged an assignation! But I asked that I should not be required to meet and acknowledge his mistress. This would be an ideal solution to the problem. To continue the affair in Paris when I am far away!* Her heart fell to the level of her satin shoes. She too put down her spoon.

'Will it be a short visit?' She kept her voice admirably calm, tried for a smile, which was not as successful, so skilfully raised her napkin to her lips to cover it.

'I do not know. A week or two, perhaps longer.'

'Very well.' *Even worse! Some would say that he is also going to ensure that there is no evidence to be discovered of the murder of poor Marianne. Many would say that. But I cannot—I will not—accept that.* The possibilities rushed into her mind, rendering her almost light-headed.

Joshua watched his wife as she licked the sugar from one finger, her skin suddenly very pale. She would never ask him what he intended to do in Paris. Of course she would not. As a partner in a marriage of convenience he knew that she would be very careful of her status, ask nothing of him other than he was prepared to give on his own initiative. The thought touched his heart with compassion. And as at Richmond when she had so desperately wanted to ride with him, a desire to give her more than she was prepared to ask. So he made his decision in the blink of an eye. What was there to decide, after all? He knew what he wanted—he would not think about his reasons for it—but he also knew what would be the best for Sarah at this crucial time in their marriage. He had tried to distance himself. That had been a disaster and he could not do it again. It would be cruelty itself to leave her here alone to face the accusations, even more for her to have to tolerate Felton's intrusive shadowing in his absence. She would assuredly think the worst of her absent husband if he abandoned her in cold blood.

He could not leave her. Had known it as soon as Nicholas had challenged him over it.

So he abandoned any attempt to eat Mrs Beddows's masterpiece with some relief and cast his napkin on the table.

'Sarah. Yes, I am going to Paris. But you are coming with me. Go and instruct your maid to pack some clothes. Not many, mind. You can enjoy the glories of Parisian fashion when you get there.'

'Me?' It was almost a squeak. She pushed aside her spoon with a clatter. 'You will take me to Paris?' Whatever she had expected, it was not this.

'You, my dear wife. I have arranged for the children to stay with Judith.' Well, he would do so first thing in the morning. 'Don't argue!' as he saw her lips part. 'Beth and John will enjoy it. Judith will spoil them inordinately. I need some time alone with you, away from the wagging tongues. Let us call it a late wedding visit, if you wish.' He built his case skilfully unless she would still refuse. But what woman would? 'I need to introduce you to Paris and you need to inspect our property there. It is Carnival, with much to entertain and amuse.'

'Well… If you think…'

'And I have suggested that Nick and Thea join us for a short time. That will be company for you when I need to be elsewhere.' He applied the layers with sly expertise.

'Yes…'

'You will spend a considerable amount of my money and enjoy it.' And before she could deny it: 'It is in our contract, so I insist.'

'But I—'

'Sarah! I think I should also have included in that damned document that you would not argue with me at every step. There is nothing for you to do but be ready to go to France within the week. I have a yacht, which is awaiting us in Dover harbour. Can you be ready?'

'Yes. Oh, yes.' A glow of colour suffused her cheeks. He could not resist, but leaned over and kissed her tinted cheek, the most gentle of caresses. And then, because the temptation was too great, and she was so close, her soft lips. They were warm and offered everything he could ask. But he drew back.

And laughed aloud as the look of startled surprise on her face struck at his senses. The likelihood of Sarah being a spy for any foreign power roused his appreciation of the ridiculous. She might mask her thoughts, but she was not that good at hiding her feelings. Wycliffe must be a fool indeed to suspect her of double-dealing! She was as transparent as the sparkling crystal on the table when jolted into happiness.

'What is it?' Her glance was one of sudden concern, of suspicion that her husband had manoeuvred her into this position, which he had, of course.

'Nothing at all, dear Sarah! You are a delight to me.'

She frowned at him, but said no more. There was no accounting for the strange whims of gentlemen, after all. So she took herself off, to organise herself for the forthcoming and entirely unexpected treat. Surely if he intended to pursue the Countess of Wexford, he would not take his wife with him. It was inconceivable! The bubble of excitement within her chest could not be quelled.

Joshua smiled at her retreating figure. It pleased him to give her pleasure. Not from love exactly—he had already made that decision, had he not? But she was enchanting when taken by surprise.

And he felt a smug satisfaction at thwarting Wycliffe's attempts to separate them, to keep Sarah alone and under surveillance in London.

Then there was only one more step for Lord Joshua Faringdon to take.

His decision to act on Wycliffe's suggestion—if *sugges-*

tion were not too mild a word for that gentleman's plain speaking—and return to Paris as the British government's eyes and ears gave his lordship pause for thought in the following days. It had never been an issue for him before. He had embarked on any number of chancy escapades with little concern for his own safety or the outcome of the mission. A thoughtless belief in his own immortality, he supposed. Now, with Sarah as his wife, he must give the inherent dangers some serious consideration. It had struck him with unpleasant force on the night when he had insisted that Sarah accompany him. There should be no danger for her in Paris, yet he must still contemplate the worst scenario. So he had some rapid plans to make.

He spent a day in careful thought and planning, partly in communication with Mr Hoskins, the lawyer who oversaw all the Faringdon legal matters, and finally the withdrawal of a large sum of money from his lordship's bank. In return he acquired a deed of property, the outcome all quickly tied up and entirely to his satisfaction.

All that remained was to present the final conclusion to Sarah. He prowled the library, awaiting her return from an outing with Theodora. And brooded over the unpredictability of women who were too independent and self-sufficient for their own good, particularly those whose well-being was fast becoming a fixation with him. However enchanting they might be, however much they might have come to fill his thoughts from one hour to the next, they were still unpredictable.

At last he heard her light footsteps in the hall and emerged to meet her, all suave elegance and composure. No one would ever question his assurance. Still in her outdoor wear, she was in process of removing her beribboned and flowered straw bonnet. The soft light through the tall windows touched her hair with pale gold. She turned to him with a quick smile.

'Joshua.' Her eyes picked up colour in the sunbeams. 'I did

not know that you were home.' Her impromptu greeting and genuine warmth filled his veins with a sudden heat.

'I was waiting for you, lady.'

She blushed deliciously. Made no attempt to walk away, as the old Sarah might have done.

'Sarah. Have you a moment?'

'Of course.'

She must have no notion of how uncertain he felt, nor would she. He would carry it off with his habitual confidence as if the outcome of the next few moments were of no real importance to him, when they concerned him very much. He opened the door into the withdrawing room, a deliberate choice, being less formal and business-like than the library. It was important to keep her at her ease, unaware.

Waiting by the window as she laid aside her gloves and her parasol, he stood and watched, then without a word he handed her an envelope. Thick. Official, with her name on the outer cover.

'What is it?' Her brows rose in typical and instant suspicion, her eyes flying to his face.

He shook his head and smiled. 'Open it.' He would not say more.

'A gift?'

'Not really. More in the way of a security.' He refused to be defensive, but saw the little line grow between her brows.

'You should not, Joshua. You have given me so much. You do not need to give me more.' But she still opened it with a very feminine curiosity.

'I know.' He watched her. 'But I thought that perhaps this was necessary for you. You will understand.'

She raised her brows at his enigmatic words, but he would say no more until she had seen for herself. So Sarah extracted a sheaf of pages. Her eyes ran down one, then the next, widened with shock. Then she began to read again, colour fluctuating in her cheeks, lips parted in amazement.

'Joshua…' At first she could not find the words.

'Sarah!' He allowed himself a smile.

'You cannot do this. You must not.'

'Of course I can. It is my right and my pleasure. You are my wife.' Perhaps for the first time, the force of the words struck home. *You are my wife and I alone am responsible for your happiness and your safety. Your peace of mind.*

'Joshua…it is too much.'

'It pleases me. You must allow me to be pleased.'

'But a house! My very own house…'

She sank to the seat beside her as if her legs had not the strength to hold her.

'It is for yourself and John. Whatever happens in the future, you will have your own home in your own name, independent of the estate. To live in or to sell, as you see fit.'

Sarah promptly shocked both of them by abandoning the document in her lap and covering her face with her hands.

'Oh, Sarah.' He sighed. What did he have to do to bring her troubled soul some degree of happiness and contentment? 'It is not worth your tears. I had hoped that it would please you and give you some security.'

Your future will no longer be entirely dependent on me.

But he could not say that, could not even admit it to himself, when his impulse was to tighten the bonds rather than loosen them.

But his instinct at this moment was to take her into his arms and dry her tears with his lips. To tell her again that she need not fear the future, or his reputation, or the terrible scandal that hedged them in—whatever it was that robbed her of comfort. He wanted her to smile at him again as she had when she had walked into the hall, a smile of sheer delight. But he held back from her, aware of his own vulnerability for perhaps the first time. If she refused this gift, it would be like a slap in the face. He did not wish to contemplate that. She might fear her dependence on him. But he was beginning to realise that his happiness was fast becoming dependent on her. And he dare not approach her, for fear that she reject him as well as his gift.

'Sarah. Please do not cry.' He raked his fingers through his hair in a typically Faringdon gesture. 'I did this to make you happy, not to deluge you in grief. You can refuse it if you wish. But, indeed, I hope that you will not.'

'Yes…no! I know why you have done it. I am so overcome.' She looked up, a wavering smile on her lips, her lashes spangled with tears as she wiped them away her hands.

What an amazing man. He had given her a house of her own. Her own house—her mind repeated it again and again. A little town house in one of the streets off the Park. Bought by him in *her name*. Not part of the Faringdon estate. With the tip of one finger she traced where her name was written on the deed of ownership, breathless with astonishment that he should do this for her, aware of her innermost fears. How could she not weep? She had never experienced such generosity in the whole of her life. Such willingness to give her her freedom if she wished to take it. Making himself vulnerable to her own choice.

He had put her future here into her own hands. What did he deserve from her? It was time that she grew up, that she stepped outside her fears and foolish insecurities.

So Sarah rose to her feet, pressing the document to her heart for a moment before laying it aside on the table. Wiped the tears from her cheeks with the heel of her hand. Then walked toward him quite deliberately. Stood before him. Watched the uncertainty on his face. Raised her hands, again quite deliberately with no tremor, to frame his face, aware of the flash of surprise in his eyes as she did so. Then placed her lips on his. Very gently, the merest breath.

'Thank you, Joshua. What a marvellous gift. How could I ask for better? I could not possibly refuse it.' She kissed him again, astonished anew at her courage in making so personal a gesture. In the cold light of day. In the withdrawing room.

The tension eased from his face, the harsh lines softened. His smile reflected hers. It was all the encouragement she needed. She kissed him one more.

'Sarah.' His voice was low, a little rough with emotion. 'Do you realise that you have kissed me three times of your own volition?'

'I know.' Her smile deepened. 'And I can make it four.'

And she did.

Later Joshua was free to heave a sigh of relief that his plan had come to a satisfactory fulfilment. Whatever happened in the future, Sarah would have her own home, over and above the settlement made for her in the legal jointure at the time of their marriage. Because it had to be faced. Sarah was unaware of the dangers, and it was his intention that she remain so, but dangers there undoubtedly were. If Wycliffe was talking of assassinations, political murder… Joshua thought about his last visit to Paris, his expression grim. It had ended in his ignominious sprawl over a balustrade with immediate pain and inconvenience, but no lasting damage. It could have ended quite differently if his assailant had been intent on taking his life. He had been careless, thoughtless of his safety. Next time—if there was to be a next time—he would be prepared against so overt an attack, but he might not be so fortunate in the outcome. It was the price he might be called upon to pay, becoming involved with those who would destroy the peace and stability of Europe. He had always accepted that. If death awaited him in the sumptuous rooms and clipped gardens of Paris and the Tuileries, so be it. But Sarah would not suffer. A grim tension settled about his mouth.

And Sarah must not know.

Chapter Nine

February 1820—Paris

It was new and overwhelming and Sarah, as she admitted in the secrecy of her heart, adored every minute of it despite having no familiarity with it or acquaintance there of her own. The city was so *old* compared with New York. So much to see, so many gracious buildings, such a variety of shop windows to gaze into, so many fashionable people. Her isolation was merely temporary. Theodora and Nicholas were expected to join them any day. Sarah suspected that Joshua had arranged it for her comfort and was grateful. Nor could she fault his own concern for her happiness. Until her sister arrived he was attentive and companionable, pleased to escort her wherever she wished to go. He bought her a copy of Galignani's *Paris Guide* and consented to accompany her sight-seeings with amused tolerance. She could almost close her mind to the many times when he was not at home, usually during the dark hours, when he left their house in the most fashionable quarter of the city without advising anyone of his destination. Almost, but not quite.

Sarah had little time to sit and think. Even to miss the children, which she did, of course, when she came upon something that would reduce John to astonishment, such as a splendid parade of the lancers of the Garde Royale, or would attract Beth's wide-eyed interest. But Lord and Lady Joshua Faringdon were in demand. As soon as it was known that the English lord had returned to Paris, they received one invitation after another to soirées and balls, intimate At Homes and Court receptions. Particularly the formal receptions at the Palais Royal in the Tuileries Gardens. Sarah made her curtsy here to Louis XVIII, his brother Charles, Comte d'Artois, and Louis' nephew, the Duc de Berri, who, with his young Duchesse, were at the centre of a lively circle who enjoyed life to the full. The Faringdons were soon drawn into the set who danced and feasted and discussed matters of triviality or importance from dawn to dusk. Sarah found it easy to admire the pretty Duchesse who remained cheerful despite her agonising failure to bear her lord, whom she so clearly adored, a son.

It was, as Joshua had told her, the time of Carnival, the days of mad revelry before the onset of the abstinence of Lent. Days of feasting and dancing, in private houses and in the streets, days and nights when no one slept. When visits to the opera or the open-air boulevard entertainments became the priority for the aristocracy. When even King Louis joined the procession of carriages and the masked revellers through the streets of the capital and the de Berris were frequently to be seen at the public festivities.

In Paris the shops were without doubt magnificent. Even Sarah could not but be entranced by the richness and beauty as she strolled along the rue Vivienne or the Champs-Elysées to the Tuileries Gardens. She could hardly wait for Theodora to join her. Meanwhile she strolled with Joshua when he visited Galignani's famous bookshop and reading room to meet and exchange news with any number of English visitors, as well as read the English newspapers and magazines delivered daily.

Although she would never speak of it to him, it could not but impress her how graciously Lord Joshua Faringdon was received. How much at ease he was. She could not but admire his address and presence as he introduced her to the Parisian *beau monde*, ensuring her immediate acceptance into the most magnificent of private homes and châteaux, at a gossipy breakfast, a fashionable and erudite *salon*, a formal diplomatic ball or a frivolous *bal costume*. Sarah might eschew the extravagant costumes worn by some—how could she possibly consider the dress of a Peruvian princess as suitable attire?—but the opportunity to wear a silver silk-and-taffeta domino over her gown with a seductively feathered mask to cover her face—how could any lady, even the quietly reserved Lady Faringdon, resist such delights? And when it came to the dancing she discovered herself perfectly adept at mastering the steps of the polka, the polonaise, and even the mazurka with its hectic Polish folk tunes. Lord Joshua was able to partner her with sure steps, impeccable grace and timing and superb sartorial elegance. How unfair it was. But her heart swelled with unspoken love and pride when he led her into a waltz and held her close, when she felt the strength and warmth of his satin-clad arm rest around her waist, to the jealous glances of any number of far more beautiful ladies than she could ever claim to be. Sarah smiled in utter contentment.

Sometimes, when at leisure, she allowed herself to recall her own upbringing in the little Jacobean manor house in Whitchurch, comfortable enough, of course, but where both affection and money were sadly lacking, from which her marriage to John Russell had been a welcome escape. Only to be forced to return to Whitchurch by a series of catastrophic events, not least the death of her husband. There was little of that naïve and shy girl to be seen now in fashionable Lady Faringdon, she mused, as she smoothed a pair of delectable lavender kid gloves over her smooth, well-cared for hands. But under the surface…there lurked the distressing lack of confidence that still struck her at the most inconvenient moments. Leaving her to feel unworthy of being noticed, much less being the recipient of affection—or even love. There was little point in her lecturing herself over it again—it just happened, rather like being struck down by a sudden heady cold. She smiled at the thought. But it afflicted her much less than it had in the past and she believed that she had learned to live with her guilt for past sins. Here in Paris she was accepted into society in her husband's name and, perhaps a little, on her own merit.

And although she was aware of and sometimes irritated by the ripple of interested gossip when they entered a room, the welcoming smiles and flirtatious glances of the beautiful women who wore their jewels with such casual assurance and hid their expressions behind feathered fans, Sarah had the relief of knowing that here in Paris she was not being followed. Not once did she feel the soft footstep of an anonymous figure behind her. Whoever had been sufficiently interested in her movements had been left behind in London. But she did not speak of it to Joshua. He would deny it anyway. She had no wish to destroy the present comfortable harmony between them.

Theodora and Nicholas arrived in Paris as expected. Sarah came upon Thea arranging the disposal of their luggage at the Faringdon house in Paris with all the skill of a lady of many and distant travels in the company of her mother and ambassadorial father.

'Sarah! We have arrived at last.' Thea embraced her sister. 'How well you look and how fashionable. It is so many years since I last visited Paris for any length of time—not since my father was with the embassy here. I expect the shops are as enticing as ever. Shall we explore them this afternoon?'

'Are you not too tired after your journey?' Sarah already knew the reply.

'When is my wife ever tired when there is the possibility of spending money on dresses and smart hats and the like?' Nicholas had entered the hall behind them and now saluted Sarah on her cheek with grace and humour. 'As my lady says, Sarah, marriage becomes you. But why you should feel comfortable as Sher's wife, I know not.' The glint in his eyes belied the sharp thrust at his cousin's expense.

Sarah blushed, but could not mistake Thea's subtle elbow in Nicholas's ribs.

'I am sure he is the perfect husband,' Theodora stated. 'Will you come with us, Nicholas?'

'No. You do not need me, I am assured.'

Thea kissed him, allowing him to curl an arm around her waist, to pull her close, in the relative privacy of the entrance hall. 'I promise not to spend too much.' She lowered her lashes, flirtatious as ever.

'Don't promise that—or we shall both be disappointed when you do.' He returned the caress to her cheek when she offered it. 'I trust Sarah to keep an eye on you, as your elder sister.'

'An impossible task to place on my shoulders!' Sarah smiled and Thea crowed with laughter, which filled Sarah with delight that her family had joined her. There was nothing now to prevent her enjoying her first experience of the fashionable and sophisticated life offered by the French capital.

Sarah's equanimity, however, at the covetous glances cast at her husband was severely overthrown during one hot and deplorably overcrowded evening at the home of Pozzo di Borgo, the Russian Ambassador. Afterwards she could not say what had made her aware, to turn her head at that precise moment. A faintest shiver of anticipation along her spine. But she felt a need to look over her shoulder—to see her lord standing at the entrance to a private anteroom. Tall, straight and splendidly handsome in the dark severity of formal evening clothes. As was now very familiar to her, her heart fluttered and her cheeks grew pink with sheer delight in his presence—until she saw that he was in close and intimate conversation with a woman. A woman whose lovely face and superb figure were horribly familiar. The conversation between the two was clearly of a serious nature and in some depth. Then her lord was bowing over the lady's hand, raising it to his lips.

Olivia Wexford. Of course.

Sarah could not see Joshua's expression, but she could view the Countess's face without interruption. Perhaps a little cool and serious at first. The faintest of frowns between her arched brows. Some sharp words from her expression. Then her face warming with a charming sparkle in her eyes and a flirtatious little smile curving her lips. She tapped Lord Faringdon's arm with her fan. There could be no mistaking so provocative a gesture for what it was. An invitation!

Sarah turned away. She did not wish to see more. The pain in her heart stabbed deeply, more than she could ever have believed. But she should have expected no less. Joshua had not married her for love. Sarah had acknowledged that incontrovertible fact at the very beginning, acknowledged, reluctantly, that he would continue to give his affections elsewhere. But she could not *like* the Countess of Wexford, remembering her sly malice and deliberate desire to harm. In fact, the gentle lady, who now stood with her back deliberately turned against the Countess and her own husband, was forced to admit that she positively *detested* the woman! Sarah's fingers curved around her fan into remarkable talons, worthy of a predator about to strike. Sensing the immediate danger to the fragile ivory sticks, Sarah took a breath and used all her will-power to force them to relax. She must be willing to accept. She could not like it, but she must acknowledge that her marriage was truly one of convenience.

But why did it have to be the Countess of Wexford who returned to such prominence in her lord's life?

She eventually brought herself to speak of the unnerving episode to Thea, desiring a sympathetic audience. But Thea shrugged, giving no credence to her sister's fears.

'I don't understand why you are so concerned.'

'He was kissing her hand.'

'Sarah! Of course he would. Joshua is all grace and elegance and perfect manners. And, after all, he knows the woman. He could hardly turn the shoulder in public, now could he?'

'No, I suppose not.' She did not look convinced.

Thea smiled. 'Joshua is no fool. Give him credit for seeing how shallow and self-centred that dreadful creature is.'

Sarah answered with unusual asperity. 'But meanwhile he might also see—and remember!—how well endowed and beautiful she is! I know for a fact that she once engaged his interest.'

'Sarah…' What could Thea say to reassure? 'That was before he married you!'

'Does that matter?'

Thea frowned at her sister with more than a little frustration. 'Well—you know him better than I, of course.' She would not refer to the rumours that, according to Nicholas, had followed Joshua all his adult life, to the despair of Lady Beatrice. 'But I would not think you had anything to fear from the Countess. Your lord is hardly neglectful of you, is he?'

For since her arrival, Thea had noted Joshua's care and particular attention to Sarah. The softness of his expression when his eyes rested on his wife, particularly when Sarah was unaware, could not be denied. How complicated it was becoming. Thea knew that Sarah loved Joshua, of course—had she not admitted the fact herself? But it seemed equally possible that Lord Joshua was fast losing his heart to a lady who had no appreciation whatsoever of that interesting development. And equally, it seemed to Theodora, a fascinated witness, that Lord Joshua was fighting against the experience. How foolish people were when they refused to accept this basic and highly desirable attraction. Not like herself and Nicholas, of course. She had the grace to blush a little as she remembered her own forward behaviour. Particularly a notable incident in the stables at Aymestry, before the disaster of the fire. But she took it upon herself not to meddle in her sister's private affairs. Or not yet, at any event. Sarah would not thank her for it and she certainly did not think that Joshua would welcome any involvement on her part. As for Nicholas… She winced a little as she imagined her lord's caustic words if she engaged in stirring the smouldering ashes between Joshua and Sarah into a bright flame. So—for a little time at least—she would simply watch and keep her own council.

Sarah, unaware of her sister's train of thought, accepted Thea's advice, but she still could not feel at ease. If she became a little uncertain and just slightly withdrawn towards her lord, he apparently showed no awareness of it.

Which perversely worried Sarah even more.

But any surface harmony between them was not to last.

For Sarah it all began with an inopportune meeting with the one woman in Paris whom she had every intention of avoiding. It could not be avoided, since Sarah had arranged to wait for Thea outside Le Domino Rouge, a mantua makers in the rue Vivienne, when out of the next-door establishment, which sold the finest of leather gloves, stepped no other than the Countess of Wexford. The two ladies faced each other. Both curtsied. Both regarded each other with smiling lips and frosty eyes.

'Mrs Russell.' The Countess unfurled her parasol with a supremely elegant gesture, entirely in keeping with her smoothly controlled voice. 'But, of course, you are no longer Mrs Russell, are you? I would not have expected to meet Lord Faringdon's…ah, housekeeper…here.' Her smile had the tiniest and most effective hint of contempt in tone and in the calculated hesitation. 'You played your cards very cleverly, did you not? I would not have expected such expertise on your part—but it seems that we must not be misled by appearances. One does not expect such skills from a mere employee.'

'I do not take your meaning, my lady.' Of course she did. It fired Sarah's blood with instant wrath. How dare the Countess patronise her!

'No? I should have realised, of course. Joshua did not seek

me out when I was resident in Hanover Square. I had thought it was his tiresome injuries that prompted his lack of interest. But now I know the truth.' The Countess's magnificent eyes flashed. '*You* were the object of his gallantry, I presume. Did you take him to your bed, Mrs Russell?'

'No, my lady, I did not.' Sarah might be suitably horrified at so intimate a conversation, so blatant a suggestion, in a public street, but as her mind absorbed the Countess's words, it was as if a heavy weight was lifted from her heart. She felt almost light-headed as an intense relief flooded through her. *Joshua did not seek me out when I was resident in Hanover Square.* She had no doubt that the Countess was speaking the truth. Why admit to such humiliation otherwise, when her intent had been to lift her finger and secure Lord Joshua's interest? So Joshua had never taken her as his mistress. It was difficult for Sarah to suppress the little bubble of delight in her throat. But she did, sensing that Olivia Wexford could still be an enemy. Further, Sarah had no intention of retreating from so insensitive an accusation about her own status in Hanover Square. But nor would she allow the explosion of fury in her blood to be evident. She opened her cream ecru parasol in malicious parody and smiled with particular sweetness. 'You must not judge me by your own standards, my lady.' The reply was quite gentle.

'No? But what woman would not welcome a man such as Joshua Faringdon to her bed? What woman would not cast out lures? Such wealth. Such an address. Between you and me, my dear, I think that we can agree that he is quite irresistible.'

'I did not have to *lure* Lord Joshua, my lady.' Sarah had no difficulty in preserving her confident little smile as she noted the tension in the beautiful face.

'Beware of being too confident, *my lady*.' A snap here as the Countess's control all but slipped in the face of such challenge. 'You hear what the rumours say of your husband. A rake and a libertine might not make for a comfortable husband.'

'I know. I have heard the rumours. I have known them from

the very beginning,' Sarah inclined her head in gracious acknowledgement. 'But I do not have to believe all that I hear.'

'Not even about Joshua's first wife? Marianne?' There was a sparkle in the Countess's eyes, almost of greed, as she watched her quarry's reaction.

She was to be disappointed. 'Certainly not of that,' Sarah replied with equanimity. 'I know of what my husband is capable. And it is not murder. I am astounded that you would repeat such an unpleasant and outright lie. It does you no credit, my lady.'

'You are haughty. Perhaps you should consider the safety of your own position—' Her words ended as Theodora made her appearance from the exclusive modiste's emporium and approached the two ladies with sharp ears and an air of deep fascination. The Countess promptly turned on her heel to put an end to any further exchange.

'The Countess of Wexford did not have the good manners to exchange greetings,' Thea observed with a bright smile. 'Not a suitable person with whom to be acquainted, I think. I could not help but overhear, Sarah. Now, where do you suppose that rumour of Marianne's fate began?' Thea raised her brows as she continued to watch the Countess's retreating figure.

Sarah too watched Olivia's departure with thinned lips. 'I cannot imagine.'

Theodora laughed. 'I see that we are in agreement, my dear sister.' She tucked her hand in Sarah's arm.

'I think that we are indeed.'

Which left Sarah with the slightest *frisson* of triumph that Olivia had not shared her bed with Joshua when they had shared a house. It gave Sarah a lighter heart—but did not heal it.

Fate began to take a more malicious hand.

The tranquil pond began to acquire even more ripples of disquiet.

Olivia Wexford's was not the only face in a crowd destined to draw Sarah's attention. The incident, trifling in itself, occurred on the following afternoon when strolling in the Tuileries Gardens with Theodora, Lord Joshua having once again cried off from accompanying them. But then, as Thea pointed out with an arch of her brows, so had Nicholas, so there was no cause for any dark suspicion—it was merely that gentlemen could always find better things to do than promenade in gardens! Sarah found herself stepping around a small group of fashionable strollers, deep in conversation, equally there to enjoy the air and the flowers, one of them, a lady in a bonnet much to Theodora's decided taste with nodding plumes and flowers and an extravagant crown. Sarah managed only a glimpse of dark hair and dark eyes and strikingly dark brows within that remarkable setting, yet she was struck by an instant recognition. But who? And where?

'Thea—the lady who has just passed us…'

'The one with the osprey feathers? What a splendid bonnet it is. But I could not wear that colour. Amber does not become me.'

'Never mind the hat! Do you know her? Your acquaintance is so much wider than mine.'

'No longer, I fear. Aymestry is not exactly the centre of the universe,' Thea admitted without discernible regret. 'I think the lady and I have not met. She has an arresting face.'

So thought Sarah. No, they had never met, yet it tugged at her mind. Perhaps indeed it was a distant acquaintance—someone whom she had seen in London who was also paying a visit to Paris. A familiar suspicion trickled into her mind. Or someone she had seen in Joshua's company. She closed her mind to that. But the lady was indeed eye-catching…

It was not important.

The face stayed in her memory. Sarah was not at ease.

Joshua also found himself beset.

His conversation with Olivia Wexford at the diplomatic reception had been totally unsatisfactory, much as he had expected. When he had broached the subject head on, with typical candour, she denied any knowledge of the source of the rumours in London. But her eyes had been cold and watchful of his reaction to her. She was not beyond throwing out lures, despite their fraught parting, making it more than evident that she would welcome any overtures from him. Joshua smiled without humour. He had no intention of making overtures of any nature to the Countess. He had never trusted her, trusted her even less now, knowing that she was capable of making any kind of mischief. He would not become involved with her again, whatever plots Wycliffe might devise. She was far too dangerous, driven by resentment at her so-casual dismissal from his life.

But the matter of the Countess of Wexford was quickly put out of his mind. There was beyond question something afoot, as Wycliffe had intimated. He could find no sound evidence beyond an uneasy calm and a variety of enigmatic observations from his many sources. He had definitely discarded the viability of the long-running plot to restore the Emperor Napoleon. It was generally acknowledged that the exiled ruler was near death. Yet it seemed to him that Paris was holding its breath, awaiting some catastrophe. As he worded to Wycliffe in a carefully neutral note, nothing was clear except the extreme vulnerability of the Bourbons. Louis himself widowed and childless, his brother also widowed. Even more a cause for concern was that Louis's nephew and his lively wife, the Duc and Duchesse de Berri, had yet to produce a living son. A carefully plotted assassination against any or all, particularly if the royal family neglected its security during the Carnival revels, could destroy the Bourbon claim in one vicious *coup* and open France to God-knew-what influences.

So Joshua worried about the lack of news and the dangers inherent in the street celebrations. It even began to tease at his mind that perhaps he should have left Sarah in London after all. It might be that there were real dangers lurking behind the costumes and masks here in Paris, not to be compared with the minor irritation of having one of Wycliffe's men dog her steps at home. That thought, growing as the days passed, troubled his sleep and scraped at the edges of his temper. He must take it upon himself to ensure Sarah's safety—after all, he had insisted that she come to Paris—but his energies were being stretched in too many directions. The one consolation was that since Thea and Nick were here it meant that she need never go out without company, if he were committed. But even so, he must stick close to his wife. It was becoming more and more important to him that he keep her safe. When his sleep was not disturbed by plots and rumours, it was troubled by thoughts of Sarah.

His troubles were multiplied a thousand times when he, too, saw a face he knew. Recognised it immediately, without any difficulty. Dark haired, dark eyed, striking features, it was a face with which he had lived for many years. So familiar that it caused him to rein in his horse with ungentle hands. The lady passed by him in a fashionable carriage, in company with a distinguished gentleman some years older than herself and another fashionably dressed couple. Before he could gather his wits and restrain his horse's lively reactions, she was too distant, so he was unable to speak with her. Besides, in truth, he had no idea what he should say to her in company, in public. He could imagine some of the repercussions with a bitter twist to his lips. The morass of scandal might deepen yet and sink everyone concerned.

Thus this chance encounter, a succession of sleepless nights and the problem of a wife who was not exactly cool but was more than a little reserved, put him out of all humour, with himself in particular and the world in general. He took himself home with a short temper and a black frown, where Nicholas came across him in the hall, leafing through his correspondence, and quickly gave an excuse to make himself scarce after the briefest of greetings. Sher's temper was legendary. Slow to burn, but inflammatory when once ignited. With the result that the one to be scorched and feel the full force of the blast was Sarah, unsuspecting and close at hand. Sarah, who was unfortunate to suffer one of her devastating moments of doubt and insecurity.

She was standing in the morning room, its door open into the entrance hall, opening an official letter, which was addressed with her name and had just been delivered. 'Joshua!' She looked up as he came into view.

'What is it?' A short brusque reply, but which did not immediately catch her attention from the sheet in her hand.

'It is a draft on your bank for me… Is this your idea of pin money?'

'What of it?' She should have realised it, made allowances, she thought in retrospect. Especially when he entered and closed the door with something like a slam. 'You need it. Particularly if you allow Theodora to encourage your spending habits.'

She should *definitely* have been warned by this unexpected sniping at Theodora. But was not.

'Not as much as this.' She was still taken up with the row of figures on the draft.

'You asked for some.'

'I cannot spend all this—not if I stayed here more than a twelve-month.'

'You must be the first woman in creation who cannot.'

'I don't deserve it.' *Oh, no! I should not have said that.* She knew it as soon as the words escaped her lips. What made her say it? It made her sound so…so pathetic! She had moved beyond such lack of esteem long ago. But she did and immediately saw the result.

A flare of anger.

'Don't! In God's name, don't put yourself down so, Sarah.' A sharp reply, intolerant in the extreme. 'If I choose to make such a present to my wife, so be it. Don't ever say again that you are not worth it.'

'No, my lord.' She watched him wide-eyed, quite taken aback. *And I should not have said that either!*

'*Joshua. Joshua—not my lord!* And this is pin money Have all your main bills sent directly to me. Do you understand?'

'Yes, Joshua. Of course I understand. I am not quite stupid.'

For a moment he simply stood and looked at her, thinking she knew not what. His face was cold and drawn, those magnificent silver eyes bleak with ice. Then he pounced, seized her by the shoulders and turned her toward an ornate mirror on the wall behind her.

'What do you see in the mirror?'

She looked, but more at the man standing behind her, temper barely held in check. Handsome, impossibly so. Imposing and dominant. But at this moment taut with overwhelming passions. She did not know what had happened to light this conflagration, but surely it was more than her unfortunate choice of words. She had never seen him so insecurely on the edge of control.

'What do you see?' he repeated, no softening in his expression.

'I see a man who is entirely out of humour!' She met his gaze squarely. She would not take the blame here.

'What else?'

'Me, of course.'

'And what do you see there?'

'I…' She had no idea where this was leading. 'I do not understand what you wish me to say.'

'Then I will tell you. I see a young woman. Well groomed, lovely, fashionable. When she smiles, the sun shines. She is as graceful as a lily.' His hands still gripped her shoulders as if to prevent her flight. The compliments were delivered in a harsh, clipped tone, totally at odds with their sentiment. His face was hard as stone. But Sarah felt no fear. Her heart beat faster at the heat from his nearness, at what he might say next. It did not make for easy listening. 'And yet she feels that she is worth nothing. It is time that she did—well beyond time. She is com-

petent, caring, loyal, worthy of respect...' *Entirely lovable!*
'Yet questions every attempt I make to show my regard or to
smooth her path. Is that true?'

'Perhaps...' She watched him, not a little shocked, much as
a rabbit would watch an approaching fox.

'It is true.' His mind still frozen with that one momentous
realisation that she was lovable—which he had always known,
of course. But that he *loved* her. And that it hurt like the very
devil when she would not accept what he wished to give her.

'I did not know that you would see me like that.'

'I married you. Of course I see you like that. It is an insult
to me that you should suggest that I am not aware of your every
asset, every gift, every superb quality. I would not marry a
woman worth less.' *And I have not spoken the most important.
The most earth-shattering. Which I have only just come to appreciate myself, fool that I am! You are totally lovable. And I
adore you!* What more could he say to her when his own
thoughts were in such turmoil? He released her so quickly she
might have stumbled.

'Don't deny me the right to make you happy!' It was all he
could manage, but delivered in a tone quite as harsh as before.

'Very well.' She still faced him in the mirror, could do no
other, could find no other words. What was wrong? What on
earth had happened to disturb his equanimity in his dealings
with her?

He saw her trepidation. But was beyond softening either his
words or his expression. What a moment to realise that he was
in love with his wife! When besieged by secrets and rumours
and those who might wish them ill. When events in Paris might
erupt to engulf and harm them both.

He took a breath, riding the edge of control. And managed
admirably.

'Forgive me. I did not mean to disturb you or shout at you.
The fault is not yours, but mine—and I should not have treated
you with so little respect. I have no excuses.'

He took possession of her hand and lifted it with a terrible formality to his lips. Then bowed with equal chill formality, before turning to stalk from the room.

To stand outside, his back to a disaster of his own creating. How could Sarah possibly hold any tender feelings towards him after such a cruel and unworthy attack? He raked vicious fingers through his hair. It seemed to him that he lurched from one confrontation to the next—and the blame was undeniably his.

Whilst Sarah, on the other side, was left to press her cold fingers against her lips, to wonder what one earth she had done to deserve such a devastating dissection of her character, even as her innate honesty demanded that she recognise the truth behind the words. Well, she would take those words to heart, accepting that it became her to exert her independence and more confidence in her relationship with her husband. She would acknowledge her own worth. She would forget the past, the guilt and the pain, the debts to be paid. She would accept her position as Lady Joshua Faringdon with all the grace that he said she possessed. She would fritter away his money—if that is what he wished! And she would continue to love him with every drop of blood in her body! Since he would never know, he would not be able to complain about that!

With which comforting thought, she left the room in his wake with a flounce of her silk skirts.

With remarkable and amazingly sly diplomacy she contacted Thea and arranged that they should attend the ball to be given by the Prussian Ambassador with Nicholas as escort. It had not been her intention to attend, but attend she would, in a new gown delivered only the day before. She would delight in delivering the receipt with the astounding figure at the bottom to her lord. If Joshua was to dine at home tonight, it would be alone. He could frown and snarl at the fricassee of lamb in his own company. If he had other engagements arranged, then it would be without her!

Her smile might be a little forced, but her mind was set.

Chapter Ten

As fate would again have it, both Lord Joshua Faringdon and his lady attended the Prussian Ambassador's ball, if separately and unaware of the other's intention. Joshua out of necessity to meet some prearranged contacts, Sarah, as she had planned, in a fit of defiance.

Joshua found it in his way to speak discreetly to a number of individuals, all of whom claimed to know nothing of subversive groups acting within the city and certainly not of any plan of assassination, but all warned that something unpleasant was in the wind.

Sarah found it in her way to dance every dance and gossip brightly with her sister and other ladies of her acquaintance in between. She agreed to go in to supper with a titled French gentleman who found the English lady both charming and elegant and willing to flirt as well as to converse at length and in a spirited manner on a range of topics.

Both Lord and Lady Faringdon, with remarkable ease, found it possible at so large an event to ignore each other and pretend that they were not aware of each other's existence. Joshua out of a frozen horror at what he could possibly say to this woman—his *wife*—whom he had just discovered was the only woman he could ever love and whom he had insulted beyond bearing. Sarah because…well, she did not quite know exactly why, but she had no wish to even recognise this infuriating man who had the power to engulf her body in flame and equally sear her soul with his harsh words. Even if she deserved them. Which, in retrospect, she was sure she did not!

'Your wife is here tonight, Sher, if you had not noticed,' Nicholas informed his sombre cousin with an expression that Joshua could only describe as a smirk.

'I am aware.' He would not rise to the bait. Of course he had seen her, in a glory of deep blue satin. Diamonds glinted on her breast and around her slender wrists, but no more than the fierce glow in her eyes. She looked quite beautiful.

'Have you spoken with her?'

'No.'

'She might grant you a dance, if you ask her. But she seems to be much in demand.' Nicholas watched Sarah execute the waltz in the embrace of a handsome dark-coated individual with assured steps.

Joshua turned his back on the sight of her in another man's arms. It was far too tempting to stalk across the floor and claim her for himself with a few well-chosen words for the man who dared hold her so close. And what a scandal that would make. '*You* dance with her, Nick. I think tonight she would prefer it.'

'I would have to agree.' Nicholas grinned at Joshua, refusing to show him any sympathy in this situation that he privately considered to be of his cousin's own making. 'You are not exactly good company.'

'No. I am not.' Joshua's lips curled in an expression not unlike a snarl.

'And, Sher, you are a fool. Go and talk to your wife!'

Joshua merely glared at his cousin, who punched him lightly on the arm, and abandoned him to take up a hand of whist with a group of like-minded gentlemen.

* * *

And then Joshua's evening disintegrated further into deep depression as a consequence of his setting eyes on the dark lady of the carriage. She was present, once again in the company of the little group of friends. Despite the very public occasion, given their previous history Joshua knew that he must speak with her, so made his way through the crowded ballroom to where she was a lively participant in a conversation, wielding a large ostrich-feathered fan with flamboyant agility. As he recalled, she had always had a leaning to the flamboyant. She turned at his approach, clearly, from her expression, waiting for him, expecting him to single her out.

'Madame?' Joshua inclined his head, his greeting posing the merest question.

The lady smiled her quick understanding. 'Lord Joshua. It is some years since we had the pleasure of meeting, is it not? Perhaps I might introduce you—this is my husband, the Marquis de Villeroi. Charles, allow me to present Lord Joshua Faringdon, from London—he is, as you would say, a family friend.'

The elderly gentleman bowed. As did Lord Joshua.

'Lord Joshua and I have a connection going back many years, have we not, my lord.' There was a pronounced glint—perhaps of mischief—in those dark eyes. Her voice was delightfully husky with its French intonation.

'We have.' There was no amusement in Lord Faringdon's face. 'I trust you are well, Madame la Marquise.'

'As you see.' She waved the fan languidly. It was clear that this conversation would be conducted in the collective eye of the *beau monde*, but the lady placed a hand on his lordship's arm to lead him a little distance for her group.

'I did not expect to meet you here.'

'No. I have not been to Paris for some years, my dearest Sher.' She kept her voice low, intimate even. 'But now my husband, who has some business interests here, wishes me to accompany him. I am not unwilling to reacquaint myself with the city.' Dark lashes swept her cheeks. 'Or with yourself.'

'I imagine not.' The lines engraved beside his lordship's mouth softened a little. 'I regret the manner of our parting, my lady.'

The lady sighed. 'And I.'

'It was not what I would have wished.'

'Nor I—but it had to be so—in the circumstances. As we both realised. We were not free to pursue our own desires, were we?'

Lord Joshua shook his head, unwilling to continue that line of conversation. 'Will you remain in Paris long?'

'It is my intention. Perhaps we shall meet again.' She laughed, a low seductive chuckle. 'But perhaps, my dear Sher, it will be best if you do not make it a formal call. It would not please everyone, if you take my meaning.'

'No, it would not.'

'Discretion is not always easy, is it?' she replied enigmatically. 'I hear that you have married recently.'

'Yes.'

'She is a fortunate woman.'

'I think the fortune is all on my side. May I say that you are as attractive as ever?' His smile a little wry.

'But a little older and wiser, perhaps.'

'Wiser, perhaps,' he agreed. 'Older I cannot accept.'

The lady turned her head as her husband approached. The brief encounter was at an end, and indeed there was nothing else for them to say to each other.

'Thank you for your compliment, Sher. It is good to see you.'

'And for me too, my lady.'

He kissed the fingers she offered him, and then, driven by impulse and strong memories of the past, which still had the power to move him, he kissed her cheek in a gallant gesture.

At which point Sarah, encouraged by some unhappy pricking of her conscience to search the crowd for a glimpse of her errant husband, watched the little tableau unfold.

And stared in horror at what she saw.

How could he! And not even in private! It was a very public

salute on the lady's cheek. And it was, unless she was very much mistaken, the dark lady from the Tuileries. The dark lady…

Sarah's memory instantly cleared, as if a candle had been lit to cast a bright image. Of course she had seen the face before. And not merely in the Tuileries Gardens. It was the face that looked out so confidently from one of the portraits in Joshua's attic in Hanover Square. So who was she—apart from being shockingly intimate with Joshua in the middle of a Parisian ball? A mistress? Highly likely! Well, if that were so, it would certainly clarify one recent development. If he was intent on taking up a liaison with this Unknown again—presumably a liaison of long standing—it would explain why the Countess of Wexford had been slighted. And that felicitous event, equally clearly, had nothing whatsoever to do with the fact that he now had a wife. No such thing! He simply had another mistress. Sarah hissed out a breath, causing Theodora to glance at her in some concern, but Sarah pinned a smile to her lips.

How dare he flaunt Another Woman before her in such a manner! With this thought in mind, Sarah lost no time and no sensible thought on the content of the looming conversation, in waylaying her husband.

'My lord.'

'My lady.'

He was immediately wary of the frigid look on her face. Now what? He truly did not need another challenging conversation today.

'I would have a brief word.'

'Can it not wait until we are private at home?'

'No!'

'Very well.' He led her to one of the little anterooms, much in demand by those who might pursue a secret liaison, away from prying eyes.

'Well?'

'Why did you bring me here to Paris?'

He waited with raised brows for further explanation. Flushed cheeks and a martial light in her eyes did not bode well. Sarah did not keep him waiting long.

'Why did you insist that I accompany you, when you obviously have no need of me? More often than not you have absented yourself, giving me no idea where you might be.' She conveniently, deliberately, overlooked his considerate presence before Thea's arrival. 'You appear to be surrounded by mistresses—' with cavalier and deliberate exaggeration '—more than willing to entertain you, so you have no need of me. I am amazed that you find the time or the energy to come to my bed at all. And I remember that I asked, quite specifically, that I need not have to acknowledge them. And you agreed.'

All delivered in a low, clipped voice, quite unlike Sarah's usual dulcet tones.

If the matter had not been so serious, Joshua thought that he might have laughed aloud at the picture painted by an irate and intolerant Sarah. His wife appeared to have amazing faith in his stamina. But there was no place for humour here. The evidence against him was growing daily, building stone upon stone, to create an insurmountable obstacle between them. But what to do would still seem to be out of his hands. He sighed a little against his own hurt, knowing that he was causing Sarah undeserved pain, and tried for words to placate.

'You asked, quite specifically, that I should not introduce you to any mistresses I might have or bring them into our house. I have done neither.' *And will not. I do not have a mistress. I love you, if you did but know it.*

'You do not have to introduce them.' Sarah looked down her nose, which Joshua recognised to be very much in the style of Lady Beatrice. 'It is clear to me by the way you look at them. It is an insult to me that you should flaunt them in this way!'

'Sarah—just who are these mythical creatures?' There was a heavy weariness in his voice.

'The Countess of Wexford, for one.'

'She is nothing to me. Neither then, despite all appearances. Nor now.'

'And the dark lady, tonight, in this very room—you kissed her cheek!'

'So I did.' What point in denying it? He was aware of nothing but the bleak chill creeping though his veins as the web of deceit pulled more tightly around him, binding his limbs, his choice of words. Ice cold, numbing, whilst his unbelieving wife burned with anger and humiliation. And it was his fault. Even if by omission, a failure to push for the truth so many years ago.

'And I know that you have her portrait hidden away in the attics of Hanover Square.'

Ah! So that is it. What could he possibly say to explain that away? In the end he did not even try. 'That also is true. But she is not my mistress.'

'Oh? So what is she?' Sarah was aware of nothing but the bleak cold in the silver eyes that held her gaze when he delivered that statement. And she would have given all she had to believe it. But how could she, with the evidence of her own eyes?

He stepped back, a clear sign of retreat, perhaps even of defeat. Such a little gesture, but it well-nigh broke Sarah's heart. She had heard nothing from her lord that might reassure her or tear holes in the weight of evidence against him. Instead he acted to put distance between them once more

'I will not answer such accusations, Sarah. Forgive me.' The sense of betrayal was as if a forged band of metal tightened around his heart and he could not stop the bitter words. 'I did not realise when I married you, my lady, that you were so suspicious, so given to unfair judgements, without true evidence. I hoped that you might trust me. It seems that I was wrong in my judgement of you.'

'Whereas I,' she retaliated, quick as the deathly strike of a viper, 'knew of *your* reputation from the very beginning, my lord. I should have taken heed of it, should I not, and should never have married you.'

After which, there was no more to be said from either side.

They left the anteroom with a black cloud of mutual suspicion and condemnation between them. And, on both sides, a terrible premonition of blighted love.

Sarah returned to Theodora's side with a swish of her satin skirts, to take a healthy gulp of champagne, cheeks becomingly flushed, but with a demeanour far from composed.

'What is it?' Thea had already caught sight of Joshua's furious figure across the room, where he stood to watch his wife with compressed lips.

'Not a thing!' She took another drink and spluttered a little against the bubbles.

'So why are you drinking that champagne as if it might save your life? And why is Joshua glaring at you across the dance floor as if he could happily wring your neck.'

'Joshua and I have had a…a disagreement.'

Theodora paused in sipping her own champagne at what was obviously a bald understatement. 'What? Only one? Nicholas and I thrive on them, at least one a week!'

That forced Sarah to choke on what might have been a laugh, which was Thea's intent as the glassy expression and the suspicion of tears in her sister's eyes were a matter for some concern.

'I think—I know!—that Joshua has just renewed his liaison with one of his mistresses.'

'And why should you think that?'

So Sarah finished the champagne in the glass and told her. A somewhat garbled tale of public kisses and pictures in attics.

'It does not sound likely to me,' Thea advised with deliberate calm and lively curiosity. 'Why keep her picture in the attic if she is his mistress, where he cannot see it? Are you sure it is the same lady?'

'Yes. Perhaps it was to hide it from me!'

'Mmm. But he did not hide the Countess of Wexford, did

he?' Thea cast an eye around the ballroom. 'And you say that the lady is still here at this incredibly tedious event?'

'Yes.'

'What does Joshua say?'

'He denies it.' Sarah blotted a stray tear with her satin glove. 'But I would expect no other.'

'Well. I suppose he would. In my experience, gentlemen do not enjoy having to admit to faults and failings.' Thea thought for a long moment, eyes narrowed on the golden bubbles remaining in her glass. 'In my opinion, there is only one thing to do. Ask the lady.'

'I can't do that!'

'Well, I would if I found a portrait of an attractive woman in Nick's attic at Aymestry and then found him kissing her.'

'Well…put like that…'

'Especially if, through marriage, they were my attics too…'

'I suppose…'

'Come along. There is nothing to be gained by dwelling on the unknown and the unknowable. We will find out what we can.' Thea took her sister in hand, very much the diplomat's daughter. Sir Hector Wooton-Devereux, she decided, would have been proud of her. 'I will come with you. All we need is the opportunity to speak to your dark lady alone…'

The opportunity presented itself only a little later in the evening when groups of people began to make their way into the banqueting room, laid out for a light supper. For a brief moment the dark lady was seen to be alone, separated from her escort. Sarah with commendable courage and considerable outrage made her way across the ballroom in that direction. Theodora would have followed, but her path was blocked by a familiar figure.

'Theodora—I know what she is about. In God's name, stop her.'

Theodora looked up at the striking Faringdon face, troubled by a range of emotions she could not even guess at. She could not help but allow her heart to soften. The difficulties might be of his making, but she found herself prepared to give him far more sympathy than had her husband. Such was the Faringdon charm, she supposed, although there was little evidence of it at present in the stern expression.

'I doubt that I can.'

'It would be better for all.'

'Are you sure of that?'

'No. I am not sure of anything at this juncture.'

'Well, I am. I don't know what you told Sarah and I don't know what the truth is, but at the moment she thinks the worst of you!'

'I know it.'

'Tell her the truth, Sher,' urged Thea, deliberately picking up Nick's affectionate family name. 'It cannot be worse than Sarah believing what she does, and Sarah can deal with the truth. Better than lies and charades. We had too many of those in the Baxendale family to accept them with any degree of comfort.' As she remembered her own attempts to hide her Baxendale connections from Nicholas. What a disaster that had been.

Theodora patted his hand and followed her sister to discover the truth.

Sarah had approached the dark lady and come to a halt beside her.

'Madame. Forgive the intrusion, but I would beg a few words with you.'

'Do I know you?' The lady appeared surprised, but not unfriendly.

'No, you do not. I am Sarah, wife of Lord Joshua Faringdon.'

'Ah.' The straight dark brows rose with some hauteur, but there was a distinct sparkle in the lady's eyes.

'So I think you know *of* me,' Sarah prompted.

'I do indeed…' The lady inclined her head. 'I am the Marquise de Villeroi.'

'Yes… I mean….' *What do I say now? Are you my husband's mistress?* Sarah discovered the dangers in Thea's plan to confront the lady. But as she became aware of Thea's presence beside her, she gathered all her courage and used the only possible opening. 'I wish, my lady, to know why your portrait is in the attic of my home in London.'

The Marquise smiled. But with no hint of shame or discomfort, or even of surprise. 'That seems a perfectly reasonable request to me,' she remarked. 'I think that we should find a private corner where we might sit—and I will try to explain what I can.'

So the little anteroom was witness that night to a second fraught conversation. The ladies drew the enclosing curtains against any who might be tempted to seek out the private space, and sat on the delicate gilded seats.

'Well, my lady…' the Marquise took up the initiative immediately as she spread her skirts and disposed her gloved hands in her lap, before embarrassment could set in '…I did not know until tonight that Joshua had remarried.'

'Yes.' Sarah was not inclined toward trivial conversation. 'Some weeks ago. But I would know—what are you to him?'

'Sarah—may I call you Sarah?' The lady lifted her hands in what could have been seen as a plea. The hauteur had vanished. Instead there was a warmth here, a depth of understanding, and not a little melancholy. 'I presume that you and Joshua are at odds over this. I am sorry for it, for the blame is partly mine. I think it will solve all your problems if I tell you my name. I am Marianne.'

Sarah's lips parted on a soundless 'Oh'. Theodora's fan paused in mid-sweep. The two ladies who heard the admission looked at each other in obvious astonishment.

'I was Joshua's wife, as you will be aware,' the Marquise de Villeroi continued, amusement now curving her lips at the stunned silence that resulted.

'We thought you were dead. The whole family believes you to be dead,' Thea exclaimed.

'Not so.'

'We thought,' Sarah added, still trying to order her wayward thoughts and come to terms with this development, 'that perhaps you had been murdered. There have been rumours to that possibility. Murdered by Joshua himself!'

'Never that!' The Marquise laughed. 'Murdered by Joshua? It is a suggestion quite nonsensical, is it not?'

Thea and Sarah again exchanged glances. 'The family was given to believe—by Lord Joshua himself—that you were struck down by some virulent disease and buried here in France.' Sarah frowned at the lady who sat before her, in no fashion discomfited, clearly in perfect health.

'No. As you see. Our marriage ended when a divorce was arranged. Discreetly and to our mutual agreement.'

'But why? Why the secrecy?'

The Marquise leaned forward to touch Sarah's hand with fingers heavy with jewels. 'Forgive me, my dear. That is not my secret to tell. You must ask Joshua. I think that he will tell you now that he knows that we have met.'

'But why could he not tell me before? Why should he deceive his family? You cannot imagine the difficulties caused by the rumour that he was a murderer!'

'I think I can.' The Marquise increased the pressure of her hand on Sarah's in eloquent sympathy. 'But as for why he would not… It was, I think, to protect me. He is a man given to gallantry. Or perhaps he was simply under orders to keep silent concerning sensitive matters. We all know what it is like to be held at the whim of those who hold the reins, do we not?' She shrugged elegantly, a particularly French gesture. 'But now it no longer matters.'

'I still do not understand,' Sarah replied, as much in the dark as ever.

'It is a complicated affair, a tapestry with many tangled

strands.' The Marquise rose to her feet. 'Tell Joshua to tell you the truth. Tell him that the truth can no longer hurt me. That I am no longer engaged in the activities I was before. Tell him, if you will, that my brother is dead. He will understand.'

'Very well.' A pause, then Sarah felt compelled to ask, 'Did you love him, my lady?'

Her reply was immediate. 'Oh, yes. He is so very handsome and so utterly charming—I could not have chosen a better husband, even if I had been given that freedom.' She shook her head as if regretting her somewhat strange admission. 'But Joshua will also explain about that too. As for the rest—it is all in the past. I have been married to Charles—the Marquis de Villeroi— for more than a year now. There is nothing between Lord Joshua and myself to concern you.'

The solemn gravity of the Marquise's assurance brought another image into Sarah's mind. The dark intensity was, of course, all Beth.

The Marquise smiled a little as if she read her thoughts. 'Tell me of Celestine. It is the one aspect of this sorry and involved tale that I regret.'

'She is well.'

'Is she happy? I had to let my daughter go, you see. I was not allowed to see her. It was not thought to be desirable.' For the first time in the conversation the lady's composure was no longer secure.

'Yes. She is happy. And she has found a friend in my son.'

'That is good. Will you care for her? Love her for me? I know that Joshua will, but she will also need a mother's care.'

'I already do love her. She is growing fast. She is a true Far-ingdon, but her eyes are yours. Now that I know, I see it clearly. I did not see it in the portrait.'

'No.' The tension in the lady's manner relaxed a little. 'I think it was not a good likeness!'

They moved towards the archway and Thea drew back the drapes, letting in the world once more.

'Shall we meet again?' Sarah asked.

'I do not know.' And the Marquise made no promises. 'But I am glad that we have done so. It has drawn a closure to something that should never have happened. I did not deal well with Joshua.' She turned quickly and, to Sarah's amazement, lightly kissed her cheek. 'It has been my pleasure to know you, Lady Faringdon.'

And then she was gone.

'What will you do?' Thea raised her hand to attract Nicholas's attention as they made their way back into the ballroom.

'Ask Joshua, of course! But not here.' Sarah frowned at the crowds that still thronged the reception, even at this late hour. If Joshua was still present, she had no knowledge of it. 'I shall go home. It seems that there is still much to be explained.' She thought for a moment or two, before adding softly, 'And we both have some apologies to make.'

Sarah waited in her bedchamber for Joshua's return. She deliberately divested herself of neither jewels nor the elegant aigrette in her hair. If this was to be a confrontation with her husband—which it undoubtedly was—Sarah decided that she would need all her confidence and dignity. Which would not be gained from donning a loose wrapper or unpinning her ringlets, despite the fact that it was long after midnight.

What in heaven's name was this morass of deception in which she had suddenly found herself? The disclosures of the evening had been shattering. Not only had her husband not murdered his first wife, she had discovered that Marianne was not even dead, that she was very much alive and obviously finding some amusement in the whole incident. Why had Joshua lied so completely and so effectively, and for so many years? What could possibly have been the motive? And one dreadful suspicion invaded her mind, to the exclusion of all else, spurred on by events in her own past. Above anything, she needed to know the truth about the status of her own marriage.

Sarah had no answers. She paced the room, kicking her fashionable skirts with their flounced demi-train at the end of each perambulation, arms folded across her breast as if to hold back the emotions that threatened to spill out and destroy her intention to face this threat with stern control. Her patience grew thinner as the clock ticked on into the morning hours and the candles burned low.

But eventually she heard him tread the stairs. Open and close the door to his room from the corridor.

She waited no longer. This conversation would be on her terms and at the time of her choosing. Such as now! She flung open the door to the dressing room, stalked though, to open the next without even the briefest and most perfunctory of knocks and enter his room

He did not look surprised to see her. He stood in the centre of the floor, arms at his side, his outer calm apparently intact as always, but in his eyes a shadow of defencelessness. But she refused to allow sympathy to cloud her judgement here. Besides, he knew exactly why she had come there and initiated the subject himself before she could summon the appropriate words.

'You have seen her and spoken with her.'

'Of course I have!'

'And you need an explanation from me. Of course you do.' Although he stood perfectly straight, shoulders firm, as if braced to ward off her angry words, he looked weary to the bone. His face was set, devoid of any expression that might give some hint of his thoughts, but the grooves beside his mouth were deep. He looked as if he would rather be anywhere than facing his wife with the weight of untruths and mistakes between them. And the weight of duty and commitment to a self-imposed goal that would still prevent him from laying it all before her.

'I think I have the right to demand an explanation. As does the rest of your family.'

'Does Thea know?'

'Yes. She was with me. And before you ask, I have no doubt that she will have informed Nicholas by now of every last detail. You cannot continue with this charade, Joshua. Whatever the reason for it.'

Without giving an answer, he unfastened the fob watch and chain at his waist, to place them gently on his dressing table, his back carefully toward her. Every movement deliberately controlled. Then he raised his head to watch her through the reflection in the mirror.

'Yes—you need to know. Marianne, as was very evident tonight, is not dead.'

'Are you still married to her?' Sarah worked hard to keep her voice even. 'Is my own position in this marriage quite legal?'

'What?' Despite her brave efforts, he caught the wavering note of panic in Sarah's voice and instantly swung round. 'Of course it is. What could you possibly think?' He saw the drowning despair in her eyes for a moment until she hid the emotion with her lashes. 'Oh, Sarah. My dear girl. I had forgotten. I would never commit an act so outrageous against you. There is no need to fear that your marriage has no basis in law.' His instinct was to close the distance between them and draw her into his arms, but there were still too many deceits and half-truths creating a barrier between them. He remained where he was, willing her to believe him. It mattered more than life itself that she did not hate him enough, distrust him enough, to turn her back and walk out of the room. Perhaps even out of his life.

Sarah closed her eyes for a long moment as nauseating memories rushed back with all the pain of the past. The anguish of a bigamous marriage had played a crucial part in her brother's devious plans against the Faringdon family, after all. But she fought back the fears, clinging to the remnants of her composure. She ran her tongue over dry lips, forcing her mind and voice to remain calm. 'No. Of course not. Marianne told me that you had been divorced. What I do not understand is why you did not tell the truth? Why did you continue with this masquerade for all this time? What would it matter if it was known that a divorce had been arranged between you?' The questions followed one after the other. 'It makes no sense!'

'It must seem so to you—a pointless masquerade.'

Sarah raised her chin, holding his eyes with her own. 'Marianne said to tell you that she is no longer engaged in…in the activities of before. And that her brother is dead. She said that you would understand.' Deadly cold inched its way through her veins to the very tips of her fingers. As insidious as a thick mist that blocked her vision, shrouded her brain so that she could not think. It numbed her senses, yet strangely she could sense the searing flames of anger begin to flicker and flare within her.

'Yes, I understand. Come here.' Joshua took a step, held out his hand to take possession of one of hers. 'Come and sit.' He would have led her to a daybed, conscious of her extreme pallor.

'No. I will not sit with you. Tell me why you allowed me to think that your wife was dead.'

He resisted when she would have pulled her hand from his grasp, shocked by the hurt in her face. But what right did he have to be shocked? The hurt was of his own making. 'Sarah—'

'Let me go!' The banked fury suddenly ignited within her, consuming in that one instant all her intentions to continue this discussion in a state of cool composure. 'You have lied and deceived me from the first day that you married me. I should hate you for that.' And instead she had loved him. Still loved him, to her shame. And he had lied. Exhaustion at the end of a long day took its toll as she was forced to accept the disintegration of all she had hoped for from her marriage. Without thought she allowed anger and despair to rule. And Sarah struck out. The flat of her free hand made firm contact with his cheek, the sharp slap sounding loud in the quiet room.

After a long moment of astounded silence, Sarah gasped, a sharp intake of breath. Joshua, equally amazed at this unexpected attack, flinched but did not step away. He dropped his hand from hers. The pain of her rejection to his heart was far greater than the sting of the blow to his face.

'I should not have done that,' her voice little more than a whisper, her cheeks even more ashen. Sarah was mortified, could have wished the ground to open and swallow her up, but held her ground. She refused to let her gaze drop but held his, her eyes full of anguish for herself, for the apparently unbridgeable chasm that now separated them 'I have never raised my hand against anyone in my life. I need to ask your pardon—'

'No! Don't ask that.' Joshua's reply was harsh, but the temper was not directed toward her. His eyes were bright with understanding of the shock that had drawn his gentle wife to so uncharacteristic an action. 'Many would say, and rightly, that I deserved it.' He inclined his head in an oddly formal acknowledgement, knowing in the depths of his heart that he deserved far worse. 'Don't let it trouble your conscience overmuch. It does not compare with the sins that I have committed against you.' *And must still hide.* His mouth twisted in bitter self-contempt.

Sarah clasped her hands together, white-knuckled. 'I should not have done it. But I think that you have married me under false pretences. I need to know what you have hidden from me.'

'I will tell you what I can.' His eyes remained on her face. 'Marianne de Colville was involved in espionage for the French government. Her role was to infiltrate our own government organisations to discover what might be British policy in France. Principally whether there were any of our own politicians who would support a rescue of Bonaparte from St Helena. It has to be said that she was not a willing spy, but her brother had been involved in some foolish enterprise and this was used by the French as a lever to ensure Marianne's compliance. If she obeyed orders, her brother—younger and ridiculously idealistic—would remain free.'

'And now he is dead.'

'So it seems. Marianne will no longer be under any compulsion.' Joshua shrugged and walked away to look down into the dying fire. 'The rest of it is not something of which I am proud, even though I had no knowledge of the deception. It was decided that I would be a useful contact for the lady. She set her sights on me, using all her female charms—of which she has many—and I was attracted to her. I asked her to marry me. Which was exactly what she and her French masters wanted.'

'She said that she loved you.'

'Did she?' He raised his head to look across the room. 'You appear to have had a remarkably detailed and intimate conversation with the lady in the circumstances. But no matter. Unfortunately the state of her heart is irrelevant. Marianne would have married me whether she loved me or no. It is what her masters desired.'

'But why *you*?'

'As a member of the English aristocracy I would automatically present Marianne as my wife with recognition and entrée into every circle in London's polite society. Both the social scene and the political gatherings. It would make her task so much easier to determine where the English interests might lie.' It was not quite the whole truth, but it would have to do.

He fell into silence as if his mind was taken up with events in the past—and with no degree of pleasure. Sarah simply waited.

'Our marriage lasted until 1817. God knows what information she passed on. But then Marianne's cover was compromised. A letter went astray and the code was broken. It was discovered that she was working for the French government. It became important that her connection with me be brought to an end.'

'So why not divorce her openly?' Sarah raised her hands, still unable to see the need for such subterfuge. 'Simply tell everyone the truth. Make up some excuse of infidelity, if necessary. Such a reason is hardly unknown.'

Joshua sighed. He had known all along that it would come

to this sticking point. 'There was a desire in…in certain circles to cover up the whole episode.' He answered carefully, choosing his words. 'The fact that Marianne had so successfully infiltrated those circles was seen as a humiliation. Not something to be broadcast or to draw attention to. It was easier for them if Marianne was simply to die a convenient and political death. To disappear quietly, rather than a more public divorce that might divulge some undesirable information. Marianne's employers wished to make use of her again under a different name. So it suited their purposes also.'

'So you divorced her and pretended she was dead.' Her voice was flat and cold.

'Yes. She retired to her family's home. No scandal, no talk, no interest. End of situation. Just as they wanted.'

'But *who*? Which circles?'

'I am not free to tell you, Sarah.'

'Why not?' She fought the almost overwhelming compulsion to shriek at her inability to batter down the wall that separated them.

'Forgive me. I am not at liberty to divulge who might be involved. All I can ask is that you have faith in me.' Now he turned fully to face her again, his eyes bleak, almost without hope. 'Trust me if you can—and accept that whatever the secrets which I am forced to keep, they do not affect my relationship with you.'

Sarah huffed out a breath and began to pace the floor as if her emotion was too great to contain within her slight frame. 'It is a great deal to ask. I am no longer sure exactly what our relationship is!' She thought for a moment, then angled a glance over her shoulder. 'Was I being followed in London?'

'Yes.'

'Did you have anything to do with it?'

'Never. On my honour.'

'Do you have any honour?' She ignored his wince and took a turn around the room. Privately he considered that she looked magnificent in her disdain for his behaviour, but his heart was filled with dread at her stark words. 'Can you tell me why?'

'I can. Because of your connection with Henry and your residence in New York. It was thought that you might have links with political groups there, particularly those with republican leanings. Perhaps you were attempting to succeed where Marianne had ultimately failed. To acquire information through your marriage to me. Our marriage was frowned upon.'

Her eyes widened in disbelief, colour creeping back into her cheeks. 'By these *same circles*, I presume. Which you are not free to discuss!' She laughed, a brief, harsh sound that expressed no amusement. Her eyes blazed with inner fire. 'I have never heard anything quite so ridiculous! Do you believe that of me?'

'No.'

'So much subterfuge. So many lies.' Her perambulations continued. Then, on another thought, with a stern frown: 'Why are we here in Paris?'

He shook his head.

'Another forbidden subject, I see. Is it dangerous?'

'Not for you.' He hoped and prayed that it would be so.

'But for you?'

'Unlikely.' He had no intention of discussing this questionable area with its threats and uncertainties.

'I see. Will you tell me one more thing?' She was relentless.

'If I can.'

'What is Marianne to you now?'

'Nothing. I have not seen her since our divorce—until tonight.'

'Do you love her? Do you still love her?' She had to know.

'No.' It was a simple denial, yet Sarah could sense the rightness in the word. As she could read the weight of pain of the betrayal in his beloved face, however adept he might be at hiding it. And she knew for certain with his final words. 'It is difficult to love where you have been used—for personal or political motives.'

'And the Countess of Wexford?' She would not let him off the hook yet, even though she suspected that she knew some of the truth in this relationship.

'Ah—the fair and vindictive Olivia.' His smile was as humourless as that of the lady who faced him with such compelling determination to unveil all. Her words had struck hard, a deadly blow, with their ring of veracity. He had no honour and she was intent on stripping away all pretence. No honour unless it was that he would give his life to protect her if it became necessary. But she must not know of that possibility either. 'No, Sarah. The Countess is not my mistress. Nor was she ever.'

'But she is somehow involved.'

'Sarah… There is so much I am not free to tell you. But I will soon. I promise you.' He would beg if he had to. 'But I would tell you this. I will do all in my power to keep you safe. I will never renege on the vows that I made on the day I married you. I will compromise neither *your* honour nor your reputation. When I can I will lay everything before you. Can you trust me? I know I deserve nothing from you, but have to ask your forbearance. I beg that you will not turn your back against me.' *And one day, when it is all finished, I will consider myself free to tell you that I love you.*

Sarah walked the length of the room and back, struck by the thinly controlled anguish in her lord's voice. And knew that it was not within her power to throw such avowals back into his face, knowing what it must have cost a man of such pride as Joshua Faringdon to bare his soul this night, to strip himself of all honour and veracity. So she made her decision, not lightly, but because she knew that she must. And because, notwithstanding all the revelations of the night, her heart was still within his keeping. 'Very well. I will give you that assurance. Since I have discovered that you did not murder your first wife.' Sarah allowed the faintest glimmer of humour to creep into her face.

For the first time that night Joshua laughed, the muscles in his belly uncoiling with the relief of her simple statement of acceptance. He would have covered the space between them, taken her hands again within his own, but knew that he must wait for her to make the decision, for her to come to him. To make that all-important step across the dark divide that could so easily have destroyed any hope for their future life together.

'I owe you so great a debt of gratitude.' He lifted a hand toward her in hope and encouragement. 'You will never know, Sarah. Your courage astounds me. I deserve neither your forgiveness nor your compliance.'

She saw the pain and hurt still evident in his face. The skin stretched taut across those magnificent cheekbones, the dark glitter of those predatory eyes as he waited for her response. Yes, he had lied and deceived. But she thought that he had not found the deception an easy task. Shadows remained between them, she knew, areas of his life still deliberately hidden from her. But he had told her of Marianne and, to some extent, of Olivia Wexford. And there, she knew deep within her that she had heard the truth. And she, poor fool perhaps, clouded by love, believed him.

So she walked forward. When he did likewise, to meet her, and bowed his head to touch his mouth to hers she did not pull away, but lifted a hand to caress the cheek which she had so recently struck in anger.

It was impossible not to acknowledge the issues that still remained to hurt and divide, yet it was with silent and mutual agreement that they came together. Their eyes spoke where their words might not. Their hands bridged the otherwise unbridgeable abyss out of a desire to comfort, out of a need to hold and be held, touch and be touched, to reassure that they could bring pleasure to each other. That the shadows could not destroy totally the fragile unity that had come to bind them in the weeks since their marriage. They knew that for a short time the demands of the world could be blotted out, erased within the smaller intimate world created by them both, one for the other, within the silk hangings and cool linen of the bed.

So Joshua and Sarah came together, clothing and costly jewels quickly discarded, with slow kisses, light caresses, murmured words of acceptance. His kisses on her mouth, on the subtle planes of her face, warmed and teased, allowing no lingering strain between them, his hands so exquisitely considerate of her sensitive skin, awakening her to her own needs. Sarah sighed and purred beneath him, stretching against him in glorious anticipation. He made her feel desired and beautiful, handling her as if she were indeed a precious gem that he valued highly. For those moments of passion in his arms she could pretend that it was indeed so. Could pretend that his emotions were as strongly engaged as hers and that he loved her. What harm would it do to deceive herself for a few short moments? Images of Marianne and the Countess of Wexford, which had haunted her days and nights, now faded into the reality of that long sweet loving. A loving that was slow and tender, all passion restrained, the fire of need banked.

Until the heat and urgency and arousal began to build under the onslaught of mouth on mouth, of searching fingertips, heightening their breathing until they shuddered in each other's arms, limbs tangled where they slid and pressed one against the other. Joshua found himself sinking, his mind overturned by his need to show Sarah his love. What use to deny it? She had, in some mysterious, incalculable way, become everything to him, become the one certainty in his life with all its shifting sands and outrageous demands. He pressed his lips to where her heart beat heavily in unison with his. So strong and loyal. So brave despite her fears. Why had he fought this acceptance of his love for her for so long? Of course he loved her—a man would be an utter fool not to. But what of her? If Sarah could not find it within her to love him with his tarnished reputation and shady past, the loss would be impossible to live with. If all she could offer was a gentle affection and tolerance… His heart felt the sharp piercing of an edged blade. That his happiness should be dependent on this one woman whom he now cradled in his arms. All he could do was banish thoughts of so terrible a future without her love to the distant recesses of his mind and let his body rule.

When he took her it was a long slow glide and she held him tight. Fire flared now to scorch and burn, ripping through both of them with heady passion. Rhythm matched to rhythm with absolute perfection as they carried each other on, driving toward oblivion. Her eyes were wide and clear on his at the culmination so that he might glimpse her soul. She remained with him until the end as he waited for her, when they reached the edge together, shattered and fell together, to lie together in that most intimate exhaustion.

Eventually Joshua raised his head from her breast.

'Sarah. I…' Words stuck in his throat. He brushed back her hair and let his fingers move with infinite lightness over her features, letting them wind into her ruffled curls. And Sarah smiled at him, eyes steady, welcoming. Joshua felt the instant response lance through him again, felt himself harden again. As did she. And moved beneath him in luxurious and sensual delight in recognition of her power.

'What?' He read a glint in her eyes as he lowered to take her lips.

'Let me give you the pleasure you give me.'

'But you do. Have you any doubt?'

'I can do better.' A flirtatious whisper, which for Sarah was a shout from the roof tops. It shook him to the core, to obliterate any further thought from his mind.

She slipped from beneath him to reverse their positions with glorious agility. Quick to sense her intent, he lifted her up, guiding her as she lowered herself to take him in. Hot. Slick with need. Silken-smooth. She rested her hands on his chest, shook back her hair. An action that should have appeared wanton, but in Sarah still had the gloss of charming innocence. The candlelight gilded her shoulders and breasts, the sleek line of hip and thigh as she looked down at him, all slender elegance. And began to move. A slow seductive rhythm against which he had no defences. The smile on her lips was all woman. He tensed his muscles against the spectacular assault.

'You make me feel so beautiful.'

'But you are.'

'Tonight I feel it. And powerful.'

The energies, the conflicting emotions that had whipped through her in a storm throughout the evening now settled, now centred in this one act of intense love. Focused on this man who had stolen her heart for no other reason than that he existed and that their paths, guided by some miraculous fate, had crossed. The man whom she loved and would always love until the day of her death. Sarah did not speak it. She could not put the burden of her love on to his shoulders if he felt unable to return her sentiments. But her body proclaimed it, a shining banner if he could but read it, as she took him and herself to distraction. Until all thought, all senses were submerged beneath their ultimate possession of each other. Until they lay spent once more in each other's arms, breathing overturned.

'Joshua?' Sarah still lay with her head pillowed on his chest, her limbs heavy and relaxed, her hair covering him in a golden skein.

He turned his head to kiss her, banding his arms tighter around her.

'What will happen now?'

'Nothing very dreadful. I will put things right for us.' He rubbed his chin gently against the top of her head. Her voice was slurred with sleep. She did not need a detailed account. Not that he was capable of giving one, not knowing what the future would bring. But Sarah, being Sarah, would need to ask. His smile was a little sad.

'I just thought…' Her voice trailed off on a sleepy sigh.

'Hmm?' He looked into the dark as the candles guttered and

burned out. He doubted that she was doing any thinking at all. He held her safe in his arms and that was all that mattered.

'Joshua?'

'What is it?'

'I love you.' Her tired mind forgot to keep its guard. 'I love you. I thought I should tell you...' And then she drifted off to sleep.

He tensed at the words, whisper soft against his skin, but not enough to wake her. His heart leapt powerfully beneath her cheek, but not enough to prevent the drag of exhaustion pulling her under.

'Oh, Sarah.' He turned his face into her bright hair. Those words had silenced all his doubts. It was more urgent than ever that he extricate himself from this life that demanded his silence, his absences, his practised deceits. Then when all was swept clean between them, he would tell her what she needed to know—that she held his heart in her hands.

But for now, 'I love you too,' he whispered against her temple. She would not hear, of course. Would not remember, but it was important none the less that he tell her. 'I love you too. Darling Sarah.'

Chapter Eleven

When Sarah awoke next morning, her lord was gone, the bed linen beside her cool as if he had never been there. Even the pillows failed to bear the indentation of his head. Yet she was aware of the scent of him, felt the ghosts of his arms around her as he had held her through the night. And loved her. Surely he loved her. He had never said those words to her, but she shivered, a delicious tremor, at the vivid memories. So tender. So caring. So passionate and arousing. Her fair skin flushed from her toes to the crown of her head at the image that sprang before her eyes, of her response to the touch of his hands, the caress of his mouth against her. The intoxicating slide of his hard body over her soft curves. Until at last she had fallen into a deep sleep, suffused with unimaginable pleasure, his arms holding her secure against him.

Completely unsettled, she blinked against the images, turning in her sensible manner to more immediate matters as her maid arrived with her morning cup of chocolate. But the immediate matters proved to be just as disturbing. Her thoughts tripped over the facts that she now knew—which she now hoped!—to be true. And skated over the areas where she was still quite as ignorant as before. And frowned at her absent husband who had left her in such a state of turmoil.

She had no idea where he had gone or where he would be for the remainder of this day. Or when she would see him again. Her frown deepened and her fingers tightened around her cup.

Because Sarah was forced to acknowledge that if she were not very much mistaken, Joshua was just as much engaged in espionage as Marianne had been. He might not be free to speak to her of such matters of national importance and security, but anyone of any sense could put two and two together and come up with the correct answer. It could be the only answer! And, having accepted that she had a husband who was a spy, she dare not contemplate the dangers with which he lived, day after day, dangers that he had denied even existed. Her heart lurched at the realisation. And it led her mind on. Just how had he acquired the injuries from which he had been suffering when he had returned home to England? The damaged hip and ribs. Sarah shrugged against her lace bedrobe. The rumours of duels and irate husbands now seemed to hold very little water.

And it would explain the concern over her own marriage to Joshua in *certain circles*. The certain circles were becoming plainer by the minute! A republican spy indeed!

Sarah finished her cup of chocolate with more haste than enjoyment, and considerable inner debate. She must decide how much to tell Thea, knowing that her sister would be avid for detail.

And also what she would say to Joshua when he finally returned. Because another thought struck home with the force of a lightning bolt as she pushed back the covers and prepared to dress for the day. Joshua had given her the deeds of a house, had he not? Just before they had left for Paris. Now she knew the reasoning behind it. Not simple kindness. Not a generous fit of philanthropy. But because he did not know that his own life was safe. And, being Joshua, he had taken steps to ensure that she would not suffer in the event of his death, but would have a home of her own, separate from the Faringdon estate. A lively fear gripped her throat, a slick of greasy panic coating her skin when she realised what he had done.

But for the rest of the day Lord Joshua was absent. Sarah was forced to deflect Thea's demands for enlightenment, contain her own impatience and torment—and accept her desire simply to see the man whom she loved, safe within their four walls again.

When he finally returned, tired and thwarted in his attempts to discover any further information of merit or importance, it was late and the house was quiet. He met up with Nicholas, who was dressed with austere elegance, suitable to grace the social scene.

'Where are they?' Joshua's question was brusque, but he was too weary to care and made no apologies.

Nicholas read his expression and made no comment. 'At Madame de Staël's salon in the Faubourg St Honoré for some intellectual discussion until an hour ago. I escorted them there as you requested. I left them comfortably ensconced with wine and sweet biscuits discussing the social position of writers before the revolution. A fascinating topic to be sure. I was delighted to leave them in such erudite company.' There was a sardonic curl to his lips. 'And from there they were engaged to join a party, well chaperoned, I assure you, to go on to the theatre. Where I am about to go, again at your request, to escort them home.' He grimaced at the prospect. 'You can do the honours instead, if you wish. A ballet or two, followed by an opera. Not an evening to my taste.'

'No. Nor mine. But you have my gratitude, Nick. I need to know that they are escorted.' He made his way into the library to pour a glass of brandy. And drank it down as if his life depended on it. Poured another.

'Some interesting family history surfaced last night, dear Sher.' Nicholas helped himself from the decanter, eyes alight with gentle mockery, unable to resist.

'I thought you would have something to say about it!' Joshua picked up a letter that lay on the desk, opened it, quickly scanning the single sheet. Then flung up a hand to stop his cousin in any further facetious comment he might be about to make.

'When did this arrive?'

'I have no idea.'

It was a short letter. A mere few lines. Unsigned. But its effect was instantaneous. Joshua crumpled it in his fist and put down the glass with considerable force, the brandy forgotten.

'Hell and damnation, Nick! This is the last thing I needed. Where did you say they had gone?'

'The opera.'

'In the rue de Richelieu?'

'Well—yes.'

'Come on.' He started toward the door. 'I need to get them home. Now.'

'But it will be in the middle of the performance. Thea will not thank us for making a spectacle of them—'

'No matter. I think it would be unwise for them to remain until the end.'

'And you are not dressed for a night of sartorial elegance amongst the French aristocracy.' Nick eyed the superfine coat and Hessian boots, perfectly appropriate for day wear, but hardly for a visit to the opera.

Joshua was unmoved. 'My clothes are of the least importance! Come *on*, Nick. I think it will be quickest for us to walk.'

At last Nicholas caught the urgency, the masked anxieties. 'What is it, Sher? Is there danger here?'

'I don't know. But I would feel far happier if Sarah and Thea were safe at home.'

Nicholas had read the situation correctly. Thea thought little of her lord's insistence, albeit *sotto voce*, that she remove herself in one of the entr'actes in the opera. She had particularly wished to see this performance of *Le Rossignol*, as had Sarah, and they had tolerated the two previous ballets in order to do so. With a shrug and raised brows, Nick indicated without words being necessary that the decision had not been of his making, but took hold of her arm in a firm grip. For his part Joshua was even more determined than Nicholas, bowing to the assembled party with infinite grace and no hint of the extreme urgency he felt pumping through his blood, but brooking no dissent. Sarah had only to glance at his face to know that there was no room for argument. Something was amiss. The ladies made their apologies to their host and hostess, gathered shawls and gloves and fans and made their way down to the street, the strains of the music following them.

'Where are we going?' Thea demanded of Joshua as soon as they were out of earshot. Clearly he was to blame for this precipitate departure.

'Home.'

'Have you arranged a carriage?'

'No. It will be quickest and easiest on foot.'

'So much for the state of my new satin shoes!'

'Is there a danger?' Sarah asked her lord in a low voice.

'Perhaps.' He pulled her hand through his arm, reassuringly warm, managing a fairly effective smile. 'That is why we will go home now.'

With that Joshua shepherded them off the main rue de Richelieu into the rue Rameau, which ran alongside the opera, where a number of carriages were drawn up. A little crowd had gathered by the first of the carriages. More early leavers. And easy to recognise. There was the Duc de Berri in the process of handing his wife into the carriage. The Duchesse saw the approaching ladies and hailed them, lifting her hand in greeting, a wicked smile on her lively face.

'Some more unenthusiastic members of the audience! Perhaps you too found the ballet—and two of them, no less—tiresome.'

Thea and Sarah smiled their acquiescence with this youthful, pleasure-loving member of the Bourbon family.

'Too many late nights for me.' She tapped her husband's arm

with her fan. 'I am going home. Alone, it would seem. When will you follow me, Charles?'

'Not yet.' He helped her into the carriage. 'But I shall not be too late.' He turned to make some comment to Joshua, whilst the Duchesse leaned from the window with an offer to take up Thea and Sarah and deliver them home, if they so wished.

Then it happened.

A disturbance from the direction of the rue de Richelieu. A running figure, slight and agile, pushing between strollers and bystanders. The opera guard looking across in surprise, stepping forward to intercept, but too late, being firmly thrust out of the way.

Joshua reacted with instinctive understanding. If it was a deliberate attack, to cause harm or even death, the prime objective would be the Duc de Berri. But then it struck him in the length of a breath, in an agonising slice to the heart with honed steel as he took in the scene. *Sarah!* Sarah stood directly between the attacker and the royal figure. With Theodora beside her.

'Nick!' he shouted. 'Get Thea out of this.'

And leapt.

Leapt forward with supreme agility, turning his shoulder, to take the full brunt of the man's speed and thus halt the impetus of the running figure, at the same time to pull Sarah out of the path and into his arms. He held her there, in the shelter of his arm as she struggled for comprehension, putting his body between her and any danger.

At the same time he flung out an arm to alert the Duc to the immediate danger. 'Your Grace! Beware!' But the assassin had the benefit of surprise and careful preparation. Not even Joshua's intervention could divert the deadly intent for more than a moment. A flash of silver. A downward stroke of a sinewy arm and Joshua flinched back with a vicious curse as pain slashed down his arm. It was all that was needed for the attacker to gain freedom of action. With another high swing of the dagger, his face alight with hatred and the inevitability of his success, the assassin buried the blade in the chest of the Duc de Berri to the right of his heart.

Shock held the little tableau in frozen immobility for a long moment, illuminated in the flambeaux from the opera, as if it were indeed a dramatic and realistic scene on the stage, the deep shadows of the street encroaching to add more drama before exploding into a burst of terrible emotion and frenzied activity. It was all too real. The assassin, small and wiry, left the dagger embedded in his victim and ran for his life, vanishing back into the rue de Richelieu before anyone could think to stop him. The Duc sank back against the carriage with a sharp cry of pain, pulling the dagger from his own flesh with a trembling hand, letting it fall to the paving with a sharp clatter. Blood, bright, shocking in its crimson brilliance, soaked the white linen of his shirt, his hand and the breast of his dark coat.

Resisting the tightness of his grip, Sarah struggled at last free of Joshua's restraining arm. Before he knew what she was about she had run to the Duc's side, ripping off her shawl as she went, to fold it and press the thickness of the material against the fatal wound to staunch the blood, for all the good it would do. The Duchesse stepped down from the carriage with a howl of anguish to stretch out her hands to her husband in hopeless entreaty. Two courtiers who had been in attendance with the Duc came finally to their senses and ran to his aid, to help him back into the opera for privacy and where his wound might be attended to. The Opera Guards, in disarray, followed him within.

Which, within a very few minutes, left the Faringdon party standing alone on the pavement beside the empty carriage. A strange hiatus of calm in the wake of such violence. Sarah, pale as wax, with blood on her hands and on the bodice of her gown. Joshua with heavy bloodstains on the coat sleeve of his left arm, blood dripping from his fingers to the ground to mingle with that of the royal duke. His lips might be thinned, but there was no hint of either pain or discomfort in his urgent words. He took control of the situation and immediate action.

'Nick. Get them home. God knows what will be the repercussions of this night's work.'

'But you are hurt.' Sarah gripped his sleeve, her face turned up to his, robbed of all colour by the flickering flames behind them. The Duc de Berri was not the only one to suffer from the blade of the assassin. She had not realised.

'Nothing much, I assure you. Will you tie this handkerchief tightly above my elbow?' He pushed it into her hands. 'Yes. That's right.' He muffled a groan as she tightened the knot with trembling fingers. Then he focused on the blood on her bosom. 'You are not harmed? The blood is not yours?' He had to be sure.

'No. It is not mine.'

'Thank God!' He would give her this moment. It was important for both of them before events tore him from her side. So he kissed her forehead very gently and would have pushed her in the direction of Nicholas if she would have loosened the clasp of her fingers on his. 'You are safe. That matters more to me than you will ever know.' Now he kissed her lips, a fierce, hard kiss. 'Now you must go home. I will join you there as soon as I can.'

'But you could be in danger.' He was injured. He had saved her life. All her instincts warned her not to leave him here on this blood-stained street.

'No. I am not the target here. Go home, Sarah. I need to know that you are safe.'

Nicholas took her arm to pull her away to where Theodora waited.

'I will wait for you.' Sarah still resisted, her eyes wide and frightened on his face.

'I know it.' Joshua nodded to Nick, who was quick to see the need to get Sarah away. 'Expect me before dawn.'

Then without another word, Joshua turned and vanished into the shadows of the rue de Richelieu in the direction of the fleeing assassin.

* * *

Too many minutes had passed since the assassin had fled the scene. But even more would pass before the Garde Royale was called out and the blood-chilling news of the attack was spread around the city. There was just a chance, Joshua decided, that he would pick up a trail before the murderer went to ground.

In the rue de Richelieu the night was still young, groups of pleasure-seeking people still strolling, laughing in these final days of Carnival before the dour austerity of Lent settled with its heavy hand. News of the terrible event in the rue de Richelieu had not yet percolated. Cafés still plied their trade. The man who had wielded the dagger to such effect could be anywhere, in any group, watching the harmless boulevard entertainments with dwarves and conjurors and fairground slides, or sitting alone to drink a final celebratory brandy in any one of the cafés. Joshua glanced about with keen eyes to where torches illuminated faces. A wild goose chase, if ever he had seen one.

Behind him, as expected, he heard running footsteps as the guard from the opera was at last dispatched to search the streets. And raised voices telling of the terrible crime. Heads turned on all sides, shock registering on faces.

And a man stood at the entrance to the Arcade Colbert, just a dark outline against a darker background. Waiting. A carriage came slowly down the Boulevard des Italiens. The man stepped out into the light.

And Joshua recognised him. Slight, thin-faced, nothing to draw attention, but an air of suppressed excitement about him.

It was the supreme anticlimax to the chase. A ridiculously easy matter to overpower him, requiring no heroic feats of strength or tactics. A short scuffle, an unequal exchange of blows, and the man lay insensible on the pavement. The assassin might have struck down a claimant to the throne, but he did not have the physique for physical combat, even against a man with a wounded arm. Besides which, there were plenty of willing onlookers. With enthusiastic assistance from a waiter from the Café Hardy, where the man had indeed been taking a brandy, apparently in all innocence, it was simple to bind him and deliver him into the hands of the guards who dragged him off to the Opera again with rough but belated efficiency. He had been far more effective in his crime than in his attempted escape.

Which left the carriage. It had come to a halt on the boulevard. Then, at a whispered instruction from passenger to driver, would have moved off again had Joshua not been sufficiently alert and interested to step up and signal the driver to halt. Without compunction he flung open the door, to recognise the figure shrouded in a dark cloak, the hood pulled up over dark hair.

'Well.' Joshua bowed with formal mockery. 'You surprise me. To murder Bourbons? I would never have suspected it.'

The Countess of Wexford looked at him with a faint smile on her shadowed face, in no way discomfited. 'Why not? They dishonoured France far more than Bonaparte ever did. I lost members of my own family at their careless hands.'

'But what is your interest, Olivia? Surely you have more political astuteness than to wish to bring Bonaparte back?'

'True, he is old and sick.' The distant torches picked out the gilt highlights in her dark eyes. They shone with a fervent belief. 'But what price for idealism, my dear Joshua? A desire to see wrongs put right. Revenge. It is very simple.' Her smile became a little sly. 'But what are we talking of? You have no proof of my involvement. The assassin is captured. I am merely making my way home from Madame de Staël's salon.'

'I doubt you were ever at Madame de Staël's this night. My wife was there, with her sister.'

'But would the little housekeeper remember me?' The sneer was well marked, forcing Lord Joshua to keep hold of his patience.

'Oh, yes. I think Lady Faringdon would remember your presence very well.'

'So do I.' The Countess laughed, a glint of white teeth. 'Your wife and I would never be friends, would we? What could we possibly have in common? What possessed you to marry her, Joshua?' She leaned toward him and touched his cheek with a satin-gloved hand. 'But no matter. You still have no proof of my interests.'

'You think not? Could you not possibly have been waiting here to take up the murderer when his vicious work was done?'

'Of course not. I know nothing of it. But I suppose you will have your revenge, my lord.'

'Yes. For spreading rumours of me having blood on my hands. You caused my family much heartache. And my wife, beyond measure. So revenge will be sweet, my lady. I think you will find that you are no longer welcome in England. Unless you wish to be taken up and questioned about your dubious political affiliations. Wycliffe will not be amused with the deception. The betrayal.'

'No, he will not. I fear that the delights of London will be barred to me now.' Her smile vanished to be replaced by a tinge of regret. 'I do not suppose I could tempt you to throw in your lot with me? What collaborators we would be. And I would be delighted to make it worth your while.' She held out her hand in blatant invitation. 'I think you do not find me unattractive, dear Joshua.'

'No.' The hand was ignored. She saw a flash of contempt in his eyes, but his words were soft enough. 'I am flattered by your invitation. But you can offer me nothing.'

So Olivia's answering laugh was bitter. 'I see that the little housekeeper has won. Who would have thought that so insignificant a woman would have the means to steal your heart and make you captive.'

But Olivia had made a mistake, a terrible misjudgement, to direct her barbs at Sarah Russell, and she knew it instantly. Joshua Faringdon's whole body stiffened, alert and prepared to attack, as a wolf prepared to defend its mate. Eyes hardened to glacial ice, his lips thinned, he now made no effort to disguise his contempt for the woman who would drag Sarah's name down to her own level. 'How dare you criticise my wife to me?' His words were little more than a whisper, but deadly in the quiet of the street. 'She is so far above you in spirit and integrity. You are not fit to speak her name. She would never stoop to the deceits that you would use. She is all goodness. Something, I suggest, of which you have no understanding.'

'Well.' Olivia's lips twisted. 'She has you well and truly wound around her fingers, does she not?'

'No. It is nothing like that. My feelings for her are beyond your comprehension, Olivia.'

'Poor Joshua.' The Countess tilted her head, a parody of rueful amusement. 'So you actually love her.'

'Yes. I love her.' It was, he realised, the first time he had spoken the words aloud, except when Sarah slept uncomprehendingly in his arms. How ridiculous, he thought, that his confession should be to the Countess of Wexford. He bit back a harsh laugh.

'And does the inestimable Sarah love you? Does she know about your less than honest activities? How entertaining it will be if she falls in love with a man whom she considers to be a hero.' Her smile became sly with a hint of threat. 'Only to discover as many lies and deceits in his past as there are in my own.'

Joshua was not to be drawn by the deliberate provocation. 'No, she does not know. But, yes, Sarah does love me. I believe that she does.' *Am I not gambling everything on that one admission, uttered without conscious thought as she fell into sleep?*

'Then you are fortunate indeed. I wish The Chameleon well of his marriage.' For the Countess knew that she had lost. She lifted her shoulders in a typically Gallic gesture of rejection of the whole matter. Her expression hardened, now all practicality. 'What now?'

'I will leave you to work out your own salvation in France. I am sure you will be able to keep your involvement secret unless the assassin talks under persuasion. And as you say, I have no proof.'

'I should thank you, but I will not. Besides, the Duc de Berri is dead or as good as. So we have succeeded despite all your efforts to save the despicable Bourbons.'

'He is not yet dead.'

'He will be fortunate indeed to survive a knife in the chest.' The glitter in her eyes was suddenly cold and cruel.

'True. But whatever the outcome, your role to undermine British espionage is ended, Olivia. Enjoy your victory if you can.'

'Oh, I will. Never doubt it. Not returning to England will be a small price to pay for the death of de Berri.' The sudden smile that touched her mouth held a clear threat. 'I could, of course, make life very difficult for you, Joshua, if you threaten my freedom. It would be so easy for me to reveal your identity and so tear your cover to rags. The value to Wycliffe of The Chameleon would be destroyed overnight.'

His instant laugh, the flare of intense satisfaction in his eyes, startled her. It was not what she had expected. 'Do it and be damned, my dear Olivia. I am not open to blackmail.'

'I think you do not realise the consequences, my lord. I can hurt you. I can tell your innocent wife of your true involvement.'

'No. You cannot hurt me. And I shall tell Sarah myself.' If anything, she saw pity in his eyes. 'It no longer matters to me what you say or do.' He bowed formally, an elegant mockery of respect. 'Because tonight The Chameleon dies. You can no longer harm me or mine. Your disclosures—to my wife or to the world at large—will be irrelevant. Good night, my lady Wexford.'

Lord Joshua stepped back, not waiting for a response, and watched the carriage draw away.

Knowing with a certainty that this evening marked the end of another chapter in his life.

It was long past the late February dawn when Joshua returned to the Faringdon residence. The day was as chill and grey as the mood of the inhabitants attempting to discover an appetite in the breakfast parlour, too worried to do more than drink a cup of coffee and look up in expectation at every sound in the street below their windows. But eventually Joshua put in an appearance. Bloodstained and dishevelled, clothes the worse for wear, face as pale and grim as Nicholas had ever seen it, and with shadows beneath his eyes.

Sarah immediately sprang to her feet and advanced. Joshua took her hands with a quick smile, raised them briefly to his lips but with no further intimacy. Indeed, he quickly put her from him.

'Well?' Nicholas had also risen to his feet.

'Dead. Some time after six. A long and agonising death. The knife missed the heart, but pierced the lung. There was never any hope.' Joshua flung himself into a chair with a groan, easing his wounded arm as the movement tore at the damaged flesh. He rubbed one hand over his face, then awkwardly took the cup of coffee poured for him by Thea. For a long moment there was a stunned silence in the room. The attractive royal couple with whom they had been speaking only a matter of hours ago, now destroyed. The young man struck down before them.

'How is the Duchesse?' Thea asked.

'Distraught, as you would imagine.'

'And the assassin?' Nicholas queried.

'Captured. Louis-Pierre Louvel.' Joshua put down the coffee untasted, stretched the taut muscles of back and shoulders. He would say nothing of his own part in the event. 'I know nothing of him beyond his name. He was being questioned last I heard in the guardroom of the opera. But it could be that he has succeeded in bringing to an end the illustrious house of Bourbon. The Duc and his Duchesse were the only remaining hope of producing a male heir for the next generation. After Louis' brother Charles, the Bourbon line is at an end.'

He retrieved the cup again and sipped the coffee in abstracted contemplation, then looked up at Nicholas, decisions made.

'I want you to leave Paris. This morning. As soon as you can gather the minimum of necessities together.'

'That bad, is it?'

'Impossible to say, but likely to ignite at any moment. The

Garde Royale is called out to search for accomplices and the city is swept with a torrent of reaction. Emotions are running high in the cafés—fights and duels even though the day is young—who knows when it will become riots in the streets? Whether the King is strong enough to enforce order and win over those who have no love for the Bourbons, I doubt. So I want you to go. Today. You will get to Calais and can wait for the next tide and fair wind.'

'And you?' They were the first words uttered by Sarah since her lord had entered the room. She searched his face. 'What will you do?' He looked tired. Drained of energy. Moved by some emotion that clouded his eyes and which he was clearly determined to hide from her. Her inclination was to touch him, just to give him comfort, but there was something in his demeanour that held her back.

'I have some unfinished business here.' He did not look at her beyond a fleeting glance. Dared not, fearing that his resolve to leave her for one last time in Nicholas's care would weaken.

'Then I will not leave. Not until you are ready to come with me. Besides, you are wounded.' She gestured towards the bloody binding around his sleeve. 'Your arm needs care.'

'A flesh wound only—easily remedied. My valet will deal with it. I would rather you made all haste to leave Paris.' He rejected her offer of help; his manner was cool, the discussion a mere matter of organising travel arrangements. 'I need to change my clothes and go out again. If you will come with me, Nick, I will give you some documents to take to England with you.'

He pushed himself to his feet and walked to the door, teeth set against the gnawing ache of the knife wound. It seemed to Sarah that he actually walked around her. He would have done exactly that—it was certainly his intent—but at the end could not leave her with such a depth of anguish in her eyes. Could not leave her without touching her once more. So with reckless longing he moved back to her, closed his fingers around her wrists in a strong grasp, his own anguish mirroring hers.

'Go with Nick and Thea, Sarah. Go back to London.'

They might have been alone in the room. His hands, gentled at last, moved in one long caress from wrist to shoulder to finally frame her face. 'Sarah.' His mouth took hers, soft and cool. He lifted his head and allowed his fingers to outline where his mouth had rested. 'Sarah. Go home.'

She thought he might have said more. It seemed that he changed his mind, for without another word he turned from her abruptly, crossed to the door. He closed it quietly behind him, leaving Sarah to stand and stare at the polished inlay, unable to take in his chill dismissal when his kiss had the power to ignite flames in her blood, when she could still feel the force of his fingers, all heated possession, around her wrists.

Whilst Joshua walked up the stairs to his bedchamber, cursing his clumsy handling of the situation. Remembering the sight of Sarah, standing in the flickering light of the flambeaux, between the assassin's knife and the intended target. Standing, face drained of all colour, with blood on her hands and on her gown when she flew to de Berri's aid. Blood which could so easily have been hers if Louvel had struck blindly and without accuracy. Or if he himself had not been aware, to snatch her from the path of the deadly blade. Before he came to her again, before he read what he hoped to see in her eyes, there was one important visit he must make.

Then at the turn of the stair he halted, his hand suddenly clenched hard on the balustrade as the thought hit him full force. He had been employed by Wycliffe to safeguard the Bourbons. And had signally failed. But he had saved Sarah. The scene in the rue Rameau played again across his mind with vivid images. In the heat of the attack, his first instinct had been to protect his wife from danger, not the Duc de Berri. He bent his head as a wave of pure love for her washed through him. And was driven to acknowledge that he would do exactly the same again, given the same circumstances. Somewhere in the past weeks, creeping up on him without his awareness, it had become impossible to contemplate sacrificing Sarah for the sake of a principle to an ideology. His love for Sarah, his care for her, far outweighed any impersonal duty to a foreign power. She meant more to him than the whole world.

With which thought, Joshua continued his steps slowly upward. He heard Nicholas come out of the breakfast parlour and begin to follow him. It was time for him to take action. And whereas, in the past, principle and political conviction had ruled his life, now he must consider the happiness of the woman he loved. For her to remain in Paris with him was too dangerous. And he had discovered that he did not wish to live here in his self-imposed exile without her. So he must make the changes.

And he owed her an explanation of the truth about the man she had married.

'We have failed. What an appalling disaster.'

Wycliffe was at the edge of his control, pacing the floor. A quiet room in the home of the British Ambassador to Paris, Sir Charles Stuart. He pinned his expected guest, Lord Joshua Faringdon, with an accusatory eye. But the gentleman who sat at his ease was not to be intimidated.

'How could we have succeeded? We could not possibly have known the man's intent. The time or the place.'

'That is not an answer which will go down well with our masters at home. We are expected to know. Expected to have our finger on the pulse.' Wycliffe's thin brows met in a formidable line. 'The third in the line to the French crown assassinated within sight of one of our most effective agents—and we could do nothing to prevent it! A disaster of the first order. When Louis dies, what are we left with? His brother Charles, and with no hope of further male descendants. Everything resting on the shoulders of a female child.'

'It may not be palatable, but it is the truthful answer.' Joshua, unperturbed, watched Wycliffe over steepled fingers. 'Louvel was an unknown. A solitary fanatic working alone. Not a liberal, not working in a conspiracy, not recognised or owned by any of the opposition groups. What chance did we have? I received the barest indication less than an hour before it was carried out. The fact that I was present at all was pure chance.' His lips tightened as he remembered shielding Sarah from the assassin's knife. 'I could barely react and the deed was done.' But the guilt remained. If only he had been able…

'A bad day for European stability.' Wycliffe shook his head. 'And for our nation's reputation as upholder of democratic monarchy.'

Lord Faringdon almost hid a smile that had about it the faintest suggestion of malice. 'I am about to make the day worse, sir.'

'I doubt that is possible. I have just had a terse note from the Prime Minister. You can imagine.'

Joshua shrugged and cast the keg of gunpowder into the flames. 'If anyone knew of Louvel's intentions, if he did have an accomplice, it was the Countess of Wexford.'

'What?' Usually soft-voiced, the sharp sound filled the room.

'I have no proof, but I wager she was integral to the plotting—both time and place.'

'Well—I knew she was a loose cannon, but…' Wycliffe poured a glass of brandy and drank it off in one abrupt gesture. 'You say you have no proof. So are you sure?'

'Olivia was waiting in an enclosed carriage—so very conveniently—to remove Louvel from the scene.'

'Was she, by God!'

'Hmm. Louvel stepped out of the Café Hardy as she approached. It has given me some pause for thought. On her possible implication in my meeting a sorry end last year. Courtesy of a stone balustrade, as you remember. She would have had knowledge of my meeting.'

'It could be.' Wycliffe pondered the possibility with no degree of pleasure. 'The Countess of Wexford passing information…to whom? To whoever suited her personal inclinations most at the time! The glitter of gold coins cannot be overesti-mated.' He bared his teeth in a grimace. 'Then if that is so, I suggest that what we need to do, my lord, is—'

'No!'

Wycliffe raised his brows. 'No, what?'

'*We* will do nothing. My services to you, sir, are at an end.'

'What?' Wycliffe sank to the discomfort of a straight-backed chair.

'I have, as you might say, suffered a change of priorities.'

'Joshua! This is not what I expected. You are invaluable to us for your efforts. I had no idea. I can only advise you to think again.' Wycliffe leaned forward as if he could physically force his agent into compliance.

'Believe me, I have thought long and hard.'

'But why? What in God's name has pushed you into this decision?'

'Any number of reasons. Shall I detail them for you?' It was Lord Joshua's turn to push himself to his feet and stride toward the window, although he turned to face Wycliffe as he spoke. His voice was low and calm, yet there was no doubting the un-derlying frustrations. Or his absolute conviction. 'Where do I start? You foisted Olivia on me, ostensibly as my mistress, on my return to London. She fooled us all, didn't she? You thor-oughly destroyed my good name to deflect any suspicions of my political interest or activity on your behalf—so effectively that my present wife finds it well-nigh impossible to trust me and my family despairs of me. And you arranged—against my better judgement, as you will remember—that particular dip-lomatic charade of a sudden death to disguise a hasty divorce—to end my marriage to Marianne.'

He held up a hand as Wycliffe would have interrupted. 'To hide the fact that she was a French spy—another terrible mis-calculation on our part! It was done to save your face, to hide that you allowed a French subject to infiltrate our tight-knit or-ganisation through marriage to me. I accept that the marriage

had to end, but your only concern was to prevent any idle speculation if a grubby divorce came to court and the true facts were
leaked. Speculation and gossip that would damage both you and
the integrity of your espionage system. Perhaps even jeopar-
dise the security of your other agents. You were simply intent
on preserving your spotless reputation, with no thought for my
own situation. You cannot imagine the complications it has led
to in my private affairs.'

He came to a halt, brooding on this catalogue of events of
which he was not proud. And finally admitted simply, 'I am not
arguing my shining innocence in all this. I went along with it,
did I not? But now I find a need to wipe some slates clean and
be able to face my wife with honesty. To look into her eyes
without deceit.'

Wycliffe frowned. 'Surely you can mould the truth, just to
tell her enough to keep her quiet. It cannot be so difficult—females rarely show interest in politics, in my experience.' It was
clear to Joshua that the Head of Espionage did not understand
at all.

'No, I will not. That is no longer enough. I have demands
on me that I cannot shirk, even in the name of my country. I
have the responsibilities of a landowner, which my cousin
Nicholas assures me I have neglected to a sad degree. I have a
daughter whom I barely know. A son by marriage who desperately wants to be taught to ride a horse. And a wife who…who
does not trust me!'

Wycliffe's face expressed his sardonic disbelief. 'But will
that be enough for you? Domestic bliss in rural England?'

'It will be.' Lord Joshua came to stand before the desk once
more, his face unreadable, unless it was relief at facing the past
in which he had been implicated. But his voice was all conviction. 'And I shall take up my seat in Parliament. I can further
my ideals there equally as well as I can in your employ. And
on present performance, with more success.'

'I see.' Wycliffe thought that he had never heard his noble

employee so impassioned. 'Then I have to respect your choice. But can I not tempt you to reconsider? I am reluctant to lose your expertise and contacts.'

'That is the second such offer in as many days.' Joshua's memory resurrected Olivia Wexford's flirtatious suggestion, but Wycliffe did not understand the dry smile. 'And this is the more attractive of the two. But, no.'

'I hope your wife appreciates what you are doing for her.' Wycliffe came round the desk to shake his lordship's hand for perhaps the last time.

'As do I. But there are no guarantees in this life. She has met Marianne.'

Wycliffe tensed. 'So the lady is back in circulation.'

'Exactly. Now under the guise of the Marquise de Villeroi. She informed Sarah in an oblique manner that she is no longer involved in spying. But I would not wager a fortune on it.'

'Nor I. Subterfuge was her element. As a duck to water. Or perhaps I should say a swan—a most…attractive lady.'

'As you say.'

A discreet knock sounded at the door. A servant entered. A note was passed that Wycliffe read and a genuine smile warmed his eyes for the first time that day.

'Perhaps not as dire a situation as we thought, my lord. Olivia Wexford and Louvel, whether in cahoots or not, did not have the success they might have envisioned.'

'How is that?'

'The Duchesse de Berri. She carries a child. An heir—if God wills it, a son. There is hope for the Bourbons yet. Please God!'

Joshua nodded, a little mollified.

'Amen to that.'

Chapter Twelve

Under strict orders from his cousin, Lord Nicholas Faringdon escorted his charges to Calais. It had been interesting to see Sher in masterful, dominant and thoroughly organisational mode. The visit to Paris in his company had been something of an education, Nick decided. Far from the dissolute and dishonourable man whom the family had been forced to accept with painful reluctance, Sher had a persona that demanded some thoughtful reconsideration. One that included personal invitations to royal receptions, free and unlimited entrée to the home of the British Ambassador, not to mention a positive obsession with keeping his wife safe from all dangers. Nick smiled at the recollection of his cousin handing out instructions and documents with terrible efficiency whilst he changed his coat and neckcloth. There was remarkable similarity, he decided, between Sher and his own brother Henry when decisions were to be made. Neither expected their decision to be questioned. So Nick did what was required and saw the ladies transported and installed comfortably in the Coq d'Or as ordered, a hostelry where Lord Joshua Faringdon was well known and respected with first call on a comfortable suite of rooms. Joshua's yacht awaited them in the harbour, the master prepared to sail at any eventuality. Now it was a matter of waiting for an appropriate tide and wind, and, despite the winter weather, all seemed set fair for an imminent voyage, leaving Sher to follow as and when business allowed.

Which, Sarah advised herself as she removed her long travelling coat in the private parlour put aside for her use, she should welcome. She longed to see the children again. It would be no hardship to leave Paris with its plots and threats of violence, its frenzied activity and its tragic bloodshed. And Joshua's involvement in heaven knew what.

For example. Where was he now?

Sarah had not the least idea, but dreaded the departure to England without him. Would have remained in Paris, uncooperative and mutinous to the last, if Nicholas had not finally threatened to remove her bodily into the carriage. Joshua had insisted that she go home to London—so go home she would. Nick refused to face his cousin to answer for his failure if Joshua returned to his house to find Sarah still in residence. So Sarah's complaints and protestations fell on deaf ears. And since Joshua was nowhere to be found to give consideration to her demands, only an implacable Nicholas and an unsympathetic sister, Sarah had felt obliged to go. But that did not imply that she accepted the situation. Her mind and her heart were torn by inner doubts and outward fractiousness. Unusual as it might be, or perhaps not when it concerned her husband—she flushed at the memory—Sarah came close, incredibly close, to losing her temper.

Theodora, still cast in the role of unfeeling sister, bore the brunt of her strained emotions with fortitude.

'How can I sit and rest as you suggest?' Sarah glared at Thea as that lady sat and poured tea with smooth competence and unruffled calm in the Coq d'Or's dining room, as if they had not just fled for their lives from a city in turmoil.

'I do not see that you have an alternative.' Thea placed a tea-cup before an empty chair. 'Until Joshua joins you, in any event. Do sit, Sarah. You will give me the headache.'

'And when, do you suppose, will my lord see fit to return?' Sarah persisted with her restless ramblings round the room, lips thinned, fists clenched.

'I have no idea.'

'And neither do I!' She rearranged one of the curtains at the window into position with a sharp tug. 'How can I live with this? The uncertainty. The secrecy. Joshua has told me some of the secrets of his past—but by no means all. Not that I cannot guess… How could I have married a man with so many hidden facets to his character, so many cobwebbed corners? Can I truly build a marriage on this?'

Thea sighed, but hid her compassion and a smile. It was a novel experience to see her sister in so unsettled and challenging a state. Cobwebbed corners indeed!

'It all depends on how much you love him. If you love him to the exclusion of all else, then you must be willing to accept how he chooses to live his life.'

'As long as it does not include the Countess of Wexford— or others like her!'

'That, my dear Sarah, goes without saying.'

'But perhaps it depends even more on how much he might care for me!' Sarah was clearly not prepared to be soothed. The window curtain suffered once more. 'He left me with hardly a word. You saw it for yourself! Nothing but *go home*! Whilst he could not wait to be gone from the house again. With not a hint of where or how long he would be occupied. Perhaps he intends never to return to London—it may be so for all I know. He certainly did not see fit to tell me!'

Which was true. But Thea could guess at the reasons, even if Sarah could not, blinded by her fears. 'He does love you, you know.'

'Does he?' Sarah frowned at her sister across the width of the room. 'There is grave room for doubt. And exactly what are his priorities? An underworld of deceit and danger of which I knew nothing when I agreed to accompany him here. A world in which I am followed through the streets as if I were a common criminal!' She took a deep breath. 'He could have been killed at the opera. Am I expected to accept this for the rest of my life?' Looking down at her hands, soft and slender, she could still see the blood from the Duc de Berri's fatal wound. It could have been Joshua's blood. She pushed the horror away and concentrated on the anger.

It was either that, or weep.

Thea put down her cup, her attention caught. 'You were followed? I did not know that. You did not tell me. How exciting!'

'Theodora! I thought that I could rely on you to take this whole matter more seriously!'

Although Theodora decided that there was no reasoning with Sarah in this mood, she folded her hands on the table and gave the advice that she thought her sister needed. 'I cannot help you to make your decision, dear Sarah. But listen to your heart. Give Joshua a chance to put things right.'

'It is easy for you to say!' Sarah's glance over her shoulder was not friendly. 'Nicholas loves you with his heart and soul. You can afford to be complacent, can you not?' Then she stopped, aghast at her words, pressing her forehead against the cold glass of the window before coming swiftly to sit beside Thea and grasp her hands, to the imminent danger of the teacups. 'That was a terrible thing to say, Thea. I am sorry I did not mean it. I am just out of sorts—and so anxious—but you should not suffer.'

'I know. There are extenuating circumstances!' Thea allowed herself the smile, which Sarah returned, a trifle rueful. 'It seems to me, my love, that this is a case of Faringdon history repeating itself.'

Sarah looked her surprise.

'Think about this. In this family there have been three women who have had to take their future into their own hands to achieve their heart's desire. Eleanor—as you know better then I—left her home, her consequence and her security here, gave it up to risk all in America to be with Henry because she could not live without him. As for me— well, if I had not travelled to Aymestry with you to make my peace with Nicholas, when we had quarrelled so dreadfully, we would have remained estranged for all time. And now it seems to me that it is your turn.'

'I had not seen it like that.'

'Well, do so. The Faringdon men are difficult, opinionated, resourceful and all with that touch of arrogance. They are also, in my opinion, impossibly attractive, impossible not to love. All you have to do is to decide if the one you love—Joshua—is worth fighting for. Even if you have to reveal your heart to him—to show your vulnerability.'

Sarah looked down at her hands to hide the stain of colour in her cheeks. 'It is true. I know it.' Her voice was low and a little husky. 'But I do not have the courage of either you or Eleanor to speak my thoughts and feelings. What if he rejects me? I do not think that I could live with that. To reveal my longing for him so there is no hiding—'

'I have never heard such nonsense!' In typically flamboyant manner, Thea swept her sister into her arms and hugged her. Then ticked off the instances on her fingers. 'You escaped from the evil machinations of our esteemed brother. You travelled to New York. You then returned to England alone with your son and no one to protect you. You took up a position of housekeeper because you desired independence above all things. You refused to take an easy life either at Aymestry with us or with Judith in London. You had the courage to marry a man of dubious reputation because you loved him—although whether that is brave or foolhardy I am unsure.' Thea chuckled. 'Sarah, throughout your life you have shown bravery of the highest order. It is simply, you foolish girl, that you refuse to recognise your own merits. Or believe that those who love you find you in any way worthy of that affection. You are well loved and respected, Sarah.'

Sarah flushed brighter at the words. 'How ridiculous you make me sound.'

'Yes. You are.' But Thea's smile was kind. 'I had the advantage of an upbringing at the hands of Lady Drusilla. She would never let me be unaware of my talents or my worth. I think our unfortunate mother did not have the same interest in her children.'

'No, she did not.' Sarah paused and then said, with a quick glance at her sister, 'I did not tell you—but Joshua bought me a house in London—in my own name—before we left for France.'

'Did he now?'

'I think he was aware of the danger to himself. So the house was for my future, for myself and John.'

'Well, then.' Thea touched Sarah's hand, the lightest of reassurances. 'And you think that Joshua does not love you?'

Sarah looked at her sister, younger, far more beautiful, far more worldly wise. 'What do I do, Thea?'

'It is so easy. Tell him what you feel. Don't use disguise or pretence. Do not allow him to think that you do not care. Tell him the truth. That you love him. That is the best advice I can give.'

And if Joshua Faringdon does not love you in return, I am no judge of Faringdon men!

Which was exactly the sentiment that she repeated to Nicholas some time later in the day when he returned from the yacht to the seclusion and privacy of their own bedchamber and Thea explained the apparent problem between Lord Joshua and his lady.

'And since you are an expert, my loved one, in affairs of the heart...' Nick grinned at the prospect of his cousin being caught in the painful toils of unrequited love.

'Exactly.'

Lord Nicholas took his lovely wife into his arms and kissed her, long and thoroughly. 'When we are back in England, let us return to Aymestry. Let us give the lovers some time and space to sort out their own problems. And decide that perhaps they do love each other after all.'

Theodora pressed close, returned the embrace, her mouth warm and inviting.

'So I think!'

The door into Sarah's parlour in the inn opened a little before ten o' clock. Although she had intended to retire to bed, she was glad of the interruption to her morbid thoughts.

'Oh, Thea…' She turned her head.

It was not Thea who stood on the threshold in dusty boots and mud-splashed greatcoat, hat and gloves in his hand.

Sarah rose to her feet.

'Joshua.'

He closed the door, but did not approach. He looked travel-weary, but his eyes were watchful and never left her face.

In that moment all her anger drained away.

'I have missed you.' It was the simplest thing in the world for her to say.

'It has only been two days.' The faintest of smiles. He had been unsure of her welcome when he walked through the door, was still unsure.

'It has been a lifetime. I did not know where you were or when I would see you again.' Her eyes were captured in the depths of his. She could not look away.

'I know.' Still he remained with his back to the door. 'When we parted I was not free to explain or say what was in my heart. Now I am. Will you sit with me and listen? Once before when I asked you, you would not.'

'Once before when you asked me, as I remember, I struck you!'

'Then I hope that you will warn me if you are tempted again.' He walked slowly across the distance.

'I promise you that I will not.' As uncertain as he, she sat. Her muscles rippled with nerves, but relief loosened the tight bands of anxiety, simply because of his presence. 'Tell me then.'

Joshua cast his greatcoat over the back of a chair and came to sit on the low sofa beside her. Sarah promptly forgot her own anxieties as she searched his face closely for the first time. In the soft light from the candles she could see the marks of strain that bracketed his mouth. She longed to smooth them away with her fingers, to touch her lips to them. But knew that she must wait. He leaned forward, arms supported by his thighs, dropping his head to run his fingers through his tousled hair. Then looked up at her.

'I have a number of confessions that I must make. I have been employed to—to collect information of a sensitive nature. That is to say…what I mean is—'

'That you are a spy.' She finished the sentence as he hesitated to tell her the depth of his involvement, the facts that he had kept from her since their marriage.

'Ah…'

'A spy for the British government, I presume.' Her fair brows rose. 'Did you think that I would not guess?'

'Wycliffe would never believe it!' Joshua rubbed his hands over his face and sat up, shaking his head when she would have enquired who Wycliffe might be. 'Yes, I have been a spy.'

'If Marianne was a French spy, as you told me, and *certain circles* wished to cover up your unfortunate marriage, it seemed logical to me that you too were involved. For the other side, I presume.'

'Yes.'

'And it probably explains why I was followed.'

'Ha! My wife, it seems, is very clever.' His eyes held a wealth of amused respect. 'What else do you know?'

Sarah flushed in denial. 'Nothing more.'

'Our aim was to protect Louis from those who would depose him, in the name of republicanism or Bonaparte. We hoped to diffuse any such attempt before it materialised.'

'And so you were told about the assassination at the opera.'

'Not exactly—or I would never have put your life in danger by allowing you to be there.'

'Thank you for telling me.' He watched her as she worried at the ruffled edging on her cuffs, as the knowledge sank in.

'Does it…does the knowledge disgust you? Shock you?' He had to know.

'No. I do not know why you did not tell me before!' Her gaze was clear and direct, no trace of distrust there. 'But what now? Can I be honest? I do not know if I can live a life where I fear for your safety every minute of every day.'

Relief at her calm acceptance of his past flooded through him. As for the future… 'There will be no need for that,' he assured her.

'You mean that you will stay here, and I will go back to London?' Her heart, all her hopes plummeted. How could he condemn her to such a bleak existence?

'Sarah…no. I did not mean that. I am coming home with you, tomorrow. After all, I have a wife and a daughter and a son.' He noted Sarah's catch of breath at this with satisfaction. 'And my wife does not seem to understand that I care for her more than anything else.'

'No. I do not know it!' Her mind was suddenly in turmoil.

'I have severed my ties, Sarah. My employment in the service of government espionage is at an end.'

'But at what cost?'

'None. There is no cost. From this moment I am my own master, to live my life as I choose.'

'Oh.'

'I had discovered that the conflicts in my life were becoming more than I could bear.'

'I see.' But she still did not.

She waited for him to touch her, the slightest brush of his fingers, to give her some indication of his thoughts. He had not done so since he had walked into the room. And still he did not. Instead, on a sudden decision, Joshua stood and walked over to the table where rested the leather satchel of documents which

Nicholas had brought with him to Calais. Opened the flap and riffled through the contents.

'What are you doing?'

'Looking for these.' He produced a number of folded sheets of paper.

'Our contracts?' She recognised them immediately, although not his purpose, which caused her to rise to her feet in a sudden ripple of panic. Did he intend to destroy them? 'I did not know you had them with you.'

'I travel with all my important documents.' Joshua smoothed them out.

'What are you going to do?'

He had set himself to discover pens and a pot of ink in a little escritoire. 'It seems to me, my love, that you have a lamentable tendency to desire everything to be stated in black and white. You seem, for some inexplicable reason, to be more certain of my intentions—and even your own—when you see them written on a page. That is what we are going to do. Come here.'

She did, reluctantly. Took the offered sheet—her own—and the pen that he held out.

'Sit there.' She did, at the little writing desk. 'Now.' His voice was suddenly deadly serious. 'You entered into this marriage with a man of soiled reputation, guilty, so rumour had it, of all manner of vice, on the strength of this contract. We have come a long way, Sarah, since you put your hand in mine and allowed me to give you my name. I think things have changed between us. So now we will update your expectations—and mine.'

Her eyes narrowed with suspicion. 'Why?'

'Do you distrust my motives still? They are entirely innocent, I do assure you. All I would ask is that you write, at the end, your heart's desire from this marriage. And I will do the same.'

He could read every emotion as it flitted across her expressive face. Fear and hope in equal measure. A desire to trust him. The instinct to throw caution to the winds and tell him the truth. Despair that he might not wish to hear the truth from her heart. Perhaps he knew her better than she knew herself. He wanted nothing more than to enfold her in his arms and reassure her that all would be well.

'Write what you truly want, Sarah. Whatever the consequences.' He must gamble everything on this one final throw, risking everything on the words she had whispered when she had tumbled into sleep, held fast in his arms. Otherwise their marriage would founder on the rocks of pride and distrust.

Sarah felt her breath back up in her lungs, a tight band around her chest. 'Even an end to it?' She did not know what made her ask, but she did. Perhaps she needed to know if he would rather tear up the documents and have done. Give them both their freedom.

'If that is what you wish.' He hid the quick thrust of pain at this unexpected question, but his eyes silvered with fear. He had not expected this, but would accept it if he must. He managed a stiff smile, but his eyes were bleak indeed. 'In God's name, you have suffered enough at my hands. I could not blame you. I have been far from honest with you. But I would wish for a different outcome.' He reached across the little desk to capture her hand. Raised it to his lips which were cold as ice. Fierce silver eyes locked with troubled blue. 'Swear to me that you will be honest. That is all I ask.'

'I swear it.' She laid the hand which he released on her heart in a quaint gesture. Then tore her gaze away from his to re-read the list of hopes and demands that she had written so many weeks before. And thought of Thea's words. Tell him. Just write: *I love you. I want you to love me.* He watched her in some amusement as her mind turned over the events and emotions of the past few days. Then, in exasperation, 'In heaven's name, Sarah, I am not asking you to sign away your soul to the devil.'

She dipped in her pen and bent her head.

'I will write what is in my heart, as you ask.'

'And I will do likewise.' Without hesitation he wrote with firm strokes at the end of his own contract. Then cast the pen aside.

And waited.

She was aware of his every movement. Very well. She would do it. Have the confidence to lay out her hopes and fears, her private dreams, in public view. Before the one man whose regard she most desired. Demand for *herself* for the first time in her life. Was it not her right after all to be loved? Thea thought so. She would grasp the future and live with the consequences.

She wrote.

He held out his hand for the sheet of paper.

Still she hesitated.

'Coward,' he whispered, but the word was soft and the smile on his mouth and in his eyes beckoned with such promise. And gave Sarah all the courage she needed.

'I am not a coward. I will tell you what I have written. I will say it aloud for the whole world to hear.' She clutched the paper against her breast, not needing to see the words written there. 'That I love you. I have loved you from the first moment I saw you walk with such pain into the hall in Hanover Square. I *hated* the Countess of Wexford when I thought you loved her. I hated any woman who might find her way into your heart. I love you foolishly and inordinately. I would wish that you loved me.' The torrent of words, so fierce and unexpected, so much more passionate than the simple statement she had written on the paper, dried up as quickly as they had overspilled. She looked at him aghast. 'I cannot believe that I just said all that. I cannot believe that you could possibly love me,' she finished on a whisper.

'Oh, Sarah.' He stretched out a hand, to stroke her cheek with gentle fingers, the most tender of gestures. 'Have I not shown you the depths of my love when I took you in my arms, to my bed. Did I not prove it—that last time in Paris when we came together with such delight? I thought that you must know my love for you, in every touch, in every caress.'

'You have never said that you loved me. I only know that you do not *object* to me—that you do not find me distasteful. You never said the words.'

'Sarah! How on earth would I find you distasteful? Let me say the words then. You are my dearest love. And if I did not make it plain to you, even without words, then I should be taken to task. It was my fault. There were so many constraints between us. I wished to obliterate them all before I spoke with you. I dared not touch you that final morning in Paris when all I could see was the blood staining your hands and your bodice. I had to end it all first. Only then could I come to you and ask for your understanding. And your forgiveness.'

'Joshua... Do you truly love me?' Her lips curved, slowly blossoming into a smile of such joy, an inner radiance. At that moment she was beautiful beyond belief.

'I love you, Sarah. Do you believe it at last?'

'Yes. Oh, yes. I think I must. If you have turned your back on that life for me.' He had done it for her. The magnitude of that decision took her breath away.

'I have. And it is my pleasure and my delight. There are others to do the Prince Regent's bidding. You are my wife. More important to me than...I cannot say. You are my very heart and soul.'

'Joshua...' And then as she became aware of the crumpled sheets still in her hand, a little frown of suspicion marked her brow. 'What did you write? It seems to me unfair if you know my innermost thoughts, but you do not reveal your own!'

He laughed aloud. 'Here, my suspicious wife. Read for yourself.'

I would surround you with my love, wrap you in its folds, hold you fast. Openly and without artifice. I would live with you until death.

'Oh, Joshua. That is so...so beautiful. No one has ever said anything so particular to me before.' Tears sparkled on her lashes until she brushed them away with her hand. 'I am so happy.'

'So why are you weeping, my foolish love?' He took the paper and pen carefully from her hands, encircled her wrists with firm fingers and lifted her to her feet. His arms slid smoothly around her waist to draw her close against him. 'I do not know what more I can do to make you certain. I shall have to tell you every day so that you are in no doubt. Or perhaps buy a parrot and train it to repeat *I love you* on the hour when I am not beside you.'

'John would like that.' She chuckled, her face turned against his shoulder as she absorbed the heat and strength of him. The wonder of his word and his closeness.

'I expect he would. Look up, Sarah.' She did. 'We have made an uneasy start together. We can do better.'

'Then show me.'

'It will be my pleasure. One thing I would ask. You painted a portrait of John, I think, when you gave me Beth's likeness. Will you give it to me?'

'Why, yes—if you wish it.' He could read the surprise in her voice, in the tilt of her head.

'I do. The two portraits should be together.' Joshua had made the decision, thought of the matter deeply and at length, so he would say what was in his heart and pray that his wife would grant him this ultimate symbol of her trust. 'Sarah—this is what I would ask—will you give me your son to bring up as my own? So that he would be mine as much as Beth is yours, in the eyes of the world. I would not wish it to be a betrayal of John Russell's claim, but—it would be my desire to give him legal recognition and for him to take my name. To love him and care for him as you would for my daughter. And as I love and care for you. Will you allow it?'

He waited, giving her a little space to contemplate his words. To decide on the debt she might yet owe to Captain John Russell. Unaware that Sarah's heart leapt with joy that Joshua Faringdon should accept and love both of them.

'I will. I will give you my son.' Her promise was as firm as the day when she had married him. 'I can think of nothing better than that you should be father to my son.'

'You have all my gratitude.' Joshua bent his head to touch

his lips to hers. Softly. A promise and a benediction. Then to her cheeks, her eyelids, the tender skin at her temples. A subtle reacquaintance with the face that now haunted his dreams. Then on, a delicious journey along the curve of her throat to where the pulse beat hard, the flutter of a caged bird beneath his mouth. To return once more to those lips that sighed under his. Sarah tightened her fingers in the cloth of his coat as if she would never release him.

'You are mine and I love you.' He murmured against her spun-silk curls.

At her reply his heart shattered. 'I have always loved you. I have waited for you my whole life.'

His fingers released her hair to fall in pale gold to her shoulders, so that he could wind his hand through it, holding her as he wished so that his mouth could fit more perfectly over hers. Drowning in her sweetness, in her ready compliance as he took the kiss deeper, more intimate still. Rediscovering the dark intoxication until she shivered in his arms. A soft sound of acceptance in her throat, which struck him with a desire to take her now and show her the depths of his love so that she might never doubt, never forget. She was his wife and belonged to him. For all time.

But he put her from him with careful hands. For one more moment before he allowed passion to rule. Took a deep breath.

'Before I take you to bed, I would wish to make one statement in my defence. I am no saint, but my reputation was never quite what you were led to believe. It was a cover—against anyone prying too closely into my private affairs. No one would expect a man without integrity to be involved in national security. So the Polite World in London views me with contempt. But as a matter of pride, I would like you to think that I have some degree of honour and principle.'

Sarah touched a hand to his lips to silence him, her heart a little sore. She understood that need for integrity very well. Had not her own life been overshadowed by her willingness to obey the vicious demands of her brother? 'Are you hoping to be accepted back with a new and bright reputation?' Her smile could not hide the sadness.

His lips twisted in wry acceptance. 'The *ton* will never believe it now. I shall have to live with it. There will always be the suspicion that I seduced innocent virgins or murdered poor Marianne. Can you still love me with all the lingering clouds of scandal?'

She tilted her head, a mischievous twinkle in her eyes. Anything to dispel this harsh moment of reality and its attendant pain. 'I think that I can. You can be a reformed rake, of course. Saved from your sins at the eleventh hour.' She reached up to kiss his mouth, still an impulsive gesture for Sarah that delighted him and did more than she would ever know to soothe the regrets of the past.

'As long as the reformation is in your hands.' He kissed her fingers one by one, then pressed his mouth against the ring she wore, his ring, the potent symbol of their unity. 'Yours and no other. For I said that I was now my own man, with the freedom to live as I chose. I think that I was wrong.'

Her eyes flashed to his, a moment of concern. But saw nothing there but love.

'No, my dear love.' He answered her silent question. 'I am not free at all. And I like the idea very much.'

Epilogue

A gentleman sat at his desk in an office in his newly built house, in shirtsleeves against the warmth of the morning. He frowned over a list of figures. Mr Henry Faringdon, joint partner in the firm of Faringdon and Bridges. Anyone acquainted with Nicholas and Joshua would immediately recognise the Faringdon cast of feature in the dark hair, straight nose and exquisite cheekbones, the predatory eyes. And in the aura of power and competence that he wore with such casual and elegant ease. The edge of ruthlessness. Henry Faringdon, Nicholas's elder brother, had no need to frown. Life was good. The business was expanding, the trade booming with new contacts both in the New World and in Europe. Faringdon and Bridges was a name now recognised and treated with respect in commercial circles. The scandal that had almost shattered the possibility of a future together for Henry and Eleanor no longer had the power to wound or destroy.

The door opened to admit the other, the most important, reason for his intense satisfaction. A gorgeous brunette with deep amethyst eyes and a sleepy baby held high against her shoulder. His pulse beat hard, just at the sight of her.

'Nell.'

'Hal.' Her smile lit her face, her eyes spoke of love. Her only love. 'Do you have a minute?'

Henry had any number of minutes for his beautiful wife. As many as she would ever demand. All his life if she would have it.

'Are you too busy?' Eleanor Faringdon wrinkled her nose at the array of account books.

'For you, never.' He stood, moved round the desk. 'What is it, my heart?'

'Here. Hold your son.' She pushed the child, Richard, into his father's arms, freeing her two hands to straighten out the sheets of a letter.

'Ah. Your mother, perhaps?' Henry's lips curled cynically at the prospect, but when his attention was drawn by the baby's tugging on his collar his smile was tender.

'No.' She chuckled. 'We are spared that. Judith!'

'Well, then.' Realising that this would not be a brief session, Henry moved across the room to tuck the baby into the corner of a sofa with a cushion, sat and pulled Eleanor down to sit beside him. 'I suppose you have to tell me. In the next hour or so.'

'Why, yes.' She scanned the contents of the closely written sheets. 'It is all very complicated. I think we must have lost a packet of letters because Judith writes of things we do not know—and she clearly presumes that we do. And you know what her letters are like at best—all dashes, exclamations and comment. So it is quite muddled—but most intriguing.'

'Then tell me all.' With an eye to the infant, he tucked his wife against his side with an arm around her shoulders and set himself to listen.

'To start with, Sarah, would you believe it, is married. And for some months, I think.'

'Ah! Now that does surprise me.'

'And to your cousin Joshua.'

'Sher?' The dark brows rose as Henry's interest was now caught. 'Sounds highly unlikely, but Ju must be right.' His lips twitched at the thought. 'The virtuous Sarah and the wicked Sher. An amazing combination.'

'I only met him the once.' Eleanor frowned at her husband. 'He was very charming, I remember.'

'All the Faringdons are charming. Had you not noticed?' He turned his head to kiss her hair. 'But Sher is highly reprehensible.'

'Judith says that they are now fixed permanently in England rather than Paris and that Lady Beatrice has forgiven him his past sins.'

'That must be a relief to him!' Eleanor could not mistake the dry note, but chose to ignore it.

'She says that something must have happened between them in Paris—she mentions a scandal of which we know nothing—but they returned to London completely besotted with each other. Sarah is in a state of permanent bliss and Joshua is very protective of her. He looks at her with passion in his eyes, as if she was his whole world. Judith says that when he looks at her it is as if he is kissing her in public and it is all positively embarrassing to the whole family. But they have gone down to Richmond where Joshua is teaching Sarah to ride.'

'Well—I suppose it is necessary…although I do not see…' But decided to say no more. Eleanor was in full flow.

'What else? Giles—Judith's son, you remember—is now beginning to walk. Marianne, Joshua's first wife, is not really dead after all—'

'What?'

'Never mind that. Just listen… Sarah was suspected of being a spy—I don't understand that either. Joshua was accused of murder, but did not do it. Well, now! Simon's horse won a race at Newmarket. I told you it was all a muddle. But listen to this. This is the best we could have hoped to hear. Nicholas and Thea are awaiting the birth of an heir for Aymestry. Isn't that splendid news?'

Henry grinned at the unlikely thought of his younger brother being settled, a prosperous landowner, with an heir. Time, it seemed, passed very quickly. 'It is. Another addition to the new generation of Faringdons. Is that all?'

'Yes. Or so I think.' She riffled through the pages again. 'I am so pleased for Sarah.'

Henry thought about the young woman with the troubled soul. 'I think that she will enjoy having the love and security of a family around her. She was never quite happy and settled here, was she? So, Judith should be congratulated—the whole family history in two sheets. Remarkable!'

Eleanor nudged him in the ribs with her elbow and tutted, taking the opportunity to remove the tasselled edge of the cushion where it was suffering from a relentless attack by her son's toothless gums. 'I am delighted for her. Sarah deserves her happiness. Judith says she is intent on restoring Joshua's reputation to a shining brilliance. So you, my love, will be the only one Beatrice can sneer at—abandoning the title and the consequence and going into *trade* of all things!'

'Beatrice and her diatribes, thank God, are too far away for me to be overly concerned. But poor Sher. Once in a woman's clutches…' Henry smiled down at Eleanor, but then narrowed his gaze at his wife's face. 'What is it, Nell?' She was looking at him, he decided, with a hint of stern censure in her lovely eyes. Or perhaps there was a sparkle there which she would hide from him.

'I was thinking—I remember the days when *you* used to look at *me* with passion in your eyes, as if I were your whole world. And probably embarrassed the family.' Definitely a sparkle!

'Do I not do that now? Every day of my life?' The possessive gleam in his eyes brought a delicate flush to her face. 'Do we not have living proof of my total adoration?' He passed a gentle hand over the now-sleeping baby's head, and they laughed when the sound of Tom's excited voice shrieked most opportunely from some distant region of the house. At eight years old, he had energy to spare and lungs to match. Henry turned his wife's hand, which he held within his and kissed her palm, his lips a burning brand on her soft skin. 'Without you my life is nothing, you know that, Nell.'

As indeed she did. She knew exactly her place in her husband's heart. 'And you are my life too.' She touched Henry's bent head with fingers that were not quite steady as she gave thanks for twists of fate which had brought them together against all the odds

'Do you miss it all, Nell? London and family? Would you wish to return?' Henry's eyes were searching. Her happiness was very precious to him.

'No.' He could not doubt the sincerity in her reply or in the love that he could read so clearly in her face. 'Your life is here. Mine is with you. I pray that Sarah has found the same security and certainty with Joshua. Just as Thea has with Nicholas.' Her fingers linked with his, an indestructible bond. 'And the same depth of love. For it seems to me that is all that matters.'

'It is very simple, is it not?' His clasp tightened on hers. She was his for ever.

'Yes.'

Of course, he did not need to ask the question. Eleanor's soft lips against Henry's told it all.

* * * * *

The Lord and the Mystery Lady

by

Georgina Devon

Georgina Devon has a Bachelor of Arts degree in Social Sciences with a concentration in History. Her interest in England began when she lived in East Anglia as a child and later as an adult. She met her husband in England and her wedding ring set is from Bath. She has many romantic and happy memories of the land. Today she lives in Tucson, Arizona, with her husband, two dogs, an inherited cat and a cockatiel. Her daughter has left the nest and does website design, including Georgina's. Contact her at www.georginadevon.com

Don't miss the second book in Georgina Devon's wonderful Regency duet – *An Unconventional Widow* is available next month in Regency High-Society Affairs Volume 12

Prologue

"Ah, chatting over the daily mutton," Dominic Mandrake Chillings drawled as he took a seat opposite his sister and on the right of his brother.

Guy William Chillings, Seventh Viscount Chillings, raised one black brow. "Witty as usual, Dominic." He took a bite of his well-prepared lamb, topped with a French sauce made by his very French chef, and chewed slowly. "I am glad you could make your way here while the Season is still in full panoply."

Dominic made a mocking half-bow. "The wishes of the head of the family are my marching orders."

"Hah!" Annabell Fenwick-Clyde, Dowager Lady Fenwick-Clyde, said. "You came only because you are curious, Dominic. Nothing more."

Dominic shrugged and cut into the mutton the butler had just set in front of him.

"Enough," Guy said, setting down his fork and rising. "I asked both of you here to discuss my betrothal."

"I beg your pardon?" Dominic said, standing, his food forgotten, his chair pushed back so abruptly that it nearly toppled. "Becoming leg-shackled? About time."

Annabell, a tall, elegant woman in her early thirties with gray, almost silver, hair and black brows like her twin, the Viscount, eyed her brother. "Dominic, I vow, you are being overly dramatic." She turned to her twin and smiled. "Whom do you intend to wed, Guy? Hopefully not one of those bits of muslin you and Dominic insist on enjoying."

Guy tsked. "Sarcasm does not become you, Bell."

He returned her smile to take the sting from his words. He knew his sister disapproved of men keeping mistresses, and she knew he would do as he pleased.

Dominic grinned. "They are not for marrying, Bell. They are for sowing one's wild oats."

Annabell set down her knife and fork. "The both of you use them."

"And pay them well," Dominic said, a small frown drawing his coal-black brows together.

"Enough," Guy said, moving from the table. "I did not invite you here to discuss my proclivities. Although, Dominic is right. The ladies are well paid and more than willing to enter into the bargain. They know the lay of the land very well."

Annabell snorted. "As though they had any choice." She rose as well. "I gather the two of you will not stay here and drink your…whisky."

Dominic stood, his blue, nearly black eyes twinkling. "You make us sound so heathen, Bell. I swear you malign us."

"I merely state the obvious," she said.

He grinned. "Not that you have much leeway in calling us uncivilized. We may not drink port till we slip under the table—"

"No," she interrupted, "you drink unfashionable Scotch whisky."

"But," he continued, "you travel to all parts of the world known and unknown. And usually with only your maid."

She eyed him. "None of my male relatives will accompany me. So I go alone."

He gave a mock shudder. "I've no wish to travel to the places you go, Bell. If you went to the Continent, that would be one thing. But I like my comforts. A tent in the heat and sand are not my idea of comfort."

"Then you have nothing to say about what I do."

She turned and marched to the door before either man could say anything more. Guy exchanged a glance with his younger brother. Both shook their heads.

"She is a widowed bluestocking, and glad of it," Guy said. "I suppose outbursts on women's right to equality are to be expected. Goodness knows she's never let being a female keep her from doing as she damn well pleased."

"Not since Fenwick-Clyde stuck his spoon in the wall."

They followed their sister into the library, where Guy crossed to the burl-walnut desk and poured two glasses of the unfashionable Scotch whisky. He handed one to Dominic and drank the second in two long swallows and poured another. Then Guy raised his glass. "Here's to the future." He downed the contents in one long gulp.

Dominic did the same, saying, "Here's to a life of wine, women and song—or something along those lines."

Annabell grimaced.

A soft knock on the door preceded the butler's arrival with the tea tray, which he set on a small kidney table near the front windows. Annabell smiled at Oswald and thanked him. The butler, his short, lean frame impeccably groomed, smiled back.

"Do either of you wish for tea?" she enquired, knowing the answer, but asking anyway. It was one of the small ways she nettled them.

Both men looked aghast at her while Guy picked up the decanter and poured each of them another generous portion. He sauntered to one of the chairs grouped around the window that looked out on to Grosvenor Square and beside the table where the tea tray sat. A fashionable phaeton driven by an even more fashionable dandy passed by. Several young ladies, followed by footmen carrying parcels, strolled along the pavement. The Season was in full swing. He sat and stretched his legs out.

"As I started to tell you, I am engaged."

"To whom?" Annabell interjected. She sat by the tea table and across from her brother.

"Miss Emily Duckworth," he said flatly.

"No, Guy," Annabell said. "She is not up to your weight."

"I never," Dominic said in disgust. He paced the room, his energy needing an outlet. "You will get no pleasure from her, I vow."

"You are both wrong," Guy drawled. "The lady is very aware of the bargain we strike and more than willing to fulfil her duty. I need an heir and she wants a husband."

"Cold, Guy," Annabell said. "You are as cold as…as…"

"Let me help you," Dominic said. "Cold as a witch's—"

"Thank you very much," Annabell interrupted before he could finish the saying.

"You are both wrong," Guy said, swirling the amber liquid in its cut-crystal glass. "I am pragmatic. I need an heir. Miss Duckworth will provide one. She needs a husband to protect her and to give her the wealth and caché to make a splash in Society. She has an impeccable lineage, but her brother is finishing what her father started by gambling away what is left of the family funds." He finished the liquor. "I, not to be too vulgar, am as rich as Golden Ball. In short, we are perfectly suited."

Annabell muttered something unladylike under her breath. "Cold as Siberia."

Dominic laughed, but it was more bitter than humourous. "So apropos. Women only marry where they see advantage. Give me the ladies of the night. They, at least, are honest in their dealings."

"You are jaded, Dominic," Guy said, setting down his empty glass.

"And what are you?" Annabell asked. "Bright-eyed and bushy-tailed?"

"Neither," Guy said, beginning to get bored with the conversation. "As I said, this is a practical arrangement. Nothing more."

"It could be worse," Dominic said. "It could be a love match, as your first marriage was." He crossed to the desk and poured himself another glass, thus missing the dark look that crossed his brother's countenance. "Care for another?" he asked.

"Just bring the decanter over here," Guy said.

"Ah," Annabell murmured, having seen the flash of pain on her twin's face. "You are doing this because

Suzanne died in childbirth and the babe with her. No more emotional risks for you.''

"That was ten years ago," Guy said, his voice flat. "I am past that. But I am thirty-three. I need an heir." He eyed his siblings through narrowed lids. "Unless one of you intends to provide me with one, since the title can pass to Dominic and then you, Bell."

"Don't look to me," Dominic said. "I have no need of an heir, so I don't need to marry—for convenience or love."

"And I cannot inherit while there is a male heir, Guy, so don't be ridiculous," Annabell said tartly.

"Just so," Guy murmured. "Hence my upcoming marriage."

"To your nuptials," Dominic said, lifting his glass as he continued to pace.

Guy raised one black brow. "Must you make a nuisance of yourself with constant movement?"

Annabell smiled. "He never could sit still. Not even in the nursery, when his reward for not moving for ten minutes was cake. You cannot expect him to have changed, Guy." She added, "Particularly considering what you just told us."

Dominic stopped momentarily and grinned. "She's right, you know."

Guy shrugged and turned his attention to the portrait of the three of them, which hung over the mantel. It had been painted when he and Bell were twenty and Dominic sixteen. Before Suzanne.

Suzanne was a subject he found hard to discuss. They had been childhood friends who married. He had been happy with her, had thought he loved her. Then she had died trying to give him an heir and the baby with her. It was only in the past couple of years that he had come to terms with the guilt he felt over her death. If he had not got her pregnant she would be alive. But that was the way of their world.

He took a deep breath, intending to speak and instead stood. He felt as pent up as Dominic looked. He poured himself another full glass of whisky, not offering any to Dominic. He downed the drink as he had the previous ones. Then poured another.

"No sense drinking yourself into oblivion," Annabell said, taking a sip of tea. "Do you even like Miss Duckworth, Guy?"

Guy smiled. "You always could change subjects faster than anyone I know. As for Miss Duckworth, I don't know her well enough to like or dislike her." Which was fine with him. She was to have his heir. Nothing more.

"Going a bit too far," Dominic said. He stopped his pacing and came to stand beside them. "Ramshackle as I am, I would not marry a woman I didn't at least like."

"He has a point, Guy," Annabell said gently.

"For him, perhaps," Guy said. "But then he does not have to marry. He can afford to do as he pleases."

Both Annabell and Dominic nodded.

Dominic said sardonically, "It is tough being the oldest. All that blunt, not to mention the title." He raised one hand to forestall comments when Annabell opened her mouth. "Not that I want the title. No, not me. Having too much fun being the black sheep of the family."

"Is that why you aren't married?" Annabell arched one dark brow.

Dominic's swarthy face darkened. "Tease me all

you like, Bell. I don't intend to marry. Besides, no respectable woman would have me.''

Dominic had been wild as a boy. As a man he was nearly a reprobate and decidedly a libertine.

Guy interrupted Bell's quizzing of Dominic, who was beginning to look harassed. ''I think we have discussed everything. Shall we go on to Prinny's gathering at Covent Garden?''

Annabell shuddered. ''Not me, thank you. There are some things I need to research before we start seriously uncovering the Roman villa we have just found on Sir Hugo Fitzsimmon's Kent estate.''

''Fitzsimmon?'' Guy said, concern entering his voice. ''He is a worse libertine than Dominic. And he makes me look like a boy still in leading strings.''

She shrugged. ''He is in Paris with Wellington. I shall never even meet him.''

''Hope not, Bell,'' Dominic said. ''He has led me down a long, dark night before. You would not like him in the least.''

''And I shall not meet him, brothers,'' she said pointedly. ''I learned more about debauchery than any woman needs to know from Fenwick-Clyde.''

A barely suppressed shudder sped through her body. Her marriage had been arranged and not happy.

Guy regretted what had happened to Bell, but he had not been Viscount then, and their parents had believed in marriages of convenience. Theirs had been one and a very happy one. Both had died in a boating accident shortly after Annabell wed and they therefore did not live to see her unhappiness.

''Well, I am going to Prinny's little get-together,'' Guy said pointedly. ''The two of you are welcome to do as you please.''

"Getting as much enjoyment from life as you can before walking down the aisle?" Dominic teased.

"Leave him be," Annabell said.

"A man has to do what he has to do, Dominic," Guy said darkly. "Some day you will learn that." He turned back to them, his lips twisted sardonically. "Wish me luck."

Chapter One

Six months later...

Guy spurred his gelding on. The sleet and wind billowed out his many-caped greatcoat and laid a layer of frost on his moustache and beard, both a fashionable *faux pas*. He did not care. He had decided long ago to do as he pleased. And if he wished to have facial hair, then he would.

The weather had trapped him in The Folly for the last week, making him irritable. He had decided this morning to visit the nearest town, where his current mistress, a widow of good standing, lived. Their arrangement was for mutual convenience. He provided the money and she provided the sexual relief. The situation suited him and he intended to enjoy it as much as possible. When he married Miss Duckworth in the coming spring, he would feel honour bound to terminate this liaison. He was not looking forward to that time. Jane was very skilled in many things.

He slowed his horse to cross a small, rock bridge that spanned a rapidly running stream. The animal slipped on the ice. Man and beast swayed. Then they were safely across the bridge and on to hard-packed earth that was fast turning to mud.

Guy leaned forward and patted his gelding on the neck. "Good boy, Dante."

The horse whickered and tossed its head in regal acceptance. Guy laughed.

They cantered up the hill until the valley spread below them. A light sprinkling of snow blanketed the moor. Gorse, a deep grey-green, was everywhere Guy looked. The wind grabbed at the muffler wrapped around his face and pulled it away. He caught the woollen scarf at the last instant.

He stopped, the muffler safe in his right hand. Below him, where a larger road ran, was a turned-over coach. The axle had broken. The horses did not look hurt from here. A man, whom guy took to be the driver, walked the animals in an attempt to keep them from cooling too rapidly. The accident must have happened recently.

Guy spurred Dante forward until they came abreast of the wreck. He reined in his mount and leapt lightly to the ground, his Hessians crunching rock and ice. "Is anyone hurt?"

The coachman paused only long enough to give Guy a quick once-over, then jerked his head towards a small outcropping of rock. "Her."

A woman lay on the cold ground, a black cape wrapped around her recumbent body. Her eyes were closed and her skin was deathly pale. Wisps of chestnut-coloured hair strayed around her face. Her lips were blue tinged.

Guy's heart skipped a beat.

He crossed the ground and squatted by her. Her chest

rose and fell in rapid, shallow breaths. Relief was sharper than he liked.

"Madam?" he asked softly.

When she did not respond, he took one of her hands. Her fingers were like ice through the black kid of her gloves. She had to be moved to a warm location. Soon.

"How long has she been like this?" he asked, never taking his eyes from her.

"Since I pulled her from the carriage," came the laconic answer.

The man's curt answer told him nothing. Impatience twisted Guy's gut. "How long ago was that?" he asked, biting off each word.

"Thirty, sixty minutes. Don't rightly know for sure."

Guy swallowed a scathing retort. Berating the man would not help the woman.

Letting go of the woman's hand, he slid his arms under her back and thighs and lifted her. She settled against his chest, curling automatically into him. The hood of her cape fell back, and her hair loosened and tumbled down until it nearly touched the ground. Guy paused instinctively, not wanting to tread on the silken strands.

She had beautiful hair. The weak winter sunlight made the thick ripples flash like diamonds tossed into copper. The weight of it pulled her head back, exposing the slim column of her neck. A pulse, weak and quick, beat like a bird's wings. She was delicate and sensual all at once.

And she was hurt.

Guy took a deep breath and looked away from her. The closest place was The Folly. His housekeeper could look after this woman better than the town's apothecary. The nearest doctor was in Newcastle, several hours away.

He whistled and Dante came. There was no way to lift her gently without help. "You, sir," Guy said to the man, who was finally slowing down the horses, "come give me a hand."

The man scowled, his brown brows forming an uninterrupted bar across his forehead. But he came.

Guy handed the woman to him. "Hand her up to me once I'm mounted."

The man hesitated before taking her. "Who'm you be?"

Totally unused to having someone ask his identity, Guy paused in the act of swinging his leg over the saddle. "Viscount Chillings."

"How'm I ter know that?"

A sardonic smile curved Guy's thin lips. "Because I say so. Besides, man, you have no choice. She cannot remain here on the ground in the cold. I am taking her to my home. I will send a groom to help you." The man still did not hand the woman up. "You may count on it." Guy said softly, his eyes narrowing.

Something in the look swayed the man for he finally lifted the woman up. Guy caught her under the arms, her cape initially keeping him from getting a good grip. Finally, after much shifting, she lay precariously in front of him, her back against his chest with his arms around her. He had tucked her glorious hair into the hood of her cape. It was a less than perfect place for such heavy and unbound curls, but it would have to do.

He urged Dante slowly forward. The last thing he or the woman needed was to take a fall. He heard the man return to the horses as he guided Dante to the track that led home. Jane would have to wait until he got this woman situated.

Guy looked down at her. Close to his chest, with his body shielding her from the wind, her face was regaining some colour. Peach blossomed on her high cheekbones, a striking contrast to the rich chestnut of her lashes that lay like a slash against the paleness of her eyelids. Her lips had relaxed into a full, plump pout that must be natural rather than caused by dissatisfaction. Her hair tangled around her face in waves before falling into the folds of her cape.

He realized with an unpleasant start that he wanted her. There was nothing logical about it, only pure desire. He never responded like this to a woman—any woman.

He told himself it was because he had been anticipating his visit to Jane. He had not been with his mistress for long enough that his body was behaving toward this woman like a boy with his first encounter, which was out of character. Guy made it a point not to let himself get carried away by his desires; being aroused by a woman he did not even know and who lay limply in his arms would be getting carried away.

Still, the occasional hint of lavender that wafted from her was enough to make him tighten. Once she stirred and he thought she would waken. She didn't.

They covered ground slowly, giving Guy more than enough time to think. Who was she? Quality from her dress. Where was she bound and why was she alone? He would find out soon enough when she woke. Patience was a virtue he had cultivated while he waited agonizingly for Suzanne to finish her unusually long labour and present him with his heir. Only she had been dying and taking their son with her. Ever since then he had waited for nothing. An event or object was either his for the taking or he walked away.

He roused from his thoughts when The Folly came into view. Without being directed, Dante turned on to the circular drive that passed by the front door and stopped when they reached the steps.

Like the superbly trained butler he was, Oswald was down the marble steps before Guy could summon him. "My lord, let me help."

The butler reached for the still-unconscious woman, and Guy gave her over. The day's cold hit him in the chest and groin, tightening his muscles. It was an uncomfortable reaction.

"Have Mrs Drummond see to her." He turned Dante around and headed for the stables without a backward glance. He would check on the woman and then, if the weather did not worsen, he would go to the village and finish what he had started out to do.

Guy entered the foyer and stamped the ice off his boots. The frozen water turned into puddles on the black-and-white marble squares.

"Tsk, my lord. You know how you dislike any imperfection in The Folly and dirty water is an imperfection," a woman said.

Already irritated with the entire situation, Guy rounded on the speaker. "Mrs Drummond, you are a favoured servant, but even you may only go so far."

She drew herself up to a very imposing height. She was a veritable Hera, her greying hair pulled back into a severe bun, her brown eyes still full of spirit. In her youth she had been Guy's nanny.

"Yes, my lord." She made him a deep curtsy.

Guy sighed and scratched at his beard. "Yes, Mrs Drummond," he said, his tone back to the indulgent one he normally used with her. "Fortunately you hold a spot in my heart."

The smile she always had for him came out. "Yes, my lord, and you in mine. Now, about the girl."

"What about her? She will have to stay here until she is able to travel."

It was not the answer he wanted to give, but there was no other. It boded no good for anyone that she aroused him even when she was unconscious, but he still could not throw her out. He would just have to resist the urgings of his body, something he was more than capable of doing.

"Just as I thought." The older woman eyed the man who had once run to her with every hurt. "I will be chaperon enough, I believe. For now, and for as long as none of your friends realize she is here."

His eyes clouded. He had been so focused on his reaction to the strange woman that he had forgotten about the proprieties. The last thing he wanted to do was compromise a woman of Quality, and he suspected that his unwelcome guest was just that. Then he would have to pay the piper with his freedom. Or, worse still, seduce her.

He had reconciled himself back in June to marrying for convenience. He needed an heir before all else since Dominic was giving no indication of ever marrying. But he intended to marry Miss Duckworth, not some strange woman whose name he did not even know simply because of the proprieties.

"She should not be here long. She did not appear to have injuries," he said, confident of his ability to avoid compromise. "Otherwise, I will need someone besides you for appearance's sake."

"She will be here as long as she needs," Mrs Drummond said, her voice a shade sharp. "She has a head injury. There is a bump the size of a hen's egg on the back of her head. That is very likely why she has not regained consciousness." Mrs Drummond shook her head. "Remember when Miss Annabell fell out of that tree, and she didn't wake up for a day? Like to scare ten years off my life."

Guy remembered only too well. That was only one of his sister's more punishing adventures. Bell had been a hellion. She was still more independent than was acceptable.

But Bell was his sister and that had been a long time ago. The last thing he wanted was for this woman to be confined under his roof for more than a couple of hours, a couple of days at the outside.

"Do you think that is what this woman will do?"

Mrs Drummond shrugged. "Only time will tell. Will you be checking on her?"

He did not need to go near his unwelcome guest any more than he needed to stick his hand in a basket of adders. But it was his duty to see that she was cared for. That meant, to him, looking in on her himself. He trusted his servants, but he was ultimately responsible.

"Later," he said, irritated at the tiny spurt of interest that held him. "After you have seen to her comfort."

Already this woman was causing him trouble. She had prevented his trip to Jane and now she was going to be a burden until she left. Heaven help her if her presence compromised his engagement to Miss Duckworth.

* * *

Hours later, Guy entered the Sylph Room where his unwelcome guest slept. Aqua and jewel-tone shades of green and blue made the chamber seem like an underwater grotto. Mahogany and rosewood furniture mixed like elegant tropical fish. Gossamer curtains done in ever-shifting shades of blue and green framed the high four-poster bed that held the woman.

By the light of the fire, he noticed a young serving girl seated in a corner, her fingers busy darning a stocking. "You may go now, Mary," he told her.

She jumped up and bobbed a curtsy. "Yes, my lord. I dinna know you were here, my lord." Even as the words left her mouth, she skittered to the door.

Guy smiled. She had only been here a fortnight or so. Given time, she would learn that none of his servants feared him. They respected him and he respected them. He found that to be a mutually satisfying arrangement. His parents had taught him the benefits and the burdens of *noblesse oblige*.

He crossed to get the servant's forgotten candle before going to the bed. His guest lay pale as the frost that rimed the windows. Her skin stretched taut and translucent over elegantly formed cheekbones and a pointed chin. Dark circles accentuated her wide-set eyes and drew attention to high arched brows and a thick sweep of lashes. Her lips were still full, pink and pouty. But it was her hair, a gloriously tumbled mess, which caught and held him. The urge to touch the silken strands, to run his fingers through their length, was nearly overwhelming.

He stepped abruptly back. The last thing he needed was to intimately touch this woman. She was alone and under his protection. She was also a woman he would be obligated to marry if he compromised her. Both were arguments that should help him keep his distance.

To hell with her hair.

He took a deep, calming breath and studied the rest of her. The cover was pulled up over her small breasts and tucked around her. Mrs Drummond had found a nightshirt that buttoned up the woman's long, elegant neck, completely hiding the vulnerable pulse he had seen when she had lain in his arms.

The scent of lavender was stronger now. Was it her hair or coming from the clothing Mrs Drummond had dressed her in? Possibly both.

A shift, a moan, and he found himself looking into hazel eyes, ringed in gold. He took a step back.

Her mouth opened and her tongue peeked out. His loins tightened in a response so automatic, so strong, that Guy cursed under his breath.

"Who are you?" His voice was harsher than he had intended.

She blinked. "I…" She closed her eyes and took a deep breath. "Could I please have a drink of water?"

Nonplussed but ever the courteous host, he picked up the jug by the bed and poured her a glass. "Of course." He held out the water. "Can you drink it on your own?"

She watched him with an intensity he found disturbing. "I think so. Thank you."

She edged up in bed and reached for the glass he still held. With a mental expletive at his own awkwardness, he moved closer to the bed so that she could grasp the glass. Her fingers, long and slim, touched his briefly as she took the drink. Her arm trembled but she said nothing, only put the liquid to her lips and drank until it was gone. He took the glass from her just as she sank back into the pillows.

"Thank you," she murmured, her voice low and weak.

"You are welcome," he answered formally, setting the empty container aside. Without asking her permission, he pulled a chair up and sat down so that his face was level with hers. "Now, who are you?"

He knew it was impossible for her to pale more, but it appeared as though she did. Perhaps it was the way she seemed to shrink into the bed.

For long seconds she looked at him before shifting slightly and staring at the fire. Impatience began to gnaw at him, but Guy kept quiet. Finally, she turned back to him.

"I..." She licked her lips. "I don't—can't..." Her eyes widened and their brilliance dimmed. "I don't know." Her voice lowered until he could barely hear her. "I don't know who I am."

He scowled. "The hit on the head." When she turned her bewildered face to him, he repeated, "You hit your head. That probably made you forget who you are. It happened to my sister, but she regained her memory the following day."

Her mouth opened in a soft circle, but she said nothing. It was as though her power of speech was gone along with her memory loss.

He instinctively took her hand and held it between his palms, regretted it as electricity sparked up his arm. Still he did not release her.

"Don't worry. This will not last long."

He smiled even though irritation and worry battled in his gut. The last thing he needed was a lady of Quality in his home, let alone one with no memory and one he was inexplicably drawn to—to put his reaction to her mildly. Yet there was nothing he could do. Until she regained her memory, he could not send her away because no one knew where her way led. And it might take minutes or weeks before she remembered.

She did not return his smile. Her hand lay flaccid in his as though with her memory went not only speech but all sensation.

"It will be all right," he said again. "These things happen."

Her eyes closed and he would swear she cried softly, the tears seeping like crystals from the corners of her eyes. But she made no sound and the light was too weak for him to be sure of what he saw. He waited.

Suzanne had not cried much, but when she had she had wanted him to hold her and just let her cry. It was a painful jolt to remember that now, under these circumstances. He no longer thought about Suzanne as much as he had. Ten years had gone a long way to easing his grief. But he still remembered the pain of losing her and the babe.

Finally the woman opened her eyes. "Thank you," she said softly. "Thank you for your patience."

She was so frail. Much as he wanted to question her further, he knew she needed a rest. He would talk to the man who had driven her coach and see what he knew.

Guy released her hand and stood. "I will send my housekeeper to you. You need to sleep. Really sleep to regain your strength. And in all likelihood when you waken your memory will have returned."

She smiled wanly at him. "Like your sister?" she said softly.

He had not yet reached the door when it opened and

Mrs Drummond bustled in. She glanced at him, saw he was fine and turned her attention and energies on the invalid.

"You poor dear. You must have the headache to end all headaches. The lump on the back of your head is as big as my fist."

The woman's smile widened slightly, but tiredness etched lines around her mouth and eyes. "It does hurt a little."

Mrs Drummond shook her head. "I dare say it hurts more than that. A good dose of laudanum will go far in easing the discomfort."

Suiting action to words, she picked up a small bottle that sat beside the jug, opened it and measured out a dose into the nearby glass. She added water, mixed the concoction and put the glass to the woman's lips.

Guy left.

She drank the opium willingly, unsure which hurt more, her head or the emptiness that filled her. Mrs Drummond smiled at her and took the empty glass from her shaking hands.

"You will feel better when this takes effect," the housekeeper said kindly.

She forced herself to smile at the older woman. "Thank you."

"You rest now," Mrs Drummond said, snuffing the candle by the bed.

She watched the housekeeper leave. She knew the laudanum would ease the pain. Her mouth twisted bitterly. But she did not know her own name and despair welled up in her.

Who was she? Why had she been travelling alone? She did not think women did that. She sighed and closed her eyes. But maybe they did. If she could not remember who she was, how could she trust the memories she did have?

And that man. Viscount Chillings. Heat flushed her cheeks. He had been so arrogant and demanding...and her heart had skipped a beat when she first saw him. Tall, slim and elegant, with eyes so dark a blue they were nearly black. His face was long and thin, aristocratic, with a nose that had the hint of a hook and a mouth that had sent shivers of awareness down her spine. She had hoped he was someone in her life, a lover or husband. But no. He had put paid to that fleeting thought.

He had made it abundantly clear that she was not welcome and would be seen out the door as soon as her memory returned. Yet, he had also been kind when she had given way to emotion and cried. She knew that most men would have lost their patience, although she did not know how she knew that.

She sighed and shifted, trying to get more comfortable. The way her senses had reacted to him, it would be to the better if she left right now. Especially if he was going to be even a little bit caring. But she could not.

The drowsy, floating sensation of the drug began to take hold. With the medication came a sense of emotional ease, the anguish of not knowing who she was fading as sleep claimed her.

She welcomed it.

Chapter Two

The coachman stood before Guy, hat in hand, finally awed by the personage who had rescued them. Behind Guy, the library windows looked out on gardens covered in a light drift of snow. The coachman shifted from scuffed boot to scuffed boot as Guy came around to the front of his desk. Hopefully, this man knew who the woman upstairs was. Otherwise she was going to be his guest for a longer time than he liked.

"The lady you were driving has lost her memory," Guy began without preamble. There was no sense in dragging this interview out. "Therefore, I need your help in finding her family. First, what is her name?"

The man grimaced. "Doan' rightly know, my lord. She gave it as Mrs Smith." He shrugged his massive shoulders while his fingers twisted his woollen cap. "Doan' rightly think that could be her name. But mayhap it is."

Guy swallowed an expletive. The man was probably right. Mrs Smith. How unimaginative. "Mrs. Smith?"

"Yes'm, my lord." Now he twisted the brim of his hat in earnest until it was a screw of material.

"You don't work for her, then." It was a flat statement that did more than any show of anger to convey Guy's growing exasperation.

"No, my lord."

Guy scowled. "You can answer in more than two- and three-word sentences, my good man."

"Yes'm, my lord."

Guy swallowed a sharp retort. He was going to have to pull every bit of information from this man. "Where did she hire you and where was she going?"

"Newcastle-upon-Tyne. London. My lord." The man's Adam's apple bobbed beneath grey stubble.

"Any other details?" Guy asked, impatience creeping into his tone.

"No, my lord."

"Did she pay you with cash or a bank draft?"

"Coin, my lord."

"I am not a bloody Bow Street Runner out to catch you for a crime," Guy said, allowing his irritation to break forth. "There are obviously details that you don't consider important. I want to know them."

"Yes'm, my lord."

Guy eyed him with dislike. Even the surly lout the man had been when Guy found them would be preferable to this oaf he had turned into who could not or would not put effort into his answers. Nothing irritated Guy more than a man or woman who shirked his duty. And it was this man's duty to help the woman upstairs. He had taken her money.

"Did she have much luggage?"

"A portmanteau, my lord."

Not a long stay, then. "Any other luggage?" Most women of his acquaintance carried more than one piece.

"A small leather one, my lord. I brought it and the other here."

Guy nodded. "Was anyone with her when she dealt with you?"

"No, my lord."

Guy leaned back on the edge of his desk, arms crossed, and decided he was getting nowhere fast. But he did not know anything else to ask this man. Ah, one last thing.

"Did she come to you in a carriage?"

"Yes'm, my lord."

"Was there any marking on the carriage? And, if so, what colour was it? Were the horses of good quality?"

"No, my lord. It was a plain black carriage. Decent horses. Probably hired." The man's lips lifted in the beginning of a smile.

Guy smiled back, tightly and not entirely satisfied, but the answer was more detailed than he had expected. The man obviously noticed horseflesh and enjoyed talking about them. He would have to be content with that.

"Thank you. That will be all."

The man's feet shuffled faster but he didn't leave. Guy waited him out.

"About my coach, your lordship."

Guy knew what was coming, but said nothing. The woman had paid coin for her journey. Unless the coach was ruined, the money should be enough to fix it. They were not that far from Newcastle that the man's expenses had taken up the compensation.

The man cleared his throat. "I needed to make a profit on this trip, my lord. Fixing the vehicle will take everything I have left from Mrs Smith's payment."

"And why should she or I pay for the repairs? You

did not take her all the way to London, so you don't have those expenses.''

The coachman's brows drew together. ''Because it was 'cause of her that we turned over. She told me to go fast even though I told her the road was bad. She said she had an appointment that she could not miss or be late for.'' His frown intensified. ''She promised me more money if I did as she bade.''

An appointment she could not miss or be late for. Interesting. ''Did she give you the extra money before you sped up?''

''No, my lord. She said she did not have enough on her. I would get it when we reached London.''

The man did have a claim and this was information that might be useful. At the least, it told him more about the woman. And, if it were true, then she was to blame for the man's broken axle. If the man lied, there was no way he could find that out until she regained her memory. There was nothing for it.

''I will have my smith repair your coach.''

The man nodded. ''Thank you, my lord.''

As though realizing he would get no more and had already tried Guy's patience nearly to exhaustion, he hurried from the room.

Guy watched the door close behind the coachman. How much more was this woman going to inconvenience him? The cost of fixing the coach was negligible. It was the time.

He stood and went to stand in front of one of a series of windows that ran the circular outside wall of the room. Outside the grounds were covered with frost. The artificial lake had a sheen of ice that might be thick enough to skate on. He would have to try it later.

Meanwhile, he had to do something. He crossed to

the fireplace and yanked the bell pull that would call Oswald. The butler was quick.

"My lord?" he said.

Guy smiled at him. "You at least have a brain and a will to use it."

Face impassive, Oswald said, "Yes, my lord."

Guy's smile widened as he told his butler about the interview. "As you can see, the man is dimwitted or lazy or both. I want someone to take the lady's luggage to my rooms. Perhaps there is something in them that will tell us who she is."

"Immediately, my lord."

"If there is nothing of note and she does not regain her memory in the next day or two, I shall send a man to Newcastle."

"Tim would be just the man, my lord. He has family there."

"Good."

Guy turned back to the window. Another inconvenience. Tim was the only Englishman the French chef would tolerate. François would raise the roof if he left.

Oswald left with a purposeful stride. Guy knew he could depend on the servant. He thought briefly about having the luggage brought here instead, but somehow the library seemed too public for her private things.

He would answer his correspondence and check with his factor on estate business and then he would go upstairs. Some things he would not put off.

Several hours later he entered the privacy of his rooms. "Jeffries," he called to his valet.

The gentleman's gentleman materialized from the doorway that led to where Guy's clothing was kept. "Yes, my lord?"

The valet was small and wiry, prim and proper. Impeccably clothed, he ensured that Guy was dressed to the nines—when Guy let him.

"I have some personal business to attend to. I will call you when I need you again."

Jeffries cast a glance at the luggage that sat in the middle of the floor. "As you wish, my lord."

Guy watched him take his leave before going to the woman's toiletry case. It was expensive; tooled leather with silver chasing. The bottles and jars inside were cut crystal with silver tops. The comb and brush were both hallmarked silver, each worked with a capital F and A. Possibly her initials. The toothbrush was immaculate. Everything sparkled. He emptied the case and turned it over, his long fingers working along the edges to see if there was a catch or lever that opened a secret compartment. That was where anything of value would be.

"Ah," he murmured as his fingers detected a tiny projection. Seconds later, a small drawer slid open.

A golden glint caught his attention. He picked up a simple band and took it closer to a candle. Winter's gloom had set in early as usual.

He turned the ring so that he could see inside. Often there was writing. As there was this time. He could barely make out the names Felicia and Edmund. Was this a wedding band? It looked like one. But was it hers? And if it was, why wasn't she wearing it? It was too small to be a man's. It could be her mother's.

Guy laid it on the table by the toiletry case and put everything else back where it belonged. He sat down in one of two large, leather wing-backed chairs that angled around the roaring fire.

She was probably married. He should be thankful.

A married woman might be ostracized if it became known that she had spent time in his bachelor establishment, but she would not be ruined like a maiden would. He would not be required to wed this woman no matter what happened.

Perhaps there was something in her portmanteau that would tell him who she was. He got back up and went to the piece, only to pause with both hands on the clasp. Her intimate apparel would be inside. Somehow that was much more disturbing than looking in the toiletry case had been. But he needed more information than Felicia and Edmund engraved on the inside of a wedding band.

With a quick flick of his fingers, he opened the case. The first thing out was a warm black woollen dress with long sleeves and a high neckline. Nothing like the thin muslins women of fashion wore in London. Guy's lips curved. She was not a slave to the current style. He set that aside.

Next was a pair of fine lawn drawers trimmed in Brussels lace. They slid across his hands like the finest silk. Lavender rose from the gossamer material. Without thought, he put the delicate material to his face and breathed deeply. Lavender, a scent as innocent as linens, yet as provocative as a partially clad woman. His loins tightened in a hard, fast reaction. He dropped the underclothing.

Taking a deep breath, he forced himself to relax. She was only a woman and one he did not even know. The last thing he—or she—needed was for him to desire her.

He left the drawers where they had fallen on the floor and reached for the next item of clothing. Stays. Again the scent of lavender clung to them. Again, he could picture all too vividly the rich material cupping below her small breasts.

This was insane.

He dropped the stays as well and paced to the window, which he opened wide to the freezing evening air. Something needed to cool his unwanted ardour for a strange woman who meant nothing to him.

His reaction was absurd. He had never had this uncontrolled reaction to Suzanne or any other woman, for that matter. He had wanted to protect Suzanne and cherish her. He had enjoyed making love to her, but he had never desired her as wantonly as his body did this unknown woman. Never.

A knock on the door interrupted his unacceptable thoughts. "Come in," he said without leaving the window and the bracing cold of the outside.

"My lord," Mrs Drummond said. "The woman is awake." Her voice lowered. "She still does not know who she is."

Weary and fed up with his unwelcome reactions to the woman, he said, "I believe her name is Felicia. Or that was her mother's. If it is hers, she is probably married to Edmund. If not, he is likely her father."

"Oh," Mrs Drummond said, entering and making her way to the portmanteau and the dropped underclothing. She picked up the drawers and stays. "These are expensive."

"Yes, they are," Guy said, turning at last and watching his housekeeper.

Mrs Drummond picked up the dress and turned it inside out. "Very nicely done. Not the height of fashion as might be seen in London, but top quality."

"I thought so," Guy said drily. A tiny smile tugged

up one corner of his mouth. "It seems she is a lady of means, whoever she is."

"These are all black," Mrs Drummond said. "As was the clothing she had on."

"I know," Guy said solemnly.

"Was there any jewellery?" Mrs Drummond folded the clothes and replaced them in the portmanteau before turning her attention to the toiletry case. She immediately saw the gold band, which lay on the table beside the case. Picking it up, she squinted to see if there was any writing.

Guy took mercy on her older eyes. "Felicia and Edmund are engraved on the inside."

Mrs Drummond raised one grey brow. "Anything about love?"

Guy shook his head, realizing this was the first time it had occurred to him that there might be a term of endearment. "Perhaps it is merely a friendship ring."

"Or a ring given in a marriage of convenience."

"That, too."

Mrs Drummond kept the ring in her hand. "The young lady wishes to speak with you. Take this and show it to her. It might jolt something loose, my lord."

"The sooner she remembers who she is the better." Guy took the ring and left.

Her room was on the floor above. He stopped and knocked on the door, then opened it before she responded.

She lay on the bed, propped up by numerous pillows, her hair spread around her like a fan. A single lit candle provided a golden glow in contrast to the orange flames of the fire. The light caught the ripples of her hair and turned them copper and gold and bronze. He ached to bury his fingers in the thick tresses.

Surely, he was going crazy.

She watched him pace towards her.

Tall, with an arrogant tilt to his long, narrow face, he was an aristocrat from the top of his head to the finely tooled leather slippers on his feet. A short black beard and full moustache softened what she thought was a square jaw. His mouth was wide and well formed, the opposite of thin and pinched.

She paused in her study and wondered where the last thought had come from. Did she know a man whose mouth was thin and pinched, almost cruel in its sparseness?

He passed between her and the fire, throwing his shadow on the bed where she lay. Her attention rushed back to him. From this distance his eyes appeared as dark as his brows, which were drawn into a frown. Yet, his hair was silver. Her senses were on edge from his nearness.

He stopped several feet from the bed and seemed to tower over her. A black satin dressing gown, picked out in a silver pattern that reminded her of chinoiserie, was belted at his narrow waist. A white shirt showed at the V of the robe and black trousers flowed from the robe's hem to his feet. With the exception of his moustache and beard, he was the height of fashion.

She frowned. She knew he was fashionable, yet she did not know her own name or where she was from or where she had been going.

The man—the housekeeper had said he was Guy William Chillings, Seventh Viscount Chillings—pulled a slipper chair covered in ice blue satin up to the bed. She watched him sit down with the grace of a man who was familiar with his own body. A shiver skipped down her spine.

She chided herself. For all she knew, she was married. The thought of marriage made her uncomfortable, as though the idea were repugnant. But there was no other sensation, no remembrance of a man touching her, kissing her. Nothing. A sigh escaped her.

Viscount Chillings leaned forward. "Have you remembered something?"

His voice was a low, smooth baritone, seductive in its beauty. Its elegant tone suited him.

"No," she managed.

"No," he repeated, his voice wrapping around the word and making it seem nearly a term of endearment.

She shook her head in an attempt to clear it of this fancifulness. His voice did unusual things to her, made her think of things better left unsaid and undone. When she had herself under better control, she spoke. "Nothing, really, Lord Chillings."

He crossed one leg over the other. "That is too bad. I had hoped you would be back to normal by now." His eyes narrowed as he held out his hand. "Perhaps this will help."

Gold flashed in the light from the candle. A wedding band rested in the palm of his hand. She stared at it for what seemed like a long time. He continued to hold the piece of jewellery towards her as though he intended her to take it. She did not want to. She had an unreasonable aversion to the ring.

She looked back at him. If he noticed her reluctance, his face did not show that awareness. His eyes, cool and detached in their impersonal perusal, were a deep blue and hooded by heavy lids. Lashes, black and thick as a mink pelt, softened his gaze—but not much.

"Take it," he said, his voice a curt command.

She reached for the ring but, before she touched it,

her hand fell back to her side. "Where did you get it, my lord?"

He lounged back and crossed his right leg over his left knee, the pose so casual they might have been discussing the weather instead of the disaster in her life. A tiny kernel of resentment formed in her.

"From your travelling case."

The kernel blossomed into a knot of irritation. Not even the insane attraction he held for her could stop the sense of having been encroached upon that left her cold.

"You went through my things without my permission? You violated my privacy."

He tossed the ring up and caught it, his gaze never leaving her. "You were asleep so could not give me permission." Her chin notched up and he added, "I do what I must. No one knows who you are or where you are from."

"That does not give you the right to go through my belongings."

"My position gives me the right."

She stiffened. Grateful as she had been before, she could not and would not suppress the anger his trespassing created. He had no right to search her things, no matter what he thought.

"To abuse your guest's privacy?"

He shrugged. "It is not as though you are invited."

"That still—"

"Enough." He leaned forward and thrust the ring at her. "Take it. The last thing I need in my life at the moment is an uninvited woman in my house unchaperoned. Yet, here you are."

She ignored the ring and glared at him. "If I am such a burden, then you should not have taken me in."

His lip curled sardonically. "When I find a woman unconscious in the middle of the road and it is snowing, I do not leave her there to freeze to death."

"Perhaps you should have since you seem to regret it so."

He looked at her, his face hard, and dropped the ring on to the bed. "Put it on and see if it fits. There are two names inscribed on the inside. One might be yours. Felicia."

"Felicia?" she murmured. "No, I don't remember that name." But it felt comfortable. She did not have an aversion to it as she did to the ring. "Perhaps."

He continued to stare down at her, his will implacable. She would have to do his bidding or they would stay like this for ever. Much as she did not want to touch the ring, she disliked this stalemate more.

She took a deep breath and picked the band up, handling it carefully as though it might snap at her. She turned it around, looking at it from all sides. Putting it close to the candle flame, she could just make out the engraving.

He had said two names. She was not sure she wanted to know the second, for surely it was a man's. Yet, this apprehension over a name was silly.

"What is the second name?"

"Edmund."

His deep rich voice clipped the name. She glanced at him, wondering why she sensed animosity in him about the name. Surely she was being fanciful. His dislike was aimed at her for the inconvenience of her being here. Nothing more. Nor did his expression tell her anything other than he was tired of this entire situation and wished it over.

"Edmund," she murmured. "It is no more familiar

than Felicia.'' But she did not feel the same warmth for it as she did for Felicia.

''Put the ring on,'' he said, impatience making his voice husky. ''See if it fits.''

''I...'' For some unfathomable reason, she felt an aversion to wearing the ring. ''Perhaps this is not mine. I don't want to wear it.''

She dropped it on to the bed and looked away from it. Why would she feel this way about the ring? Her reactions made no sense.

''It might be your mother's.''

She looked at him to see if he might actually think so. As she was beginning to expect, his face showed nothing of what he thought. The irritation of seconds before was gone as though it had never existed. He did stroke his beard, something she had not seen him do before.

She told herself she was being silly. The ring was only an object. If it fitted, then it might be hers, in which case her name would likely be Felicia. Edmund would be her husband. Even should it fit her that did not definitely mean it was hers, only that it was her size. Still, her reluctance to put it on was surprising.

Enough. She grabbed the ring and jammed it on to her wedding finger. The perfect size. She looked up at her reluctant host.

He watched her. ''In your travel case there is a brush and comb set with a mirror. The initials F and A are the centre of the design. They are also on the lids of all the vials and bottles. The case is not old. Perhaps several years.''

Her mouth dropped. Not in surprise, but anger. ''How dare you? Finding the ring was not enough. First you violate my privacy, next you take your own time telling me everything you have found. You knew from the start that this ring very likely was mine and that my name almost assuredly is Felicia.''

The fingers of his right hand drummed on his thigh. ''I wanted to see if the ring would bring any memories before I told you anything else. I did not want to create preconceived ideas in you.''

She glared at him. ''You are the most arrogant and thoughtless man.''

He drew himself up. ''As I told you before, I do what I feel necessary.''

Bitterness welled up inside her. It was sudden and far exceeded what this man had done. It seeped out in her voice. ''Don't all men, regardless of who they hurt in doing so?''

''Someone must do the difficult things in life.''

Another comment like that and she would be hard pressed not to throw something at him. For some reason, she responded more strongly to his arrogant assumption that he could do with her and her belongings as he saw fit than she had responded to the ring or the initials...or even her loss of memory.

Strange. She did not think she was an unreasonable woman, but then she did not know who she was. Her chest tightened. If he had not been here, she knew she would cry. She would cry from fear and anger and... and loss.

Instead, she sank back into the multitude of pillows, the anger seeping from her to be replaced by exhaustion. ''Is there anything else, Lord Chillings, that you know about me from snooping in my belongings? Something that I, perhaps, should know as well?''

His eyes narrowed, but he made no comment on her sarcasm. ''One other thing, yes.''

When he did not come out and say what it was, she said, "I suppose you will tell me when you are good and ready. Perhaps tomorrow?"

He studied her for long minutes. "That might be better."

His voice was low and without a hint of snideness or even coldness. She could almost think he was considering her vulnerability and trying to protect her from something that would be even more trying than what had just transpired. But she would have none of that.

"Tell me now. In for a penny, in for a pound, as the saying goes. Nothing can be worse than losing my memory and being an unwelcome guest in a strange man's home." ·

"You think not?" he murmured, his deep baritone sounding like a beautiful dirge. "I hope so, for your sake."

His mouth, which had been a straight line of disapproval, softened, showing sensual curves and a fullness she had not expected. She could almost think he felt sorry for her.

"Well?" she prompted.

"Don't you think you have gone through enough for one day?"

His sudden compassion and the words he used set off alarm bells. Her pulse quickened.

"Been in a wrecked carriage and lost my memory. Is there something worse?"

He stood and put the chair back in its place. "Perhaps."

"You are making this harder."

He turned to her. "I suppose I am, and I had not intended to do so. Fortunately, you seem to be a strong woman."

There was nothing to say to that. She did not know if she was strong. She did not know if she wasn't.

"All your clothes are black," he said softly. "Unrelieved."

"Mourning," she murmured. "I must have lost someone close to me and within the last year."

He nodded.

Somehow, she knew that to be true. There was a sense of emptiness that rushed in on her. She had not noticed it before in her preoccupation with her memory loss. Now that void loomed like a chasm ready for her to fall into. His words must have triggered her response. But whom had she lost?

The tightness that had caught her chest earlier returned. Her stomach clenched. She turned her face from his gaze. This grief, for someone she did not even remember, was too private for him to witness.

"Please. Please go," she said, holding back tears by sheer strength of will.

"I will send Mrs Drummond to you," he said quietly.

"No. Please. No one." She took a deep breath. "Not yet."

The housekeeper would want to give her laudanum. Laudanum would numb her pain and her emotions. She did not want that. Not yet. Hurtful as this was, it might jar her memory. She could hope.

"Are you sure?" he persisted.

"Yes," she whispered.

She could not look at him. She did not want him to see the hurt she knew was in her eyes. Her vulnerability. Or the tears that were flowing now in spite of her determination that they not start until he was gone. It was as though something inside her had broken.

"As you wish."

Relief flooded her at his agreement. She heard the door close and knew he was gone. She felt a sudden and inexplicable sense of terrible aloneness. At least while he was with her, there was the chance of human warmth and kindness. Never mind that he had shown neither—this time.

Drat the man. Drat him for invading her privacy. Drat him for telling her she was in deep mourning and opening this abyss of grief. And drat him for leaving her to suffer through this alone.

Then she was lost. She fell into the dark chasm of grief over a loss she could put no name to, but sensed was immense. Tears flowed. Her chest rose and fell in gasping little sobs. Her hands twisted the sheets and she burrowed her face into the pillows, not wanting to see the world.

Her heart knew what her mind did not. Whatever it had been, her loss had been devastating.

Guy stayed outside her door to insure that no servant intruded on her and listened to her sob as though her heart was breaking. More than anything, he wanted to go back in and comfort her. He wanted to hold her and stroke his hands down the thick fall of hair that seemed heavier than her delicate neck could hold. He wanted…

He wanted things that he should not even think about, let alone desire.

Her crying lessened, jogging him from his unwelcome thoughts. He had not known he was so attuned to her that he would realize she had quieted.

He should have been gentler with her, but she had goaded him with her anger over what he had done. Then she had called him arrogant. Suzanne had often called him that, and high-handed, and many other things that all meant the same thing. This woman saying the nearly exact words had made him uncomfortable.

Yes, he was autocratic.

Silence came from the room at last. The urge was strong to go back in and make sure she was okay. But it would do no good and probably harm. He reacted to her in ways that might provoke him to do more than he wanted.

He crossed the hall to where a sconce held a flickering candle. He plucked the light free and headed to his own room.

Chapter Three

She woke with a sigh. She still remembered nothing, not even her name. Mrs Drummond came in as she was getting up, and helped her to dress.

She glanced at the bottle of laudanum sitting on the table by her bed. Yesterday she had been grateful for its numbing of her pain, both physical and emotional. But yesterday was gone and she needed to move on. Somehow, she had to discover who she was.

Still, her head hurt with a dull throb that made it hard to think. The opium would be welcome, although she knew it would dull her concentration as well as the pain.

But no. She did not like being dependent on the drug. She sighed. Had she been this way before her accident? Was she always loath to take medication? Or just laudanum? She did not know.

To take her mind off the discomfort, she turned back to study herself in the full-length mirror, framed in mahogany inlaid with rosewood. She looked like a crow. Black shrouded her from top to bottom. Her hair was scraped back and knotted at the nape of her neck into a thick chignon. Even so, tendrils escaped. She was paste white and dark circles under her eyes made her look sick. Black did not become her.

Mrs Drummond hovered in the background, tsking. "You must be in deep, deep mourning, ma'am. Everything in your portmanteau is solid black. Nothing in white and black stripes for half-mourning."

She continued staring at herself. "This is not a becoming colour, but somehow it seems familiar. I think I have been dressed like this for a long time."

Mrs Drummond shook her head. "If only we knew. His lordship was talking to Oswald, the butler, only this morn. Seems he is going to send someone to Newcastle-upon-Tyne." At the younger woman's raised brow, she added, "The coachman you hired said you started there."

"I did?" She turned from her unbecoming reflection. "The only thing that comes to mind about the city is that it produces a large quantity of coal. But anyone would know that."

Mrs Drummond pursed her lips. "Perhaps. I know that, but I've lived my entire life here. His lordship probably knows."

She shrugged. "Well, that is all I can think of about the place."

She reached for a black wool shawl trimmed in black tassels. Mrs Drummond helped her drape it over her shoulders. The heavy weave would keep her comfortable. As modern as this house seemed, this room was large and even the state-of-the-art fireplace did not send its heat to all the corners.

"His lordship is in the breakfast room, ma'am. I will show you the way."

"I am sure you are much too busy to be spending time with me like this."

Mrs Drummond smiled. "I am busy. But his lord-ship has instructed me to see that you are well taken care of. A lady needs a lady's maid, but none of the young girls have the skills. As for escorting you to his lordship, I could leave that to a footman, but I wish to show you myself."

She returned the older woman's smile. Mrs Drum-mond was obviously a loved and respected servant who did her job well and then did as she pleased. Fortu-nately for the Viscount, anything the housekeeper wanted to do would only benefit him.

"As you wish, Mrs Drummond."

Instead of going to the door where the housekeeper stood, she moved to the dressing stand where her toi-letry case sat. As though from long practice, her hand went to the lever that opened the hidden drawer. The compartment slid out and the gleam of gold caught her eye.

She had returned the ring last night after she had woken from her grief-induced sleep. Silly as it seemed now, in the morning light, she had not wanted the thing on her finger.

"There is no doubt the case is yours, ma'am," Mrs Drummond said. "You know your way around it like his lordship does this house."

Momentarily distracted, she paused in the act of reaching for the piece of jewellery. But her attention came instantly back to the ring. The case was hers. The clothes she wore fitted her as though they had been made for her so they had to be hers. The ring also fitted her perfectly.

Her fingers brushed the gold, but stopped short of picking it up. She shook her head. What was the matter with her? Putting the clothes on had saddened her, but when they were on she had felt right about wearing them. But the ring had never felt right. Why?

Overreacting. She was overreacting. Nothing more. She picked up the plain band and slipped it on her left ring finger, where a wedding ring should be. A shudder ran bone deep through her. This ring had to hold unhappy memories for her.

Very likely she was a widow, hence the deep mourning and this sense of great loss. That had to be it. She removed the ring from her left hand and shifted it to her right.

She hastened to the door and through it, eager to be somewhere else now that she had made a decision. She strode into the hallway where elaborately chased silver sconces each held two lit candles. Walnut panelling rose to midway on the walls where it was met by sage green watered damask that went to the high ceiling. She marvelled at the wealth needed to create this beauty.

"This way, ma'am."

Mrs Drummond's summons and stately figure led her down a long corridor to a set of curving stairs. A silver banister, designed like ivy, led the way to a small foyer floored in creamy marble. Mrs Drummond continued across this area and into a hall, which formed a half-moon until the apogee where it spilled into a sumptuously furnished games room done in shades of blue. A billiard table held pride of place. They passed around the table and through the room to where the hall continued its half-moon course. Windows stood every ten feet, framing what she knew must be a very lovely garden during the spring and summer. Right now, the lawn and shrubs were dusted with snow. The trees stood bare, their gnarled limbs in stark relief against the grey winter sky.

They walked into the main entrance and she gasped. The ceiling was three storeys above them where a circular stained-glass window fashioned into a coat of arms formed the dome. The weak winter sun sent pale beams of blue and green light drifting to the white marble under their feet. It was like being in an underwater grotto.

"Did Viscount Chillings build this place?" she asked in awe when Mrs Drummond paused. "It seems very modern."

"His lordship's father, the Sixth Viscount, started The Folly, but the current Viscount finished it." Her face glowed with pride. "He was such a mischievous boy and accomplished young man."

Some of her former animosity toward Viscount Chillings faded in light of the other woman's emotion. "You must love him very much."

Mrs Drummond nodded. "I raised him and would do anything for him."

"How very fortunate for him," she said sincerely in spite of her own opinion about the man.

She could not help but smile warmly at the older woman. Mrs Drummond radiated love and devotion. There must be more to the Viscount than the one act of kindness buried in among the actions of aggression that he had shown her yesterday.

"The door across the foyer is the breakfast room," Mrs Drummond said. "Where the footman is standing."

"Thank you very much for your help," she said.

Mrs Drummond gave her a brief curtsy and left. She looked across the open expanse to the footman. He was young and attractive in his suit of sage green piped with silver. His white stockings were pristine.

She crossed to the young man, her slippered feet making no sound. He bowed deeply when she stopped in front of him.

"His lordship is expecting you."

She nodded and smiled at him.

He opened the door, and announced, "Madam Felicia."

She gave him a startled glance. *Madam Felicia?* Then she gave a mental shrug. There was nothing else to call her. She was obviously the Felicia of the ring and must have been married and now widowed. There was no other explanation she could think of.

She nodded to the footman as she passed him. The room was delightful, light and airy even though it was winter. French doors opened on to an orangery and the green growth lent the warmth of living things. The walls were done in sage green, as so much of the house seemed to be. It must be his family colour.

Viscount Chillings stood by the table, monogrammed linen napkin in hand, and waited for her. She made him a brief curtsy.

"Your lordship."

He nodded. "Call me Chillings."

"As you wish."

"Please have a seat. Oswald will bring anything you wish." He waited till she sat before resuming his place.

The butler was at her side immediately. He was as short and round as Mrs Drummond was tall and slim. His sparse grey hair was combed from one side to the other and smoothed down with a pomander. A twinkle lurked in the back of his grey eyes.

"What may I get you, ma'am?"

She smiled. "Toast and tea, please."

"Kippers, eggs, kidneys, chocolate?" he recited the list.

"No, thank you. I am not a large breakfast eater." No sooner were the words out of her mouth, than Felicia paused. "How can I know that—for I do—when I don't even know my name?"

Chillings took a sip of black coffee. "How indeed? I believe the human brain is a cipher." He cut a piece of kidney and ate it slowly, his attention never leaving her. "Have you remembered anything else?"

"No. Or if I have, I don't realize it yet."

Oswald appeared with her tea and toast. She put a generous helping of sugar and cream into the beverage. Then spread marmalade on a triangular wedge of toast.

"It is delightful to have something solid to eat." She swallowed the toast and followed with a sip of tea.

"You tire of sickroom food."

The cynical gleam in his eyes made her realize how ungrateful she must sound. "Mrs Drummond was perfectly right to feed me calve's-foot jelly and weak tea, but surely you will agree that those are nothing compared with what you are eating now."

"True." The ghost of a smile lifted one corner of his mouth, softening the harshness of his face. "I remember eating that particular diet many times. She swore it would make me feel better." His smile became a grin, showing strong white teeth. "Perhaps she was right. I always got better."

Felicia laughed. "Perhaps you would have got better anyway."

"Perhaps, but I would never have suggested that. I would have got my ears boxed."

"I doubt she would have gone so far as to do that."

"Mrs Drummond would go as far as she deemed necessary to keep my brother, sister and myself on the path of health and honour."

He finished his kidneys and drank the last of his coffee, the hard angles of his face no longer the arrogant slashes Felicia remembered so well from the previous night. He was a totally different man from the one who had questioned her so unmercifully.

She found herself smiling broadly at him before she realized what she was doing. His sharing this bit of his childhood with her, and doing so with humour, charmed her.

As she waited for him to continue talking, he leaned back in his chair and templed his fingertips. The amusement left his countenance. Seeing the change come over him, Felicia's sense of ease fled.

"I have started some inquiries about you." His baritone was flat, the music gone, as though the sharing of moments before had never happened. She was back to being the strange, unwelcome woman to whom he was a reluctant host. "Or they will start as soon as my man gets to Newcastle-upon-Tyne."

"Newcastle-upon-Tyne?" she echoed him. "Mrs Drummond said the coachman had brought me from there, but I don't remember the place or seem to know much about it."

"Nothing?" The cynicism she remembered so well from the night before crept back into his tone.

"Nothing much. As I told her, I know that it is a large coal centre."

"Most people know that." He took a drink of fresh coffee. "Most educated people, that is, with an awareness of the world outside their own village or home."

"I realize that." Exasperation made it easy to be

curt. "Perhaps you have forgotten that I have lost my memory?"

He set his cup down with a clink. "No, I have not."

"So, as I said before, why there?"

"It is the most logical place to start. The man whose coach you were in said that is where you hired him to take you to London as quickly as possible." He stopped a moment. "He blames your haste for the accident."

She drew herself up. "That is all very convenient since I cannot gainsay him."

Ill use over the entire situation welled up in her. No memory, and now some strange man was blaming her for an expensive wreck that might have killed them both, and she could say nothing in her own support. And he might very well be correct.

"Did he say why I wanted to go to London in such a hurry?"

"You have or had an urgent appointment and you paid him handsomely."

Her brows drew together. "Where did I get the money?"

Chillings's mouth curled sardonically. "From your dress and travelling case, I would say you are not a woman in poverty."

"But am I wealthy enough to hire a private coach to take me all the way to London?"

"It would seem that way. Although, it appears not wealthy enough to have a travelling chaise of your own."

She sighed. "Another piece of the puzzle, and like the others it does me no good."

"Yet." He stood. "With luck, someone in Newcastle will know who you are."

"And how will you find that out?" She stood so that he would not tower over her. The resultant feeling of being overwhelmed was not one she wanted to repeat.

"My man will put an advertisement into the papers. Farfetched, but a start. He will also visit solicitors. If you are a woman of means, you will have a solicitor."

She nodded her understanding. Much as she was not sure she even liked him, she had to give the devil his due. "Very smart of you, my lord. I am not sure I would have thought of those things."

He looked down at her, his eyes inscrutable. "I am sure you would have eventually." To ruin the compliment, he added, "You are not a stupid woman."

She clamped her mouth closed to keep from making a scathing comment. She looked around the room, searching for something to discuss other than how he annoyed her. She found it in a portrait over the fireplace's pink marble mantel. She had noticed it earlier, but before she could comment on it, she had seen him waiting for her. All else had fled from her mind. Much as he irritated her, he drew her. Not a good thing. Even now, determined as she was to change the topic of conversation, just thinking of him made her lose her thread of thought. She forced herself to study the portrait.

A young woman sat in fashionable dishabille, her pale blonde hair falling around her shoulders like fine lace. Large blue, almost grey, eyes looked out on the world with confidence. Her mouth was a red cupid's bow. The white gown she wore draped a full bosom and hinted at a tiny waist. She was a Beauty.

Felicia looked from the Beauty to her host and saw him looking at the portrait. There was a stillness about him that she had not seen before. Who was this woman?

As though he heard her unspoken question, Chillings said flatly, his voice barely audible, "My wife."

The tension in him made Felicia incredibly uncomfortable. But if she was honest with herself, and she thought that she normally was, she must admit to a twinge of something very like jealousy. Surely not. How could she be jealous of a woman in a portrait and over a man she did not even know and was not even sure she liked?

She wished she had not even looked at the portrait. She wished she had left and gone to the boredom and safety of her chamber. But it was too late.

She had to say something now. "She is lovely." Her words were inadequate to describe his wife, but Felicia wanted nothing more than a change of topic.

"Was," he said softly.

Felicia gasped in dismay. Chillings had suffered a loss as great as her own. Sympathy for the man, and a sense of connection with him, overwhelmed her. She reached a hand to his arm, only to draw it abruptly back. She did not know him well enough to touch him, and she sensed that he would not welcome her compassion.

Instead, she settled for more inadequate words. "I am so sorry."

He looked at her now, his face grim. "It was a long time ago."

She nodded, helpless to ease his pain or the tension that was so thick it could be cut with the proverbial knife. Of all the things Mrs Drummond had talked about, Felicia wished strongly that this had been one of them.

The need to comfort, and knowing she could not, knotted her stomach. Desperate to change the subject, she said, "I would like to speak with the coachman I hired. I don't wish to impose on your hospitality longer. It is time I continued to London."

He turned to face her. Emotions moved across his face, the most prominent being anger. "Are you always so difficult?"

She took a step back, not having expected his attack. "I beg your pardon, Lord Chillings. I am trying to do the right thing. You have been more than plain about the inconvenience of my staying here, not to mention the impropriety."

He pivoted on his heel and stalked to the door. "A woman on her own, with no memory of who she is or where she is going or why, should not be on the road alone. I would have thought you intelligent enough to realize that."

The knot in her stomach tightened. His hurtful words put up her back. "Not when you are constantly reminding me of how unwanted I am. I have no wish to further discommode you. Please summon the coachman for me."

"He left. Yesterday." He bit the words off.

She gaped. "You let him leave? After I had paid him to take me to London and without asking me? You are very high-handed."

He gripped the doorknob with enough strength to turn his knuckles white. "I did what I thought best. You were in no condition to travel. Furthermore, where would you go in London? You did not even know you were headed there."

She tossed her head and to her chagrin one of the pins holding the thick roll of hair secured to her nape flew out and landed on the carpet. A strand fell to her shoulder, and with it, she was sure, fell her dignity. Instinctively, her hands lifted to tuck the errant piece back in. She stopped herself. Let it be.

"No, I did not, but now I do. Surely I also told him where I wished to go in London."

"No, you did not. Evidently you planned on telling him when you arrived."

She frowned. "Why was I so secretive?"

He released the doorknob and took a step toward her. "I've no idea, but you have certainly made it difficult for us to find out who you are."

She drew herself up, refusing to let him intimidate her with his approach. "Whatever I was doing, it must have been extremely important to me and I obviously did not want anyone to know I was doing it. Perhaps if I saw the coachman I would remember something. Surely I would not entrust myself to a man I could not depend on not to harm me."

"One would hope," he said, his lip curling. "But that is neither here nor there. He is gone. If you continue to London, I or one of my people will escort you."

This was becoming more and more surreal. "You most certainly will not. I am not your responsibility."

He took another step towards her. "Much as I dislike it, you became my responsibility the minute I picked you up from the snow unconscious."

"You put far too great an importance on your rescue."

"Do I?"

His voice was dangerously low. His eyes seemed to devour her, his gaze lingering on the strand of hair that tumbled down her shoulder. She tried desperately to ignore the tremors running through her body, but it was nearly impossible. She was not afraid of him. No, never that.

"Yes, you do. Anyone could have found me and brought me to their home." Her voice rose the tiniest bit. "I am obviously able to care for myself. And I must be a woman alone and used to being so, otherwise a man, or at the very least a maid, would have accompanied me."

"You are certainly foolhardy. A maid should have accompanied you regardless of whether or not you have male relatives."

He was right and she could not refute it. Her memory of who she was might be gone, but she knew well enough what propriety demanded. Why had she travelled without a maid? She shook her head and some of her bravado dissipated.

"Yes, I should have had a maid."

A glint of something that might be humour entered his dark blue eyes. The tension that had radiated from his body seconds before lessened. Against her better judgment, she was disappointed.

"Capitulation?" he asked, his rich voice low.

"Agreement."

"Ah."

He was so smug. She notched her chin up. "But that does not excuse your high-handed dismissal of the coachman. How am I to get to London now?" He opened his mouth, but she forestalled him. "And do not say you or one of your people will take me, for I won't allow it. I am not your concern."

"I will not argue the point with you any more. My sister, Lady Annabell Fenwick-Clyde, will be here in several days."

"Not for my sake," she blurted out. "I shall be gone by then."

He took another step towards her. She took a step back. The last thing she wanted was to be more indebted to this arrogant man. She did not want to cause him or his family any more inconvenience than she already had. Nor did she want to remain in such close proximity to him. He disturbed her too much.

"Not for your sake, ma'am. Mine."

"Yours? Whatever do you mean?"

"Exactly that. Mine. If word gets about that you have been under my roof unchaperoned, the pressure will be brought to bear on me to make a respectable woman of you."

"What?" Her voice rose in earnest. "Make a respectable woman of me?" Her shoulders straightened. "I may not remember who I am, but I know what I am. I am a respectable woman already, whether *your* reputation is compromised or not. Nor would I marry you."

She stopped in full tirade. Her eyes widened as she realized what she had said. He took another step toward her, bringing him much too close. She could almost feel the heat radiating from his lithe body. She was a fool twice over.

"I could not marry you, even should we both wish it." She raised one white hand to forestall the comment she knew was on the tip of his tongue. "I am a widow of recent bereavement."

All her bravado and energy seeped from her. It was an effort not to sit back down and put her face into her hands. She fought the urge, remained standing and looked him square in the eye.

"Yes, you are. And I am engaged. Totally out of the

question, no matter what anyone might say." His voice had a husky quality that made her think of loss and something else she could not, would not, name. "Consequently, my sister is coming as soon as possible."

She nodded, all words gone. *He was engaged.* Of course he was. And she was a recent widow. Silly to have imagined anything else.

His gaze remained on her. "If you will excuse me, ma'am. I have work to do."

She nodded again, her emotions numb. Too much was happening, too fast. He strode from the room without a backward glance at her.

She turned back to the portrait.

Chapter Four

Being lonely was not a good enough reason for accepting Viscount Chillings's invitation to dinner, Felicia decided. This was her seventh day here and she had long ago decided she was far too attracted to him—and he was engaged to another woman. This was refined torture. Nor did it do her any good to tell herself that she was a widow. She did not feel like a widow, she felt like a woman sitting far too close to a man she found exciting.

She was on his right side at a beautiful satinwood-inlaid walnut table that went the length of the large dining room. Behind her, ceiling-to-floor windows, draped in cream and sage velvet curtains, looked on to the grounds and could be opened in warmer weather for access to the terrace. Across from her, the fireplace filled nearly one-third of the wall. Above the imported Italian marble of the mantel, and flanked by gilt candelabra that were at least four feet tall, hung a portrait.

The late Viscountess Chillings.

This time her pose was formal. Her dress was high-waisted and pale pink silk over a white muslin under-skirt. The style was from years before when Grecian simplicity was the height of fashion. Her hair was cut short and curled around her face, accentuating her wide-set eyes and full, red cupid's bow mouth. Her complexion was the traditional roses and cream. If anything, she was more beautiful in this portrait than in the one in the breakfast room.

Yet, as lovely as her face was and as perfectly formed as her figure was, it was the necklace that held Felicia's attention. A triple strand of large, perfectly matched white pearls circled the Viscountess's slender neck. They were caught at the base of her throat by a magnificent emerald that had to be the size of a goose's egg. That gem was surrounded by diamonds. A piece of jewellery one would never forget. A piece of jewellery that would pay to feed a thousand or more people for their entire lives.

She had known from the estate that Viscount Chillings was wealthy. This necklace told her he was rich as Golden Ball. No wonder he worried about women trying to trap him into matrimony. He must be the most eligible bachelor in England or, if not that, close.

The butler set a bowl of turtle soup in front of her, making her look away from the portrait. "Thank you, Oswald." She smiled at him.

His mouth curved in the hint of a returned smile. "You are very welcome, ma'am."

She looked at the array of cutlery set before her and marvelled that she knew which one was the soup spoon. She had no personal knowledge of herself, but she seemed to know everything pertinent to the world around her.

She took a sip of soup. "Your cook is excellent, Chillings."

He nodded. "François is French. Returned with me from Paris."

"Paris? Were you there after Waterloo?" She took another sip while Oswald poured her white wine.

She sensed rather than saw Chillings tense. His face flushed a deeper tan. But when he spoke there was no sign of emotion in his voice, other than that of polite conversation.

"Yes. I was one of the Duke's aide-de-camps. I went with him to Paris when he left Brussels."

She longed to ask him for stories of his travels, but sensed that this, like the topic of his wife, was not one he wanted to dwell on. She was surprised when he continued on his own.

"I enjoyed Paris very much. It seemed that the entire British aristocracy went there with Wellington. Parties went on round the clock, given by us and the French aristocrats who had been restored to their lands and titles." He laughed. "The things that were done in the name of entertainment."

She watched animation ease the lines at his mouth and decided that she must have been mistaken earlier when she thought the topic bothered him.

"I had heard that everyone was giddy with victory."

His eyes narrowed and he watched her carefully over the rim of his wine glass. "You had? From whom?"

Nonplussed, she stopped eating. "I…" She shook her head. It was as though a wisp of memory came to her only to disappear like fog on a hot morning. Frustration was like a cord around her throat, choking her. "I don't recall. Only that I heard such."

As though he realized her discomfort, he finished his wine and set the glass down. "Anyway, the goal was to see who could give the most elaborate ball or which woman would wear the most *outré* clothes. I remember one chap riding a fully caparisoned horse up the front steps, through the hall and into the ballroom of one of Paris's most grand and old hotels. The owner was not thrilled, but could say nothing when all his guests cheered on the brazen fellow and his mount.''

Felicia felt indignant for the poor host. ''I dare say he did not appreciate such treatment. I imagine you would not like anyone doing such a thing here.''

''I would have the churl horsewhipped.''

She blinked. He had gone from amiable to blood-thirsty so quickly. ''I beg your pardon?''

He smiled, thin and cruel. ''I would have him horse-whipped.''

Her appetite for turtle soup gone, she sipped the fine, dry French wine Oswald had poured. ''You have a magnificent estate. I can understand that it would upset you to have someone do such a thing.''

''Yes, it would.'' He set down his glass and sig-nalled Oswald to bring the next course. ''The Folly was started by my father, but he died before finishing it. I had it completed and the grounds landscaped. Capa-bility Brown started them, but fashion has changed.''

She nodded, following what he said. ''In what way has fashion changed?''

Oswald delivered the next course, which comprised several meats and removes. He poured a clear red wine this time.

Chillings warmed to his topic. ''We are more infor-mal than our fathers were. In the past years, I have had the course of the Rye River diverted by weir dams so that it runs closer to the house. There is even a lake within several minutes' walk, which you can see from the library. The plantings are wilder and less structured, more casual. Things like that.''

Felicia understood what he was saying, but was positive that she had no personal experience of these changes. "That sounds very different. Something the Prince Regent might do.''

Chillings smiled. "Something he has already done at Brighton.''

"Ah, the Pavilion.''

Chillings sipped his wine and watched her over the rim. "You have no memory about yourself, but you are remarkably well versed with many other subjects. Strange how the human mind works.''

She cut into her roast beef with its fine French sauce. "It is disconcerting, to say the least.''

"I can imagine so.''

He finished his wine and Oswald immediately poured more. Seeing the butler's attentiveness, Felicia told herself to remember not to drain her glass. Somehow she did not think she had a head for drink of any sort.

"Well,'' she said, wishing to take the talk away from her, "you seem very interested in your estate.''

"It has occupied a great deal of my time in the past ten years or so. I have even considered building a seaside cottage, but have contented myself with building a small lakeside cottage for picnicking and such.''

"If it is anywhere even remotely as well done at this house, then it must be delightful.''

"Thank you. If time permits, I will take you there tomorrow. It is just outside the terrace.''

"I don't wish to cause you any more trouble, Lord Chillings, than I already am,'' Felicia said steadily, looking him in the eye.

"As you wish," he drawled.

Oswald removed the latest course and set out the dessert trays. There was a dizzying array of sweets. Felicia found herself tempted to try everything, so she did.

She laughed lightly. "I must have a prodigious sweet tooth."

"It would appear that way," Chillings said, helping himself to a syllabub.

Felicia rose after dessert. "Thank you so much for inviting me, Lord Chillings. I have greatly enjoyed talking to you about your estate and the building and improvements you have done."

He rose and bowed. "My pleasure, ma'am."

She turned to go and noticed the painting hanging above the door she had entered. It was a single portrait of a young man in a dashing Hussar's uniform. Chillings.

He was debonair and rakish all at once. Posed with one leg crossed in front of the other and his shoulder propped against his horse's shoulder, he was the classic military officer that any woman would be interested in. His dark blue uniform crusted with gold braid made his shoulders look broader than they already were. The scarlet sash around his waist drew attention to his lean hips and strong thighs.

Felicia found herself mesmerised. Her breath was suddenly shallow and her heart beating rapidly. He was magnificent.

"That was in my younger days," Chillings drawled.

His words were like cold water on a fever victim's forehead. She snapped out of her preoccupation.

''Very well done, my lord,'' she managed in a credible imitation of nonchalance.

Without looking back at him, she stepped through the doorway and managed to smile at the footman who held the door open for her. An image of Chillings in his uniform seemed printed on her eye. No wonder he was engaged. He must have avoided all eligible females to have remained a single widower this long.

She needed something to take her mind off of him or her sleep would be fitful and unrestful. She headed for the library. Something in Latin would be just the thing.

She had not been in the library yet, but knew the direction. She stopped in the entrance and gaped. The room was, if possible, more impressive than the rest of the manor. Like the other public rooms, it was in the rotunda, so the outside wall was circular. Windows marched around the exterior with floor to ceiling bookcases spaced between them. As with the rest of the house, sage-green velvet curtains shut out the cold night.

A roaring fire warmed the room, but failed to light the corners where shadows held sway. As with every other room she had been in, a picture hung over the fireplace. This time it was a grouping of two young men with a woman posed between them. All three laughed at something the picture did not show.

She recognized one as a younger Chillings. The woman was very like him, with silver-blonde hair and dark eyes. She had his height and slim elegance. The second man was darker. His hair was black as pitch and his complexion was swarthy as a tinker's instead of being pale as fashion dictated. Unlike the other two in looks, he did have their high-bridged nose and the same dark blue eyes. All were dressed in the fashion of the first part of the century. Beau Brummell would have been proud of them.

Her host had a brother as well as the sister who was coming to chaperon.

She looked around some more and was relieved not to find any portraits of Chillings's wife. She told herself that it was no concern of hers, but she pitied the woman who fell in love with him. There was no room in his heart for anyone but the wife who was gone.

The thought caused moisture to prick her eyes, which was silly. He was nothing to her, and the unknown woman who would some day love him meant even less to her.

With more determination than she had felt on entering the room, she scanned the many books until she found a copy of the *Odyssey* in the original Latin. She opened the cover and began reading. She knew Latin.

Stunned, she sank into the nearest chair. She knew so much that many people would not know, yet she could not even remember her name. It was disheartening. She even knew that most women could not read Latin.

This was more than she could take. On legs grown weary beyond belief, she rose and started walking the seemingly endless distance to her room.

She reached the entry to the game room and stopped. Chillings stood bent over the billiard table holding a long, thin stick. To get to the hall that led to her room, she had to pass him. There was nothing for it. She was tired.

He used the stick to hit a white ball with black marks that then hit a red ball. The red ball ricocheted off the edge of the table while the ball he had hit stopped. It looked like a very boring way to spend the evening.

"Good night, Lord Chillings," she murmured politely as she passed by him.

"Ah, Madam Felicia. Would you care to play?"

She shook her head. "Thank you, but I don't believe I know how."

"I will teach you," he said, standing straight and setting one end of the stick on the ground so that the pointed end rested against the table. "My pleasure."

She eyed him narrowly. He had made it abundantly clear that nothing about him was her pleasure.

"Thank you, but I am tired."

She kept moving, although her steps were smaller and slower. There was a magnetism about him that made her want to be close. The attraction had been there from the start, ridiculous as it was.

"Afraid?" He drawled, lounging with his hips against the table, his legs crossed at the ankle.

Yes, she thought. I am afraid of what you make me feel. Out loud, she said, "Merely tired."

A slow, lazy grin lit his blue eyes. "Of course."

He turned away as though she had ceased to exist for him. She bit her lip in chagrin. She should leave.

Instead, she said, "Well, it might be interesting."

He turned back. "It can be."

Felicia looked around the game room and wondered what she had let herself in for. Unlike most of the house, this room was done in shades of blue. For a place where competition would be rife, it was very peaceful. Placed between two windows was a card table with sconces on the nearby walls and a candelabrum on the table itself. Cards were serious business.

"I think," Chillings said, "a smaller cue would suit you."

He took a long stick down from a device on the wall that held many sticks, some longer and fatter around than others. Felicia had no memory of any game like this.

"Now," he said, "the object is to hit the red ball with this ball."

She nodded.

"To do so, you use this cue to strike the first ball in such a way that it hits the second one."

Felicia nodded again. She could tell already that this was a game of hand-and-eye skill. She did not know if she would be able to play it. Chillings held the cue out to her. She took the stick, wondering if he would become angry if she played badly. For some reason, the possibility made her hands clammy, as though someone in her past had been that way.

She looked at him and saw him watching her. She knew he had a temper, but she also knew he controlled it.

"If you don't wish to do this, just say so," he said quietly, his voice smooth and beguiling.

"No, no…that is, yes, I do wish to try."

Her pulse increased, and she knew she would be hard pressed to refuse him anything he asked for in that voice. She was so susceptible to him. It was an unnerving realisation.

"I think to start, you should just practise hitting your ball."

She nodded. Lifting the stick, she put the pointed end against the ball as she had seen him do. She pulled the stick back and pushed it forward. It hit the ball lopsided, sending the ball bouncing across the table and on to the floor.

She frowned. "It is not as easy as it looked."

"No, it is not."

She whipped her head around to look at him. "Are you laughing at me?"

"I am merely enjoying the situation."

Part of her felt she should be insulted. But he was right. She must have looked ridiculous, bent over with this stick and then sending the ball flying.

He stooped and retrieved her ball, which he put back on the table. He quirked one black brow. "Again?"

"Again," she said firmly.

The need to master this skill lent her determination. Positioning the stick, or cue, again, she wondered if she had always been this stubborn. Was this part of who she was? From her desire to show Chillings and show herself that she could learn billiards, she rather thought it was.

Ten times later and ten flying balls later, she admitted defeat. "I don't think this is my game."

He studied her with a curious glint in his eyes. "But you want to learn it." It was a statement, not a question.

"Yes. I find that I don't want to be someone who gives up easily." She shrugged. 'I don't know if that is a trait of mine or just something that has come on since the amnesia."

"You have probably always had it. I believe the general thought on conditions like yours is that the person does not change. He merely does not remember."

"You are very well versed in my condition," she said a trifle tartly.

"I saw a number of men suffer from it during the wars."

His tone said he did not want to discuss the wars. He had made a statement of fact as he knew it and that was that.

Felicia counted to ten and lifted the cue again. Her exhaustion of earlier was gone. She took aim, shot and hit the ball on the left.

"A little left slide," Chillings said.

"What?"

"The way you hit the ball, although you did not intend to do so, is called putting slide on the ball."

"I see." But she did not and she knew that he knew.

"How badly do you want to learn?" he asked, leaning lightly on his cue, which was planted on the floor.

"I don't really know." She felt helpless, a feeling she was experiencing too much lately. She did not like it. "I suppose I would like to at least be able to hit that silly white ball so that it hits the red one."

"Right."

He pushed off, coming towards her. "Let me help you, then."

"How?"

She was getting a sense of unease. There was something about the way he was looking at her that made shivers skip down her spine.

"Pick your cue up. Now, use your left hand as a guide. Like this." He showed her. "Then pull back slowly on the cue and shoot forward."

She tried.

"You are angling your elbow too far out," he said, touching her upper arm so that she pulled the offending elbow to her side.

She tried again.

He frowned. "If you will let me."

Instead of waiting for permission, he went behind her and brought his arms around so his body cupped hers. Her posterior pressed into his loins. His chest lay fully along her back. Slowly, he bent her forward as he moulded her into the position he wanted.

Felicia thought she would pass out from the blood rushing away from her head and to other parts of her body. She tingled in areas she had not noticed before.

His breath was warm on the nape of her neck. His scent engulfed her. She gulped hard and hoped she could concentrate enough to hit the red ball so that he would release her. Her senses could not take much more of this.

"Now," he said, his voice a husky rasp, "let me guide you."

She licked dry lips. "Yes."

She leaned forward more until her back end pressed tightly to him. She gasped as she felt him stir against her. He jerked.

Without thought for the possible consequences, she turned her head to see his expression. It was a mistake.

His pupils were dilated. The angles of his face were knife blades of hunger, sharp enough to cut to her core. He tensed around her so that she could not have escaped had she wanted to.

She stared up at him.

"Felicia?" he said, his murmur a request.

Her eyes widened as he lowered his head the few inches that separated them. His mouth touched hers. His lips moved against hers, demanding and giving all at once. His beard scratched her skin and then she forgot all about it as her senses exploded outwards. She responded with a fervour she had not known she possessed.

He deepened the kiss until she whimpered with rising desire. As he plundered her mouth with his, he turned her in his arms so that her breasts pressed against his chest. One of his hands burrowed into her hair. The other slid down her back to cup her hip and pull her tightly to him.

He moved against her, an action so natural that she responded without thought. He groaned deep in his throat.

His hands skimmed over her body, coming to rest on her waist. He lifted her on to the billiard table in one easy flexing of muscles and straddled her so that his inner thighs embraced her on the outside. Her head fell back and her hair tumbled from the pins to fall in a golden puddle on the table.

He trailed kisses down her arched neck.

She had never felt like this. Even with her memory gone, a deep part of her knew that no man had ever done this to her. It was as though the ardour he created in her rose up from her depths and burst outwards to consume all thought, leaving only a woman in the throes of an uncontrollable response to a man's lovemaking.

One of his hands skimmed up her ribs to fold around one of her breasts while his other hand held her steady. He kneaded the aching mound of her flesh until all she wanted to do was rip her clothing off and press herself into his embrace.

She slid her hands to where his shirt lay open at his throat and started undoing the buttons until she could slip her palms inside the cloth and feel his flesh hot against hers. She began to shiver in earnest as he gasped.

He broke away from their kiss to stare down at her. His eyes were wild and his mouth was moist from her lips.

"I want you, Felicia."

His voice was so deep and so hoarse that she could barely understand him, but she knew instinctively. Her body could feel the tension that held him against her, his loins straining against her stomach.

"Now," he said with more force.

"Now," she murmured. "Yes, please."

A shudder ran through him. Holding her eyes with his, he started unbuttoning her bodice. He licked his lips and his eyes suddenly closed as stark hunger moved over his features. By touch alone, he pulled her clothing from her shoulders and slid the sleeves down her arms until the only thing between her and his passion was her thin cotton chemise. Only then did he open his eyes again to look at her.

He drew his breath in sharply as he gazed at the pink pricks of her nipples visible through the gossamer material. Her breathing became rapid and shallow as she watched his arousal. Every part of her ached with suppressed need.

He lowered his head until his mouth closed over her nipple. He nipped her gently with his teeth and she thought she would die. Through the cotton material he pulled and sucked and bit her until she was ready to scream. Then he went to the other breast.

She was lost.

Her release was a spasm that ripped through her entire body. She gripped him with arms grown so tense they hurt. Tiny gasps of pleasure and surprise escaped her. Her head collapsed on to his shoulder, his mouth still pressed to her bosom.

When she had stopped shaking, he released her. She lifted her head and met his gaze. His lips were swollen from suckling her and his eyes were glazed with un-released passion. He caught her face between his palms seconds before he caught her mouth with his.

He kissed her long and deep. Her head whirled.

Then she was free.

He stepped back abruptly. His chest rose and fell in rapid, deep gulps.

Dazed, she swayed but managed to get her hands pressed to the top of the billiard table where she still sat so that she was balanced. Lethargy held her.

''I believe,'' he said, his voice not quite steady, ''that you had better go to bed.'' He closed his eyes and added, ''Alone.''

Felicia slid from the table to stand on wobbly legs. Without a word, feeling a hot blush of shame mount her skin from the top of her chemise up her exposed bosom to the top of her hair, she walked away.

She reached her room, thankful that no servant waited for her. She could not stand to face someone after what had just happened. She finished unbuttoning her dress, which was easy because Chillings had done most of the work for her. The black bombazine fell from her to crumple on the floor. She left it there. Next came the stays.

She crawled into bed with the chemise still on. The cotton was damp where her breasts poked upwards. She brought one hand slowly to her bosom. Chillings's— Guy's—mouth had been pressed here. Her nipples ached.

"Lord, what have I done?" she whispered into the silent night.

She had behaved as a wanton. Not only had she let him ravish her, she had encouraged him. The breath caught in her throat. She had…she had… She had no word for what had happened to her.

She twisted to her side and curled tightly around her stomach. She was a widow so she must have known a man before. Somehow she did not think she had ever had that overwhelming experience that was a pleasure unlike anything she could have possibly imagined.

No wonder men wanted to make love. But tomorrow she would have to face him in the bright light of day.

She groaned in embarrassment and buried her head in the pillow, as though by doing so she could as easily bury the desire that ran unabated through her blood. Somehow, she had to find the strength to look at him and not throw herself into his arms, begging for more.

Somehow, she had to leave here before more happened between them. Not only was her virtue in jeopardy, but so was her heart. Neither was a possession she could give into another's keeping.

Chapter Five

Guy woke, his entire body tense and feeling as though he might explode at the slightest provocation. Then he remembered.

He had made love to Felicia, or very nearly done so. They had come so close that not finishing what they had started was the reason he felt so irritable this morning. Although, he thought wryly, she had got more pleasure than he had. A heavy fullness settled in his loins at the knowledge. He had enjoyed many women, but never had he had one who responded as completely as she had.

He flung his arm across his eyes, only to have the scent of lavender—of her—fill his senses. She had been eager and responsive, as anxious to go where they were headed as he had been. He still did not know how he had managed to stop. Probably when she had experienced her release. Her total involvement had aroused him at the same time as it had sobered him.

He groaned.

If he hoped to accomplish anything today other than going to her room and taking her without regard for the consequences, then he had better get up and find a way to release the pent-up energy that held him tight as a bowstring.

"Jeffries," he bellowed. "I am going riding."

The valet appeared. "Yes, my lord. Your clothes are laid out."

Guy eyed the valet. "You seem to know what I intend to do before I know myself. It is not always a comfortable habit."

Jeffries shrugged. "I try to always be one step ahead of your needs, my lord. If I fail to please, I beg your pardon."

Guy got out of bed, thankful that his nightshirt covered his reaction to the memory of last night. Jeffries was too aware by half as it was.

"You know you are indispensable. Now, just help me get dressed."

After what seemed far too long a period, Guy found himself dressed and on his way to the stables. Dante stood ready, pawing the ground in impatience.

"Easy, my friend," Guy said, stroking the gelding's strong neck. "We will be gone shortly."

And they were.

Hours later, the sun fully risen, Guy decided to visit his mistress. Jane could easily help him get rid of the physical discomfort that rode his loins like a harpy. He was surprised that he had not thought of her first.

He arrived at Jane's modest dwelling on the village outskirts cold and more than willing to be made warm. She answered his knock quickly.

"My lord," she said, delighted surprise making her prettier than she actually was.

He smiled at her. "May I come in?"

She smiled back and opened the door wide. "Please."

He stepped past her, catching her earthy scent that had always made him more than ready to enjoy their joining. Today he felt nothing. He was still tense with unreleased passion, but he was experienced enough to know that his condition was not caused by this woman. But he was here.

She wiped her flour-covered hands on the apron that was tied around her small waist. He appreciated the sight of her. Petite in height, but buxom and wide-hipped, she was a woman made for lovemaking. He had always been able to lose himself in her ample charms and skilled hands.

As usual, she waited for him to take the initiative. He closed the distance between them and wrapped his arms around her so that her breasts pressed into the hard muscles just below his nipples. His mouth took hers and her fingers found their way to the buttons of his shirt.

He was naked from the waist up when he gave up.

"I am sorry, my dear," he said, feeling true regret. "But it seems I have started something I cannot finish."

She gave him a bewildered smile. "That is perfectly fine, my lord. We have never fully completed our lovemaking. That is, you have never—"

He put one finger on her lips. "I know that, but this is different. It has nothing to do with you, Jane." He gently took her hands from the tabs of his breeches. "I wish there were an easier way to say this."

She stepped away from him. "I understand, my lord. It is over between us."

He nodded.

She took a deep breath, her ample bosom rising and

falling under the brown wool of her dress. Always before the sight had aroused him. Now he watched with regret only.

"It is just as well, my lord. Farmer John has asked me to marry him." She flushed. "I was not sure what to tell him because of what was between us. Now I will accept."

"Is that what you want, Jane? I will provide for you so that you need never marry if you don't wish to."

She nodded. "I want children and a home. I am ready."

It was just as well. He had never had anything to offer her other than money and the physical pleasure he could give her. Now he had nothing.

"I understand. I am engaged to marry because I need a son."

"I wish you very happy," she said, formally.

"And I you," he replied.

He turned away and pulled on his shirt, his coat and greatcoat. When he was fully dressed, he went back to her.

"I will see that you have a tidy nest egg for you and your farmer, if you wish to share." True regret darkened his eyes. "I have always enjoyed my visits."

She smiled wistfully. "And I, my lord. But I always knew it would end."

He took her hand and raised it to his lips. "I wish you the best of everything, Jane. Let me know when the first child arrives."

He released her and left. There was no sense in lingering. They had each made their decisions. He did not even regret that they had not slept together. Somehow it had not felt right to do so.

Damn Felicia. What would she change in his life next?

* * *

A good hour later, Guy cantered Dante on to the circular driveway in front of The Folly and noticed a travelling carriage. The Fenwick-Clyde coat of arms stood starkly against the black door. Annabell was here at last, and not a day too soon and almost a night too late.

He handed Dante to a groom and strode towards the travelling chaise.

He was in time to help her out of the coach.

"Guy," she said, pleasure lighting her face. "I came as quickly as I could. I hope I am not too late." She smiled at him as though her words were to tease him, but her eyes held concern.

He chose to respond to her humour. "Minx." Then glanced at her luggage. "You seem to have brought everything you own. I swear, I will never fathom how you have travelled the globe when you seem to take half of the British nation with you."

She laughed. "I travel in luxury while here. Otherwise, I travel like a Bedouin, with the clothes on my back and my tent and tea kettle, only they drink coffee. Nasty drink," she finished, wrinkling her nose.

He shook his head. "However you travel and however much paraphernalia you bring with you, there is room in your old suite." He put his arms around her and hugged her tightly. "Thank you for coming, Bell, and for being so prompt."

She hugged him back. "I gathered from your uninformative note that it was rather urgent."

He grimaced as he led her to the front door. "I am in a potentially compromising situation and through no fault of my own." He grinned. "For once."

She raised one black brow, so much like his. "Not of your making?"

"No, dammit." He rubbed his jaw, feeling the short growth of his beard. "I have only done what any decent person would do. Taken her in and given her shelter."

Annabell's brow rose higher. "Her?"

"Yes, Bell, her."

"The plot thickens," she said, her voice lowering into an exaggeratedly conspiratorial tone.

He grinned in spite of his worry. "Melodramatic as always."

She shrugged out of his embrace. "You are the one who is carrying on as though this situation will be the ruin of you, not me."

He allowed her to put some distance between them as she mounted the steps to the entrance. Her making light of the situation irritated Guy. What had happened between him and Felicia just the night before over billiards had not been nearly enough for him. And he thought she felt the same. No matter how Bell might tease about the situation, it was serious.

"Good morning, Miss Annabell," Oswald said, bowing.

She grinned at him as she stepped into the foyer. "Good morning to you, Oswald. And it is Lady Fenwick-Clyde."

"Yes, Miss Annabell," the always-perfect butler replied.

The exchange lightened Guy's mood. "He always thinks of you as the small girl you used to be, running wild around here. I doubt he will ever call you by your new title."

Annabell shrugged. "That is fine with me. I often

wish that I were still that small girl." She shrugged off her heavy wool-and-beaver cape, giving it to a footman who had appeared. "My trunks are still in the carriage."

"I will have them taken to your rooms, Miss Annabell," Oswald said.

She thanked him and turned to her brother. "So, where is this beastie who has you scared for your honour?"

Guy glared at her. "This is not a laughing matter, Bell. The woman has lost her memory, and I am stuck with her until I learn who she is."

"An onerous burden indeed," Annabell said. "But that does not answer my question."

Guy gave a long, put-upon sigh. "She is likely in the library. The room seems to have ensnared her."

"She has good taste." Annabell moved in that direction.

Guy kept pace with her. "What are you doing?"

"I am going to meet her."

"You can do that later."

She stopped and looked pointedly at him. "No, I cannot. If she has got you in such an uproar, then I need to find out what she is like."

He knew there was no keeping her from something she had decided to do. He moved aside. "You always were the most stubborn of us."

"I was also the most practical."

Guy watched his sister sail away, the skirts of her silver-grey travelling dress swishing behind her. He might as well have tea and refreshments served in the library. It would be some time before Annabell went to her rooms.

* * *

Felicia looked up from her book to see a woman framed in the library door. She was tall with silver-blonde hair and black slashing brows. High cheekbones and a strong chin gave her face character. Her clothing was the height of fashion with a high waist and grey piping. A grey spencer made her elegant figure look trim.

Felicia stared. She was a female version of the Viscount, even to her well-defined, sensual mouth. She was the young woman in the portrait.

"Good morning," the woman said in a husky contralto. "I am Annabell Fenwick-Clyde. I dare say my brother has not told you he has a twin sister—or a younger brother, for that matter."

Felicia set the book aside and stood. She returned the woman's smile. "No, he has not, but the portrait over the mantel told me such."

Annabell's gaze went to the picture. "Ah. It is a reasonable likeness. Especially considering that it was nearly thirteen years ago."

Annabell took off her gloves and spencer and tossed them on one of the many blue-and-green velvet upholstered settees. "So, you have lost your memory."

Felicia nodded and sat back down, resigning herself to another interrogation. She cast one wistful glance at the book she had been reading before focusing her attention on the other woman.

"But you know your first name," Annabell continued.

She sank into a leather chair with a natural gracefulness that reminded Felicia of Chillings—Guy. After what they had done last night, using his title seemed too impersonal. She felt herself flush from the remembered passion, his lips, his hands, everything.

"Ahem," Annabell said. "You seem to know your first name."

Felicia felt like a child caught where she should not be. With an effort of will, she put last night's sensations aside.

"It seems that my toiletry case has my initials and a wedding band..." She paused, wondering why every mention of that ring caused her stomach to tighten uncomfortably. She raised her right hand. "There was a wedding band with mine and my husband's names engraved on the inside. Or so we think." She shrugged, uncomfortable with the situation. "It seems that I am likely a widow because of my black clothing."

She hoped she was a widow. What she had done last night would nearly be adultery if she were still married. The fact that Guy was engaged paled beside the knowledge that she might have been unfaithful to a man she could not remember. But she had wanted what they had shared. Even now, in the cold, sparse light of day, she knew she would do it all over again. Her body was in control, not her reason.

Annabell pinned her with a piercing look. "Is that what you really think?"

More uncomfortable than ever, Felicia shrugged. "I don't know."

"Don't know or don't want to know?"

Exasperation at the other woman's pointed questions made Felicia's voice sharp. "I don't know. Plain and simple. If it is because I don't want to know, then so be it. If it is simply because of the hit to the head I took, then so be it. I do not know."

Annabell grinned, so spontaneously and genuinely, that Felicia returned it without thinking.

"You are feisty," Annabell said. "That will stand you in good stead here."

A knock on the door preceded the entrance of Oswald with the tea tray. "His lordship thought you might like some refreshments."

"My brother, the perfect host," Annabell said.

"I try to be," Chillings said smoothly, following the butler and tray in. He glanced from one flushed face to the other. "I hope we don't intrude."

Annabell waved a long-fingered hand. "Of course not. I was merely quizzing your guest, much to her irritation. I would wager that Felicia is grateful for your arrival."

Felicia, already warm, turned warmer. Just looking at him, she felt his lips on hers and his hands doing things to her that had nearly made her crazy with longing for more. She wanted things that would be improper under any circumstances, but because of her situation were doubly so. Yet, she could not help herself.

He cast her an inscrutable look before crossing to the desk where a decanter and several glasses sat on a silver tray. He unstoppered the container and poured himself a drink.

"Whisky, as usual?" Annabell said.

Felicia glanced sharply at Annabell. Did she disapprove of her brother's drinking? Most men drank liberally.

Guy raised his glass. "To my sister and our guest." He downed the contents in one long swallow.

"You don't even cough or gasp," Annabell said. She turned to Felicia. "That stuff burns all the way down your throat and it explodes in your stomach. Normally. But when you drink it constantly, it seems the effects are not so strong."

Felicia said nothing. There were undercurrents here that she did not understand and was better out of. Just as she was better out of this room and away from the Viscount. The last thing any of them needed was for her to make a fool of herself over him in front of his sister. The other woman was here to preserve their reputations, to keep them from doing what they had done last night. Definitely to prevent them from consummating what they had started.

She rose abruptly. "If you will excuse me." She looked at Annabell, unwilling to see what the Viscount's face might reveal. "But I am tired and my head is beginning to ache."

Not waiting for a reply, she grabbed her book and skirted the table where the tea tray sat. She caught a glimpse of movement from the corner of her eye.

Guy stood at the door, his hand on the handle so she could not open it herself. She hardened herself to meet his gaze. His eyes were dark as the sea during a storm and his mouth was a sensual slash bared in a predatory smile. Her knees weakened and it was all she could do to remain standing.

"Yes, my lord?" she said, her voice barely a whisper.

"I will send Mrs Drummond to you."

His melodic baritone made her nerves sing. She remembered all too clearly how he had spoken to her last night, telling her how desirable she was, how beautiful she was. Need, hot, heavy and sudden, engulfed her.

"That is a very good idea, Guy," Annabell said loudly, breaking Felicia's concentration just in time.

Felicia pulled herself up short and ground her nails into her palms in an effort to take her mind off of the Viscount. "Thank you," she murmured, slipping through the door he now held open and not looking back.

Heaven only knew what she would do if he continued to watch her with eyes that spoke of shared passion, because *she* did not know what she would do.

Guy waited until Felicia was no longer visible before closing the door and turning back to his sister. Condemnation met him.

"What have you two been doing?" Annabell demanded.

He shrugged. "What does it matter? You are here now."

Annabell shook her head. "It matters to her, Guy. And unless I miss my guess, it matters to you. You looked ready to devour her."

He crossed to his empty glass and refilled it. "That is why you are here."

She sighed in resignation. "I doubt that my presence is going to do much after what I just saw. There is an electricity between the two of you that is palpable." She rose and went to him. "And you are engaged."

"And she is a widow," he said, downing his whisky.

"That is not the point. If Miss Duckworth hears of this, your engagement will be over. If the *ton* gets even a hint of this, it will be all over town." She put a cautionary hand on his arm. "Are you prepared to marry this woman whom you know nothing about?"

He scowled at her. "You always were adept at calling a spade a spade, Bell. I am marrying Miss Duckworth. That is settled and the notice in *The Times*. Nothing can change that. A gentleman does not jilt a lady, no matter what the provocation."

"Then you had best find out who this Felicia is as quickly as possible and get her out of your house," Annabell stated flatly. "Or else, you will find yourself where you do not want to be."

Chapter Six

"Faugh!" Annabell threw her cards onto the table. "You are unbeatable, Guy."

Felicia laid her cards down more sedately. "He certainly has the Devil's own luck tonight."

He smiled faintly. "If I were at Brook's tonight, I probably would not lose my inheritance."

"Definitely not," Annabell said, rising. She sobered. "Have you heard about Dominic's latest?"

Guy raised one brow and cast a quick glance at Felicia. "Is it polite conversation?"

Annabell looked at Felicia, who still sat at the table with her hands folded calmly in her lap. "No. Nothing Dominic does is ever acceptable conversation for a drawing room."

Felicia, realizing they were discussing their younger and feckless brother, rose. "If you will excuse me, I will retire."

"No, no," Annabell said quickly. "I should not have brought the subject up. I am just restless."

She paced to the fireplace, picked up the poker and jabbed at the embers. Having excited the fire so that sparks shot out and landed on the tile surround, she moved to the window. She threw wide the window and stepped on to the terrace that ran the length of the house. Cold wind whipped into the room.

From outside, Annabell said, "The moon is full, Guy, and your lake is frozen. What do you say to ice-skating? We can see well enough."

Guy rose and joined her. "Sometimes you are as volatile as Dominic."

She slanted him a look full of meaning. "And you, brother."

Felicia stayed inside, bundled tightly in her shawl, and moved to the fireplace. She should go to her room, but she was not sleepy and the idea of ice-skating under a full moon was appealing. It smacked of something slightly dangerous and exciting. She even thought she knew how to do it.

"What do you think, Felicia?" Annabell said, coming back inside. "If you want to skate, then I know Guy will agree."

Felicia blinked at Annabell's words. "You jest, I am sure. But, skating does sound exciting. Only I have no skates and not enough clothing to stay warm."

Annabell let loose her infectious laugh. "I have everything you will need." She turned on Guy, who was closing the French doors behind him. "What say you now?"

Guy looked from one woman to the other. Annabell had colour in her cheeks from the cold. Felicia had colour in her cheeks from the fire, and her eyes danced with interest. His inclination was to decline. But he said nothing.

"No answer is a yes," Annabell said. "Come along," she said to Felicia. "Some of my old clothes that are stored here should fit you."

Felicia looked at Guy, who shrugged his shoulders. His eyes watched her with an intensity that put the lie to his casual gesture. She shivered, but not from the cold.

"It seems I have no say in this," he said. "Shall we meet back here in thirty minutes? I will have Oswald dig up our old skates."

Both women burst into smiles. He watched them hurry down the hall and knew why he had agreed to something so ridiculous. Felicia's face had told him that she wanted to skate. Nothing else would have swayed him, certainly not Bell's restlessness. He would have talked with his sister instead. Very likely Dominic's latest escapade was bothering her. But he had said nothing, and now the three of them would freeze on the ice and might or might not have fun doing it.

Annoyed at himself, he stalked from the room. There was no telling what he would do next. He had already done things that if someone had told him a fortnight ago he would do, he would have laughed until they slunk away in embarrassment. He did not like to think what he would do next.

They met back at the game room's French doors in exactly thirty minutes. Annabell grinned in anticipation. Guy looked bored and Felicia wondered if she was doing the right thing.

Oswald joined them with three pairs of skates hanging from his gloved hands. "I hope these fit, my lord," he said, handing them to Guy.

"If they don't," Felicia said, "we will make do."

As she had made do with Annabell's old clothing. The other woman had lively tastes and there had been no black for Felicia to wear. She had settled on a navy spencer and matching pelisse and a cape lined with rabbit fur. The second pair of stockings she wore were pink and the two extra petticoats were cream and white. At first she had been uncomfortable in the colours. Now, she accepted them. At least her outer clothing was dark.

Guy gave her a quick perusal. "It appears that you found something in Bell's castoffs."

Felicia smiled. "She has lovely things."

"Mostly out of fashion," Annabell said.

"But they will keep me warm," Felicia said calmly. Somehow she knew that she had made do most of her life. This was nothing new and it did not bother her.

Guy opened the doors and they all walked outside. Felicia caught her breath at the cold and the beauty. Moonlight limned the terrace in silver and sent moon shadows to dance along the frost-tipped grounds. It was like a fairy-tale world, and Felicia was suddenly glad they were doing this.

"It is as though we have left the world behind," she murmured.

No one responded, but that was all right. She was happy.

They reached the artificial lake quickly. Willows towered above the shore with their limbs dipping like maiden's hands to skim the ice. Ornamental bushes in casual clusters provided texture.

"This is truly beautiful," Felicia said, knowing she sounded redundant, but unable not to comment on the magnificent simplicity Guy had created. "You have made this into a magical place."

"Thank you," Guy said. "It was done over the past few years. I wanted the grounds to reflect the more casual aspect of country life. Not like the stately and staid vistas from my father's time."

"Come along, you two," Annabell said. "You can talk about Guy's passion for landscaping and building another time."

Nestled next to an elegant little pier was a bathhouse done in Grecian lines with a more casual green-and-white striped awning that seemed to float over the lake's edge. At the moment, frost and snow made the awning sparkle as though diamonds were strewn across it.

"Do you swim in the summer?" Felicia asked.

"As children we did all the time," Annabell answered without looking back at them.

In a lower tone, like rich thick chocolate, Guy said, "I still do. When it is hot, the cold water against my skin is like a refreshing tonic."

Felicia glanced at him, only to be caught by the dark hunger in his eyes. She knew they reflected the emotion in her own. For some reason, when she pictured him swimming, he was without clothes. His wide shoulders and lean hips would slice through the water, and then he would stand up.... She licked suddenly dry lips.

"Really?" She forced herself to look away, but could do nothing about her breathlessness.

"Yes, really," he said, a hint of laughter in his voice now.

Disconcerted by his abrupt change of mood, she turned back to him. "You are the most contrary man."

"The same might be said of you," he murmured, holding out his hand to help her over an icy patch.

Without thought she placed her hand in his. When he was near, she felt safe. Then the heat from his body penetrated his glove and hers. She sucked in cold air that did nothing to cool the curl of smoke in her stomach. Her sense of safety fled.

She made it across the slippery area, but he did not release her. Instead he pulled her closer until she could smell the clean fresh scent of lime. It was a scent she would always associate with him, no matter what happened.

They reached the stone bench where Annabell sat donning her skates without Felicia realizing it. She smiled at the other woman and saw that the Viscount's sister was studying her through narrowed eyes. But Annabell smiled back.

"Are you sure you know how to skate?" Annabell asked, as she stood.

"No," Felicia said, laughing lightly, "but I think I do. Surely I do. I can picture people skating."

And she could. She really could. She stared at nothing as her mind played back a scene. It was daytime, but the sun was in her eyes and she could not make out any of the figures she saw skating. They were all blurred, although some seemed smaller than the others. Children, perhaps?

"What do you see, Felicia?" Guy asked.

"People. Some are small. Children?" Then the image was gone. She shook her head. "I must have been seeing people I know." She sighed. "But I could not see them clearly."

"That makes sense," he said, releasing her hand.

She felt bereft. But she should not. To take her mind off the unexpected sense of aloneness, she sank to the bench Annabell had just vacated. Guy handed her the skates to be strapped to her boots. She took them and started to attach them only to realize that she did not know how, and there was not enough light from the full moon for her to figure out how to do so. She frowned.

"Having problems?" Guy said, squatting down in front of her.

"Yes," she said, impatient with herself. Her hands fisted. "I don't know how to attach these. I thought I did or would or something. And now, it is as though I know nothing."

"Easy," he said soothingly. "I will do them for you." He looked up at her and a frown marred his patrician forehead. "You may never have had to fasten them. A man might have done it for you."

She returned his frown. "If I am a widow?"

"That seems likely, as we have discussed."

"Then that makes me a very silly woman if I did not learn how to fend for myself but always depended on a man."

His brow smoothed. "Many women would disagree with you."

"I suppose."

He finished fastening the skates and sat beside her. His thigh met hers and, even through the multiple layers of clothing, she could feel his hard muscles. She inched away until she was barely on the bench. Better to fall on to the ground than touch this man in a manner that felt intimate enough to spark a desire in her that would burn with the intensity of an inferno.

He paused a moment in fastening his skates, his face shifting so that his dark eyes met hers. She looked away and jumped to her feet, determined to put some distance between them before she lost all sense of propriety and threw herself into his arms.

She wobbled and her left ankle buckled. She fell sideways, right into Guy's arms as he stood to catch her. She leaned into him, telling herself it was only for support. Still, her side felt scorched as awareness of him radiated out to every fibre of her body.

Memories of what they had done just several nights before, and of what they had not done, played through her mind. He had lifted her on to the billiard table, scattering the balls to the floor, then he had touched her. His fingers had caressed her in places so intimate that she had not realized what it would feel like to have someone stroke them. And she had done the same to him. Tremors of desire took her and she wondered if she was the only one remembering. She looked up at him and knew she was not alone.

There was a wild look about him. His eyes were a little more narrow than usual, his jaw a little firmer, his body tighter.

His head angled down until his breath brushed across her cheek. "I would do it all over," he murmured.

She gazed up at him. Part of her wanted to tell him she would not. The part that did not know who she was or if she might be married. The part of her that was her heart told him, "So would I."

His grip on her tightened and she thought he would kiss her. His lips were nearly on hers.

"Guy," Annabell said loudly, "we came here to skate."

Guy moved back, but did not release Felicia. "So we did, Bell."

As though he had not just nearly seduced her with nothing more than the promise of a kiss, he helped Felicia with all propriety until they stood side by side on the ice. Frustration took Felicia as her ankles gave out and she slid down, saved only by Guy's arm around her waist.

"Easy," he said.

"It seems that I don't know how to skate after all." Her fingers tightened on his forearm.

"Come along, you two," Annabell called from farther out on the lake. "Come skate in the moonlight."

Felicia looked at Annabell and forgot her irritation for the moment. Guy's sister did figures of eight and glided by on one foot with the other held gracefully in the air, and all on a lake of ice that sparkled like molten silver in the moon's glow. Annabell's elongated shadow swept behind her like a swan gliding across water.

"Oh," Felicia breathed, "how beautiful. She is so graceful."

Guy did not glance at his twin. "Yes."

Felicia's gaze snapped back to him. "Again?" she asked softly. "Annabell will see us, you know."

"To hell with Annabell. She is a grown woman."

Felicia shook her head. "No, it is not comfortable."

"Nothing about this is comfortable." He bit off each word.

"No," she murmured, "it is not."

"Shall we return to the house?" Annabell asked from not more than four feet away.

Felicia had been so involved with Guy that she had not noticed Annabell approach. The realization of how mesmerized she was by him was sobering. She stepped away, forgetting she was on ice skates.

Her feet slid and slipped. Her arms windmilled as she tried to keep her balance. She squeaked.

Guy caught her to his chest and held her tight until her breathing returned to normal. A thick strand of hair had come loose and hung like spun copper down the back of her coat. She brushed futilely at it before giving up.

"Leave it," Guy said, his voice deep.

She nodded. "You can let me go now. Or just hold my hand."

He released her and skated back only far enough to put some distance between them, but he continued to hold her hand. "Move slowly," he said. "And don't look down."

She scooted her feet along in tiny slides. Her fingers gripped Guy's hand like pincers.

"That's the way," he crooned. "Slow and easy."

She darted a glance at him, wondering if he knew how seductively suggestive his words and tone were. The knowing glint in his eyes told her that he did. She tried to ignore him. Next to impossible, but she tried.

Then, as though by magic, she got her balance. "You can let go," she said, her voice barely above a whisper. "I think I have it now."

His fingers loosened on hers, but he did not withdraw his hand. Slowly, so as not to lose her newfound balance, Felicia let his hand go. She found it felt safer if she held her arms slightly out at her sides. Elation filled her as she moved on her own.

"Bravo, bravo," Annabell said, skating up to Felicia. "I believe you have got the idea now."

Felicia did not dare nod. She was not even comfortable speaking in case her concentration broke. Instead, she skated towards the centre of the lake where Annabell had been. She reached the spot where the moon shone down like a spotlight. Giddy with delight, she did circles, her arms held wide. Her skirts belled around her. Her coat flared out. Her hair escaped from the pins that had only managed to barely hold it in proper confinement.

Guy smiled at her exuberance. This was a side of

her he had not seen yet. But then, he had only known her for a matter of weeks. It seemed longer.

"She is lovely," Annabell said, coming up to Guy's side. "It is a pity you are already promised to Miss Duckworth."

Guy tensed. "A pity for whom?" he drawled. "Not for me."

"Hah. I have seen the way you look at her. You would devour her if you could." She paused to let her words sink in before adding, "And she feels the same."

"Rubbish."

Even as he said the word, Guy knew in his stomach that he did not mean it. Nor could he lie to his sister. Not that she would not see through the lie, for she would, but simply because he and Bell had always been honest with each other. He thought it might come of being twins.

"It is better this way," he finally said. "She does not know who she is or what her life is. I am looking for a marriage of convenience, not passion."

"Or love?" Annabell queried softly.

"Or that."

Felicia, gaining confidence with every second she remained on her feet, did a twirl. Guy watched her, noting the way the moonlight emphasized her elegant cheekbones and the fine way she tilted her head back so her long neck showed graceful as a swan's.

The next instant she fell.

Felicia shrieked in surprise and consternation. She hit the ice with an impact that knocked her breath out.

Guy watched her slam into the ice and bounce up from the force of the fall. Then, to his horror, dark lines started forming.

"Felicia," he shouted, "get up. Now. Come back."

She rolled to her knees and looked around. "Oh, no," she moaned. She tried to stand and fell back. More cracks appeared.

Guy's heart sped like a galloping horse as he rushed to her, stopping just short of the cracks. He did not trust the ice with his added weight.

"Don't try to stand again. Crawl toward me. Quickly, now," he finished, keeping the panic he felt from showing in his voice. The last thing she needed was his fear added to her own.

Felicia looked up at him. She knew that when she reached him she would be safe. On hands and knees, she scrambled towards him.

The ice cracked again, the sound reverberating in Felicia's ears. Distantly, logically, she knew the noise had not been great, but she also sensed that this crack was crucial. Seconds later, she sank. Cold water closed around her. She gasped and freezing liquid rushed down her throat and filled her lungs. She thrashed until her head broke the surface. She coughed and gasped and went under again.

"Oh, my God, no," Guy said.

He inched forward, afraid to go too far and fall in with her. He would not be able to help her if he was submersed.

He looked back at Annabell. "I am going to lie on my stomach and move slowly toward her. The less weight on the ice near her, the less chance that it will break too."

Annabell nodded, too stunned to speak.

Guy sprawled on his belly. He was distantly aware of the cold seeping through his clothes and into his muscles. He inched forward. He had to reach her. He was almost to her when the ice beneath him started to creak. He did not have much time. He pushed himself to the edge and looked into the dark water. He could see Felicia just below the surface.

The ice creaked again. A fresh crack started.

Time was against him. He shoved his arms into the freezing black water as deep as they would go. He felt her fingers but could not get a grip on her. He inched forward and took a deep breath then plunged his head in along with his arms so that he was in the water to his chest. He caught her.

His heart pounded until he thought it would burst. His muscles clenched until they ached, but he held on to her. Slowly, ever so slowly, he used the strength in his legs to move him backwards. Too slowly.

He felt hands on his ankles and realized that Annabell had come out behind him and grabbed him. She pulled and he slid backward more than he could do on his own.

His head broke the water and he gasped for air. "More, Bell. More. She is like a dead weight with all her clothing."

Annabell grunted.

Felicia's head popped above the surface. She gasped and coughed and choked.

Relief was a sharp pain in Guy's chest. "Come on, Felicia. Help me if you can."

Her eyes opened wide. "I…I.."

Her teeth chattered and her fingers were stiff in his. He could see her fear. "I have you." Without looking back, he said, "I need more help, Bell. I don't think it is safe for me to stand yet."

"Yes," Annabell said breathlessly. "I am trying."

"I know, Bell."

He kept his gaze on Felicia. Her eyes had closed and she looked lifeless. Fresh fear speared his stomach. They had to get her out. Now.

"To hell with it," he muttered. "Let go, Bell. This is taking too long."

Annabell barely released him when he worked his way to his knees, keeping a firm grip on Felicia's hands. He changed his hold to her wrists and stood, pulling her up with him. The weight of her clothing was enough to bend him over, but he persevered. Then she was out and in his arms. He gripped her tightly. The ice under his feet cracked.

"Move," he shouted at Bell. "Now."

He leaped away from the breaking ice, landed precariously because of his skates, and sped toward shore. He saw Bell safely ahead of him. At least he did not have to worry about her.

He knew it had only taken seconds to reach the shore, but it had felt like an eternity. Bell was beside him instantly.

"How is she?" his sister asked.

"Cold and still," he said quietly, keeping his voice calm. The last thing any of them needed was for him to give in to the fear he felt. "We need to get her to the house."

Bell knelt down and undid his skates without being told. He smiled. She had always been one to take action. Sometimes it was the wrong action, but she never stood by and did nothing.

He started up the path as quickly as he could. Felicia lay in his arms like a leaden weight. She did not move or open her eyes. Her glorious hair, sodden and heavy, fell nearly to the ground in lank strands. Her breath came in shallow little puffs that looked like smoke in the cold air. He sped up. His feet slipped on the frosted gravel but he did not slow down. He did not dare.

He heard Bell behind him. "Go ahead and notify Mrs Drummond."

"Right." She passed him running.

Guy's arms ached and the cold from Felicia's body and wet clothes penetrated his own clothing. The closeness of their bodies and the warmth he exuded from exertion did not make a difference to the chill he felt in her.

He was at the door just as Oswald opened it. "Mrs Drummond is in Madam Felicia's room, my lord."

"Thank you," Guy said, hurrying past. "See that a hot bath is prepared."

"Mrs Drummond has already ordered one, my lord."

Guy heard Oswald's words as though from a distance. He was already rushing down the corridor. He passed through the games room. One more set of stairs to climb up to the first floor where the guest chambers were. He was nearly out of energy. The door to Felicia's room stood open. He burst through and made straight for the bed where he gently laid her. She did not stir.

"Dear me, dear me," Mrs Drummond said, coming up behind him. "She is drenched to the skin." She spared a glance for the Viscount. "And so are you. Go change. You cannot do anything for her that I cannot do better, my lord."

A wry smile twisted Guy's lips. Mrs Drummond was nothing if not confident of her skills.

"I will stay here and help." He took off his coat and tossed it on to a chair. The housekeeper opened her mouth to speak, but he cut her off. "Two pairs of hands are better than one. Someone used to tell me that.''

''Using my own words against me, my lord. It is not playing fair.''

He shrugged. ''I don't intend to play fair where this woman is concerned.''

Mrs Drummond gave him a startled look before focusing her attention on the frighteningly still woman. ''Her lips are blue and her breathing is shallow and irregular. Best get her out of those wet things.'' She all but elbowed her way past the Viscount. ''You had best turn away, my lord.''

He gave her a fleeting grin. ''I don't believe I will do that. I have seen and undressed enough women to know what to do here.''

Mrs Drummond's sharp intake of air was loud in the quiet room. ''As you say, *my lord*.''

He did not even look at her. ''We have more important things to do than waste words.''

''True.''

Mrs Drummond started unbuttoning Felicia's coat even as Guy put an arm around Felicia's back and raised her enough that they could pull the clothing off. It hit the floor. Next was the pelisse. After that a spencer. Now her dress.

The buttons and ties were at the back so Guy held her propped forward, resting on his chest. He continued to hold her thus while Mrs Drummond stripped the chilling material from Felicia's skin.

''She is clammy and cold as an eel.''

Guy grimaced. ''Not a very flattering description.''

''But accurate. Hold up her hips, my lord, so I can slide this off.''

He did as ordered. Under it all was a simple set of

stays over a thin chemise, which was transparent from the water. The pink aureoles of her breasts thrust upward, the nipples taut as though she were caught in the throes of passion. As they had been several nights before. The breath caught in Guy's throat.

He had to look elsewhere while Mrs Drummond unlaced the stays and the ripe fullness of Felicia's bosom tumbled loose. The urge to touch her, even now, was nearly undeniable. He berated himself for his lack of control.

"My lord," Mrs Drummond said sharply. "I need you to help me undress her, not hinder me by holding her so that I cannot get her chemise off."

He jerked. But her scold had broken the spell. For the moment. He knew it would not last. He desired Felicia too greatly.

He clenched his jaw and did as directed until Felicia lay naked on the coverlet that was now wet and needing to be replaced. Her skin was pale as alabaster. It had been that way the last time he had seen her naked, although he had not seen more than her bosom. Without forethought, his gaze travelled down the length of her.

Full, tip-tilted breasts led to a slim ribcage and tiny waist. Her hips flared in lush welcome. Her legs were long and her ankles neat. She was lovely.

She was also a mother. There were nearly transparent stretch marks across her abdomen. They were not easy to see. The light had to hit them just right as it did now. His gut clenched. A fleeting memory of Suzanne crying out in pain from birthing sped through his mind and disappeared. The sight of Felicia was too immediate for anything else to matter.

He traced one of the spidery stretch marks that told

him she had birthed at least one child. Other men might think it an imperfection, but to Guy it added to her beauty. His finger skimmed the line from her right hip to her belly button where another barely visible mark started. This one went to silken hairs—

"Stop that." Mrs Drummond swatted his hand.

Guy jerked back and took a deep breath. Closing his eyes to Felicia's beauty, he carefully covered her with the sheet. "Thank you, Mrs Drummond," he murmured, not sure he truly meant it.

This was the second time tonight that his passions had got the better of him, and he had acted indiscreetly with other people around. What was this woman doing to him?

Then the realization hit him. This was proof that she was a widow. But where was her child?

Mrs Drummond sniffed. Once more she disrupted his thoughts. "I will go get clean bedding myself. Calling a maid will take too long." She eyed the Viscount. "See that you do not do anything. It is improper enough that you are seeing her like this. Not that I can do anything to stop you."

Knowing her reprimand was deserved, Guy said, "At least credit me with the decency to realize that she is too sick for me to seduce her."

"Miss Annabell should be here," Mrs Drummond said pointedly.

"And she will be," Guy said. "She is changing before she catches an inflammation."

Mrs Drummond turned reluctantly away. Felicia's eyes flickered open. Guy leaned forward, gripping her hand hard.

"Felicia?" he said. "Do you hear me?"

Her head moved in a nearly imperceptible nod.

"You are safe," he said.

"Don't leave me," she whispered.

"Never," he said.

Chapter Seven

Her eyes drifted shut again. Her body relaxed.

Mrs Drummond, who had stopped when she heard Felicia's voice, started out again. She reached the door just as two footmen, supervised by Oswald, arrived with the hip bath and cans of steaming water. She waved them in and turned back to stare at the Viscount.

"I will be back before they have the water poured, my lord."

Guy understood what she was not saying. He was to wait for her before putting Felicia into the bath. He did not deign to answer. Favored and loved servant she was, but he would do as he determined best.

Painfully aware of Felicia's nakedness under the sheet, Guy hastily grabbed the corner of the coverlet from the opposite side of the bed and pulled it over her still form. Only then did he direct them to place the bath by the fire, something they were already doing. This woman had addled his brain along with his body.

They poured the water into the bath and left. The door closed behind them before Guy uncovered Felicia again. The hot water would take some of the cold from her flesh. Something needed to. If she remained like this, she would catch an inflammation of the lungs or worse.

He would bathe her while Mrs Drummond was gone. He flipped back the coverlet and picked her up as gently as possible and carried her to the tub. Careful not to get her hair into the hot water, he lowered her. Her skin flushed like a pink rose as the water enveloped her.

He folded a towel and placed it beneath her head so she was not resting on hard metal. Next he fanned her hair out so that it hung down the back of the tub where the heat from the fire would dry it. Unable to resist, he combed his fingers through the thick mass. It was like stroking the finest silk. His loins tightened instantly.

He groaned. Heaven help him. His response to her was beyond reason.

When he was sure she would not slide under the water if left unattended, he positioned a screen around the tub so she would not be seen by someone entering the room. He wanted to protect her privacy from other people. His mouth twisted. He could appreciate the irony. He had dug through her belongings without a thought for her feelings. Now he intended to bathe her, an act almost more intimate than making love. He was not her maid and he was not her husband. He wanted to be her lover, and he wanted to keep others from seeing her this vulnerable.

Guy turned back to her.

She watched him, her eyes half-closed. Her lips drooped. But she was awake.

He knelt by the bath. "Felicia."

Her mouth twitched in a weak attempt at a smile, but she did not speak. Her eyes drifted shut.

"Felicia," he said, projecting confidence into his

voice. "I am going to bathe you. The warm water will help bring heat back into your body. Next we are going to get you into dry clothes and into bed with a posset."

He did not often feel helpless, but he was close to that emotion now. To occupy himself, since the purpose of the hot water was not to clean her but to warm her, he fetched her brush.

Sitting to the side of the tub so that his body did not block the heat from the fire, he began brushing her hair. The damp tendrils did not take well to the bristles, but he slowly worked out the knots.

"Ahem," Annabell said, looking around the screen. "I thought Mrs Drummond was here."

"She was. She is fetching dry linens."

"And left you alone with Felicia?"

He shrugged and stood up. "I am the master here. She did as I told her, which is more than you have ever done."

He was irritated at himself for not having heard Bell come in. He had been so enthralled by Felicia's hair that nothing else had registered. This had to stop.

"Here," he said, handing her the brush, "you finish."

She raised one quizzical brow. "Is that an order? A maid could do it."

"No." He gave his twin a hard look. "She is ill and floating in and out of awareness. I won't have someone tending her whom she does not know."

Annabell said nothing, but took the brush from him and sat in the chair he had vacated. Guy nodded before going around the screen. He stopped, his jaw clenched tight and his hands fisted until the knuckles hurt. He had to get control of his reactions.

Felicia was only a woman. A desirable woman, but

only a woman. He had had his share of women, many more lovely than her. Suzanne had been a beauty. If his wife were alive today, she would eclipse Felicia without even trying.

But he knew, in some part of him, that it would not matter. Suzanne had never held him captive as Felicia did. He had cared for Suzanne, even loved her, but he had never been consumed by passion for her.

Mrs Drummond entered, stopping his thoughts and making him glad to see her. "About time," he grumbled unfairly.

She cocked her head to one side. "Where is madam?"

He waved a hand at the screen. "In the hot water with Annabell brushing out her hair."

The housekeeper gave him a sharp look, but said nothing. She quickly changed the linen. That done, she went to join Annabell. Guy knew his help would no longer be needed. If he stayed, the two of them would hound him and let him do nothing. Mrs Drummond he could have overrode, but not Bell.

It was better this way. No telling what he would do next. He left without a word.

Guy sprawled in the same slipper chair he had sat in several weeks earlier while questioning Felicia. His unwelcome guest. He laughed, but it was more sardonic than humourous.

The fire crackled and leapt up the chimney, but its heat was faint by the time it reached the bed. The bath had warmed Felicia, but that had been temporary. Since the small hours of the night, he had watched her get worse. Her teeth chattered and she tossed and turned.

The next thing, she was hot with perspiration on her brow.

She turned towards him and he thought her eyes were open. There was no candle, only firelight, so he stood up and moved to the bed.

"Guy?" she said, her voice a hoarse whisper.

"I'm here," he murmured.

She smiled at him, but it was weak. Dark circles made her eyes appear huge. He smoothed the hair back from her face, delighting in the feel of the silken strands. He did not think he would ever tire of running his fingers through her hair.

"I am so cold," she said, her jaw clenched to keep her teeth from chattering.

Consternation gripped him. They had done everything they could. There were extra covers on the bed. An earthenware hot water-bottle nestled near her feet. Warm stones had been put in with her.

"So cold," she said, her voice cracking with exhaustion.

He studied her carefully. She looked so frail, as though she was too weak to fight off the chills that wracked her body. Mrs Drummond had been afraid this would happen. If they were not careful or were unlucky, Felicia would have a severe inflammation of the lungs.

There was only one other thing to do.

He stood and slipped out of his robe and shirt. He went to the other side of the bed and slid under the covers. Then he moved to her side and pulled her into the curve of his body. She felt like ice, as she had when he'd pulled her from the lake. This had to work.

A soft sigh came from her as she snuggled into him. Lying on his side, he wrapped his arms around her.

The flare of her bottom flush with his loins, the smooth flow of her flank running the length of his thighs and the heavy fullness of her breasts resting against his forearm all combined to make him groan.

He chastised himself. He was here to take the cold from her body and hopefully help her recover. He was not here to make love to her. The last thing he wanted to do—or needed to do—was make love to her. That basic act would complicate too many things. And he could not, would not take a chance on getting her pregnant.

No, he had to control himself better than he had in the past. But this was temptation so great that it was torture to resist.

She wriggled in closer. He thought he would explode. And her breasts. Even through the nightdress she wore, he could feel their fullness. In his mind, he could taste their sweetness and delight in their response to his touch.

Madness.

"Guy? Guy?" She twisted in his arms until she faced him. Her eyes were wide, her mouth a soft blur. "Hold me. Make the cold go away. Please."

He knew she had to be delirious. "I'm trying, Felicia. I'm trying." His voice was hoarse with desire, his loins tight with the need to love her.

She burrowed into him until her lips pressed against the bare skin of his chest. Her arms slid up and around his neck. Her breasts pushed against him. Her nipples were hard pebbles that abraded his sensitized flesh. She might as well be naked for all the barrier her nightdress provided. They touched in every area that mattered. Guy ached and still she clung to him as though she were trying to absorb him or be absorbed by him.

"So cold," she murmured, her breath hot and moist against his flesh.

He groaned, all his good intentions beginning to evaporate in the heat she created in his body. "Felicia," he said, his voice cracking on her name. "Stop. Perhaps this was not such a good idea."

She held him tighter. She tipped back her head to look at him and her eyes glittered feverishly. "This is a very good idea. Very, very good."

Her lips parted and her eyelids drooped, but her body clung to his. Guy knew he was lost.

No longer able to resist the temptation of her, no longer caring about why he had first entered her bed, Guy lowered his face. His mouth met hers and the shock of it rocked through his body, more intense than the first time. Her lips moved beneath his, opening and welcoming him. The pulse pounded in his loins as he accepted her invitation.

Little soft sucking sounds punctuated each kiss. He nipped her lips, then gently suckled them. She sighed in pleasure. Her fingers tangled in his hair, holding him close.

"More," she demanded, straining against him.

Guy did not know if she meant more kisses or just to hold her tighter. He was beyond himself with desire. All reason fled as his body rose to meet her need.

He undid the ribbon at her neck and then slid his hands down her side, revelling in the sleek feel of her under his fingers. He caught the hem of her gown and started working it up her body. She moved to help him until the clothing was over her head and on to the floor with his robe.

He shuddered as the silken flesh of her bosom rubbed the raw nerves of his chest. It took all his control not to push her to her back and enter her then and there. Her mouth sought out his neck where she suckled until he thought he would go crazy.

It became harder to breath. "Damn these trousers," he cursed.

He fumbled with the buttons, his fingers all thumbs. She continued to kiss him and nuzzle him until he thought he would go crazy if he did not take this to the next level. Finally his trousers were undone and he pulled them down his legs, taking his stockings and underclothing with them.

He sprang free and lodged in the soft warmth between her legs. He jerked and nearly ended everything then.

"Guy." She stopped kissing him long enough to look at him. "I want everything."

Her eyes held a glittering intensity. He stared back at her, wondering if she knew what she was saying. She was sick and had been freezing. Dimly he remembered that her coldness had started all of this. Right now, she felt like a flaming brand in his arms. Her face was flushed and her skin was hot against his.

She moved, trapping his hardness between her thighs and it no longer mattered. Nothing mattered but being inside her.

"I will give you everything I have," he promised.

Determined to pleasure her until she cried out for him, he slid down the length of her, kissing and nipping her as he went. In each hand, he held a breast and gently kneaded them, revelling in the firmness and the way they responded to his touch. Her entire body seemed to hum.

He reached the juncture of her thighs and regretfully released her breasts. She made a soft sound of protest.

"It is all right, Felicia," he said, his voice deeper than he had ever heard it. "You will like this."

He spread her legs and positioned them so he could reach her soft core. Then he began to kiss and lave her with his tongue.

"Guy," she gasped, her body bucking.

"Easy," he said, holding her hips firmly.

He used his fingers to massage her belly, never stopping his mouth and tongue. When her gasps became soft and quick and her stomach knotted, he knew she was ready. He rose to his knees, ignoring her protest, and slid into her. Her back arched and her nails bit into his thighs. He pulled out and thrust deeper, setting up a rhythm that she followed as though they had been lovers for all eternity. It was bliss.

Sensation overwhelmed him. He lost control. He tightened to the point of near pain, the pleasure was so intense. Shudders racked his body and he knew he was near his end.

"Guy…" Her voice rose, her nails raked his skin.

A glimmer of sanity entered his brain. He could not—he panted, trying desperately to gain control of himself—would not lose himself in her. She would not bear his child and all the danger that entailed.

Somehow, some way, he pulled out of her. His body protested, his muscles spasmed. He released his seed on the soft whiteness of her belly.

"My…" He trailed off, spent, with no breath to speak.

"Guy," she moaned. "Please, please, help me."

He realized with a start that he had ended it too soon for her. "Easy, Felicia," he said, rolling to her side and gathering her close. "I will make it right. I promise."

He caught her hungry mouth with his and slid his hand down. He stroked her with a passion that reignited his own. This time, he controlled himself. He might have spent himself once already, but he would not take another chance of being able to pull from her in time. Instead, he increased his motion to match the movement of her hips.

He felt her muscles clench and knew she was almost there. She thrust hard against his hand. Her mouth left his as a high moan escaped her. She exploded around him. Only after he was sure she was satisfied did he ease his stroking and bend to kiss her gently. Her sigh of relief filled his lungs.

He turned her so that her back fitted against his chest and pulled the covers around them, careful to see that she was tucked in. Instead of cold coming from her now, she radiated the hot heat of satisfaction. He shifted her hair aside and kissed the nape of her neck. She murmured something he could not hear and then her body relaxed. She had fallen asleep.

He lay awake into the early hours of morning.

Guy started awake. Where was he? What had woken him? Felicia. He was in her bed.

Memory flooded back. Felicia falling into the lake. Making love to her. Her calling out. Words he could not make out. That was what had woken him.

She tossed. "Nooo... Please, Lord, no." Her breath caught on a sob. "Not Colleen, please. Ced..."

She was calling out to someone. He rose on one elbow to see her, but the fire had died and she was only a darker shadow in a dark room. The covers fell from his shoulder. A cold dark room. Her body was in complete contrast. She was like a smouldering cinder. Something was wrong.

He had to see her better. He crawled from the bed. Naked as the day he was born and covered in goose-flesh, he went to her side and fumbled at the nearby table. He found a tinder box and the candle. Soon there was enough light to find his clothes where they lay strewn on the floor. Her nightdress tangled with his trousers as intimately as her body had tangled with his.

Instantly, uncontrollably, he hardened. It was as though he had not quenched his ardour no more than a couple hours before. He groaned as he pulled his trousers up and fastened them.

He went to Felicia. She was drenched in perspiration. Her beautiful hair lay in tangles on the pillow, its shine dulled.

"Dammit," he muttered. "This is not good."

"Please," she begged, eyes closed, body twisting. "Don't take them."

Tears streamed down her face. Her lips moved as she continued to plead. She was delirious. He had to get her temperature down.

He pulled back the covers and tucked an extra sheet that Mrs Drummond had left around Felicia, then went to the washbasin and soaked a cloth with the icy water. Mrs Drummond had left instructions to bathe her like this if her temperature rose, which it had.

He pulled the covers from her again and the musty odor of their lovemaking met him. His body responded instantly. He grimaced. He had to stop this. She needed his help, not his passion.

Gently, and more aroused than he wanted, he washed her heated skin. Already the cloth was warm and needed to be dipped in the cold water. He brought the washbasin and its stand by the bed.

Next he rinsed her face. The flush left her skin as the coolness touched it, only to return as soon as he stopped. He dipped the cloth again and moved down her body.

He bathed her without stop, starting at her forehead and going to her toes and then repeated it, again and again. The repetition eased some of his aching desire for her. She was so sick, he felt like a heartless rogue to want her so badly. But he did.

The water in the basin was lukewarm when someone knocked. "Come in," he said.

"Guy?" Annabell said.

He glanced over his shoulder as she stepped into the room. Before she could speak again, he said, "Bell, please go for more cold water and have a maid come in and start the fire. I am freezing."

Instead of immediately doing what he said, which was usual, she came to the bed and stood beside him. "She looks bad."

"I know," he said.

"But even so, she is lovely."

"I know," he said, wondering why his normal sardonic answers would not come.

Annabell glanced at him. "Are you in love with her?"

Guy tensed and with an effort of will looked his sister in the eye. "Don't be a silly romantic, Bell. I am not in love with her."

"A good thing," Annabell said drily, "since you are engaged to Miss Duckworth."

Her words were a blow to his solar plexus. He had forgotten. He had not thought about Emily Duckworth since he left her in London wearing the engagement ring he had just bought. He had not given her his mother's, the ring that passed from bride to bride. Suzanne had worn it and now it stayed in a safe here at The Folly.

"Go get the water and maid, Bell," he said, his voice sounding more tired than he wanted.

She gave him one searching glance before leaving, but said nothing further. Guy was thankful for that.

He looked down at Felicia. Her lashes were a sweep of chocolate above her cheeks. Her lips were swollen and scarlet. The dark circles under her eyes were deeper and blacker than they had been just hours before.

He had told her about Emily Duckworth, intending to put distance between them. It had for all of a day. And now they were to this point. It was no good. Emily Duckworth was the woman he intended to marry and have an heir by. Felicia had been an unwelcome houseguest.

Now she was his mistress.

This was not what he had planned. Widows frequently became men's mistresses—Jane in the village had been his for some time. But somehow he did not think Felicia was the type of woman to be a man's lightskirt.

That did not answer what he was to do about Felicia. Ideally, he would apologize to her and walk away. He knew he could not do that. Not yet. Not while she was in his house. Not while his need for her was greater than his reason. He groaned and rubbed his jaw where his beard itched.

The arrival of Bell, a maid and more water turned

his concentration. He yanked the covers over Felicia's nakedness and turned to his sister.

"Thank you for hurrying, Bell."

"A better greeting than before," she said, a smile in her eyes. "But you still look like something Dominic dragged home with him."

Guy laughed. He could not help it. He had seen some of the strays—four-legged and two—Dominic had brought home with him.

"Then I must look like something to scare children."

Now she smiled with her lips. "Or worse. Get some sleep." When his jaw tightened, she added, "I will stay with her until you are able to return."

He looked at Felicia. She seemed to be resting more comfortably. "Good advice, Bell, but call me immediately if her condition changes."

"I will," she promised with an indulgent look on her face. "Although I should not."

Chapter Eight

Guy woke feeling like he had drunk too much whisky the night before. His head felt like it was stuffed with wool and his limbs had no strength. He forced one eye open and then the other. From the faint light peeking through the drapes, he knew it was late afternoon.

He staggered out of bed and instantly regretted it. He wore no clothes and did not even remember removing them. His room was as cold as the lake Felicia had fallen in or so it seemed.

"Jeffries," he said, his voice louder than normal but not a shout.

His valet responded immediately. "Yes, my lord?" a very proper gentleman's gentleman answered from one of the many shadows.

Guy twisted around to see Jeffries crossing the room towards him. The valet was a short, trim man with a pointed chin and a decided dapperness about him. At the moment, he was impeccable in a plain black coat and pantaloons with a white shirt. Even his shirt points stood tall. A gentleman's gentleman of the first water.

Guy grinned.

He and Jeffries had been together a long time. Prior

to his elevation, the valet had been a footman at the Chillings's mansion in London. When Guy had chosen him, the man had contacted Beau Brummell's valet on his own initiative in order to learn his new job from the best. There were many men of fashion who would do anything to lure Jeffries from Guy, but the valet was loyal. However, he never failed to mention his desirability when Guy would not follow some dictate of Brummell's.

"Jeffries, I need to bathe and dress immediately."

The valet nodded. "As you wish, my lord, but she is no worse than when you left her."

Guy stopped in mid-step. "What did you say?"

Jeffries coughed. "I merely thought you wished to know that Madam Felicia is still sleeping and seems in no immediate danger. Her fever is down. I believe Mrs Drummond has a mustard poultice on the lady's, ahem...chest to ward off any inflammation."

Guy nodded. That was exactly what he wanted to know, but he did not like it that his valet knew the answer before he asked the question.

"Thank you."

"I am always glad to be of service."

Guy eyed the other man. Jeffries could be tongue in cheek when he chose. It was his only failing.

"Then you will be glad to arrange for my hot water to come immediately." Guy turned away with a grin. That would put Jeffries on his mettle.

"Absolutely, my lord," the valet said, his tone only the slightest bit huffy.

Twenty minutes later, Guy sank into the welcome heat of the bath. "Ah," he sighed. "This is perfect, Jeffries."

"I know, my lord."

Guy shook his head slightly. "As will be my clothes."

"You arrange a beautiful cravat, my lord."

Guy laughed outright, some of the night's worry leaving him. "Generous of you."

A knock interrupted them. Guy heard the door open.

"Lady Fenwick-Clyde," the valet said in his most disapproving tone. "His lordship is indisposed."

From behind the privacy of the screen, Guy said, "I am bathing, Bell. Can't this wait?"

"I don't think so," she said.

Guy caught the anxiety in her voice. He sat straight up and grabbed for the bath sheet laid across the hearth. He stood and wrapped the length around him.

"Has Felicia got worse?"

He heard Bell sigh and could picture her selecting a strand of hair and starting to twirl it around her fingers. "This is not about her. We—you—are in a pickle. Miss Emily Duckworth is here."

"What?"

Guy nearly dropped the bath sheet into the water. He managed to catch it with only one corner sopping. Securing it so that it covered his hips and legs, he stepped out of the tub and around the screen.

"What the devil is she doing here?"

Bell shrugged, but she twirled the strand of hair. "I have no idea. She won't speak to me, other than civilities."

"Fine pickle indeed," Guy muttered. "Jeffries, fetch my things. Bell, go back and keep her company." Bell raised one black brow. Guy caught her action just before turning away. "Please go back and stay with her."

"That is much better. I am not one of your servants

or horses," Annabell said. "I don't like her showing up like this either. It makes me think that she knows about Felicia, but I don't see how she could."

"Neither do I," Guy said, nodding to Jeffries his acceptance of the clothing the valet had selected. "But I did not invite her."

Annabell groaned. "Oh, dear. Well, I had better get back. No telling what is happening while I am here. Perhaps I can get something out of her before you come down."

"Let us hope so," Guy said.

"This is a very uncomfortable situation," she said tartly, retreating to the door.

"Yes, it is, Bell, and not one of my making. I did not bring Felicia here to flaunt the proprieties. I brought her here because she was hurt. Nor did I invite Miss Duckworth," Guy said, his mouth twisted.

Fifteen minutes later, Guy stood outside the door that led to the north drawing room. He was dressed in the height of fashion and knew that no matter what kind of physical and emotional mayhem had been going on between him and Felicia, he looked the part of the consummate aristocrat without a concern in the world other than the perfection of his cravat, which was done in a perfect Chillings Crease.

When the footman moved to open the door and announce him, Guy shook his head. Miss Duckworth should not be here. He wanted to see her face before she saw him. Perhaps he could learn something from observing her.

Guy entered the room quietly. Annabell sat at her ease, feet on a stool and posture anything but elegant. Miss Duckworth, on the other hand, sat with back straight, hands folded in her lap, and head held high. She was the perfect picture of a highborn lady. She also looked uncomfortable, as well she might. Ladies of Quality, which she was, did not call on unmarried gentlemen who were not their relations.

He scowled. ''Miss Duckworth,'' he said in a voice that carried the distance of the room to where the two women sat in chairs grouped around a roaring fire. ''So pleased to see you.''

Miss Duckworth started, her head and upper body jerking around so that she could see him. He studied her dispassionately. She was not a Beauty, but she was striking. Her hair, red as a rowan berry, was pulled back from her strongly angled face and into a chignon at the nape of her long neck. He knew her eyes to be grey. Her figure was tall and slim. She would make him a more than acceptable wife.

She would also be biddable, or so he had thought. This visit, however, made him think he needed to re-evaluate her. Not that it mattered now. He had offered for Miss Duckworth and she had accepted. It was a bargain only a man of no honour would break and he was many things, but not honourless.

Annabell rose and came toward him. ''I was just telling Miss Duckworth that you would be with us shortly.''

Miss Duckworth also stood, and her brown sarcenet pelisse trimmed with ermine moved gracefully with her. Beneath she wore a plum kerseymere carriage dress. Brown was not a popular colour, but it became her. Her ermine muff lay on a nearby chair. She wore Wellington boots. Her style was what had first attracted Guy. He still admired it.

''Lovely, as always,'' he said.

Annabell linked her arm in his and pulled him to the other woman. Guy felt his sister's tension. He shrugged slightly so that his coat settled better on his shoulders and some of the tightness in his muscles eased. When they were within feet of Miss Duckworth, Bell released him. He stepped forward and took his fiancée's outstretched hand and brought it to his lips. The fine leather of her gloves was soft.

She smiled at him, but it did not reach her eyes. "Courteous, as always."

If he did not know better, he would say she was irritated, not nervous. He realized that, much as he hoped differently, she very likely knew about Felicia. News travelled quickly in their world, even here in the country in the dead of winter.

"Is tea on the way?" he asked Annabell, deciding to ease some of the discomfort that was so palpable.

"Of course," his sister said in tones that implied he had insulted her by asking.

"I never doubted you would organise this, Bell. The issue was timing." He ignored his twin's scowl and turned to Miss Duckworth. "You must be frozen after your trip."

"December is not the best month to travel in," she conceded and cast a quick look at Annabell. "But we cannot always choose when we must visit."

He raised one eyebrow, a trick that normally quelled most people. However, it had never worked with Felicia, and he realized, as Miss Duckworth returned his look without flinching, that it did not work with his fiancée either.

Tea came and Annabell poured. After handing Miss Duckworth hers, she turned to Guy. "Would you care for some?"

She was being provoking. "Thank you, Bell, but you know it is not a favourite of mine. Did Oswald bring coffee?" He knew the butler had done so. Oswald was meticulous.

Bell poured the coffee black and handed the cup to him. She shuddered dramatically. "I don't see how you can stand to drink this without cream or sugar. It is a bitter drink. Even in my travels I never developed a taste for it."

He drank the beverage down. "It cuts the sweetness of the cakes and gives me a jolt of energy. Something I may need." He looked at Miss Duckworth as he said the last. His gut said he was not going to like the reason for her visit. Deciding to bring this meeting to a head, he asked, "What brings you here, Miss Duckworth?"

He caught her unawares, and she choked on the tea she had just sipped. She set her cup and saucer down just in time to keep the liquid that spilled over the edge from landing on her clothing. Annabell glared at him at the same time as she handed Miss Duckworth a white napkin embroidered with the Chillings arms. His fiancée dabbed at her mouth and then her spotless clothing.

Nerves, Guy decided.

"I think," Miss Duckworth said, her cultured tones back, "that my reason for being here is best discussed in private, Chillings."

"That bad?" he drawled.

Miss Duckworth's ivory skin reddened.

Annabell sighed and shot Guy a reproachful look. "I shall be in the Sylph Room." What she did not say was, with Felicia.

He cast his twin a minatory look. Bell grinned roguishly, her expression telling him that tit for tat was fun.

He could be pushy and rude to Miss Duckworth, but Bell would put him in his place.

As soon as the door closed behind Annabell, Miss Duckworth rose and started pacing. She reminded Guy of Dominic, and he nearly told her to sit back down just as he would have ordered his brother. She stopped on her own and looked squarely at him.

"I can hedge and simper and beg you to tell me this is nothing but a Banbury tale," she sighed. "But I do not think it is."

The reproach in her grey eyes told Guy she knew about Felicia. How much more she knew remained to be revealed. But she could not know about last night. No one but Felicia and he knew about that.

Memory rushed through his mind and body without his volition. The feel of her hair against his bare skin, the touch of her lips on his and the ecstasy of their joining. A shudder of desire racked his body.

"Are you quite all right?" Miss Duckworth asked, her brows drawn in worry.

"Of course," Guy said, his voice deeper than he liked, and wondered if he truly were fine. "A draught. Nothing more."

Her expression remained skeptical but she said nothing else on the matter.

"You were saying..." he prompted, his tone normal, his mind once more in control of his treacherous body.

"It has come to my attention, and goodness only knows who else's, that you have a female guest here." The words were a spurt that ended as abruptly as they had begun.

Guy lifted one black brow. "Yes?" He invited her with his tone to confide in him.

Her eyes narrowed slightly. It seemed she had more spirit than he had thought.

"I know you very likely think it none of my business, Chillings, but I must disagree with you. We are betrothed."

His jaw tightened. "But we are not married."

She took a step back. "True. Is this how I can expect you to go on after we are wed?"

Guy rubbed his bearded jaw with long fingers as he considered his answer. The tone of this conversation would tell how they would deal together. He had thought she knew his terms better than this. And he had not decided what to do about Felicia.

"Annabell is here to chaperon."

She nodded. "My information did not have her here."

"Ah." So the tale had reached her early in the unfolding. "Might I ask how you found out?"

Her sigh was deeper, and she turned on her heel and walked to the window where she stared outside. "One of your footmen is stepping out with a maid in another house. The maid is a distant cousin of one of the dairymaids on my father's estate. And so the thread of connection goes."

He understood perfectly. The aristocracy and their servants lived in a small world, intertwined in so many ways. The links of relationship were not surprising. This was also another reason why he had been fairly sure from the beginning that, while Felicia was a lady of Quality, she was not from his circle. He would have known her otherwise.

"She was in a carriage accident." He told his fiancée what had transpired over the past weeks, leaving out only his growing involvement with Felicia. "And there you have it, Miss Duckworth. The lady is upstairs now with a fever and delirium.'' He paused to let the information sink in. ''Would you like to see her?''

Emily Duckworth shook her head emphatically. ''No, thank you, Chillings. I did not come to quiz the woman.''

''Only me,'' he said with a cynical twist of his lips.

She shrugged. ''You have a reputation.''

''Which you knew when you accepted my offer.''

''Yes, I did. I did not think it would matter.'' She gave him a candid look. ''We are not in love. We don't even know each other beyond a passing acquaintance.''

''Enough for you to know of my proclivities.''

''True. But then, most gentlemen of the *beau monde* share your *proclivities*. It is a trait a married woman must endure.''

He did not like the direction of this discussion. ''A marriage of convenience is like that, Miss Duckworth.''

''Yes, I know.'' She took a deep breath. ''Does she mean anything to you?''

He stared at her. ''You are impertinent.''

''Yes, I suppose I am,'' she said softly, turning away. ''I had not intended to be. As I said before, ours is not a love match. Yet, I find my pride pricked.''

''Then accept the situation as everyone else of our acquaintance does, even the gentlemen.''

His cynical words dropped between them like stones. He knew he should tell her that Felicia was a houseguest, nothing more. He should reiterate that Bell was here, had been here before anything happened. He said nothing. Instead he stood so she would know this interrogation was over.

She turned back to him. ''I wish that I could, Chillings. But pride is my besetting sin. Even Lucy says so, and she is barely old enough to come out this next Season.''

His shoulders hunched. This was the moment for him to tell her that nothing had happened, that gossip—if it reached the *ton*—would die soon. The Quality lived life to the fullest and then moved on with very little thought for the past. Again, he said nothing. He had many faults, but he did not lie.

Her hands, buried in the folds of her pelisse, moved as though she could not control them. He wondered why he had not noticed before that she was not truly the calm and reasonable spinster he had first thought her. She hid herself well.

"Pride can be difficult," he agreed. "But I repeat, ours is to be a marriage of convenience. All I ask of you is an heir. After that, you may go on as you please. Just as I will.''

He watched her straight back stiffen. Remorse and a hint of sorrow that their marriage would be so sterile took him. "I am sorry if you wished for more, Miss Duckworth. It is not too late for you to call off.''

Even as the words left his mouth, he found himself hoping she would do so. Suddenly, a marriage of convenience was the last thing he wanted.

She turned back to look at him. Her face told him nothing of her feelings. "I understand what you want from me, Chillings. I knew it from the start and am willing to comply. I just did not think you would throw your infidelities in my face, and I hope that once we are married you will not bring your mistresses home with you.''

His eyes narrowed and the urge to lambast her was strong, but she had not said anything that was not the truth. And she had a right to be angry, no matter what he had said earlier. But he was not willing to stay and receive more of her sharp tongue.

He gave her a curt bow. ''If you will excuse me, Miss Duckworth. I will send Oswald to escort you to your rooms.''

She still said nothing, so he pivoted on the heel of his Hessian and left. The jangle of the boot's gold tassel was loud in the silent room.

Felicia lay still with her eyes closed. She was kept warm and cocooned by the covers. The scents of lavender, lime and musk mixed in the air along with the smell of burning coal.

She opened her eyes and looked around for Guy. When she did not see him, her spirits fell. She told herself not to be a goose. There was no reason for him to here. The lime and musk had misled her and meant nothing.

She sighed and closed her eyes, thinking she would nap. She was so tired. But her mind insisted on racing so that she could not mentally relax no matter how badly her body needed rest.

The last thing she remembered clearly was skating on the frozen lake. Everything after that was a blur. Cold, freezing cold and then hotter, hot as flames. Guy, Chillings, Viscount Chillings was mixed in with everything.

And before that. An accident in a carriage on her way to London where she was to meet with…

She sucked in air.

She remembered everything, who she was, why she was in mourning, why she was going to London in such a hurry. Everything.

She heard movement, sensed someone by the bed. She had been so lost in her returning memories, that she had not heard the door open.

"Felicia?"

A man's deep voice folded around her like the thickest, most desirable of honey. Her chest ached with longing. She opened her eyes.

"Chillings?" she whispered. "Guy."

"Felicia." She heard gladness in his voice and relief.

He leaned over her so close that she could see the fine lines that bracketed his mouth. There were dark circles under his eyes, accentuating their deep blue colour. His hair was dishevelled and his shirt open, the cravat untied and hanging down on each side of the collar. His pulse throbbed strongly just below his Adam's apple. Felicia's senses quickened with desire for him.

He was her safety, her warmth—her passion.

She forced a smile but knew it was weak. She was so tired. She said the first thing that came to her mind. "I love you."

"What?"

His voice held surprise and...and withdrawal. Her head hurt, whether from his rejection or her illness she could not tell, nor would she make herself decide. Some things were better left alone.

Her smile faded and she turned her head just enough so she would not have to look at him, see the rejection spread across his face. She remembered too many losses and too many rejections already to be able to watch him push her away too.

"Felicia," he said softly, his tone commanding her to listen to him. "You have been ill. We were worried about you."

She nodded, a barely perceptible movement, but still could not bring herself to look at him. She had to come to terms with the memories that poured into her before she could face him with equanimity and acceptance of the fact that she loved him and he did not feel the same. Her mouth twisted. Not that any of this mattered. She was married to a man very much alive.

Her stomach cramped sharply and painfully. Now she remembered that this spasming occurred when she was upset.

"Mrs Drummond has left some laudanum for the pain she says you will feel in your chest. You have been coughing so much when you were not drenched with a fever." She heard glass clinking and the slosh of water. "Drink this. It will help."

"Yes, it will lessen the physical pain," she murmured. "But I don't wish to take it." She had never liked blunting her senses with drugs. "I remember who I am."

She could not see his face. She sensed rather than saw his shock. Finally, knowing she could not continue to hide behind her sickness, she turned back to him.

He stared at her, his expression unreadable. The stark lines of his cheeks and jaw showed his strength and his determination. She might be stupid and have told him she loved him, but she knew in this moment that he would never feel the same for her. He desired her. He had proven that when he taught her billiards. Instantly, she was hot, something she realized that came from her memory of what they had done.

Fortunately for her and her vows of marriage, Chillings was not as susceptible as she. His body was involved. Her heart was involved. Two very different organs.

Quietly, he asked, "Who are you?"

In a barely audible voice, she told him. "I am Felicia Anne Marbury, married to Edmund Douglas Marbury, mother of Cedric and Colleen Marbury." Tears blurred her vision, as unexpected as they were painful. "Or I was their mother. They…" Her voice trailed off and no matter how she tried, the words would not come out. "I…mourning."

Sobs welled up inside her to spill over as a torrent. Her shoulders shook and her stomach bunched. Breathing seemed impossible. She curled into a ball. The remembered loss was as sharp and torturous as though it had happened yesterday instead of nearly a year ago.

"Felicia," Guy said.

She could not answer him.

A part of her felt him wrap his arms around her and bundle her and her covers up. He carried her to a chair and sat down with her in his lap, held securely against his chest. She turned her face into his warmth.

One hand held her shoulder while the other burrowed into the depths of her loose hair. His fingers began to massage the tight muscles at the base of her skull, bringing comfort and the healing power of touch.

Guy held her tightly, wishing there was something he could do to ease her pain, wanting to protect her from this agony. He knew only too well how heartwrenching it was to lose a child. But to lose two children she had borne and raised must have been horrendous.

He also worried. This bout with grief could not be good for her in her frail condition. She needed all her strength to heal.

But she remembered.

They could go forward from here. He stopped himself from going down that road. She could go forward from here. There was no future for them, even if she did think she loved him. She was married. He was betrothed.

He continued to stroke and massage her scalp even as he held her close. The fire crackled, providing more warmth than he needed with her on his lap and the covers, coverlet and all, from the bed draped over them both. But the last thing he wanted was for her to get sick again. As it was, they would be lucky if she did not suffer a relapse.

He heard her hiccup at the same time as her head rose from his chest. He looked down into her tear-drenched eyes and it was nearly more than he could resist not to kiss her. But she did not need his passion right now. She needed his strength and protection. Instead of taking her lips with his, he stroked the tangled, damp hair from her forehead. She burned.

Then she smiled at him, a wavering one, but still a smile. He smiled back.

"I am so sorry," he murmured, continuing to stroke her hair back. "So very sorry."

She closed her eyes as though to shut out the memory, but soon reopened them. "Thank you, Guy. For holding me." She hiccupped again. "I've ruined your shirt. And it is—was—spotless."

"It doesn't matter," he said. "You needed to release your grief."

She sighed and leaned her head against him. "It was as though I had just lost them. As though nearly a year has not gone by."

"Your amnesia. I would be surprised if it has not

played strange tricks with your mind and your memories."

She nodded, her hair tangling in his shirt buttons. "Ouch," she muttered.

"Careful," he murmured. "I will free you."

She gazed at him with trusting eyes as he carefully worked the strands loose. "I wish all my pain could be so easily dealt with."

"So do I," he said, finding that he truly meant it.

The realization made his fingers still. But it was too late for them. He hardened his resolve.

"It is best if you get back in bed. You need sleep and rest to get well." He stood and carried her to the four-poster where he laid her gently down.

Her hands fell away from his neck as she sank into the mound of mattress and pillows. Her mouth tightened. "I owe you an explanation of who I am and what I was doing when you found me," she finally said.

He stayed by the bed. "Later. You need rest right now."

Her mouth twisted. "Rest. I feel like I have not rested for a year. Even here, with no memory, I knew something awful had happened to me. No, I need to talk more than I need to sleep. Perhaps telling you will free me."

He saw her slender body shift as though her mind moved her to physical action. Perhaps this was better. Talking might release some of the pain, like lancing a festering wound let the poison flow out so the wound could heal.

"Go ahead," he said softly, taking her hand and squeezing carefully.

"My full name is Felicia Anne Marbury. I was born Felicia Anne Dunston."

He sucked in his breath. "Dunston?"

"Yes. My father is Nathan Dunston."

"The coal baron." Guy whistled softly. "He is one of the richest men in Newcastle."

"Yes, again," she muttered. "And one of the most single-minded. My mother died giving birth to a still-born boy—" Guy jerked, releasing her hand, his reaction beyond his control. "Oh," she murmured, looking stricken, "I did not think. I am so sorry. I did not mean to bring you pain."

"It happened a long time ago. Keep talking," he said firmly.

"My father raised me. He was not always a coal baron. But he was always ambitious and always doing whatever it took to get ahead in the world. He said it was for me, but I always knew it was for himself. He sent me to the finest schools so that I would look and speak like Quality." Her fingers twisted in the soft, feathery squares of the coverlet. "He forced me to marry Edmund. Or rather, he explained to me why I was going to. Edmund is of the gentry. My children would inherit my father's wealth with Edmund's land. Then their children would marry into the aristocracy. My father has it all planned out." She gazed at nothing. "Had it all planned out."

Her thumbnail went through the silk covering of the coverlet and she began to pluck out the feathers. One by one, they fell to the floor. Guy did not think she even knew what she was doing. Her gaze was on something in the past.

"Then I lost them. Measles. Scarlet Fever. They were gone before I realized it. That was, oh, eleven, twelve months ago."

Fresh tears welled from her eyes to drip over softly.

The violent emotions of earlier had been drained from her.

"Edmund accused me of carelessness." Her jaw twitched. "It did not help that I had denied him my bed since Cedric's birth. There was no other heir." More feathers drifted to the floor. "My father was furious. He told me to reconcile with Edmund. To have another child." Her fingers shook so that the feathers drifted everywhere. "I could not." She looked up at him, her eyes huge in the pinched pallor of her face. "I know how important an heir is to a man, but Cedric was my son. My child. Not just someone to inherit my father's money and my husband's land. You understand, don't you?"

He nodded, unable to speak. If her father were here, this moment, he would murder the man for his brutality. He sat on the edge of the bed and pulled her close. All he could do was hold Felicia and try to comfort her. Frustration was an emotion he had not felt since Suzanne's death. It was not an emotion he enjoyed.

Guy lost track of how long he held her. He had not thought himself capable of giving just comfort to a woman who aroused him as this one did. Especially after last night. Yet, that was all he did. She was too vulnerable for anything else.

The fire popped and the mantel clock chimed. They seemed to rouse Felicia.

"Guy?"

"Hmm?" He was nearly asleep, content just to have her close.

"There is more."

Chapter Nine

Guy sighed. "There always is, Felicia." He felt her stiffen in his arms and regretted his unsympathetic words. "Tell me."

"I am—*was* on my way to London because Edmund is divorcing me."

Her words fell between them like weighted stones. For one instant, elation held him, then was gone. It did not matter. He was marrying Emily Duckworth. He needed an heir, just as her father and husband had needed one. Dispassionate and impersonal as that might sound to the woman responsible for bearing the child, that was a fundamental fact of life in his world.

A rebellious voice that he cynically attributed to his loins said that Felicia could give him an heir. The Lord only knew how much he wanted her.

He looked down at her face, raised so she could watch his expression as she told him her story. She was not beautiful. Emily Duckworth was more distinctive-looking. But Felicia had a delicacy about her that stirred him. And she had that glorious hair that lured his senses like a siren lured unwary seamen.

No. Felicia would never stop other men in their

tracks, but they would grow to love her when they came to know her. She was a gentle soul who had the spirit and strength of her convictions.

She also aroused him like no other woman ever had. But he could not, would not marry her. He needed an heir, and he would not impregnate a woman he cared greatly for. Never again.

"Say something, please," she whispered when he did not comment on her last words.

Guy's arms tightened around her. "On what grounds is he divorcing you?"

Her usually soft lips twisted into a hard smile. "My failure to provide an heir."

A sharp, short bark of laughter escaped Guy. The irony was exquisite. "As much as he might wish to divorce you for that, my dear, he cannot."

Her mouth twisted. "True. That is his real reason. But one cannot get a divorce because one's wife has failed to produce an heir, so Edmund has accused me of adultery."

A sharp twinge of anger was quickly followed by guilt. He might not have completed his lovemaking to Felicia, but he might just as well have. He did not think she was an adulteress before last night. But she did not remember and now was not the time to tell her.

"Your husband is the lowest form of life," he said, his voice cracking. "And why were you going to London? To fight it?"

"No. At first I was shocked and angry beyond bearing. Now I am glad. I want to be free of him." Her disillusionment and hurt tinged every word. "But he is determined to keep my jointure because I have failed to give him an heir. He is telling the courts that he is entitled to my money because of my infidelity." Her cheeks burned with indignation. "He knows very well that I have not been unfaithful. He is greedy. I need that jointure, or at the very least a part of it, more than he does. With it, I will be free of my father, as well."

Fresh guilt ate at Guy, but the last thing she needed to know right now was about last night. Yet, there was such yearning in her last words that Guy reacted without thought. "To hell with your jointure. I will give you enough money that neither one of those bastards will ever have any hold over you again."

She gaped at him.

He silently cursed himself. What was he doing? He had as good as asked her to become his mistress. But he did not stop.

"I will give you enough money that your jointure, whatever it is, will be as nothing." She looked stricken, as though he had wounded her. Then her face hardened, and her eyes glittered. "You don't have to do anything, Felicia. I am offering because I hate to see you in this situation because two men control your financial security." He smiled ruefully. "Bell would certainly applaud that reason."

She pushed hard against his chest so that he released her. "I cannot and will not take your money, Viscount Chillings. No matter what magnanimous reason you have for offering." Her voice was quiet and cold. "I would not accept your offer even if refusing it meant spending the rest of my life under Edmund's or my father's control."

He looked away from her at the fire, unwilling to decide if the knot in his stomach was from relief at her refusal or disappointment. "You are wise, Felicia. I spoke from anger at what those two men have done to you. They should be protecting you, not using you as a pawn for their own ends.'' He looked back at her. ''But remember, the offer is always there if you have need of it.''

The look in her eyes softened and she withdrew one hand from the covers and cupped it around his cheek. ''You are generous, Guy. I should not have misjudged you so.''

He said nothing. She had not misjudged him so badly. He wanted her for a mistress, in his house, in his bed, beneath him. Heaven help him, he just wanted her.

A knock preceded Annabell. She stopped cold and looked at them.

''What are you doing?'' she demanded in a harsh whisper, glaring at her twin. ''What if someone besides me came in?''

''Anyone else would wait to be asked in,'' Guy drawled, but he knew she was right.

''Mrs Drummond would not and you know it,'' she stated flatly. She reached them and studied Felicia. ''I see you are feeling better.''

Felicia blushed from the roots of her hair to where the pale flesh of her skin disappeared beneath the covers. ''Much, thank you, Annabell.''

''Humph! No thanks to my brother, I am sure.''

''No, Annabell, your brother has helped me more than I can say.'' Felicia's soft voice, firm in its conviction, caught and held Annabell's attention. ''I have regained my memory.''

Annabell started. She glanced at Guy. ''When did it happen?''

''When I woke up.''

It was a long, hard story for her to repeat. Some things she left out. Annabell did not need to know about her father's dynastic plans. That was too personal for anyone but Guy to know.

Hours later, Felicia watched Guy and Annabell leave. Even exhausted as she was, she could not sleep. She remembered everything: the children, Edmund, her father...Guy's lack of response to her declaration of love.

And why should he have responded? He did not love her, and he was engaged. She had known that from the first. He had not hidden it from her. Yet, she had fallen in love with him, nearly let him make love to her that evening in the games room.

And there were other images that refused to go away. Pictures of them here, doing things she could not believe. Making love.

She was crazy. Regaining her memory had made her crazier than before.

She tossed from side to side, unable to get comfortable, unable to stop thinking. The best thing was for her to leave as soon as possible. She had to get to London. She had to find a solicitor who would speak in her defence, since she could not do so herself, when Edmund accused her of being an adulteress and tried to keep her jointure. She had to have that money. She had to get away from her father and start a life of her own, and that money was her only chance.

And she was late. She should have been in London weeks ago.

There is always Guy's offer of money, a small voice insisted. Money with no strings attached. He could not—would not—marry her, but she sensed in her heart that he would make her his mistress if she would let him. She could not do that.

She would soon be a divorcée, an accused adulteress, a disgraced woman. That did not make her a fallen woman, and she would not become one. Not even for Guy.

Still, fury at the injustice of it all burned inside her. A woman had no rights. Edmund was accusing her of infidelity and as long as he found two witnesses he would be believed. She could not even testify in her own defence.

She turned to her side, then, unable to get comfortable, propped herself up on the pillows. The fire burned orange, its flames seeming like dancers leaping for the stars before falling back to earth. That was how she felt right now, wanting something she could never have.

Life was not easy. First the loss of her children… Her chest hurt to the point that drawing a breath was nearly impossible. She closed her eyes and forced her mind to keep thinking, willing away the emotional pain that nearly overwhelmed her. Then there was Edmund shaming her and dragging her reputation through the muck for his own ends. And now Guy. She loved him and it was too late. She was a woman with a reputation beyond the pale, and he was engaged to another woman. She did not think things could be worse.

With a sigh, she curled into a tight protective ball.

Felicia shifted the curtains just enough to see the gravelled drive way below. This was the last thing she should be doing, spying on Miss Duckworth's departure, but here she was. The other woman had only stayed one night. She had not met her, and her curiosity had got the better of her.

Guy walked beside Miss Duckworth with Annabell

on the other side. All three talked with much enthusiasm. Guy laughed at something his fiancée said. Felicia's nails dug into the thick velvet fabric of the curtain. Guy took the woman's hand and raised it to his lips. Felicia's nails ripped through the velvet. From this distance she could not see the expression on anyone's face.

She dropped the material and turned away.

It was time for her to leave. Past time.

A knock on the door made Felicia start guiltily. She had told no one of her intention to leave immediately and every creak or crack in the room made her think someone was coming to stop her. A ridiculous fear, considering that Guy had made it plain from the start that she was unwelcome.

"Who is it?" she finally asked.

"Mrs Drummond, Mrs Marbury."

Felicia gripped the leather straps of the portmanteau and considered what to do. If she let the housekeeper in, Guy would know her plans before she even finished packing. Not that it mattered. Her business in London was urgent and did not concern him.

She tossed her head, suddenly defiant. "Come in."

The older woman entered, took one look at what Felicia was doing, and gasped, one hand going to her mouth. "Never say you are leaving without a word to anyone, ma'am. His lordship will be that upset, he will."

Felicia's jaw clenched. "His lordship has other concerns." She forced her muscles to relax enough so she could smile. "What can I do for you?"

The housekeeper shook her head. "Never be asking what you can do for me, ma'am. I am here to see if there is anything I can do for you.'' She moved closer to the bed where Felicia stood. ''His lordship sent me.''

Felicia's first inclination was to say something un-ladylike, but that would not be fair. There was no reason to take out her sense of loss on this woman. Mrs Drummond had always been more than kind to her. Today the housekeeper looked particularly old, her grey hair seemed dull and the lines around her eyes and mouth were more pronounced. No, she did not deserve Felicia's hurt anger.

''Thank you, but I am fine. Please tell his lordship so.''

''Yes, ma'am,'' the housekeeper said, casting one last comprehensive look at the portmanteau and travelling case.

Felicia watched the other woman close the door before sinking down on to the chair by the bed, the same chair Guy had sat in to watch over her. She had thought the loss of her children was still more than she could bear, and now she had this.

She was in love with a man who could never marry her. He was engaged to another woman, an arrangement that no man with honour would break. She was about to become a divorced woman, so that even if Miss Duckworth broke off the engagement Guy still could not marry her. No matter what, she could not marry the man she loved.

She could become his mistress.

The thought was as insidious as it was tempting. It was the only way she could see to be with him.

But she wanted more children. She wanted more children so badly she ached from the need. She did not want those children to be illegitimate.

No, she could not become his mistress. She had to find her own way in the world without him.

The door crashed open without any warning.

Felicia jumped to her feet, her heart skipping a beat. "What?"

Guy strode into the room, slamming the door with one violent push. "What are you doing?"

Heart still pounding, arms akimbo, she faced him. "Don't you believe in knocking?"

He reached her. "Don't you believe you owe me notification that you intend to leave my home and my protection?"

She could barely breathe around the tightness in her chest and her voice was squeaky. "Surely you jest? You have wanted me gone since the moment you brought me here."

He grabbed her upper arms and yanked her to him. She gasped in surprise.

"I...sto—"

His mouth crushed hers. The fury that drove him, communicated to her. Her body tingled and sparked as she responded to him.

His hands slid up her arms, cupped her neck in passing and burrowed into the depths of her hair. Shivers held her as she felt the thick strands come loose from their pins and tumble to her shoulders. They were heavy and pulled her head back. He took advantage and deepened the kiss.

Desire welled up in her, desire as she had never experienced it, not even with him. A desperate hunger seemed to drive him and made her respond against all her better judgment.

"I want you so badly I hurt," he said against her mouth, his normally smooth baritone a rasp.

She felt him against her, pushing and teasing even through the layers of her petticoat and skirt and his breeches. They were like two animals caught in a passion neither could control. Nor did she understand the intensity of her response.

"Don't leave," he said.

He lifted her into his arms and strode to the chair where he had held and comforted her just days before. He sank down, his lips never leaving hers. She clung to the lapels of his jacket, needing the security of his strength in her growing weakness.

Heat consumed her. The heat of the fire and the heat of her response to him filled her so that she did not realize he had undone the buttons of her dress and pulled the material from her shoulders until his mouth left hers and descended on her exposed flesh. She gasped as his tongue slid along the line of her collarbone until his mouth found the hollow at the base of her throat.

She gasped. "What are you doing?" A soft moan escaped her as his mouth found her breast. "What…?"

"I am making love to you," he murmured.

His words seared through her being. This was everything she wanted, but not enough. She wanted more.

Her body had a will of its own. Her nipple tightened and her stomach tensed. Her heart pounded.

But she had to stop this. She had to.

Felicia took a deep breath, pushing her breast deeper into Guy's waiting lips. She sucked in sharply as his teeth nipped her and a bolt of electricity shot to her loins.

"Oh, stop, please stop," she managed, wondering why her voice sounded so strange and distant, yet knowing why. She wanted to make love to him.

He lifted his head and his eyes, dark and stormy, looked at her. His cheeks were blade sharp. His mouth was swollen from consuming her. Slowly, she saw reason return to him. His dilated pupils no longer glittered with passion.

He stood and set her carefully from him. "My apologies, Felicia. Mrs Marbury."

She gulped hard, her throat feeling like it was closed. "I..."

"There is nothing to say. I took liberties." He stared above her head. "We are both committed elsewhere. I should have remembered that."

He pivoted on his heel and left without a backward glance. Felicia crumbled to the floor. She buried her face in her hands.

She had to leave. There were no other choices. She loved him too much, while he only desired her.

The next morning, Felicia stood in the breakfast room gazing at the portrait of Guy's first wife while she waited for the travelling coach to be brought around. The other woman seemed to gaze down at her in mocking humour.

"She was a Beauty," Annabell said from behind.

Felicia whirled around, taken by surprise. "Yes, she was," she managed to say calmly.

The last thing she wanted anyone to know was that her heart was breaking. That would be too humiliating, and she had already been humiliated enough by her unbridled response to Viscount Chillings's lovemaking.

Annabell gave her an oblique look. "They were childhood sweethearts. Or rather, Suzanne was crazy about Guy from the moment she could walk well enough to follow him. He did not notice her until much later." She smiled. "I believe that is typical."

"I suppose," Felicia said.

She remembered how her daughter, Colleen, had followed her older brother Cedric like a puppy follows the master it adores. It was a bittersweet memory, no longer the painful wrench it had once been. It was a relief to remember the good things without feeling such pain that she wanted to remember nothing.

"Then Suzanne had her London Season," Annabell continued, drawing Felicia's thoughts back to the present. "She was the toast of the town. Every man courted her, even Prinny, although I dare say his intentions were far from honourable. Still, it was a great feather in her cap."

When Annabell paused, Felicia said, "I can see how that might have been."

She wanted the other woman to continue. She wanted to learn about this woman whom Guy had married. She wanted to learn about the younger Guy, to perhaps understand the present Guy better.

"Yes, well, Suzanne was still madly in love with Guy." Her eyes narrowed as she studied the portrait. "This truly is a good likeness of her. Guy finally saw that delicate beauty and began to pursue her. Or so I've always liked to think. But it might have been that he coveted what every man of his acquaintance coveted."

Felicia realized she must have made a sound of distress, for Annabell turned to her, concern writ across her features. She knew this all happened years before, but it might as well be this minute for her emotional response to the story. Still, she wanted to know what had happened. Felicia managed to force a smile.

"Please go on."

Annabell nodded. "He proposed, she accepted. They married and within the year Suzanne was breeding. Everyone was happy."

Felicia knew what happened next. "He never re-married."

"No. But he has never lacked for female company."

"That seems to be a universal trait," Felicia said, remembering Edmund.

"True." Annabell said. "He is only remarrying now to get an heir." Softly, she added, "I thought you should know that."

Before Felicia could say anything, Annabell turned away and sat at the breakfast table where she poured herself a cup of tea. She laced it liberally with cream and sugar.

"I would like to say that Suzanne would wish nothing but the best for Guy. I know she truly loved him as much as a young woman, fresh from the school-room, could love a man. But I am not sure." She drank the tea down and carefully laid the cup in the saucer. "She was over-possessive of him. I believe that had she lived, it would have driven a wedge between them. Guy goes where he will."

Their eyes met and Felicia understood what the other woman was telling her. "Thank you, Annabell. I shan't forget."

"Right," Annabell said, standing abruptly. "I believe the carriage is ready. That is why Guy sent me in here."

"Thank you all the more for risking his wrath to take the time to tell me," Felicia said with a smile.

"We must hurry. Guy has never liked to wait and we have left him cooling his heels quite a white."

There was a gleam in her eyes that did not speak of contrition.

"Not even when all he has to do is bid someone goodbye?"

Annabell gave her a funny look. "Don't you know?"

"Know what?" Felicia felt a sense of foreboding. "He is not supposed to come with me."

"I am coming as well. To chaperon."

Felicia came to a standstill, her hands clenched at her side. Her stomach roiled. "I told him I was going alone."

Annabell spread her hands wide to indicate that the situation had not been of her doing. "He is stubborn when he thinks he is doing the right thing. He always has been." She smiled wistfully. "I remember when one of the servants was accused of stealing some silver and Guy thought him innocent. He confronted our father over the issue and would not let the servant be punished. Impressed with Guy's determination, Father waited until the real culprit was found."

"Not many people would have defied their father for a servant," Felicia said.

Annabell started walking again. "No, and Oswald has been fiercely loyal ever since."

Nonplussed, Felicia blinked. The next thing she knew, Oswald was in front of her holding open the door. She smiled at him.

"Thank you for everything you have done," she said to the butler. "And please tell Mrs Drummond how much I appreciate her care of me."

He came as close to a smile as he could. "I believe she is here to say goodbye, madam."

Felicia turned around and there was the housekeeper,

tall, imposing and looking as though she really was sad to see Felicia go. "Thank you, Mrs Drummond. Without your expert care, I doubt I would be able to leave now."

The housekeeper beamed. "I was that glad to help you, madam. And I hope your trip to London accomplishes everything you need."

"Hurry up, will you?" Guy's impatient voice called from outside. "We haven't all day, and I want to be well on our way before we stop for the night."

Mrs Drummond tsked. "You had best hurry. He has spent his entire life trying to be patient. There are times when it is impossible."

"Goodbye again," Felicia said, moving quickly outside.

The cold wind slapped her in the face and billowed out her cape. She looked at the cloud-covered sky and knew it would rain before evening. This did not look like a good day to travel, but there was nothing for it.

She stepped down to the gravel where Guy stood flicking his riding whip into his left palm, each contact making a sharp slap. A scowl told Felicia that he was in no mood for dallying.

"Viscount Chillings," she said, her voice as cold as the weather, "I thought we had agreed that I was to travel alone? I do not need your protection, and had you told me this would happen, I would not need your carriage. I would have hired one as I did before."

"And have the ham-fisted driver wreck you again?" His tone brooked no argument. "Annabell is already inside. I will help you up the steps."

She eyed him with ill-concealed irritation. If she refused him, then it would be that much longer before she reached London.

As though he read her thoughts, he said, "If you refuse my protection, I shall see to it that you are hard-pressed to hire a carriage in town. I won't have you setting out alone again."

Her lips compressed into a tight line that kept back the scathing words she wanted to fling at him. Still, some slipped out. "You are not much better than the other men in my life. You think you know what is right for me and so you ignore my wishes."

His face darkened dangerously. "I think it in everyone's best interests that you get inside the carriage now."

He turned away and went to his horse, Dante, who stood nearby pawing the ground in his eagerness to be off. Guy jerked his head at a footman who rushed to Felicia. Chin high, knowing there was nothing else she could do that would not put her further behind schedule, Felicia allowed the young man to assist her.

Entering the carriage, she took the seat facing the back of the vehicle. Her fingers twisted tightly together inside the warmth of her muff.

"I thought I told you he is impossible to deal with when he thinks he is doing the proper thing," Annabell said mildly.

Felicia said with asperity, "So you did. I must not have listened very well."

Felicia was cold and hungry and tired when she felt the carriage slowing. Sitting up, she pulled aside the velvet curtain that had kept out the grey daylight and some of the cold. The Swan hotel proclaimed its ability to put up weary travellers and their mounts.

Annabell, who sat across from her, opened her eyes and yawned. "We must be at the Swan."

"How do you know?" Felicia asked. "You have not even looked outside."

Annabell rolled her eyes. "Guy always stops at the Swan. Always."

"Oh."

Felicia's stomach felt like a hollow pit. She knew almost nothing about the man she had fallen in love with. It was a sobering thought. Not that it mattered. She was never going to see him again after she arrived in London.

Guy opened the carriage door. There was frost on his moustache and a sprinkling of snow on the shoulders of his greatcoat.

"Come along, Bell," he said, offering his hand to his twin and helping her out. He turned to Felicia and asked softly, "How are you feeling?"

"Perfectly fine."

"Liar," he murmured. "You have circles under your eyes and your mouth has that pinched look I have come to associate with exhaustion." He took her hand before she could extend it and pulled her toward him. "Now, shall we start again? Unless you are still mad at me."

She gave him a rueful smile. "I am tired and very glad to be stopping for the night. Nor am I still angry with me. There is something about a jouncing carriage that puts everything else into perspective."

He helped her down the steps, giving her the strength she lacked. Before she could ease away from him, he slid his arm around her waist. Heat and security and desire welled up in her. Somehow she managed to resist her own urges.

"Please, Guy, let me go."

"You are on the verge of collapse," he stated the obvious, his voice hard. "You should have given yourself more time to recuperate before making this trip. Now I am taking care of you, whether you wish it or not.'' He edged her towards the entrance. ''And we have Bell. She will see to it that nothing happens between us, so you need not fear that.''

Felicia sighed. She knew she should continue to protest, but he was right about her being out of stamina. And, as he said, they had Annabell.

The innkeeper met them at the door, all smiles and profuse bows. ''My lord Chillings, welcome.''

''Glad to be here, Jim,'' Guy said. ''The weather isn't the best for travelling.''

''No, my lord.'' The innkeeper motioned to a boy. ''Take his lordship's things up to the first-floor room with the view.''

''I will need three rooms tonight,'' Guy said, still holding Felicia. ''And a private parlour.''

The innkeeper gave Felicia a discreet look before once more focusing on the viscount. ''Yes, my lord. The rooms will take a few minutes. But the parlour is ready. If you would follow me, please. I will have tea and coffee sent.''

They found Annabell already in the parlour, poking at the coals, trying to build up the fire. She turned when they entered.

''I vow, this place is nearly as cold as it is outside.'' Without waiting for an answer, she turned back to her task.

Guy stuck his head out the door and said, ''Innkeeper, we need a blanket and a hot water-bottle.''

The innkeeper, who had just reached the end of the hall, hurried back. ''Yes, my lord. Immediately.''

''And the makings for punch. And dinner.''

''Yes, my lord.''

Guy went back in the room and took off his coat, which he draped around Felicia, who sat in the chair closest to the fire. "I am sorry, but that is the best I can do until he returns."

"Thank you," Felicia murmured, burrowing into the heavy folds of cloth that were still warm from his body. They smelled of him too, a heady mix of lime and musk. She shivered.

"Are you still cold?" he asked, leaning over her so that his breath was a hot whisper against her cheek.

"No," she whispered, forcing herself to turn away from his concern. "No. If anything, I am the opposite."

Annabell snorted. "Leave her be, Guy."

He did not bother to acknowledge Annabell. Instead, he stepped away as though he had not just set her pulse pounding. Felicia resolutely turned her attention to the fire.

"It seems to be warmer than when we entered, Bell."

"Some."

There was a knock on the door.

"Come in," Guy said, moving to the mantel. He propped one Hessian-covered foot on the grate.

The innkeeper entered with a maid behind him. The servant carried a tray laden with a punch bowl, cups and the makings. She set her burden on the table the proprietor had pulled away from the wall and positioned between the several chairs and the fireplace.

"Thank you," Guy said in dismissal.

"Dinner will be along shortly," the landlord said. "Nothing fancy, my lord, but plenty of it. Roast beef with vegetables and Yorkshire pudding."

"That will be fine," Guy said.

The innkeeper bowed himself out.

Guy crossed to the table and started preparing the punch. Claret and brandy went in first, then a pinch of nutmeg, more sugar and some lemon juice. He swirled the mixture around before dipping a cup in and tasting it.

"I think more nutmeg," he murmured. "What do you think?" He handed the cup to Felicia.

She took the cup, careful not to touch his gloved fingers with her own. She was so strongly attracted to him that the gloves were no barrier to desire.

"Punch?" Annabell asked. "What happened to whisky?"

Guy shrugged and gave her a roguish smile. "I knew neither of you would drink it, and it is too cold for you to have only tea. This will warm you up better."

"Make us tipsy, more like," Annabell retorted, but she returned his smile.

Felicia sipped the concoction. "I believe it needs more nutmeg and lemon juice. But just a pinch of nutmeg."

He nodded and took the cup from her. He added the rest and stirred.

"Don't I get to sample it?" Annabell asked, her tone implying that she knew her taste was of little account with her twin.

"Of course." Guy produced another sample and handed it to her.

"Perfect," Annabell pronounced after finishing off the entire cup. "And exactly as you said, brother. It warms me to my toes."

Guy laughed. "Careful, or you will totter over into the fire."

He took back the cup and refilled it. After handing

it to Annabell, he tossed some toast into the bowl so it floated on top of the punch.

Felicia took the cup of punch Guy handed her. It warmed her fingers and the aroma of claret and brandy told her it would ease the tension that held her shoulders tight. She took a sip, and then another and another. Her coldness and sadness began to dissipate.

Another knock on the door and dinner was served.

Watching the meal being laid out, Felicia realized how hungry she was. Her stomach growled.

"Oops." She flushed and put her hand over her mouth.

Annabell laughed. "No more punch for you."

"What you need," Guy said, "is food."

The innkeeper and serving girl left and Guy started carving the roast beef. He put a helping of everything on her plate.

"I am not starved," Felicia protested. "That is far too much food, but I would like some more of that very delicious punch." She saw Guy and Annabell exchange amused glances. "Well, it is very good."

Guy dipped her another cup and sat it beside her plate.

Annabell said, "I think you need tea more than punch, Felicia." Suiting action to words, she poured Felicia a cup, adding plenty of cream and sugar.

"Thank you," Felicia said, intending to drink the punch first. The wine eased her emotional pain. The tea would not.

Everyone was served by the time Felicia finished her second cup of punch. Guy raised one black eyebrow but said nothing.

"We have a long day tomorrow and must be up

early," he said, eyeing Felicia as she raised her empty punch cup. "I think not," he murmured.

Felicia felt like a small girl being told no more sweets. But she knew he was right. Drinking alcohol was no different from taking laudanum, and she had never taken the latter unless she really needed it.

She sighed and rose. "You are right. This only numbs one's senses for a few hours and I am quite numb as it is."

She made her way to the door where the maid waited to show them to their rooms.

After the maid had left, Felicia and Annabell helped each other undress, neither having a lady's maid. Felicia had left hers in her husband's house, determined that no servant hired by Edmund would spy on her. Annabell rarely travelled with a maid. It was easier since most servants did not want to go to the unusual and exotic places Annabell frequented.

As soon as Annabell left the room, Felicia crawled into bed. The punch had fuzzed her emotions and she fell instantly asleep.

Tomorrow was another day.

Chapter Ten

The travelling chaise pulled to a stop in front of an imposing Georgian townhouse. The fashionable May-fair address spoke of money and position. Felicia gazed out of the carriage window and realized they were at Guy's London home. Guy opened the door and held out his hand to her.

Instead of putting her fingers in his, Felicia shook her head. "We have already discussed this, Lord Chillings." At her use of his title, he frowned. "I will not stay with you. Even with Annabell in attendance, it would not be the thing."

"Bell is plenty enough respectability. Aren't you?" He flashed his sister a look that said 'agree with me'.

Annabell looked from one to the other and shook her head. "Felicia is right, Guy. And you know it."

His scowl deepened, but he dropped his arm and stepped back. "Where will you stay?"

Felicia hugged her cape about her shoulders. She was sure her sudden sense of chill was due to the weather and nothing else. The inside of the vehicle was cold enough that the hot water-bottle was no longer hot.

"I shall stay with my father as I had always planned." Her voice cracked on the last word and did nothing to make her feel more confident of what lay ahead.

"You would do better in an hotel." Guy's words were as flat as his voice.

"Guy," Annabell remonstrated. "Do not make this more difficult than it is, and not in so public a place. Now step back and give the coachman the address. I shall accompany her so that you may be sure she is delivered safely."

Guy stepped back and closed the door. Bell was right and he knew it. His enacting such a scene in front of his townhouse was part and parcel with every other rash act he had committed with Felicia and because of her. But he would not let her go alone to her father after being weeks late. From what little she had said about the man, he did not imagine her welcome would be warm.

He mounted his gelding and gave directions to his coachman.

Felicia barely kept herself from sighing in disappointment as Guy closed the door. Annabell was right and had not told her brother anything that Felicia had not already said. Still, she felt bereft and vulnerable. Emotions she had felt for so much of her life and even more so in the last year.

"Thank you, Annabell," she said softly. "His accompanying me would only make a difficult situation nearly impossible."

"Don't fret," Annabell said stoutly, putting her gloved hands over Felicia's clenched ones. "I shall accompany you in. I have no fear of your father, having faced down more than one irate male who thought he could tell me to jump and that I would do so without further ado.''

Felicia smiled in spite of the growing tightness in her throat. ''I am sure you can do anything you set your mind to.''

''That is what I tell my brothers.''

They fell silent as the coach made its way through a labyrinth of streets. Her father was wealthier than many aristocrats, but he did not live in a fashionable part of London. He lived where the merchants did.

Felicia had never been to London before. Neither her father nor her husband had ever thought it necessary for her to accompany them. She was a country girl, educated at well-respected boarding schools in all the social niceties, but a country girl none the less.

Her eyes widened as she saw the sights. Elegant carriages, marked with the crests of their owners, passed them nonstop. A few hardy souls walked the West End streets, dressed in the height of perfection. Women wore warm capes and pelisses trimmed in fur. Jaunty bonnets, obviously designed by a milliner of the first stare, and delicate parasols protected them from the light drizzle. Gentlemen strolled along, their many-caped greatcoats buttoned securely against the cold breeze, their beaver hats sitting at rakish angles on top of their short-cropped hair.

Shop windows glowed so that the merchandise stood out like many-coloured jewels behind the glass. Peddlers pitched their wares everywhere. An urchin hawked roasted chestnuts.

Newcastle was considered a large industrial town, but it was as nothing compared to this. Doctor Johnson had been right, when he had said that to tire of London was to tire of life. She was enthralled.

A servant was lighting the gas lamp outside Felicia's father's residence when they pulled up. She did not recognize the man, and only knew this was where her father lived because of the address. Her stomach cramped and she wished for the umpteenth time that she did not have to be here. But unless she stayed in an hotel, this is where she had to reside.

If she was to have any chance of convincing Edmund to give her the jointure settled on her when they married, she would do well to have no breath of scandal attached to her name. Edmund knew very well that in order to prove her guilty of adultery he would have to bribe two people to testify to a lie. She had never been unfaithful. She would tell him that she would not naysay him if he returned the money that was rightfully hers.

She cut a quick glance at Annabell who sat across from her, her back straight and her face composed in the look of confidence she always wore. No, even with her presence, it would not do for her to be in Guy's London residence where all would know. Particularly since her father was also here.

Nor could she stay with her husband.

She pulled her cape closed, wishing it were armour and knowing that it would not even give her adequate protection against the storm moving in. The only defence she had against the fury she knew her father would direct at her was her determination not to be left destitute by this divorce and thus back on the mercy of her parent.

She picked up her case and moved to open the carriage door. Someone else opened it ahead of her. Guy blocked her exit.

''What are you doing here?''

He took her hand before she realized what he intended and pulled her out. "The obvious."

"I told you not to."

"You told me you were staying with your father. Bell told me not to come."

She stumbled on the coach's lowered stairs and would have fallen if he had not caught her. His arm went around her waist, burning like a brand. Her feet tangled in the hem of her cape and she clung to him. He was her safety and her love.

Then she was free.

He moved his arm away, keeping a firm grip on her lower arm. "Easy. I did not mean for you to trip like that."

"Yes," she managed to say around the sudden lump in her throat.

Much as she knew it was not wise, she was glad he was here. It would give her a few more minutes with him than she would have otherwise had. Soon they would part and she would not see him again.

"Can't you two keep away from each other?" Annabell asked drily, stepping around them.

Felicia shook her head to clear it of the pain of losing him shortly and the desire that his nearness always created. She felt her hair loosen from a pin.

Guy reached up and caught the errant strand. He ran it through his fingers, his expression saying that he felt the silken softness even through the fine kid leather of his gloves. Then he tucked it behind her ear, careful not to tip her bonnet.

"I am going inside with you, Felicia," he said softly, his tone implacable, his eyes unyielding. "I intend to meet your father."

She shook her head, not trusting herself to speak for

fear she would say what she should not, afraid she might thank him for this meddling. Another strand of hair came loose.

"You will be in complete dishevel if you continue that," he murmured.

The coldness left his eyes, replaced by the heat she remembered so well. Her knees turned to jelly and she would have sagged against him if he had not still gripped her arm tightly. Her gaze locked with his.

Desire and more flared in her. She loved this man. His offer of enough money to support her flitted through her thoughts, lodged in her conscious. She loved him, but she did not want to be his mistress. She would be second best in his life or worse. She would not be able to have the children she craved.

"This is not going to help me," she finally managed. "If you are with me, it will only make matters worse."

"Why?" His eyes, nearly black in the increasing dusk, pierced to her heart. "Why will my being here make it worse, Felicia?"

"Guy!" Annabell said sharply. "Enough."

Felicia blinked in surprise at Annabell's voice and then because she lost her balance when Guy released her. She wavered, but managed to stay standing.

"You are right," Guy said. "This is not the place to be doing this. Again." Disgust filled his voice.

He turned sharply on his heel and went to the door where he rapped smartly. Felicia waited behind him, feeling like all control of the situation had been stripped from her. She felt like a spectator, not the person whose future was being put in jeopardy by Guy's actions.

The door opened and a tall, imposing butler filled the entry. "Yes?"

The servant looked down his very long nose even though Guy was his equal in height. The butler's gaze travelled from Guy's mud-splattered Wellingtons up his road-stained trousers to his damp greatcoat. But his look of barely concealed contempt was reserved for Guy's unfashionable beard and moustache.

Guy returned the butler's perusal with the flick of a dismissive glance. "Tell your master that Viscount Chillings is here."

The butler's eyes widened a fraction before the same supercilious air settled once more over him like a mantle. His glance went to Felicia and Annabell. Just as Felicia did not recognize the servant, the servant did not recognize her.

"And Lady Fenwick-Clyde and Mrs Marbury."

The butler's gaze riveted on Felicia. He made a curt bow. "Please come inside, my lord. Ladies."

Annabell hung back. "If you are going inside, Guy, then I will stay in the carriage. Better yet, I will return home." She cast a regretful look at Felicia. "I am sure that Felicia feels one of us is more than enough. I had intended to stay with her for moral support." Her voice turned ironic. "I am sure you will provide more solid support."

Much as Felicia had come to like and admire Annabell, she could only feel relief at the other woman's decision. She did not want Annabell to be subjected to the scene she knew was coming. Her father was quick to lose his temper and even faster to start yelling. It would be bad enough with Guy here.

Knowing she would likely never see Annabell again, Felicia did not follow Guy immediately into the house. She turned to the other woman and held out her hand.

Annabell smiled at her before stepping forward and hugging her.

"I am way too forward," Annabell said, stepping back. "Guy never fails to tell me. But I have enjoyed meeting you and will miss you." Her eyes, so much like her brother's that they twisted Felicia's heart, turned serious. "Be careful and good luck."

"Thank you for everything," Felicia said. "I shall never forget you."

"Nor I you."

Without waiting to see Annabell get back into the coach, Felicia squared her shoulders and clenched her hands into fists inside her muff where no one could see. Thus fortified, she marched up the steps and through the door the butler still held open. There was no turning back.

The interior was dark with heavy wood panelling. Even the furniture was dark and heavy, nothing like Guy's country house had been. Felicia felt her spirits drag down. She instantly chided herself. She should not have expected anything different. Her father's house in the country where she had grown up had been like this. Her father was a driven man, not a happy man, and he surrounded himself with substantial things. From furniture to horses, he preferred large.

She followed the butler down the hall to the back of the house and into a small room with a smaller window that looked out on to a spit of garden. Nothing bloomed in the winter cold. Guy sat at his leisure in a chair drawn up to a small fire. He still had his coat and beaver hat on.

She shivered and gave Guy an apologetic smile. "My father believes in the saying 'waste not, want not'."

"That is how I have made my money, Felicia," her father's voice boomed from behind her.

She jerked and spun around. He stood in the doorway, his lips stretched in what he considered a smile. Tall and rotund, he was formidable. In shades of brown, he dressed in the style of an earlier age. He did not wear a wig, but his hair was long enough to be pulled into a queue instead of the current sporting Corinthian cut or, more to Beau Brummell's liking, the Brutus style.

"Father," she said, her voice breathless. She frowned. She sounded like a child caught with its hand in the biscuit barrel. She had nothing to feel guilty about. "Father," she began again, "I would like to introduce you to G— Viscount Chillings."

Her father's hard, brown eyes turned to Guy who stood now. "What are you doing here with my daughter? She is a married woman."

Guy's right hand fisted, then relaxed as he extended it. "Mrs Marbury has a great deal to tell you, sir. I merely escorted her here to ensure that she arrived on your doorstep safely."

Felicia looked from one man to the other. Guy's words were polite enough, but there was an air about him that spoke of danger, as though he were warning her father instead of trying to reassure him.

Nathan Dunston stepped to the Viscount. "Then thank you for your service, my lord."

Felicia flinched. Polite words with no genuine thanks behind them. This meeting was going exactly as she had anticipated. She moved forward so that both men looked at her.

She held her hand out to Guy. "Thank you so much for your care and concern, my lord. But I am tired after the journey.'' Her gaze held his, and she begged him with her eyes to understand and do nothing rash. ''I know you will understand when I ask you to leave.''

Guy flicked a freezing glance at her father before taking her proffered hand. Raising it to his lips, he murmured, ''I understand quite well, Mrs Marbury.'' He released her hand and moved back. He gave her father a curt bow. ''Good day, sir. I hope to have the pleasure of meeting you again.''

''And I, my lord,'' her father said, a challenge in his stance.

Felicia turned away, unable to watch the two of them any more. She was surprised at the relief she felt when she heard the door shut behind Guy. Her relief was short-lived. Immediately a sense of overwhelming loss, an emotional pain she was too familiar with, engulfed her. He had said he would call on her, but it was better for both of them if he did not.

''Well, gel, you came against my orders,'' her father said, his loud voice jarring through her tense nerves. ''Now you can just turn around and go home to Newcastle.''

Felicia's neck muscles bunched into painful knots. She took a deep breath and then another. She had only defied her father twice in her life. The first time was when she would not give Edmund more children. The second was in coming here. To turn around and face him now was nearly more than her remaining strength could support. But she had to do so for her future.

But she moved slowly, not wanting to confront him for confrontation it would be. When she was completely turned, she forced herself to meet his angry gaze with her own, willing her eyes not to look scared.

''I am not going home, Father.''

She was pleased that there was no wobble in her voice. If there had been, he would hear it and use it against her as he had so many times in the past. Still, when his bushy grey brows drew into a furious line across his forehead, she could not stop herself from trembling. She hoped he did not see it.

"What did you say, daughter?" His voice boomed at her, his displeasure like a slap.

She licked her lips and cravenly wished that Guy had stayed. But there was nothing he could have done that would have changed this.

"I said that I am not returning home until after the hearings."

"You will do as I say or regret it."

He grabbed her upper arms and shook her until her hair tumbled from its pins and her already stiff neck hurt. She bit her bottom lip to keep from crying out. When he released her, she fell back against the windowsill. She licked her bleeding lip before speaking.

"Then I will go some place else, Father."

He sneered. "Go to your husband."

Slowly, anger began to replace her fear. He was goading her, belittling her. "You know Edmund will not have me any more than you will."

"If you had been a good wife this would not have happened."

"Bred for him like a mare?" The vulgar words spewed from her in a torrent she could not stop, did not want to stop. "Like you did Mother, until it killed her?" The old hurt and anger rode her.

"That is a woman's job. To have children. To give a man an heir." His face was puce, his brown eyes bulging. "Had you done so, Edmund would have an heir instead of getting one on another woman so that now he is trying to divorce you so he can marry her. Calling you an adulteress in the process. You'll be ruined, gel.''

"Let him," she said. "I wish no part of him. I never did.''

"That was not your decision, just as this is not.''

"You cannot stop him. Or me," she added. "All I want is to ensure that my jointure comes to me.''

"Get out.''

She notched her chin up, refusing to let the fury radiating from him scare her. Nor would she beg him to let her stay here. She would find some place. An hotel. There were reputable hotels where a woman alone could go.

She left without a backward glance. Standing on the doorstep, her case in one hand and portmanteau in the other, she gazed into grey fog. What had been a drizzle an hour ago was now a downpour. The feather in her bonnet hung limp and clung to her right cheek. Her half-boots were soaked through.

For a second her shoulders slumped. This past year had been so hard. And now this. But she was not going to give in.

"Felicia," Guy said, materializing in front of her, "let me help you.''

"I thought you had gone," she said inanely.

She had thought he was gone and that, in spite of what he had said, she would never see him again. Even shivering from rain and wondering if her next breath would be liquid, she felt light hearted. With Guy beside her, anything was possible. He would care for her and keep her safe.

"Thank you," she murmured.

His smile seemed to break through the dreary

weather. "I had to make sure that if this happened I would be here to help you." He held his horse by the reins. "Where are you going now?"

Water ran down her face in tiny rivulets. "I don't know. An hotel. Surely there is one where a respectable woman can go alone."

"The Pulteney in Piccadilly. Tsar Alexander and his sister, the Grand Duchess, stayed there the summer before last."

She nodded and went down the steps to the street. "Could you, please, hire me a hackney?"

With his free hand, Guy took her portmanteau. "I have been out here for thirty minutes or more and have seen none. I think you would do better to mount my horse and let me lead you to a more fashionable part of town. We will be sure to find one there. Hopefully, not taken," he added.

"I can walk, but thank you."

"It is foul weather, Felicia, don't be stubborn."

"I am not." She wiped the rain from her brow with her handkerchief, only to have the water immediately replaced by more. "I can walk as quickly as your mount can take me with you leading it."

"You will tire quickly in this weather and carrying your case."

"And while we argue, both of us will get wetter. If that is possible," she added wryly.

"Were you this obstinate with your father?"

She gave him a resigned look. "Why do you think I am in this position? I refused to do as he said. He does not take defiance well."

Instead of saying something derogatory about her parent, Guy set the portmanteau down and shrugged out of his greatcoat. He moved to Felicia and draped the garment over her shoulders. The hem was a scant inch from the ground and the mud.

"This will help keep some of the water away and perhaps provide a modicum of warmth."

Her free hand gripped the coat's collar. "I cannot wear this. You have nothing."

"For once, do as you are told," he said, stepping away so she would have difficulty returning the garment. "Now come along. We have a distance to go."

She trudged after him.

After five minutes, he stopped and looked back. She trailed him, her right arm and shoulder pulled down by the case. His heavy coat did not help her, although it was keeping her drier and warmer than she would otherwise be.

"You look like a bedraggled kitten someone has dressed in ribbons and thrown into the rain."

She stopped before running into him and looked up so she could see him instead of the road that, in spite of being cobbled, had tiny rivers of mud running through it. He radiated exasperation.

"I have let you have your way, but that is over." His voice brooked no argument. "Put down your case. You are going on the horse. We will go much faster."

He was right and she knew it. Still… "It is not right that I should ride while you must walk."

"It is perfectly right. You will be able to carry the two cases. It will be easier on us both."

Before she could do anything, he took the case from her hand and set it down beside the portmanteau. Both pieces of luggage were going to be badly damaged. She sighed. That was the least of her problems. Then, while she was busy telling herself things could only get better, he grabbed her waist, his coat included, and lifted her to the saddle. Her rear end hit with a plop. She teetered precariously, holding tightly to his lower arms.

She looked down at him and the urge to slide off the horse and into his embrace was strong enough that not doing so made her shake. If only he could be the man she had married. If only he were not engaged. If only. If only.

"I am balanced now," she whispered, hoping the longing she felt for him did not show in her voice. "You can let me go."

He released her slowly. "Can you hold the luggage?"

She nodded. "I can try."

"It won't be easy. Sitting side saddle with no side saddle is something I could not do, let alone hold things."

She smiled. "You are being modest. Besides, men don't ride side saddle so they don't know how to do it." Still, it was hard with no horn for her to lock her leg around.

"True."

He picked up the pieces and handed them to her one at a time. As he had thought, it was next to impossible for her to hold both. She would be lucky to remain in the saddle holding nothing.

"Straddle him," Guy finally said. "The last thing we need is for you to fall off."

"I cannot do that." She felt every inch of her skin heat. "My skirts would come up to my calves."

"Probably higher," he said, his gaze going to where her clothing covered her legs. "You have lovely legs," he murmured so low she was not sure she heard him.

"What?" Embarrassment flooded her.

What had they done that he had seen her legs? To

her knowledge, she had never shown him. The time he had nearly seduced her on the billiard table, her legs had remained completely covered.

His gaze met hers. "You have beautiful legs."

"How...how do you know?"

He smiled, a smile full of knowing and promise and desire. "I have seen them, caressed them, got lost between them."

Heat, fast and furious, consumed her. "Never."

A fresh blast of wind drove rain into her face. She gasped. She had forgotten where they were, what the weather was like—everything. And, heaven help her, she knew nothing of what he spoke of.

"We must go," she said, her voice tight.

He nodded and the hunger that had sharpened the angles of his face receded. "Straddle him, as I said. If too much of your legs show, take my coat off and drape it over them. Although there will be bloody few people out in this to see you."

If straddling the horse was the only way to get him to stop looking at her like that, she would do so. It was awkward and unladylike, but with Guy's help to keep her steady, she managed. Her skirts rode up to her thighs, revealing her black silk stockings and satin garters. She saw him tense his hands, his gaze riveted by her exposed flesh.

"Guy," she said, painfully aware that she responded to him as he did her. "This is not the place. Or the time."

He looked up at her face, his eyes haunted. "It never is and never will be." He took a deep, shuddering breath. "Give me my coat. I will help you get it across your legs."

Somehow they managed. She did not know how,

when his touch heated her entire body even though the rain continued to pour down on them. This was madness. Her life had fallen to shambles a year ago, and now this.

For her own sanity, she had to be thankful they would never see each other once he got her to safety. Or that is what she told herself, as the horse followed slowly behind Guy and they made their way to Piccadilly.

Chapter Eleven

They arrived at the Pulteney Hotel without once seeing an available hackney. Felicia was wet and miserable, her bonnet a sodden mess. Guy did not look much better, but at least his hair did not hang down his back like drenched ropes.

She sighed and pushed a strand of hair off her face. She had been in worse situations. Guy was with her now, so embarrassing and uncomfortable as this was, she felt protected and safe. That was all she asked.

He turned to her and smiled. "We are here and not a minute too soon. We shall quickly have you dry and warm."

She returned his smile. She did not have a lot of clothing with her and hoped this hotel had a good staff.

Somehow she managed to get her left leg over the saddle and keep the greatcoat positioned so she could slide down to Guy's arms without showing her thighs. Unfortunately, her modesty had kept her from being as warm and dry as she might have been.

"Your lips are blue," he said severely, setting her carefully on her feet. "I knew this trip was premature. I will send my doctor to tend you."

"I am perfectly fine. A hot bath and plenty of hot tea will fix everything." She returned his scowl with one of her own, suddenly bone tired. "Stop fussing over me as though you have a right."

As soon as the words were out of her mouth, she wished she could take them back. He did not deserve such ingratitude from her. Nor did she like having said the words. They implied that perhaps he should have a say in what she did, that perhaps she wanted him to have a say.

She had told him once that she loved him. He had ignored her. She never intended to tell him again no matter what happened. They could never be together.

"I am sorry," she murmured. "You did not deserve that."

His face unreadable, he said, "No need to apologize. You were perfectly correct. I have no right to tell you what to do." He picked up her two pieces of luggage. "Having said that, will you please precede me into the hotel?"

She did so without a word.

The lobby was everything that is elegant. She felt like a fish out of water. The man behind the desk watched her enter with such a look of distaste on his long face that Felicia turned around, intending to leave. Guy was directly behind her, blocking her exit.

As though he sensed her unease, Guy lifted one black brow. She forced a feeble smile.

"I think this is not the place for me," she said, barely loud enough for her to hear, let alone him.

His attention shifted to the man behind the desk. At the man's supercilious look, Guy carefully set the luggage down, ignoring the puddles they made on the expensive carpet.

He strode up to the man. "I am Viscount Chillings, and I require a room for Mrs Marbury." When the man hesitated, Guy added in tones that would have frozen an inferno, *"Now."*

The clerk's eyes widened a fraction before he moved out from behind the desk and snapped his fingers. A young man, barely more than a boy, rushed up. "Take the lady's things to the second-floor room with the balcony. The one where her Royal Highness the Grand Duchess stays."

The boy gave Felicia a curious look before rushing to do as he was ordered. She swallowed a sigh of relief. For a moment she had thought the clerk would refuse Guy, and then she would be hard pressed to find another place to stay. Nor did she wish to go back out into the inclement weather. Had she been alone, the man would have turned her away without a second's hesitation. Now she was going to be in what were likely to be some of their best rooms.

"Come this way, please, my lord," the clerk said. "I am sure you and madam will be pleased with the accommodations."

In a voice laced with irony, Guy said, "I am sure we will." He motioned for Felicia to go ahead of him.

Felicia followed the clerk, feeling uncomfortable because she left a trail of water behind her. But after a quick look the clerk said nothing, so neither did she. They climbed the stairs silently.

They reached her rooms and Guy looked in. "This will do," he said. Turning to her, he asked, "Are you sure this is what you wish to do?"

She nodded, not at all sure, but not willing to tell him. This was all she could do except return to Edmund or to her father's home in Newcastle, which were not choices for her.

He turned to the clerk. "See that a hot bath is prepared immediately and that hot tea and dinner follow."

"Yes, Lord Chillings," the man said, his long nose all but twitching. He looked at Felicia. "When can we expect madam's maid?"

Felicia's gaze dropped.

"Mrs Marbury's maid will be here this evening," Guy said. "Until then, have one of the serving girls here help her."

Felicia said nothing, realizing that Guy intended to send someone from his own establishment. How many times would she regret not finding a maid to accompany her? But she had not wanted a woman on this trip who had been hired by her husband and whose loyalty belonged to him.

"Thank you," she murmured, remembering to add, "Lord Chillings."

"Take care," Guy said. "I will call on you tomorrow."

She nodded, her bonnet slipping forward, its ribbons finally giving up and coming undone. Guy caught the ruined confection as it fell from her head. He held it out to her.

Felicia took the hat from him. Their fingers brushed. All she wanted to do was rush into his arms. Instead, she stood like a statue, watching him walk away. When he was no longer in view, she entered the room and closed the door behind her.

Guy wished he could stay with her, but that was totally unacceptable unless he wanted to ruin her and he did not want to do that. So, he left.

He took long enough in the lobby to approach the

desk clerk. "If I hear that the slightest discourtesy has been given to Mrs Marbury, I will see that you and the Pulteney Hotel regret it."

The man nodded, his movement jerky. "Yes, Lord Chillings. There shall be none, my lord."

"See that there isn't."

The next day Felicia woke up tired and aching. Her throat felt as though she had screamed for the entire previous day without respite. All she wanted was to stay in bed and sleep. That was the last thing she could do.

She dragged herself out of bed and hoped her clothes had been dried and pressed during the night. This was the day she needed to call on her husband.

The light in the room was dim. A single candle sat on a nearby table. There was a fire in the grate. Felicia looked around dazed. She had not lit the candle or started the fire.

Movement in one of the corners caught her eye. A young woman stepped forward and curtseyed.

"Pardon me if I startled you, ma'am. His lordship sent me."

The woman, little more than a girl, was thin and anxious-looking. Her blonde hair was pulled back from a face with large blue eyes and a pointed chin. She looked vaguely familiar.

Felicia smiled at her. "What is your name?"

"Mary, ma'am." She bobbed another curtsy.

"You are from Lord Chillings's country estate, aren't you?"

She bobbed another curtsy. "Yes, ma'am. I came in the baggage carriage."

"No need to carry on so," Felicia said. "I am not some fancy lady."

"Yes, ma'am." She started to dip and caught herself. Instead, she twisted her hands in the folds of her immaculate white apron.

"Come along, Mary," Felicia said kindly. "I need to be somewhere soon, so must dress quickly. I am afraid I overslept."

"Yes, ma'am. Your clothing is in the wardrobe, ma'am. His lordship had it picked up last night. He had it dried and pressed and brought back here, ma'am."

"How considerate," Felicia murmured. And so like him.

She undid the ribbon at her throat and pulled the nightdress over her head. Before she got the fine muslin off, she felt Mary's hands fumble in an attempt to help her. After a little difficulty, Felicia was dressed.

"I am that sorry, ma'am," Mary said, bowing her head to look at her clasped hands. "I am not a lady's maid."

"You did just fine," Felicia said. "I am not used to having a fine French maid, so I am most comfortable with you. Give yourself time, Mary. We will get along well."

Watching the girl relax enough to smile, Felicia knew she had spoken the truth. She was a simple country girl herself, and would not know what to do if she had a fancy maid. It was better this way.

"You may have the morning to yourself, Mary."

"I will go with you, ma'am, if that is all right. His lordship said I was not to leave you."

The girl was wringing her hands again, obviously expecting Felicia to tell her no. Felicia's first inclination was to do just that, but she held her tongue. Much as she might be tempted to send the girl back to Guy after this much meddling, it would not bode well for the girl. And Guy was right. She did need a maid with her. Mary would lend her respectability.

"As you wish—or as Viscount Chillings wishes," Felicia said. "Let us get some tea and toast and then we will be on our way."

The maid bobbed another curtsy. Felicia shook her head, wondering how long it would take before Mary's eagerness began to be tiresome. But the girl was doing her best.

After a light repast, Felicia had a hackney cab waved down and set off on her visit. She had not seen Edmund in nearly a year. Not since the children... She pushed the memory away. She wished she did not need to see him now.

The coach pulled up at a very nice row house. It was not in the Mayfair area where Guy's London residence was, but it was still very attractive and respectable. Edmund had found enough money to set himself and his mistress up very well. Another thing she could use against him in court. He was supposed to be blameless.

Felicia got out of the coach followed by the faithful Mary. Together they mounted the steps. Felicia took a deep breath. Much as she did not wish for this meeting, she knew she had to go through with it. She lifted the knocker and rapped it smartly. It seemed a long, cold time before she heard footsteps.

An impeccable butler opened the door. He stood as tall as Felicia's chin and half again as round.

"Yes?" Somehow, he managed to look down his hooked nose at her.

Glad that her clothing had been dried, cleaned and

pressed, Felicia drew herself up so she was now a good foot taller than the servant. "I am Mrs Marbury, here to see Mr Marbury." She handed him her card.

He read the simple print. His eyes only widened a fraction. Otherwise, his features were completely impassive. He was indeed a good butler.

"If you will be so kind as to follow me, ma'am, I will inform the master that you are here."

Felicia stepped into the house. Her husband had spared no expense for his paramour. No wonder he now wanted to keep his unwanted wife's dowry. The interior was done in the popular Egyptian motif, almost flamboyant. Not Edmund's style at all. He was a country squire with a country squire's tastes.

She did not love Edmund, had never loved him, but she could not keep from feeling a pang of envy. He had never cared what she thought or desired. He had wanted her to bear an heir and leave him to his pursuits. And she had done so.

The butler indicated a chair in the hallway where Mary was to wait. The maid looked to refuse, but Felicia said, "It is all right, Mary. I will be fine."

The maid looked doubtful, but she sat where instructed. Next the butler ushered Felicia into a small dark room with no window and no fire. Felicia was grateful for her heavy pelisse and cape.

The room was an insult. She should have been shown into the drawing room or parlour. She told herself the slight did not matter. It was so typically Edmund and how he treated her.

It was not long before she heard voices raised in anger. One was her husband, the other…her father. Her father was here. This was going to be much worse than she had imagined. Her stomach twisted in dread.

The door banged open. Felicia flinched uncontrollably before getting herself in hand. There was nothing her father or husband could do to her that would hurt more or impact on her more than the loss of her children. The only person who could hurt her now was Guy.

She drew herself up and stepped towards them. "Good day, Father. Edmund."

Their looks of surprise that she dared to be the first to speak did wonders for her courage. She told herself she could survive this and, possibly, even come out of the discussion a winner.

"Felicia," her father nearly shouted. He turned to Edmund. "I thought you said she did not come to you yesterday."

Edmund eyed her with dislike. "She did not. This is a visit and nothing more, unless I am mistaken."

"Absolutely correct, Edmund," she said with more bravado than she felt. "I came to meet with you. I did not realize Father would be here."

"And why shouldn't I be, gel?" Even his thick, grey whiskers seemed to bristle.

She shrugged. "No reason. I just had not thought it."

Her father puffed up in his fury. "I came here to offer Edmund twice the amount of your dowry if he will stop this fool divorce." He glared at her, his face close enough that she could see the red veins in his eyes. "I told him you would give him an heir."

Her inclination was to step back, to cower under his attack. That was the last thing she should do. This was her future, not her father's—or Edmund's.

"Did he agree?" She looked at Edmund who appeared as angry as her father. "Because if he did, he will be disappointed. I will never, ever, give him another child. Never," she repeated for emphasis.

"Hah! I told you," Edmund said, satisfaction at being right mingling with the anger caused by her vehement rejection.

"Then make her, damn you," her father bellowed. "I will give you three times her dowry."

"Father!"

"You are my property, gel. The law says so." He gave Edmund a sly look. "Or, more correctly, you belong to your husband. He can use you as he wishes and you have no say."

Felicia blanched. Her father's words hurt more than she would let either man see.

In a bitter voice, she said, "Then it is fortunate for me that he has started divorce proceedings. If I understand correctly, he has found two witnesses to say I was unfaithful. I won't contest that if he will give me my jointure. Then the only thing left is for Parliament to approve after the courts."

"Bah!" Her father spat at the empty fire grate. "It is not final. Edmund can stop it."

Edmund, a greedy gleam in his eyes, studied Felicia. She met his look defiantly.

"You would have to force me, Edmund," she said softly, her voice carrying with the force of her conviction. "You have a more willing woman now. One who already is with child. And if you ensure that I get my jointure, I won't contest your petition on the grounds that you are not blameless."

The greed remained, but she knew him well enough to know her words had had the desired effect. "No, Dunston," he said to her father. "I don't think that even three times her dowry would be enough." His thin lips curved slyly. "If you gave me half your estate, I would consider it."

Her father blanched. Then he flushed a violent shade of red. She could imagine steam coming from his ears.

"You go too far, Marbury." He stormed from the room.

Felicia felt as though someone had pricked her with a pin and all the bravado that had sustained her was seeping out. She went to the nearest chair and sank down. But before she was fully recovered, Edmund spoke.

"Why are you here, Felicia? I had not thought to see you ever again."

She looked at her husband, truly looked at him for the first time since he entered the room. He was not a handsome man. Not much taller than she, he was slender and robust. His hair was a nondescript brown, cut in a fashionable Brutus. His eyes were also brown. His nose was a beak over lips that were well shaped but thin. His dress was casual, his coat looser than style dictated and his shirt points not high enough. But he was more than presentable.

Too bad he had not been a good husband and father. Although to do him justice, theirs had been a marriage of convenience. And as for the children, he had done by them the same that had been done by him.

"Well?" he asked, impatience showing in the set of his mouth.

"I came to ask you for my jointure. I—"

"No."

Felicia held down her anger at his interruption and refusal without hearing her side. This was so typical of him.

"I need it to live on, Edmund. Since you are divorcing me, my dowry is forfeit and Parliament has the choice of whether or not to give me my jointure. Surely you can afford to give me the jointure or a settlement.''

''No. I intend to use the money from your jointure to pay for the divorce. I have already spent a good portion of it going through the courts. The remainder and a significant amount of my rents this year will go for the Act of Parliament.''

She did not want to beg, but without the dowry she would be destitute. Nor did she want to threaten him, but as a divorced woman she would not even be able to get a job as a governess.

''For the children I gave you, Edmund.''

''For the heir you cost me? I think not.''

His words cut like a knife. He had always been able to hurt her more with words than another man might have with his fists.

''Then give me part of my jointure because while you can bribe two men to lie about me, you cannot keep my representative from telling the court that you are already living with your mistress.'' Satisfaction was a small comfort as she saw him go completely still, her words getting through to him. ''You are not blameless and the law states that you must be.''

His eyes narrowed. ''I see you have done some research. I will think about your request.''

He moved to the door. She remained sitting, unable to stand at the moment while she dealt with the fresh pain he had just inflicted. Not that anything she did mattered. He was done with this discussion and intended to end it like he had so many before by leaving. Still, he had listened to her last words. Perhaps she would have a chance.

She stayed in the dull, dim little room long enough

to regain her composure. As so often in the past, her pride was all she had. She did not intend the servants to see how Edmund's treatment of her hurt.

After several long minutes, she rose, knowing she should not feel disappointed or anything. She had not expected Edmund to agree, he never had. But she had had to try.

It was her father who had taken her unawares. He had always made it plain that his interest in her was to further his own plans. She had known he did not want this divorce, but she had never expected him to go to the lengths he was.

She left the room, not surprised that the butler was gone. Edmund's contempt for her would have been communicated to his staff.

The scuff of a shoe on the wooden floor drew her attention. A woman stood in the doorway of what must be the front parlour, a room Edmund's butler had not seen fit to take her to. The woman was blonde with striking blue eyes, pretty in a robust way. Felicia's gaze dropped. The woman was breeding.

Her heart squeezed—the pain was as sharp and fresh as though she had lost her children yesterday instead of nearly a year ago. It took all her concentration to keep tears of bereavement from filling her eyes. This was all so hard.

The woman stepped into the hall so that Felicia could not pass her without pushing her aside. Felicia stopped.

"Felicia Marbury," the woman said.

Her voice held a hint of brogue. Felicia had heard that Edmund's pregnant mistress was Irish.

"I am Felicia Marbury," Felicia answered, adding, "for the present."

The woman ran a speculative gaze over Felicia. "He said you were attractive, but cold as the fish in the sea."

Felicia flushed before feeling the blood drain from her face in anger. Edmund had discussed her with his mistress. Now he was divorcing her to marry this woman. What other insult had he heaped on her?

"You are fortunate. He has said nothing about you other than your condition and his intentions."

The woman smiled, showing a crooked front tooth. Her face lit up. She loved Edmund.

Amazed, Felicia moved past her husband's mistress and to the door. She glanced back at the woman. She could tell her husband's mistress that his case could be thrown out of court because she was pregnant. But she would not. There was no reason to hurt and worry the woman.

Best to leave. The sooner she was gone, the better. There was nothing for her here. Both Edmund and her father had made that plain. The woman had confirmed it.

Chapter Twelve

Felicia woke to her second day in London and the first day when the winter sun shone through the window. She heard Mary rustling around.

Rising up on one elbow she watched the maid. "Mary, what are some of the sights I might like seeing?"

Mary dropped the poker she had been using to stir the fire. "Lordy, ma'am, but you scared me. I thought you was sound asleep."

"I was. But now I am restless. I have two days before Edmund testifies in court." She threw back the covers and swung her feet off the bed. "I am ready to eat something and go out."

What she did not say was that she had to get out or go mad enough for Bedlam. She could not forget what her father had done yesterday. Nor could she work out what she was going to do without the money from her jointure—even a small portion would be enough. Strange as it felt, she might be better off if the courts refused to accept Edmund's petition because then he could not take it to Parliament for a divorce. In that case, he might insist that she move out of his country house so that he and his mistress could move in. That would not be as good as a divorce and her reputation would be sullied, but not ruined. And by the terms of their wedding agreement Edmund had to give her a certain amount of money as long as they were married.

But she would not be free. If she was free and Guy was not yet married, there might be a chance he would turn to her. She laughed, but it was mirthless and more like a cry from her heart. Guy would never break his engagement.

Guy did not love her.

Mary's voice drew her thoughts back. "What did you say?" she asked the maid.

The young woman gave her a quizzical look. "Tea and toast is on its way, ma'am." She picked up the poker and returned it to the fire set. "His lordship sent this message over earlier."

Felicia took the thick vellum writing paper that had been folded and sealed with wax. She read the contents and threw the note into the fire.

"Ma'am," Mary exclaimed.

Felicia gave the young woman a smile. "His lordship will be here in thirty minutes to take me for a ride in the park."

She should send a message right back, refusing. She did not want to. After yesterday and the abuse she had taken, she longed to be with someone who wanted to be with her. He might lust after her, not love her, but he enjoyed her company. There was a lot to be said for that.

And the thought of seeing him made her blood sing. She did not want to love Guy Chillings, but his constant pursuit of her made it hard to forget him. Her lips curled in self-derision. As though she would ever forget him. She might tell herself any number of Banbury tales, but in her heart she knew she would never, ever forget him, no matter what happened in the next couple of days.

She made her decision. It was just a few more days. After that she would leave London and never see him again. She was going driving.

"I don't have anything to wear," she muttered, forcing her mind to the present and more mundane concerns.

"Begging your pardon, ma'am, but I took the liberty of having the hotel clean your dress while you slept."

"You are a jewel," Felicia said. "I don't know how I got on without you. And I shall be sad to see you return to Lord Chillings's household."

The girl blushed. "Thank you, ma'am. No one's ever said such kind words to me. 'Ceptin' me mum."

"They are only the truth, Mary, and praise you deserve for your good service. Now, we must hurry. I would like a bite to eat before his lordship arrives."

Between the two of them, Felicia was dressed just as the toast and tea were delivered. She wolfed down the toast and gulped the tea, scalding her tongue in the process. She barely noticed, so strong was her desire to see Guy again.

She reached the lobby as he entered. She did not see the desk clerk frown as she went straight to Guy.

"Punctual as I have come to expect," he said, taking her outstretched hands.

She smiled up at him. "Mary is such a gift. I shall be sad to see her return to you."

He tucked her left hand into the crook of his elbow and escorted her outside. "She may stay with you as long as you wish."

She halted when she saw his vehicle. "Oh, my goodness. You cannot mean for us to ride in that?"

"I am considered a fair hand with the reins," he said, a slight chill in his voice.

"But it is so high."

"It is a high-perch phaeton, and I assure you that I have yet to turn one over."

She swallowed another protest. "Of course. I have no doubt."

He helped her on to the seat and tucked a blanket around her legs. There was no help for the rest of her body. She would freeze.

He hopped in and took up the reins. "You may let go their heads," he said to a diminutive tiger dressed in sage green livery with silver trim.

The young man jumped away and Felicia felt the horses step forward, eager to move. She took a deep breath and kept her eyes open, even though every sensibility urged her to close them. She did not want to see the ground rushing by so far beneath her.

"Stay here, Jem," Guy said. "Have something to eat and drink."

The tiger touched the brim of his hat before disappearing inside the Pulteney Hotel.

Felicia sat stiffly, her outside hand gripping the side of the carriage as though her life depended on how tightly she held on. The hand closest to Guy hung on to the front edge of the burgundy leather seat. She kept her head up and her eyes forward.

"You can relax," he said. "I promise not to turn us over. It is not as though we will be on bad roads. We are going for a drive through Hyde Park. If anyone sees how stiff you are, they will think I am making importunate comments."

She forced a smile to lips that felt numb.

He flicked the whip lightly and the horses jumped forward. She fell backward, a small squeak of alarm escaping her clenched teeth.

Guy slowed their movement. "Are you really that scared?"

"What a ninny you must think me," she said, her voice tight.

"Is it because of your accident?"

She had not even thought of that. "Absolutely not. It is just that we are so far from the ground. I have heard of high-perch phaetons, but never expected to see one, let alone ride in one."

"They can be dangerous driven by someone with ham-fists, which I am not. I assure you, the members of the Four-in-Hand club consider me skilled enough for this."

She risked a quick glance at him. His mouth curved up slightly at the corner. "I am sure you are."

She looked forward and gasped. A heavily laden wagon stood in the middle of the road. With a flick of his wrist, Guy had them around the seeming barricade. She swayed from side to side and renewed her grips.

The weather was much better and others were taking advantage of the unusual sunshine.

"Everyone is out," Guy said in explanation. "There will probably be people in Rotten Row as well."

Felicia recognized the derogatory term for Hyde Park.

Guy guided them smartly through the arch and into Hyde Park. There were several hardy walkers, a group of riders and a few other carriages. Nothing like the crowds that thronged the park during the summer Season.

Felicia looked around at the infamous Rotten Row. "Somehow I pictured this differently."

Guy smiled knowingly. "It is during the summer. The winter, even when Parliament is in session, is slow." He glanced at her briefly, before returning his attention to his driving. "And speaking of Parliament. When do you hear about your husband's court hearing?"

Felicia sighed, her breath forming steam in the cold air. "Not for two more days." She burrowed her hands deeper into her muff, more relaxed with Guy's driving. "That is when Edmund goes before the court."

Several riders approached them, two women and one man. Felicia felt a pang of discomfort when they matched their pace to the phaeton.

One of the women was Miss Duckworth. She nodded at both of them. "I see you are out for a drive, Chillings."

Her words spoke the obvious, but her eyes said more. She looked pointedly at Felicia.

"Miss Duckworth," Guy said smoothly, "let me introduce you to Mrs Marbury."

"Good morning, Mrs Marbury."

Felicia put on her most gracious face, but it was hard. Seeing the other woman reminded her of all the reasons why she should not be here. She was a married woman and Guy was engaged to this woman. The divorce Edmund was asking for only made matters worse.

Still, she tried to be pleasant. None of this was Miss Duckworth's fault. "The same to you, Miss Duckworth. It is a pleasure to meet you."

"This is the first fine day we have had in some time," Miss Duckworth said.

Guy slowed the carriage to a stop and the riders halted with him. "Mrs Marbury, may I introduce Miss Lucy, Miss Duckworth's younger sister."

Felicia nodded. "How do you do."

The other woman—or girl, more like—giggled. "I am very well indeed, Mrs Marbury. I do so love London." She grinned conspiratorially. "I am new to Society."

Miss Duckworth nearly groaned. "My sister is giddy with delight at being freed from the nursery."

Miss Lucy flushed scarlet and her full, red cupid-bow mouth pouted. "Now, Ducky, don't be dreadful."

Miss Duckworth gave her young sister a minatory look. "Then don't behave like a child."

Guy interrupted them. "And may I also present my brother, Dominic Chillings."

Felicia studied the younger man. He had a raffish air about him. His beaver was cocked at a jaunty angle over curls as black and glossy as the finest polished jet. His deep blue eyes sparked with mischief. Even his clothes were less than respectable. Oh, he was dressed in the height of fashion, but there was a sense of dishevelment in the looseness of his coat and the unpretentious twist of his cravat. Unless she missed the mark, he was a rake.

"Most pleased to meet you, Mrs Marbury."

He reached for her hand and before she realized what he was about, he raised it to his mouth. The grin he flashed was conspiratorial, definitely inviting.

She found herself grinning back without conscious volition. He was as charming as he was dangerous. Was he pursuing Miss Lucy? If so, she pitied Miss Duckworth the job of chaperon. Between the two of them, Miss Duckworth would undoubtedly find herself always a step behind.

Clouds scudded across the sky, obscuring the sun. A breeze started. Cold penetrated Felicia's pelisse. She was glad of the blanket over her legs.

Miss Duckworth looked up at the greying weather. "We had best get home. It was nice to meet you, Mrs Marbury. I hope you enjoy your stay in London. Chillings."

"Miss Duckworth," Guy said, bowing lightly from the waist. "Miss Lucy." He looked pointedly at his brother. "I will see you later, Dominic."

"You can bet on that, brother," Dominic said, tipping his hat to Felicia. "Mrs Marbury."

Felicia watched the three ride away before turning to Guy. "I think I should go back to the Pulteney."

He expertly turned the phaeton and headed them back the way they had come. "I will send my coachman around this evening. Annabell has asked if you will dine with us."

Felicia hesitated. "Please give her my regrets."

He handled the team as smoothly as before, but Felicia could feel the tension in his thigh that touched hers. "Why? Have you other plans?"

"No." She sighed and turned away from him. "I don't know anyone in town. I just do not think it wise for me to spend too much time with you. You are engaged. I am married."

"Do you really think anyone in the *ton* cares?" His words dripped cynicism. "No, I take that back. Everyone would love to discuss us as the latest *on dit*, but Annabell will be our chaperon so there will be nothing to discuss."

She heard the sarcasm he did nothing to hide. She

knew he was correct as far as it went. "What if rumour starts that I stayed at your estate alone with you?"

"That would be a different situation."

"I thought so," she said drily. "Nor would it be nice to put Miss Duckworth through the scandal."

"Do you really care?" he asked, his lip curled sardonically. When she did not immediately reply, he glanced at her. "I believe you do."

"I don't wish to hurt anyone. Particularly a woman who has done nothing to deserve being hurt." She clenched her hands inside her muff. "I know how devastating it is to be in pain from something over which you had no control. I don't ever wish to be the cause of pain to another."

Fresh memories welled up of Cedric and Colleen playing in the garden or fishing, catching nothing but enjoying themselves immensely. Then she remembered them as she had last seen them.

"No," she whispered, "I would not wish pain on anyone."

Guy laid a gloved hand on her arm. "Let it go, Felicia. There is nothing you can do. You have your entire life ahead of you."

"Yes. I know."

She could not share her fears for the future with him. He would offer her money again. She did not want that.

He pulled up in front of the Pulteney Hotel. The tiger who had stayed behind immediately appeared and went to the head of the horses. Guy tossed down the reins and jumped lightly to the ground. He circled the phaeton and held up his arms for Felicia. She looked down at him.

The sharp angles of his face, softened by his beard, were dearer to her than anything else in her life. Yet, she could not have him. Her chest tightened and her stomach twisted. She would leave London as soon as the court made its decision. It would be better for all of them.

"Well?"

She put her hands lightly on his shoulders as he gripped her waist and swung her down. For a brief time, she felt giddy with pleasure. He was so close she could smell his lime and musk and see the fine lines around his eyes. He was so close that if she tilted her face up her lips would touch his.

She looked away. "Thank you for taking me. I enjoyed it much more than I would have enjoyed staying in the hotel."

"Look at me," he said, his tone brooking no denial.

She bit her lower lip but did as he wished. "What?"

"I will send my coachman for you."

"I..." She pushed away from him, regretting her freedom the second his hands fell away from her. "I don't think that is a good idea."

"To hell with what you think." His voice was implacable. "My coachman will be here. I will be with him. Don't make me come and fetch you."

She moved away from him, saying over her shoulder, "I will consider it. Thank you and goodbye."

Guy watched her enter the hotel and saw the desk clerk come forward to meet her. Only then did he get back in the phaeton.

"Stand away, Jem."

The tiger stepped back, seeing that the Viscount had the reins before moving quickly to the back and hopping on to his perch. They set off at a smart pace.

With only half his mind on his driving, Guy thought about their situation. He wanted her more than he had ever wanted a woman. He laughed, a harsh bark. He wanted her and he could not have her.

His stomach tightened with desire and anger. He put them both aside as best he could while his loins ached and his jaw was so tense it twitched. It was better this way. If he could have her, he did not know how long he could trust himself not to take her completely and risk getting her pregnant with his child. For if she came to him, it would not be for convenience.

He pulled the phaeton to a stop in front of his London townhouse, handed the reins to the tiger and leaped out. Knowing that Jem would take care of the horses, he strode into the house and stopped in his tracks. His brother and sister stood in the hall, arguing. The butler looked on with a worried frown.

"What is going on?" Guy moved to them.

"We were discussing Mrs Mar—"

"Hush," Annabell said. She turned to Guy. "Miss Duckworth is here."

Guy stopped the expletive that came to his lips. "How long?"

Dominic shrugged. "Ten minutes at the most. She must have taken Lucy home and then come straight here." He eyed his brother. "Not that I blame her. Don't you think you were doing it up too nicely taking Mrs Marbury around Rotten Row?"

Guy thought of a scathing retort and swallowed it. Dominic was right. "I did as I wished. I would do it again." His words and the look in his eyes told them not to pursue this topic.

"As you will," Dominic said. He focused on his sister. "You and I have a discussion to finish, Bell."

She grimaced. "You are the pot calling the kettle black, Dominic."

"I am your brother."

"Go somewhere private to finish your discussion," Guy said, irritable because he knew that he must meet with Miss Duckworth, and he knew what she was here for. "Where is my guest?"

The butler answered without a second's hesitation. "In the front parlour, my lord."

"Good luck," Annabell said softly.

"Be careful," Dominic said, his eyes alight with a knowing glint. "Single women who call on bachelors are up to no good."

"That has been my experience." Guy left them to their argument and entered the room where his fiancée waited.

Miss Duckworth sat, back ramrod straight, in the chair nearest the fire. The weather had got colder. She rose and came to meet him.

"Miss Duckworth," Guy said. "What can I do for you?" He raised one brow to let her know that her presence was very unusual.

Her gaze held his. "We need to talk, my lord."

"As you wish," he murmured. He moved past her to the chairs where she had been. "Won't you be seated?"

She sank on to her original seat. "Not to beat around the bush, Chillings, for we are both busy people."

"Please don't," he murmured, stopping before he said something more sarcastic than she deserved.

"I have two reasons for being here." She raised two fingers for emphasis. "First is your brother, Dominic Mandrake Chillings."

"Really?"

"Yes, really. You may stare me down all you want, Chillings, but that will not erase the fact that he is paying marked attention to my younger sister, Lucy. She is barely out of the schoolroom and your brother is a libertine.''

Inwardly, Guy groaned. ''Are you saying that Dominic's attentions are unwelcome?''

''By me. Lucy is too flighty and immature to realize that he is only amusing himself at her expense.'' She sat straighter. ''As the responsible member of my family, I am asking you, as the head of your family, to speak with him. It must stop.''

''You are right, of course.'' And she was. Dominic was dallying where he had no business. ''I will speak with him.'' And hope it does some good, he added silently. He rubbed his beard with one finger. ''And what is your second reason?''

Her peaches-and-cream complexion deepened. ''The second is about us. That is, you and Mrs Marbury.'' She took a deep breath and faced him squarely. ''If you wish to end our engagement, I will understand.''

''Do you mistake me for a man without honour, Miss Duckworth?'' he asked, his voice cold enough to freeze water.

Her face stiffened. ''No, my lord. I take you for a man who is showing a marked interest in a woman who is not his wife or fiancée, and who, in fact, is married to another man.''

He was furious with her, but he was more angry with himself because she was right. ''If you wish to call off our engagement, Miss Duckworth, I will understand. Otherwise, I believe this discussion is over.''

He watched her for several long moments. Emotions moved over her features. He did not think pain was one of them.

Finally she spoke. ''As we said before, ours will be

a marriage of convenience, Chillings. You are marrying me for an heir and I am marrying you because my father and brother's gambling debts are beyond our financial ability to pay. In short, we are both marrying for family. I don't fancy myself in love with you, so that will be fine. But my pride bids me tell you that if you should decide our agreement is something you no longer wish, I will accept ending our engagement.''

He was tempted. Very tempted. But he needed an heir, and he needed one from a woman he did not care greatly for. He liked and respected Miss Duckworth, but she did not make his blood boil so that his body wanted to do things to her that his mind knew were wrong. Miss Duckworth was the perfect wife for his needs.

"If that time should arise, you will be the first to know," he said firmly. "But as you say, we are both entering this marriage for reasons other than our own happiness. Therefore, we must both accept that there will be times and actions that we are not pleased about.''

She nodded, a slight grimace twisting her lips. "You are entirely correct, Chillings. My pride bids me to break our engagement now, my family's needs tell me I cannot.'' She stood. "Thank you, Chillings.''

"You are more than welcome," he murmured to her retreating back.

The door closed behind her, and he went to a side table where a decanter of whisky sat. He poured himself a strong helping and drank it down, staring outside without seeing anything.

She had given him a way out of their engagement. Felicia would be a divorced woman soon. He could marry her.

He shook his head and poured another glass. No, he could not wed Felicia. He needed an heir. That was the only reason he was marrying now. And he needed a wife he did not love.

Suzanne's death had nearly ruined him. He had blamed himself for years afterwards. Even now, this moment, a small part of him still blamed himself for it. It did not matter that women died in childbirth, that it was one of the hazards they all faced. He had felt responsible for her premature death.

Guy sighed and turned away from the window. He had loved Suzanne as a big brother loves a sister, but he had not realized that when he married her. He had not truly realized that until Felicia.

He had felt desire for Suzanne, but it had been born more of necessity than passion. While with Felicia, it was nearly impossible for him to keep his hands and body from her. He wanted her day and night, like an ache that never ended.

But he could not, would not, marry her.

He had to do something to stop this road of thought. He would speak with Dominic while he was here. That would take his mind off Felicia. He strode from the room.

He found Bell and Dominic in the library, as he had expected. Both turned in surprise when he entered.

"You are not needed here," Annabell said.

"You can side with me," Dominic said at the same time.

"I am here to speak with you, Dominic, not get into the middle of your argument." He stopped in front of them and looked from one to the other. "Although, perhaps you need a referee."

Annabell snorted. "Nothing of the sort. Dominic is out of line and knows it. Our discussion is over."

"Not by a long shot," Dominic said. "And Guy will support me in this."

"I will?"

"Absolutely," Dominic said. "This Roman excavation she is so set on doing is on Fitzsimmon's property. Totally unacceptable."

"Which you already knew," Annabell retorted.

"I did not think you would actually do this," Dominic said, fists on hips.

"And?" Guy knew Dominic's reasons, but goaded him anyway. Perhaps if he vocalized his objections and then was reminded of what he was doing to Lucy Duckworth, the lesson would sink in.

"And? He is a notorious rake. No woman is safe from him." He shot his sister a severe look. "Not even a bluestocking widow."

"How dare you," Annabell blustered. "You make me sound as though I am ripe for the picking, and Fitzsimmon will be the one to harvest me."

Dominic shrugged.

Guy decided it was time to intervene. "Bell is old enough to take care of herself, Dominic. Something that cannot be said for every woman."

As though he sensed more than Guy said, Dominic bristled. "So you say. Bell is my sister and it is my duty to protect her."

"From men like yourself?"

"Low blow," Dominic said.

"Is it?" Guy asked. "Miss Duckworth was here on behalf of her young sister."

Dominic had the grace to look chagrined. "What about Miss Lucy?"

"Miss Duckworth feels your attentions are too marked and not welcomed."

"Ah hah," Annabell said. "I thought you were coming it too brown over Fitzsimmon."

"Not half enough," Dominic shot back. "As for Miss Lucy, at least she is an amusing chit. Not like Mistress Sourpuss."

"Sourpuss?" Guy and Annabell said.

"Sourpuss," Dominic repeated. He turned back to Annabell. "Mark my words, Bell, you will rue the day you tangled with Fitzsimmon."

She sighed dramatically. "As though I am not all of three and thirty, financially independent and unattractive to men. You worry too much."

For one brief moment, Dominic met her eyes without anger or humour. "I hope so."

"Bell must go her own way," Guy said.

Dominic rounded on him. "And what about you, brother? Was Miss Sourpuss's visit only about my unwanted attentions?"

Guy took a step back from their triangle.

"I thought not," Dominic said. "She did not like your drive in the park with the lovely Mrs Marbury."

Annabell laid a hand on Guy's arm. "Be careful, Guy. Felicia is a married woman about to go through divorce proceedings. The last thing you want is for your name to be linked with hers. Or for Miss Duckworth to cry off your engagement."

"Heaven forbid," Dominic said.

Guy moved away from Bell's touch. She was right and he knew it. That still did not make it any easier to reject Felicia.

"I have invited her to dinner tonight."

"What? Who?" Dominic asked. "Mrs Marbury?"

"Surely not," Annabell said.

"Surely I have," he said. "I told her you would be our chaperon, Bell."

She rolled her eyes skywards. "As Dominic said, heaven help you. For you don't help yourself."

Chapter Thirteen

With growing dismay, Felicia listened to Edmund. He had made an unannounced visit to her here at the Pulteney.

"Furthermore—" he stopped pacing and faced her "—you were in Hyde Park with him today."

She nodded. "We were in a high-perch phaeton. There is no impropriety in that."

Thank goodness he did not know she had stayed at Guy's country seat for over a week unchaperoned. Her mouth twisted. If he had cared about her enough to inquire about when she left Newcastle, he would know her trip took nearly three weeks longer than it should have. It was bad enough that he was prepared to pay two male servants from his own country home to testify against her in court, lying about her supposed infidelity. What would he do if he knew about Guy, demand the Viscount to testify? She could not allow that.

He glared at her. "Your father persists in offering me large sums of money if I will stop the divorce proceedings."

He stopped speaking, waiting for her to say something. There was nothing she could say. A month ago she would have agreed with her father, if for no other reason than the disgrace of being divorced. Now she wanted one, no matter what it did to her reputation. Edmund had gone too far.

"I know," she said. "If you remember I was here when he offered you up to three times my dowry."

"Well, he has been back." He paused to let her suffer in ignorance. "He has agreed that, if I stop divorce proceedings, he will see that I am given the revenues from half of his holdings."

She gasped. She could not help it. Her father, who was tighter with his money than the Prince Regent's stays, had agreed to that?

"What did you say?" She was almost scared to ask. Edmund had married her for money in the first place.

"I told him I need an heir."

Her fingers twisted in the folds of her skirt. "Your mistress is breeding."

He nodded, satisfaction easing the thin line of his mouth. "But she does not bring me any money."

Felicia's heart skipped a beat. "Nor do I," she said softly.

He advanced on her. "Your father told me to make you give me an heir."

She blanched. "You would have to use force."

He inched closer. She moved to put a chair between them. He had never hurt her, but she did not want him near her. As it was, she could smell the faint sourness of him, a distasteful contrast to Guy's clean lime and seductive musk.

"Something I would not do even for the amount of money your father is talking about." Disgust dripped from every word. "However, I told your father that I would give you one more chance. You have refused."

She gaped at him. "What about your mistress? Would you have cast her off?"

He shrugged and ran his gaze over her. "You could give me the heir I need if you had a mind to it. And you would bring more money. A country estate always needs money."

Her lip curled. "I think it best if you go now."

"One more thing," he said, stuffing his hands into the pockets of his coat. "Your father told me you left Newcastle over three weeks ago."

Her eyes widened. Satisfaction softened his face and she knew she had given herself away. "My carriage had an accident."

"He also said you arrived at his house escorted by Viscount Chillings."

Each word fell with the bruising intensity of a stone lobbed to hurt. Even if he did not say another word, she knew her father had told him everything he needed to know in order to ensure that he got the divorce. Not only would Edmund drag her name through the muck, he would pull Guy in with her. It was her father's way of trying to force her to stay with Edmund.

"Where is this leading?" she demanded, her voice more forceful than she felt. But she had a sick feeling in the pit of her stomach that she knew exactly where this was going.

He pulled his hands from his pockets and picked up his beaver hat, which sat on a table. A small, detached portion of Felicia's mind registered that Edmund wore his beaver like a plodding man forging ahead. Guy wore his with dash. The Viscount was the type of man who made the hats so fashionable.

Edmund fixed the beaver on his head. "Since you will not bear me an heir, I am forced to present Viscount Chillings as an accomplice in your adultery. This way I will be sure to be awarded a divorce and your dowry to pay for the expense I have incurred. I hope to retain your jointure as well."

She had known this was coming, but it still felt like he had knocked the air from her lungs and left her helpless. She gripped the back of the chair until her knuckles turned white. She told herself she should not be surprised.

She took a deep breath. "You have not been blameless, Edmund, and I believe in order to get approval from the courts for divorce, you must be unsullied."

He scowled. "Are you threatening me?"

"No," she finally said.

Nor was she. It went against everything she was to use this against him even though he deserved it.

"That is good," he said. "For I would just send her out of town until this is over. No one would bother to track her down."

He was probably right. She was the only one with any interest in the condition of his mistress, and she would not push this further. It was not in her to do so.

"Please don't drag Viscount Chillings into this, Edmund."

She hated begging him for anything, but this was not about just her. Guy was involved. Testifying in court like this would ruin his good name. Miss Duckworth would be sure to break their engagement.

Edmund gave her a smile that was more like a sneer. "Afraid you will lose your dowry? Well, it was never yours after you married me. And your jointure is something I agreed to give you, but I will do everything in my power to keep it now."

She looked at him, noting the closeness of his eyes

and the way his nose turned red at the tip when he was upset. She knew it would do her no good to appeal to his noble side. He did not have one. But she had to try.

"The Viscount is engaged. If you drag him in to testify, it might ruin his future marriage."

Edmund's sneer widened. "He should have considered that before making you his mistress."

"How dare you." He had gone too far. She whipped around the chair that separated them and slapped him hard. Her fingers left a red imprint on his ruddy cheek. "I am not his mistress."

Edmund put one hand up to his face and the look he gave her was deadly. "A momentary fling."

"Neither," she stated. "We have done nothing. Nothing. How can you even say that we have? I am married. He is engaged."

"A Banbury tale."

Before she could respond, Edmund stormed from the room. She sank into the chair. This was horrible. Guy was going to be dragged through the mud for something he had not done. They had never been lovers. She would remember something as momentous as that. Surely.

She flushed. They had wanted to make love that night on the billiard table. But they had not. Yet... She had a sense of more between them, as though, perhaps, they had made love.

She shook her head. Clearly she was upset about the situation to even think they might have done more than she could remember.

She could stay with Edmund, give him an heir and everything would be fine, except her heart. She would be with a man she did not love or even like or respect.

But it was not as though by staying with Edmund she gave up Guy. Guy would never be hers, no matter what she did.

What was she going to do? She had to stop seeing Guy. Somehow she had to control her response to him and refuse him no matter what her heart wanted. She had to, for both their sakes. Not that it would change Edmund's plan. Not that she would keep her dowry. But perhaps if nothing happened in London that could be brought out in court they would be all right. No one knew for certain that she had spent one unchaperoned week under his roof.

That would have to do. For now.

Guy entered the lobby of the Pulteney Hotel. The clerk was by his side instantly.

"How may I help you, my lord?"

"Please inform Mrs Marbury that I am here."

The man gave him a funny look, but hurried away. The unease that Guy had managed to keep in check since Miss Duckworth's afternoon visit returned. He had learned while Wellington's aide to trust his instinct. Something was wrong.

The clerk returned. "Mrs Marbury sends her regrets, my lord."

"She does?" he said dangerously.

The clerk nodded, his Adam's apple bobbing. "Yes, my lord."

Guy headed for the stairs.

"My lord," the clerk said, his voice hesitant.

Guy wheeled around. "What?"

The clerk licked his lips. "She had a male visitor this afternoon. He was with her for quite some time."

Guy's eyes narrowed. "What are you implying?"

The man took a hasty step back. "Nothing, my lord. Merely telling you what I know. Nothing else. My lord."

"See to it that you keep your mouth shut."

The clerk jerked his head up and down. "Yes, my lord. I won't say a word."

Something was very wrong. Guy took the stairs two at a time. He reached Felicia's door in seconds and wondered if he was too late.

The girl he had sent over to care for Felicia answered his knock. She bobbed a curtsy, her eyes wide with fear.

"I am here to see Mrs Marbury," Guy said, stepping forward with the intention of going inside.

The maid held her ground. "I am that sorry, my lord, but she don't wish to see anyone."

The girl twisted her apron until Guy thought she would rip the material. He scowled at her. Eyes downcast, she did not budge. He had to admire her courage. Evidently she had developed a loyalty to Felicia. It spoke well of Felicia.

He reined in his anger. "Mary—that is your name?" She nodded. "You should go downstairs and get something to eat. Mrs Marbury and I have something to discuss."

Her mouth crumpled. "I'm that sorry, my lord, but I can't let you in." Her voice lowered. "I can't, my lord."

Guy's patience ran out. "Get out of my way, Mary. I won't harm your mistress, but I will speak with her."

Felicia's voice came faintly to them. "Do as his lordship says, Mary. It is not fair that you should take the brunt of his anger when I am the one who is the cause."

The maid cast a frightened glance back at her mistress. Guy shifted so she could get out the door. What she saw must have reassured her because she slipped between him and the wall and out into the hall. She gave him one scowling look before scurrying to the stairs.

Guy stepped through the doorway. "She is devoted to you."

Felicia stepped from the shadows by the window. "She is very loyal. I could not have asked for better. Thank you."

She looked haggard. Something had happened. The urge to go to her, enfold her in his arms and kiss her until nothing else mattered raged through him. He nearly groaned aloud at the need he had to fight so desperately.

Finally, when he was sure his ardour would not show in his voice, he asked, "What has happened?"

"You should not be here," she said, her voice barely above a whisper.

"Is it because of the man who visited you earlier?"

He could not stop the cold blade of anger that entered his voice. Jealousy was an emotion he had no experience of. She started, but there was a sadness about her that tore at him.

"Yes. It was Edmund."

"Ah," he said.

He wanted to go to her, but dared not for fear of what he would do. He wanted to erase the hurt look about her eyes and replace it with one of satiation. He wanted to lay her on the bed and make love to her until they both forgot about the rest of the world.

She gave him a wan smile. "My husband." She moved to the side table where a decanter sat. She poured a glass of something red. "Sherry," she said. "Would you care for some?"

"I think not."

She sipped the sweet wine. "I had never had it until this afternoon." She twisted around until he faced him again. "Edmund is going to force you to testify in court." She took a deep, sighing breath. "He is going to accuse you of being my lover. He is going to drag your name through the mud on a lie so that he can be assured of getting my dowry." Her mouth turned sour. "Your testimony is infinitely better than that of two servants."

He went to her, unable to see her suffer and not comfort her. She backed away, using the full glass as a shield.

"I am so sorry." Her voice trembled. "I don't know how he can do so dishonourable a thing as lie about what has happened between you and me." Her hands shook so that sherry slopped over the edge. "I know we nearly became lovers that one night, before my accident. But we did not. Now you are going to pay for something we have not even done."

She turned away, her head bowed, the glass forgotten. He took it from her fingers before she dropped it and set it on the table.

"Felicia," he said gently, "look at me."

She shook her head. "Go away, Guy. There is nothing we can do—or you can do." She took a great shuddering breath. "I can stay with Edmund and give him a child. My father offered him more money than he can refuse." She turned to Guy, her eyes glistening with unshed tears. "But I cannot bear the thought of him even touching me, let alone kissing me and...and doing other things to me."

He gathered her into his arms even though her fingers splayed against his chest in an effort to stop him. He gripped her chin and forced her to look at him when she would have buried her face where he could not see her.

"Felicia, don't. Don't ever think of being with Edmund again."

Jealousy ripped through him even as his arousal tightened his loins to painful intensity. The picture of Edmund touching her as he had touched her was more than he could tolerate.

He lowered his face to hers. "Don't ever think of another man."

He crushed her mouth with his, driving away all his anger and jealousy in one searing union. Her lips opened to his and he plunged in, willing to drown in the passion she offered so willingly.

Driven by the need to make her forget Edmund, he lifted her into his arms and took her to the bed. His lips never left hers as his fingers moved nimbly down her back, undoing the multitude of tiny buttons that held her bodice on. He slid the black fabric from her shoulders as she lifted to give him better access.

Her arms wrapped around his neck, keeping him close as her clothing peeled away. "If he is going to ruin you, then let us at least experience the joy he is accusing us of."

Guy lifted his head to look at her. "Do you truly mean that?"

"Yes," she whispered, raising her lips for his kiss. "Yes, with all my heart."

Guy felt a pang of guilt. It was obvious she did not remember what they had done the night she lay cold and delirious. He had not told her.

Then her arms brought him down to her and everything else fled except the feel of her body pressed hot and urgent against his. Her breasts, covered only by her chemise, felt full and soft beneath his chest and sent hot tingles through him.

Minutes later, she lay naked and he stood by the side of the bed, caught up in her beauty. She smiled at him with her arms held up to welcome him. He discarded his clothes without thought. Something ripped, but he did not slow down.

Then he was beside her, her right thigh running the length of his left thigh. His nerves sparked. He leaned over her until his mouth found hers. He slid his fingers into the luxuriant length of her hair and revelled in the supple silk.

He held the back of her head as he teased her with his tongue. She responded to him like a woman too long unloved.

"Oh, Guy," she murmured. "This feels right."

He opened his eyes to look down at her. She was flushed and her mouth trembled with passion. "Yes," he finally whispered. "Perfect."

And heaven help him, it was. She was everything he wanted.

She arched her back until they were chest to chest and he was lost. When her hands slid down the ridges of muscle along his spine and her fingers hooked into his hips and pulled him to her, he went. And when her thighs opened for him, he entered.

Exquisite pleasure. Exquisite pain.

They were joined. He gasped and felt her stiffen beneath him. Slowly, afraid to break the bonds of delight that connected them, Guy began to move. She encouraged him with her hips, her hands and her lips. He tried harder.

He opened his eyes, wanting to see her face in these moments of passionate intimacy. Her eyes were half-closed, her pupils large enough that he could see his own reflection in them. Her lips were parted and plump. She smiled up at him just as he felt her spasm.

Her eyes widened. She gasped. He pushed.

Then she was over and he was so close it hurt.

His back bowed. Sensation shot down his legs. Instinctively his hips bucked. He was nearly...

He gasped just as he pulled free.

Later, she lay in his arms, her legs tangled with his. Guy rested his forehead on hers and breathed deeply of the lavender scent that clung to her, mixed now with their lovemaking.

She ran her fingers down his ribs. "Guy, why won't you—I mean, you did not..."

He looked down at her, saw the unease in her eyes even as he felt the tension begin to mount in her body beneath his. "I won't do that to you. I won't get you with child."

"But it is only one time."

He closed his eyes, unwilling to see the emotions moving over her face. "It is the second time, Felicia."

She stiffened beneath him, her legs gripping him tightly where he lay cradled between her thighs. In spite of everything that was going on, he hardened. She drove him crazy without even trying. Why? He did not know, he only responded.

"What do you mean? Look at me!"

He opened his eyes and met her accusation with a

calmness his body did not feel. "When you were sick. You begged me to warm you, to love you. I did."

She shoved him—hard. He allowed her to push him off. He lay on his back, oblivious of his nakedness, one knee drawn up, one arm flung across his eyes.

"We have done this before." It was a flat statement.

He nodded, not bothering to speak. There was nothing else to say. He felt her sit up and then get out of the bed. He heard her fumbling and figured she was putting on a robe.

"So, Edmund is right."

"Yes, Felicia." He did not bother to keep the tiredness from his voice. He opened his eyes and stared straight at her. "We both wanted it, Felicia. Just as we both wanted what just happened."

"I am your mistress," she said, her voice barely above a whisper. Her eyes closed and he barely heard her next words. "My imagination was right."

"I would not go that far," he said. "I have not set you up in your own establishment. We do not do this on a regular basis. But Edmund has every right to call me to testify."

Her fingers knotted into the sash around her waist. "When were you going to tell me?"

He got out of bed and gathered his clothes before putting them on. "I tried telling you once, but being in the frozen rain after being turned out of your father's house was not the right time." He shrugged. "I don't know when I would have told you, just that I would have." He stilled, his fingers on the buttons of his trousers. "You have to believe that, Felicia."

He could see her indecision in the angle of her head

and the pinched look around her mouth. Then she nodded.

"I do, but we are ruined."

He finished dressing. "We were ruined anyway."

Chapter Fourteen

Felicia woke up the next day with a splitting headache. Her mouth tasted like dried ashes, and her limbs felt as though she had been stretched out of alignment. Yet, a strange lethargy held her, a sense of complete satiation.

Then she remembered—everything. Her entire body throbbed. She had to stop what was happening between them, for it was plain that Guy had no intention of doing so.

"Ma'am." Mary's meek voice intruded on Felicia's memories.

"Yes," she managed to say in a normal voice.

"A man is here. A big man. He says he is your father."

What more could happen? Felicia thought. First last night and its revelations and now her father fast on the footsteps of Edmund's threat and Guy's lovemaking. She was not sure she could continue to be strong enough to see this through. But she had no choice. She had to stay in London until she knew whether the courts would agree to a divorce so that Edmund could go to Parliament.

Then she would have to find a way to make her living. She had no skills other than those a housekeeper or governess might use. And she would not take anything from Guy. Especially now. She might have made love with him—twice—but she would not become his mistress.

"Felicia, you in there, gel?" her father's voice boomed through the door separating her sleeping room from the parlour.

She dragged herself from bed. "I am coming, Father."

Mary helped her to hastily don her clothing and pin up her hair. She took a quick look in the mirror. She was presentable.

Smoothing her skirt as she went, she entered the front room where her father paced. She could tell he was angry. Her first reaction was apprehension, but she drew herself up. She was no longer the little girl who cringed every time her father lost his temper.

"What do you want, Father?"

He stopped in his tracks and scowled at her. "What do you mean, turning Marbury down again?"

"He was quick to tell you," she said derisively. "But I am not surprised."

Her father's scowl deepened until his bushy brows were one thick bar across his forehead. "He was right to tell me. You are going back to him, gel, make no mistake."

"No, I am not."

Even as she defied him, she took a step back. Refusing to do as he ordered left a strange sensation in the pit of her stomach.

He towered over her. "You will regret that decision."

"I don't think so," she said, forcing all the conviction she felt into her voice. "Edmund only wants one thing from me. Two, now that you have offered him so much financial incentive. I want nothing from him. We are better apart."

"You will be ruined," her father stated. "A divorced woman. No other man will have you."

His face edged forward, as though he were trying to get a better look at her. It made her feel uneasy. Her father had never cared what she looked like or what she felt.

She made herself shrug. "I can live with that, Father. All I want is my dowry back."

"You won't get that, gel. Not now." There was a strange light in his eyes that told her there was more to come. "Edmund says he's going to have that Viscount brought forward. Says you have committed adultery with the man." His small brown eyes bored into her. "Is it true?"

Felicia was not a liar and much as she wanted to deny Edmund's accusation, she could not. Instead she turned away. Better to refuse to answer.

"Tell me, gel."

The force of her father's voice nearly had her speaking. She had thought defying him before was hard. This was next to impossible, but she could not admit to anything.

"If it is true, it will come out at the hearing," her father said.

She shuddered as dread took her. She and Guy would both be shamed. But the alternative... She shook her head.

"Don't shake your head at me, gel. If it is true, I

will see that the man weds you.'' Her father laughed, not a nice sound but one full of power.

She whirled around. ''You would not dare.''

''Watch me, gel. Just watch me.''

She stood paralyzed as he left. Things were going too fast, changing too rapidly, and none of them for the better. She had to warn Guy of this latest development. He did not deserve this. All this had come about because he'd rescued her from a carriage accident, and now his reputation was about to be ruined.

She sank to a chair and dropped her head to her hands. Her neck and back ached. Her entire body ached. Her temples throbbed. She knew it was all because of frustration and fear over what might happen next.

If only she had not fallen in love with Guy. If only he had not made love to her. They should have never met. Their lives were being tangled in knots by one another.

Felicia felt tears welling up and could do nothing to stop them. She had become a watering pot.

Felicia stopped pacing when she heard the knock. Guy must be here. Thank goodness he had come promptly. Mary answered the door and the next thing Felicia knew, Guy was striding across the room to her.

''Felicia,'' he said, grasping her hands. ''Whatever is the matter that you send me a message saying I must come immediately?''

''Oh, Guy,'' she said. ''It is my father.'' His fingers tightened until she squeaked. ''He was here this morning. He is threatening to force you to marry me because I won't go back to Edmund. He means to ruin you.''

Guy laughed. ''He is full of himself.''

She pulled her hands free only to start wringing them. "He is rich. He can do anything he wants. He always has."

"Felicia," Guy said firmly, "you are overreacting. Your father cannot make me do something I don't wish to do."

"You don't know that," she said, turning away and going to the window. She looked out on the street, seeing the carriages and people passing by. "He can do a lot of damage."

Guy shook his head in amazement. "Not to me, Felicia." He crossed to her, stopping without touching her. "You think he is all powerful because he has controlled your life and your decisions. He is not."

"He said he will ruin you." She turned to him. "I have thought seriously of going back to Edmund. That would make Father happy. You would be safe from his threats."

"Don't you dare." He grabbed her upper arms and shook her gently. "If you do that, I will call out that miserable excuse of a husband you have. That will take care of everything. You will be a widow and beyond your father's touch."

"Guy!" She stared at him, nearly not recognizing the man she had fallen in love with because of the fury that contorted his features. "You cannot do that."

He released her and stepped back. "Then do not make stupid statements. You are not going back to Edmund and your father can do nothing to harm me." A dangerous gleam entered his eyes. "Just let your father try and see how he likes it when someone who is stronger and more influential than he makes him do what he does not want to do."

"But what of your testimony? Father and Edmund

both have assured me you will be called on to—" It was so hard to say the words, even though the act had been the easiest and most pleasurable thing she had ever done. "To tell about our liaison. That will ruin you in the eyes of Society."

He shrugged. "Let it. I have been a marginal participant for years. If I never came to London except to sit in the Lords, it would not bother me. It is you who will be truly hurt by my testimony."

She took a deep breath. "Miss Duckworth might break your engagement."

It was out. Just saying the words exhausted her. She knew that no matter what happened, he would not marry her. But...but if Miss Duckworth called off, he could.

He looked at her, his face devoid of emotion. She had no idea what was going through his mind.

When he finally spoke, his voice was calm and matter-of-fact. "Miss Duckworth will do as she thinks best."

No hint that he might want Miss Duckworth to break their engagement. No intimation that he might, just might, want to marry her.

Felicia took a deep breath and willed herself to speak as dispassionately as he had. "As we all will."

He quirked one brow and took a step toward her. She warned him off with her eyes. He did not come closer. Instead he made a curt bow.

"I had best go."

She nodded, doing nothing to stop him. She turned back to the window so she would not see him leave. If only he had desired to marry her given the chance, but no. He did not.

Sometimes life was so hard, so disappointing. She

lifted her head, even though her chest hurt abominably. There was nothing she could do except keep going and hope that her dowry would be returned to her. When the petition reached Parliament they appointed a Lady's Friend and a gentleman from Parliament who would represent her when the divorce petition was presented. Otherwise, there would be no one to speak on her behalf. Then she would leave London and Guy behind. He would become her past just as so much this last year was now her past.

If everything became too complicated, she could go back to Edmund. There was safety in that decision. One could live with a broken heart. She had done so all this year. One could not live without food and shelter.

Guy left the Pulteney. He had not told Felicia he was due at the law courts shortly to testify. She was troubled enough without knowing how close everything was to blowing up in their faces. He signalled his tiger to follow him with the phaeton. He was feeling too reckless to drive at the moment.

He entered the building, with its dark panelling and smell of beeswax. The hearing was to be held in a small room for privacy. He entered and looked around. Edmund Marbury was already here. He knew some of the other men.

One lord came over and shook Guy's hand. "Didn't expect to see you involved in this, Chillings. Dominic, possibly. Rum business."

Guy shrugged and resisted the urge to cut the man for his derogatory reference to Dominic. "It happens to the best of us."

There was no time for social niceties. The hearing started.

Edmund Marbury spoke first. "She has been my wife for ten years. She bore me two children, one a boy. Through her negligence as a mother, they both died just a year ago. But that is not the reason I want a divorce," he said with feigned contrition. "She has been unfaithful. This man here…" he waved his hand at a man who was obviously a servant "…saw her at the Pulteney with Viscount Chillings. Also, I have named the Viscount as my wife's accomplice."

The urge to throttle the man and the determination needed not to do so turned Guy's stomach. The most cynical part of him noted that Marbury no longer intended to use the two male servants from his country estate. He had caught a bigger fish.

Guy glanced around at the others to see how they reacted to the statement. No one blinked an eye. The man wanted a divorce and he was paying thousands of pounds to get it. They would give it to him, unless Guy missed his reading of their countenances.

Then it was his turn. He could lie. Deny that he had even touched Felicia. No one here could prove differently. The servant's testimony would be damaging, but alone it might not stand. It would be his word against Marbury's. The men here would believe him. Then he would have to live with his act of dishonour.

In his thirty-three years, he had only told one lie and Mrs Drummond had blistered his bottom and sent him to bed without supper. He had been five and it had been to protect Bell who had really been the one to climb down the apple tree outside the nursery window. Even thinking of not telling the truth closed his throat.

But the truth would ensure that Marbury got his divorce. It would ruin Felicia. No man would marry her. By law, her dowry would not go back to her. She would be completely dependent on what the final decision makers gave her for funds. Usually something, but it did not have to be much. Nor would she be able to work for money. No respectable household would hire her. She might get work as a maid for someone in the deep country who had no ties to London, a well-to-do farmer or clerk. Or even factory work. Both would be condemning a woman of her intelligence to a life of bare existence.

Then there was his situation. His reputation would be ruined. There was every possibility Miss Duckworth would call off. Then he would be without a wife to provide him with an heir.

It would be better for everyone if he lied.

He made eye contact with everyone in the room, lingering on Marbury, before he spoke. Felicia's soon-to-be ex-husband gloated, he was that sure of success. No matter what the cost, Guy could not lie, but he could make very clear where the blame lay.

He stood and started speaking. "Mrs Marbury came to my country estate after I found her in a coach wreckage. She was hurt. When she woke, she did not remember who she was. She thought she was a widow. I thought she was a widow." He told about the ice-skating accident and Felicia's subsequent fever and delirium. Now came the moment of truth. "While she was unaware of what was really going on, I seduced her."

Everyone stilled. Hands that had been fiddling with a pen, sheet of paper, or just twiddling, stopped. One man had been fidgeting in his chair. He froze. Marbury was stunned, his mouth hanging open like a beached fish.

No one had really expected Guy to confess to adultery. They had definitely not expected him to confess to taking advantage of a woman who did not know what she was doing. He was doubly ruined.

The Lord Chancellor rose before Guy could say anything else. Almost as though he wanted to forestall Guy from saying anything further that might be damning.

''Thank you, Lord Chillings. That will be all.''

Guy stood and without another word, left. He had done what he could for Felicia. Somehow, he did not think it was enough.

Chapter Fifteen

Felicia set down the cup of tea and took the note from Mary. Her hands shook as she ripped open the envelope. Edmund's scrawl covered the enclosed sheet of paper. *The divorce petition has passed the courts. Only a matter of time before it goes to Parliament. Your dowry is mine.* The fine vellum fell from her nerveless fingers.

She was as good as a divorcée. The courts had approved, there was no reason for Parliament not to agree.

Emotions overwhelmed her. On one level she was ecstatic about the news. On another she was sad. She had spent the last ten years of her life with Edmund, had borne him two children. Still, she was glad for her freedom.

Drained and exhausted, she let her head fall back onto the chair. She plucked the handkerchief from its place up her sleeve and blew her nose. She felt almost anticlimactic.

It was time for her to go home, except that home was Edmund's country estate. Well, she would go there and pack her belongings. She had some money left from the quarterly allowance Edmund had given her. She doubted he would give her more now. With any luck, Parliament would make Edmund give her a stipend of some sort, possibly her marriage jointure. But that was in the future. One thing at a time.

She rose. "Mary," she called.

The maid came scurrying from the bedroom. "Yes, ma'am?"

"Pack my things. We are leaving in the morning." Felicia stopped as she realized what she had said. "I will be leaving in the morning, Mary. You will return to Viscount Chillings."

"Never say so, ma'am." The maid's mobile face twisted in sadness.

Yet another loss, Felicia thought, her emotional exhaustion weighing on her like a ton of coal. "I wish I could take you with me, Mary, but I cannot. I don't even know how I shall care for myself. I have not means to care for another person. I am truly sorry. I will miss you."

The maid wrung her hands, her eyes wide and dazed. "Yes, ma'am. If it ain't too presumptuous, ma'am, did you get yer divorce? Is that why you be leaving?"

"I will. It is almost guaranteed. That is why I am leaving. I am done with my reason for coming to London. The sooner I leave, the better for all of us."

She had to turn away from Mary's anguished face. The servant only reflected back what she, Felicia, felt in her heart. It was better this way. She had failed to convince Edmund to give her support. She knew what Parliament would decide. There was no reason to linger.

Not even for Guy. In truth, it would be better for

him if she left. He had his own life to lead and he had
made it obvious that his future did not include her.

Felicia took a deep, shuddering breath. "I am going
for a walk." She needed to get out of the hotel. She
felt contained and claustrophobic.

"Yes, ma'am."

Mary went into the sleeping area and returned with
Felicia's pelisse and cape, which she helped Felicia
don. The maid then shrugged into her own outerwear.

Felicia looked at her. "I am going by myself."

"Ma'am?"

"By myself," Felicia repeated. "I need to be
alone."

"Beggin' your pardon, ma'am, but his lordship said
I was to go everywhere you went." The girl flushed
and her gaze dropped to the floor.

"His lordship is not my keeper, Mary. I am going
alone." She realized how harsh her voice had been and
forced herself to smile gently at the maid. "I will be
all right."

The maid watched her leave, helpless frustration writ
on her countenance. Felicia could sympathize. That
was exactly how she had felt about everything this past
year.

Passing through the lobby, she nodded briefly at the
desk clerk, the same one who had been on duty when
she had checked in two days before. It seemed an eternity ago. He made her a brief bow and his gaze went
to the stairs she had just descended.

Felicia knew he was looking for her maid. Out of
sheer perversity, she said, "I am going out on my
own."

A frown marred his previously impassive features.

"I am sure that madam knows what is best." His tone implied just the opposite.

"Yes, I do," Felicia said, the perversity still riding her.

She stepped outside into a blistering wind. Lifting her head proudly, she set off at a brisk pace towards Hyde Park. It would be dark soon, but she had plenty of time to walk there, go down some of the paths and return to the Pulteney without mishap.

She had many plans to make. Somehow she had to get out of London, but this time she would go by mail coach. As it was, she could barely afford that.

She grinned. She would have her bill for the Pulteney sent to Edmund. He was such a stickler that, hopping mad as he would be, he would pay the price. Besides, she had incurred the expense while his wife. He was legally responsible.

That was the only bright spot in her future.

Guy set the newspaper down with a snap. They had printed a lurid story of how he had been called to testify before a private hearing, telling how he had committed adultery with the soon to be ex-wife of Edmund Marbury. Failure to produce an heir was an underlying cause, but infidelity was the reason for the petition.

Marbury had promised to drag his name through the mud, and he had done so with a vengeance. Guy could have no more lied under oath than he could have kept from making love to Felicia. It was his bad luck that she was married to a man of Marbury's stamp.

Not only was his reputation ruined along with Felicia's, but he could expect a visit from Miss Duckworth shortly. Probably tomorrow, if not later today.

He stood and strode to the window, his Hessians

clicking sharply even through the thick Aubusson carpet. He yanked open the heavy green velvet curtains and stared out at the overcast day. Night would fall soon. One of the servants lit the gas-fed light in front of the house so that it cast a yellow glow into the gathering mist.

A small, slim figure hurried past, head bent. The servant he had sent to Felicia. Something was wrong or she would not be here. His heart skipped a beat.

He turned to the library door and waited, his patience a hard-won thread that threatened to break. At the first knock, he said, "Come in."

Oswald came in and said, "The girl, Mary, wishes to speak with you, my lord."

"It is fine, Oswald," he responded to the butler's look of disapproval. "Send her in."

"Yes, my lord."

Mary entered with her head down and her hands clasped tightly in front of her. Even though every nerve screamed for him to demand that she tell him why she was here, he did not. The girl was already afraid.

"I am glad you came, Mary," he said gently. "This is what we arranged."

She nodded. "Yes, my lord."

"So, tell me," he said, trying to keep his fierce need to know from making his voice harsh and scaring the girl. It would do no good and probably make her stumble around and take longer telling him.

"Mrs Marbury. She received a letter this afternoon. She threw it in the fire immediately she read it. Tomorrow she leaves town." Her voice broke. "She won't take me."

Leaving town? She must have got word about the court's decision. It had to be in favour of her husband.

As though it could have been anything else, given the reason Marbury was seeking a divorce.

"Thank you for coming so promptly, Mary. I will see that she does not leave without you." The girl looked up, her face alight with hope. "I promise."

"Thank you, my lord. Thank you so much. She means that much to me. She is kind." The words tumbled from the servant's lips.

Guy smiled, although he wanted the girl to leave. But he did not want to send her away until he was sure there was nothing else.

"Is there anything else I need to know?" He spoke calmly when he felt anything but.

"Yes,'m, my lord. I don't rightly know as it matters, but Mrs Marbury went out by herself. She would not take me."

"What?" Guy surged forward and it was all he could do not to shake the chit. "When? Where did she go? Why did you not follow her?"

Her eyes widened and she edged away from him. "She told me not to. She said she wanted to be alone, that she would not be gone long. She was going to a park. I came here."

He tamped down on his irritation. The girl had done her best, there was no sense in punishing her or making her feel worse than she already did.

"You did right, Mary. You may go now. Cook will see that you get something warm to eat and drink and a footman will take you back to the Pulteney. It is getting dark."

He turned his back to her, listening for the sound of the door closing behind her. Felicia was going to a park, probably Hyde Park since that was where he had taken her. Surely she would be back at the hotel by now, but he would make sure.

He strode from the room, calling, "Oswald, have the phaeton brought round. Jeffries," he yelled for his valet, "I need my greatcoat."

Five minutes later the carriage waited with two fresh horses and Jeffries helped him into his coat. The valet handed him his beaver and cane.

"Thank you," Guy said, already forgetting everyone but Felicia.

It was a quick trip to the hotel. The tiger jumped down and went to the horses' heads. Guy leaped gracefully to the ground.

"Walk them until I return, Jem."

"Of course, my lord," the tiger said, affronted that his master had even felt it necessary to tell him what to do.

Guy heard the tiger's tone and looked over his shoulder as he strode into the lobby. "I know you will do so, Jem, without my telling you. Habit."

And worry about Felicia and what foolhardy plans she was making. The desk clerk saw him immediately. A long-suffering look came over the man's face, but he smiled and came out from behind the desk.

"My lord, how may I help you?"

Guy glanced at him and kept going towards the stairs. "I am calling on Mrs Marbury."

"Mrs Marbury is not here, my lord."

Guy stopped. "Damnation." He whirled around. "Are you telling me she has not come back from her walk?"

"Yes, my lord."

"I am going after her. If she returns before I do, tell

her to stay here. I will be back.'' He glared at the other man, who remained impassive. "Do you understand?"

"I will tell her that you wish her to remain here, my lord, but I cannot make her do so against her will." He was stiff as a poker and about as emotional.

"See that you do," Guy said, scowling.

He strode from the building and signalled to the tiger who had walked the horses down the road. Determined to waste no more time, Guy lengthened his stride and went to them. He jumped into the phaeton before the tiger managed to stop the horses.

"We are for Hyde Park," he said, setting the carriage in motion.

"Yes, my lord," the tiger said, just barely catching hold of his perch in the back and leaping on to it.

Guy drove at a fast clip. Dusk had already set in. Most of the street lamps were lit, their golden glow a haze in the gathering mists. It was a bone-chilling damp that went through layers of clothing as though they were non-existent. Felicia should not be out in this weather.

Guy increased his speed.

He thought he saw a lone figure up ahead. He strained to see better, but all he could make out was something billowing out that must be a cape. Very likely a female, then.

Even as he caught sight of the walker, he heard a group of men, their voices raised in merriment—and inebriation, if their slurring and vulgar language were any indication. They were cultured. Young bucks on the town early.

Nearing, he heard a woman's voice—Felicia's voice—say, "Excuse me, please."

There was an absentmindedness in her tone that told

Guy she was thinking of something besides the group of young men who blocked her way. He spurred his horses on.

One of the men, his words less than distinct, said, "Excused all you want, mistress. Demme if we don't."

His cronies laughed.

Another one said, "You are about late without an escort."

Guy bristled at the leering note in the man's voice. He pulled the phaeton to a rocking stop and sprang down. He'd be damned if any man made importunate remarks to Felicia.

"You are in my way," Felicia said, her tone forceful now as though she finally realized the situation she was in.

"Not without a little sport," the first said.

Guy saw the group of drunken bucks close around Felicia. He was just in time.

"The only sport we will have here," he said dangerously, taking hold of the shoulder of one of the men and flinging him backwards, "is when we see how well you bounce."

The other man whirled around. "Just havin' some innocent fun. She's alone. Must be looking."

"You are mistaken," Guy said, his voice deathly cold.

"Guy," Felicia said, relief seeping from her words.

"Come away, Felicia," Guy said, keeping his attention on the two men.

The one he had flung to the ground now stood, brushing off his trousers. "No cause for violence," he said. "We did not know she was taken."

It was all Guy could do not to give the lout a facer.

"You should know not to accost any woman. A gentleman protects ladies. He does not molest them."

"Well—" one of them sputtered.

Guy turned his back on them, judging them harmless when confronted by a man. He took Felicia's arm and hurried her to the phaeton where he helped her up. He quickly joined her and set the horses in motion with a light flick of the whip.

"Thank you," Felicia said a little bit breathlessly. "I never thought something like that might happen."

"You did not *think*," Guy said harshly, his relief at finding her unharmed making him sharp. "You had no business being out alone. It is not done in daylight, let alone at dusk and night. This is not the country."

"I did not expect to be gone so long," she said, drawing away from him.

"That is no excuse."

His tone brooked no argument and she gave none. Neither one spoke.

With a supple movement of wrists, he guided the horses down the streets and around the corners while his mind was on Felicia. More aptly, his thoughts were on his worry for her and subsequent relief on finding her.

They arrived at the Pulteney Hotel before he realized it. He gave the reins to the tiger and went around the carriage to help her down. She ignored his hand and managed to clamber down without catching her skirts or falling.

She stalked by him, head high. He let her go. To stop her now would only cause a scene and the two of them were already providing more than enough fuel for the gossips' fire.

Instead, he followed her, fully intending to accompany her up to her room and see that she was safely behind the door. When he had learned she was out alone and then found her in a situation that might have harmed her if he had not shown, his only thought had been to protect her.

"I am perfectly capable of going on by myself from here, Lord Chillings." She gave him a look over her shoulder that would have made a less determined man leave.

He studied her, noting the mutinous look on her face. Her cheeks were red from the cold or her anger, probably both. Her glorious hair was dishevelled, looking as though a lover had run his fingers through the long strands and then haphazardly pinned them up in an effort to restore her look of respectability. He nearly groaned aloud as desire rose hot and heavy in him. Instead, he pivoted on his heel to leave.

"As you wish," he said, his voice heavy with sarcasm that he made no effort to soften.

He heard her soft gasp behind him but ignored it. She had told him to go, and this time he would. She was safe, and he needed to think, something he would not do if he stayed here.

It was a matter of moments before he was once more in the phaeton. Too irritated to go home, he directed the horses towards Brook's.

He entered the club and handed his hat and coat to the waiting butler. "Bring me a bottle of port." He took a step forward before adding, "Make that two."

The servant nodded and left to do Guy's bidding. Guy found a large leather chair in a dark corner and flung himself into it. The last thing he felt like was company.

The servant quickly delivered the two bottles and

poured Guy a glass of the dark red wine before leaving. Guy drained the glass and wondered if he should have ordered whisky. He would get that next.

The mood he was in, two bottles of port would not be nearly enough. He was furious with Felicia, but he was more angry with himself and the way he forgot everything but her. He had never been this way.

"Another night of inebriation, brother?"

Guy looked up to see Dominic. The younger man was immaculately dressed in evening wear. He had to admit that his brother cut a dashing figure.

"And what about you, Dominic? You don't normally haunt Brook's."

"Well," Dominic drawled, pulling up a chair and straddling it with his hands crossed on the back. "I just left Almack's and decided I was not ready to go home."

Guy's eyebrows lifted. "You? At the Marriage Mart? Whatever for?"

"Escorting Miss Lucy Duckworth." His voice lowered and he said in tones of disgust, "And the Sourpuss. She is like a burr on a horse's backside."

In spite of himself, Guy chuckled. "I fear she will pay me another visit tomorrow." He sighed, the humour gone, and poured another glass. "And she will be perfectly right to be upset."

"She ain't the only one," Dominic said. "Best check the Betting Book."

Guy groaned. "An entry about yesterday's proceedings?"

Dominic nodded.

Guy remembered only too well what entries in the Betting Book had caused his friends the Duke of Braborne and the Earls of Ravensford and Perth to do.

Marry their ladies. He was not eager to see what the entry about him said. It could be scathing in the extreme.

He levered himself up. "I suppose it will do no good to ignore it."

"Probably not," Dominic said, following him. "But I don't think you will call anyone out either. Big enough scandal as it is."

Guy shot him an irritated glance. "That bad?"

Dominic shrugged. "See for yourself."

It was a matter of minutes to the book. Guy emptied his glass of wine before opening the cover.

Viscount C. Engaged to one, fornicating with another. A monkey that he marries neither.

Guy closed the book very carefully, his glance going around the crowded room. Some of the men scattered around at tables and lounging in chairs watched him back. Others paid him no mind, whether from respect for his privacy or embarrassment over what they knew he would find in the book.

"Time I left, Dominic," He did not realize he used his brother's full name, something he only did when he was beyond anger.

"Right," Dominic said.

Guy took his coat, hat and cane from the waiting doorman and strode into the night, oblivious to his tiger standing ready with the phaeton.

"Pace us," Dominic said to the servant, for it was obvious Guy was beyond being aware of anything but his anger.

Haze hung over the streets, making it difficult to see more than a length ahead. Cold permeated everything, and ice was beginning to form.

"That entry was not made in jest or goodwill," Guy

said through clenched teeth. "Nothing like what Perth did."

Dominic nodded. "No. It was meant to hurt." He looked at his brother out of the corner of his eye. "I didn't know you had an enemy."

"Everyone has people who don't like them." He slapped his cane against his thigh in rhythm with his pace. "Very likely it is someone who thinks he is about to come into five hundred pounds. Bastard."

Dominic said nothing for some time. "What are you going to do?" he finally asked.

"What can I do? I am guilty of the charges. I even confessed before all the world because I could not bring myself to lie, no matter who the truth might hurt."

"You always were too honourable," Dominic said with only a hint of teasing in his voice. "I thank everything sacred that I am not like you in that aspect."

"And I can almost agree with you after that entry," Guy said wryly.

They walked on. The only sounds were those of the horse's hooves clopping behind them. It had started to drizzle minutes earlier, and still neither of them noticed.

"You are in for a hell of a day tomorrow, I wager." Dominic said.

Guy shrugged, the capes on his greatcoat lifting in the wind. "Unfortunately, nothing I don't deserve."

"What are you going to do about the Sourpuss?" Dominic asked, his voice curiously flat.

"Miss Duckworth?" Guy asked, intentionally using her proper name.

Dominic sighed gustily, his breath billowing out in frosty smoke. "Yes, her."

"I am going to let her berate me."

"Are you going to break off your engagement?"

"A gentleman does not cry off, Dominic," Guy said firmly.

"In your position, it might actually be better for her if you did."

"I can't argue that." Guy gave Dominic a curious look, noting his brother's fixed interest on the ground. "Why do you care? Afraid that if the family connection is severed you will be unable to court the fair Miss Lucy?"

"It would make it difficult if none of us were any longer welcomed in the Duckworth establishment."

"That has never stopped you before."

"True." Dominic seemed to perk up at the thought and started whistling a jaunty tune more often heard in pubs.

"We are here," Guy said, surprised at how quickly they had walked home.

"It is too early for me, brother. I have a gaming hell to supervise, so I'll be on my way since you seem to have everything under control."

"Take the phaeton," Guy said, signalling to Jem. "The weather is too nasty to be out and about. Not that an open carriage will be much better, but it will be faster."

"I wish you had thought of that thirty minutes ago," Dominic said, leaping into the carriage and waving with the whip.

Guy watched Dominic tool off down the road.

Tomorrow was going to be hellish. He had made a botch of everything. But worse, by his lack of control, he had ruined Felicia. Not only was she now a divorced woman, no longer acceptable to Polite Society, she was a confessed adulteress. People would not invite her to their home, nor would they hire her to care for their children or themselves.

Lord Holland had married his lady, but that had always been his intention. He, Guy, could not marry Felicia even if he wished. He was engaged, and as dishonourably as he had behaved towards Felicia, he could not compound his trespasses by jilting Miss Duckworth. He had given his word to Miss Duckworth.

Lord, but his passions had made a damned mess of everything.

Guy groaned aloud as he mounted the stairs to his front door. Felicia had been delirious that first time. He should have never got into bed with her and then he surely should never have made love to her. That experience had opened the floodgates of his passion, and he had never been able to get enough of her since.

He went through the door Oswald held open.

"Good evening, my lord," the butler said.

Guy nodded and continued to the library. What was he to do? He had ruined Felicia and could not marry her himself. He was engaged. Even if he were not, he could not marry her. He could not keep his hands off her or his body from wanting her. If he married her, he would have her pregnant within a fortnight, even though that was the last thing he would want to do. He knew he would.

He crossed to a side table and poured himself a tumbler of whisky. He had started this night determined to get drunk and forget all his worries. So far, he had been unsuccessful. But no more.

Tomorrow he had some hard decisions to make.

Chapter Sixteen

Guy studied himself critically. "I shall have a number of visitors today, Jeffries."

The valet twitched Guy's shirt points so they stood a little straighter. "Beau Brummell himself would approve of you, my lord."

Guy took the cravat Jeffries held out to him and carefully wrapped it around his collar. When he was satisfied, he slowly lowered his chin to set the crease. The Chillings's Crease was perfect.

"Very nice, my lord."

"Thank you," Guy said with only a touch of irony. He held out his arms and Jeffries helped him into a bottle-green coat perfectly tailored by Weston. "I shan't disgrace you. At least not in my clothing," he finished.

"You are a credit to my skills, my lord."

A knock on the door told Guy that his first visitor was here. He did not need Oswald to tell him Miss Duckworth was in the front drawing room. He had fully expected her to show as early as decently possible.

"Come in, Oswald."

The butler entered and held out a silver tray with a card. "You have a visitor, my lord." He raised one expressive grey brow.

"Miss Duckworth," Guy stated without looking at the card.

"Ahem, would that it were, my lord. This is a gentleman caller, or so he styles himself. A Mr Dunston." He sniffed. "He says he has urgent business with you."

Felicia's father. He had not expected this. But with hindsight, he should have.

"See that he is treated with all respect." When Oswald did all but look down his nose, he added, "He is Mrs Marbury's father."

If Oswald could look shocked, he did. His eyes widened a fraction and his shoulders drew up. But he said nothing scathing.

"Yes, my lord."

Guy watched Oswald walk stiffly to the door and leave. He wished he was sending the butler to deny Dunston's request for a meeting, but he could not. Felicia's father was here because Guy had admitted to adultery with the man's daughter. This promised to be a very awkward visit.

Guy headed out. The sooner he got the accusations and recriminations over with, the better. He still had to deal with Miss Duckworth when she arrived. After that, he had to go to the Pulteney and reason with Felicia.

He found Felicia's father where Oswald had put him, in the front drawing room. The man probably did not even know the honour accorded him. Oswald always put tradesmen in the small, dark antechamber nearer the back of the house. It was the butler's opinion that tradesmen did not visit lords.

"How do you do," Guy said, striding into the room. "I see you have been offered refreshments."

Dunston rose from the chair where he had been eating cakes. "Very nice, too."

"I am glad," Guy said. There was no sense in wasting time on polite nothings. "What can I do for you?"

Dunston took another bite of cake and studied Guy. His stare was an impertinence, but Guy admitted that the man had a right to be angry. The testimony had not been pretty.

"I'm sure your lordship knows why I am here."

"I have a good idea."

"You admitted yourself that you have been Felicia's lover. Bad enough her husband was divorcing her, you had to go and ruin all her chances of possibly making a good remarriage."

Guy kept quiet. There was nothing to say. But he felt the tension creeping into his shoulders and making them ache.

"It is your duty to make reparation." It was a statement that was more of a command.

Guy's sense of guilt evaporated to be replaced by mounting irritation. "To whom?"

"To me. To Felicia." Dunston smiled, but it was only a stretching of his lips while his eyes looked greedy.

"And what do you suggest?" Guy asked, his voice deadly calm.

"Marriage."

Guy managed not to say anything. Felicia had mentioned that her father was talking marriage, but he had never really thought the man was serious. Money and lots of it would have been more in keeping with his impression of Felicia's father. And money he could have given her.

"Marriage is out of the question," he said, his face drawn into sharp angles. "I am engaged."

"Break it," Dunston countered, his round face hardening. "You ruined my daughter, Viscount Chillings. I know you lords don't believe in paying the piper for your indiscretions, but this time I mean to see that you do. And the only acceptable payment is marriage."

Guy's eyes narrowed. "Does Felicia know you are here?"

"Ain't her business. She's about to be a single woman again. I am her father. I decide what she does, not her." He scowled and stuffed his beefy hands into the pockets of his old-fashioned breeches. "Ain't like she's a respectable widow with a jointure, her dead husband's name and mother of his children. She's disgraced. She's mine again. She's marrying you."

Guy drew himself up so that he looked down on Dunston. "You are despicable. But that is neither here nor there. I am not free to marry your daughter."

Dunston stepped up until he was chest to chest with Guy. "I mean to change that."

The urge to give the man a facer was nearly greater than his personal acknowledgment that Dunston had a right to be here demanding marriage for his daughter. Guy was not sure what angered him more, the fact that this man was toe to toe with him or the knowledge that he could not marry Felicia.

Guy did not step back as he stared into Dunston's close-set brown eyes. "Leave my fiancée out of this."

"I will do as I think necessary," Dunston stated.

With grim haughtiness, Guy said, "You have overstayed your welcome."

"Throw me out," Dunston challenged.

"I would throttle you if doing so would not send me to prison," Guy murmured, his voice low and colder than the outside weather. "Get out."

A knock on the door interrupted them.

"My lord," Oswald said entering without waiting for a reply. He stopped and looked at Guy. "You have a visitor."

Guy never took his eyes off Felicia's father. "Oswald, escort Mr Dunston out. Use a pistol to encourage him if needed."

"Yes, my lord," Oswald said with relish.

Guy glanced at his butler. "Bloodthirsty? I am surprised." He turned back to his adversary. "You heard my butler, Dunston. I have another guest. You are *de trop*."

Knowing that Oswald would see their unwelcome guest out, no matter what it took, Guy left. Miss Duckworth would be in the library. That was Oswald's second-favourite place to put people.

He paused outside the room long enough to adjust his coat so it lay more smoothly across his shoulders. Oswald had not named this visitor, but Miss Duckworth was the only one left except for Felicia, and she would not come to him.

He waved off the footman who waited to knock and announce him. He opened the door and walked in. She stood at a bookcase, looking over the titles.

"Miss Duckworth," he said.

"Chillings," she replied without looking in his direction. "So good of you to see me yet again on such short notice."

There was an edge to her voice, from tiredness or ire, Guy could not tell. He did not know her well cnough. Although he expected it was due to the situation he had landed her in. Betrothal to a man with his reputation could not be easy for a very proper woman.

"Please have a seat. Oswald will serve tea shortly. He is busy at the moment." He waved to a small grouping of chairs and tables.

She shook her head and finally turned to face him. "No, thank you. I won't be staying long." She pulled open the reticule that dangled from her wrist and fished something out. "I have come to return this."

The engagement ring he had given her sparkled on her palm. He had not expected this, but yet again, was not totally surprised. He had added insult to injury with his testimony.

"I see," he murmured. "You don't have to do this, you know."

She smiled sadly at him. "Oh, but I do. While ours was to be a marriage of convenience and neither one of us was in love with someone else, it was fine. But now, things have changed drastically."

Her wording was a little discommoding. "How do you mean?"

"Come along, Chillings. You are in love with Mrs Marbury, or as close to that emotion as you are capable of."

He drew back in affront. "I beg your pardon, Miss Duckworth. My attachment to Mrs Marbury is private."

Her mouth twisted wryly. "Very private indeed."

"My testimony was behind closed doors and supposed to have been confidential. Someone obviously felt he could derive some benefit by leaking the information to the press. I am sorry for that. I never intended to embarrass you like that."

She turned away again, her hands clasped behind her back. "As to that, I cannot say. The damage is done." She whirled back around and thrust out her fist. "Will you take this, or should I leave it on a table?"

He sighed. "On a table."

She did, the ring tinkling as it hit the polished wood and rocked from side to side. The centre diamond glittered like ice.

"I wish you only the best," she said, angling so that she would walk past him with more than enough distance separating them.

"Miss Duckworth," he said, causing her to pause. "I will send a notice to *The Times*."

"Of course."

She left without a backward glance. Guy stood where he was for several minutes, wondering if what he felt was joy at being freed from an engagement that had been getting more and more burdensome or disappointment that she had released him.

Now he truly could marry Felicia.

It was not a totally joyful realization. Wedding her was fraught with too many possibilities, not all of them pleasant or happy.

He crossed to the table where the ring lay and picked the piece up. The large centre diamond was flawless as were the smaller circling stones. He had gone to a jeweller with the intent to have them make a new ring for Miss Duckworth, but they had had this one already done. He had purchased it without a second's thought.

His family's traditional engagement ring was in a safe in this very room. He took the set wherever he went. His mother had given it to him when he asked Suzanne to marry him, thus when his parents had drowned the ring had been on Suzanne's finger.

He went to the fireplace and ran his fingers along the trim that went down the right side until they found the spot. A soft click and part of the wall opened. Behind was a lead-lined safe. He opened it and reached inside.

He pulled out a velvet bag and put the diamond ring into the safe. He sat in a chair and emptied the contents of the bag. A blood-red ruby, large as a thumbnail and set in platinum, fell into his palm. A thin band with channel-set rubies followed. The Chillings engagement and marriage rings.

He sat looking at them for a long time.

Felicia held tightly to the mail coach's strap. They were travelling the York Road, and she had got up at five-thirty in order to do so. The hackney she had ordered the day before had, thankfully, been waiting for her as she said farewell to a tearful Mary. She had been in this smelly coach since she boarded it at six-thirty at the George and Blue Boar in Holborn. She was more than ready to get out of it.

There were eight of them and they were squeezed in like fish wrapped tight, heads and tails touching. Most of them smelled worse than sardines. Felicia took as shallow a breath as she could and pressed her nose to the window.

The sun was well up and they had already changed horses several times. Hopefully, they would stop for lunch soon. She had had nothing to eat today and very little yesterday. She had been too upset over everything that had happened.

With luck, she would reach Edmund's country home before word of the divorce did. Although in all fairness to Edmund, his servants would not kick her out or refuse to allow her in to pack her belongings. She just did not want to go through the mix of stares, conjecture and pity that would be directed her way.

The coach hit a particularly bad rut and everyone went up in the air. Felicia came down with a hard thump and hoped her luggage was still strapped to the top.

Over the babble of her fellow passengers, she heard the crack of a whip. The carriage sped up.

"What is going on?" bellowed one of the male passengers, his ample form taking up more than his share of the seat. He stuck his head out of the window nearest him, having to lean over a woman who frowned fiercely. "Coachman, what are you about?"

Another man on the opposite side, who sat near the roadside window, stuck his head out. "Damn. The fool driver is racing a high-perch phaeton driven by some town swell. We are all in for it now."

The woman who was being squashed by the fat man, who still had his head out the window beside her, rolled her eyes. "Heaven help us. Plenty of innocent people have perished in mail-coach accidents caused by this very thing."

Another woman, thin, angular and plainly dressed, closed her eyes. Her lips moved with a fervency that spoke of prayer.

Felicia groaned in unison with the coach's springs and clung tighter to the strap. The vehicle rocked from side to side, the passengers hanging on for dear life. Heaven help the people on the roof. They would all be lucky to get out of this with only a few bruises.

Bang!

A gun. Someone was firing a gun. What was going on?

As suddenly as they had begun their mad dash, it ended. The coach started slowing down. They hit a rock or hole or something and she herd a crack. But they still moved forward until, finally, they stopped.

"You've no call to be firing at us." The driver's angry voice carried. "I thought you was wantin' to race, what with coming up on me all asudden like and trying to pass, nearly forcing me into the ditch."

"Count yourself lucky that I don't turn you in for reckless driving," another man said angrily in a deep, melting baritone.

Guy.

Felicia caught her breath. Her heart seemed to stop before starting again at a painfully fast pace.

The door farthest from her banged open, and Guy peered inside. "Felicia."

She stared at him. "I... Go away, Guy. Leave me alone. I won't become your mistress."

The prim woman gasped. "Well, I never. And on the King's road."

One of the men snickered.

Felicia came to a belated awareness of the people around her. In her shock at seeing Guy, she had forgotten she sat in a crowded carriage.

The door closed and Felicia sighed in relief. He was going to let her go. Yet, even though she knew this was the only way it could be, her relief quickly disappeared. Knowing what was right and reasonable was a far, painful cry from what she longed for.

She heard activity on the roof and shortly after a piece of luggage thumped to the ground. Suspicion began to grow.

Before she could step outside to see if it was her portmanteau on the ground, the door nearest her opened. Guy stood there. He reached in, grabbed her and hauled her outside.

Her momentum carried her into his chest. She looked up and his face was right there. She could see the individual hairs of his beard and the fine lines around his eyes.

"You are coming back to London," he said, his tone brooking no argument.

She squirmed against his hold, but quickly realized he was not going to let go. She stopped moving, but held herself stiffly and as far from him as she could, which was not far. She could smell the lime and musk that was so essentially him.

"And do what?"

He took a deep breath and his eyes closed. He looked like a man faced with a life and death decision. His eyes opened and he looked down at her.

"Marry me."

"What?" Startlement followed by pain followed by anger gave her strength. She wrenched herself from his hold. "Your jest is cruel."

He shook his head, making no move to grab her. "It is no jest. Miss Duckworth broke our engagement today."

"She… Over your testimony," Felicia said, all the fury draining from her. She was the cause of his misfortune. "I am sorry."

"Don't be. I am the one at fault, not you."

He rubbed at his beard, a habit she now knew that showed he was upset over something or thinking deeply. He did not touch her, but his gaze held her as surely as his arms could have.

"That does not mean you have to marry me."

He sighed. "No, it does not. I need a marriage of convenience and a wife to give me an heir."

"A marriage of convenience," she echoed faintly.

He did not offer love. But then he never had. She bit her lower lip. He was offering her security, which was nothing to disdain. But no love.

"Come away, Felicia." He finally reached for her arm. "This is not the place to discuss this."

She followed him without thinking. Her portmanteau was being loaded on his phaeton. Her travelling case was on the front seat. The other passengers in the mail coach had their heads out of the window, watching. The driver was on the ground, fists on his hips, frowning.

"You shoulda said you was after a female, gov'nor."

Guy flipped him a coin that flashed golden in the meager sunlight. "I did not have the opportunity," he said drily.

"Right-o." The driver deftly caught the piece of gold and pocketed it in one smooth gesture. That accomplished, he climbed back into the driver's seat. "Ever'one get ready. We're off." His whip cracked and the carriage set off one person lighter.

Felicia stared after the coach. What was she doing? But she knew. Guy might be offering a marriage of convenience with no love, but she was sorely tempted to accept. She loved him with enough passion for the both of them. It might be enough. It might have to be— for now.

Chapter Seventeen

Felicia's teeth chattered in spite of the blanket over her lap and the one around her shoulders. Her feet, in their half-boots, were like blocks of ice.

She took a surreptitious look at Guy. He had to be colder than she because he had already been driving this open carriage for hours.

As though sensing her study, he glanced at her. "I have changed my mind, we are going to The Folly. It is actually closer than going all the way back to London. A serious consideration in this weather."

"Ah," she murmured, "I shall be able to feel my feet soon."

His mouth twisted in a wry grin. "I was more concerned with catching up to you than in practicality. A closed carriage would have been better, but not as fast. I am sorry for the resultant discomfort."

She kept her gaze straight ahead. She had to know why he had made this decision, even though she was sure that she would not like his answer. Some things were better left unknown and this was probably one of them, but she could not marry him under the current conditions.

"Why did you come after me?" she finally managed to ask, her hands gripping the seat of the phaeton until she thought they would snap.

"I told you." His tone was clipped and no nonsense.

"Even though Miss Duckworth has broken your engagement, that does not make it necessary for you to marry me. Any woman would be glad to wed you and give you an heir."

His eyes narrowed as though what she had said angered him. "I am not marrying you to have an heir."

"But…"

Irritation radiated from every part of him. "I am marrying you because it is the right thing, the honourable thing to do."

His words hit a chord and she responded tartly, "Then don't bother. For I won't marry someone whose only reason is *honour*. You can just turn this carriage around and catch up with the mail coach, for I am not going anywhere with you."

His mouth tightened and his words were clipped. "You are coming to The Folly. As soon as your divorce is final, you will marry me. I have the Special Licence in my pocket."

"What? You are certainly confident."

His lips curled. "You have given me every indication that I am not repulsive to you."

She flushed and for the first time since clambering aboard the phaeton, she was warm. "Not very gentlemanly."

He flicked his whip over the lead horse's head. "As I told you long ago, I do what I must."

"And so do I. You can take me where you will, but you cannot force me to marry you."

"This is a pointless conversation."

She immediately bristled. "I don't agree." They entered a town before she could fully berate him. "Ah," she said as they pulled into the courtyard of a hotel. "The Swan. Annabell said you always stop here."

He glanced at her. "We cannot get to The Folly today, just as we could not get to London. Dark will be here shortly and, in this weather, we are better off here."

The fact that he was right did nothing to make her less disgruntled. He was being high-handed and autocratic. Traits she had nearly forgotten he had.

Ostlers grabbed the reins as the tiger jumped down to help. Guy climbed out and went around to help Felicia, but the mood she was in, she was already putting a foot on the ground. The innkeeper rushed out to greet them and stopped dead.

He bowed. "My lord Chillings." He turned to Felicia, "And madam." His gaze went beyond her as though he looked for someone else.

It was obvious he remembered her.

"We need two rooms," Guy said. He glanced at Felicia. "Dinner in our rooms."

A servant came out and Guy directed the boy to Felicia's luggage. It was then she realized Guy did not have any. She gave him a questioning look.

He shrugged. "I was in a hurry. I can make do. I've done so under worse conditions than these."

They followed the innkeeper inside to warmth and the smells of dinner. Instead of going to the private parlour, they went directly to their rooms. Felicia realized with a start that Guy's room was directly across the hall from hers. Embarrassment was her first reaction. The innkeeper, not seeing Annabell this time, had decided she and Guy were intimate.

She cast one fulminating look at Guy and went into her room. Her luggage was already here and she quickly got dressed for bed. The day had been long and all she wanted was food and sleep.

Tomorrow she would deal with Lord Chillings. She was not going to his estate to await his pleasure on marrying her.

Felicia descended the inn's stairs the next morning feeling human. Her clothing had been brushed and pressed while she slept. She had had plenty of tea and toast and was ready to face Guy. To her chagrin, she found him outside, impatiently waiting for her.

"We have a long way to go," he said in greeting.

The same boy who had carried her bags upstairs the night before scurried around her and deposited her luggage in the phaeton. Guy tossed him a coin for his effort. Felicia frowned.

"I am positive I can catch a coach from here to my destination, my lord," she said, staring defiantly at him.

He glanced at her. "I am sure you could. But you are not. Now get up."

She ground her teeth. "I think not," she muttered.

He stalked up to her. "If you persist in this, you will cause a scene. Believe me, they will remember it when word reaches them of my testimony, as it will. You and I are the latest scandal."

His words took the fire out of her. He was right. A fight here would just be more trouble. She shook off his helping hand and climbed in on her own, only catching her skirt once. The boy handed up the blankets, which she draped around herself. This promised to be another very cold ride.

Fortunately, it was not raining. The roads would have been quagmires. As it was, the ruts were still deep and in their way just as bad because the ground was frozen. They moved slowly and steadily in spite of the conditions.

Felicia, determined to work things through before they reached The Folly, said firmly, "I am not marrying you under the circumstances."

He did not even bother to look at her. "What will you do? You have no money, and I doubt your father will take you in."

"I will become a governess," she said with more bravado than sense.

He laughed, curt and harsh. "I doubt that. No one will hire you after the divorce and my testimony. You should know that someone leaked to the press what I said, nearly to the word. We are both doubly ruined."

The breath caught in her throat. "I did not know that."

"I did not think you did."

She stared at nothing. "Well," she finally said, "I did not really think anyone would hire me. I will just have to think of something else. There must be something. I am a good seamstress. I could do that."

He snorted. "Now you are grasping at straws. Face facts, Felicia, you have to marry me. You have no other options unless you wish to starve."

She closed her eyes and wished she could as easily close her ears to his words. Her voice shook. "I can go back to my father. He won't like it, but he cannot turn me out."

"He can and he will," Guy said, his voice laced with anger. "I can guarantee you that he will."

"How?" Much as she hated saying or even thinking

the next words, she did. "If I agree to remarry at his choosing, he will be furious with me now, but he will take me in. I am a commodity to him."

"And who could he find to marry you?"

"I don't know, but I imagine that if he offers enough money, someone will take me off his hands. Edmund would have done so if I had agreed to give him more children."

By the time the words were out of her mouth, she felt totally defeated. Everything she had hoped to gain by going to London was ashes.

"Have you spoken to your father?" Guy asked, a funny note in his voice. "Since the testimony?"

She shook her head. "No. I left."

He did not speak for some time. "Then you don't know that your father has already picked your new husband."

She jerked. "What? How could he?" An awful suspicion caught her. "How do you know?"

"Because Dunston told me."

"You?" she asked, aghast, her voice barely loud enough to hear.

"Yes."

She collapsed back in the seat. "He has gone too far," she said. Then another thought hit that brought with it more pain. "That is why you asked me to marry you."

He did not answer.

She turned away, wishing she could jump out of the carriage and never have to face this man again. Through no fault of his, he had been dragged into the sordid details of her life. And now her father had tried to make him marry her.

When she thought she could speak without sobbing, she said, "I am sorry. Truly sorry."

"Don't be," he said curtly. "Your father cannot make me offer marriage unless I wish it. I have offered."

Felicia sat, dazed and hurt. She did not know what to answer. She wanted to marry him. Had wanted to do so since the moment she saw him, coming towards her bed, when she did not even know who she was.

"Why?" she finally asked.

He shrugged, the capes of his greatcoat filling with the breeze. "Not for an heir."

"Why?" she asked again, wanting him to say something she knew he would not, yet unable to resist the need to try and make him say he loved her.

"Honour, as I already said."

His gloved hands tightened on the reins and the horses shied just a little. He was too good a driver to lose control.

"Honour and nothing else?"

With an abrupt twist of the wrist, he pulled the phaeton to the side of the narrow road and stopped. Still gripping the reins in one hand, he reached for her with the other. Hope rose in Felicia's heart.

He pulled her to him. His mouth descended on hers. "Passion, Felicia, passion such as I have never known before."

His kiss was brutal, consuming and arousing. She sank into sensations. Still, a part of her cried. Passion, not love. It had never been love for him. But at least he felt something for her, a powerful emotion that might become love—some day.

He finally released her and Felicia swayed. Fortunately, he kept hold of her arm, or she would have fallen backwards and tumbled to the ground. Her mind still whirled.

"That is why I am marrying you, Felicia," he said, his deep voice a harsh rasp.

She lifted her gloved fingers to her swollen lips, her eyes, wide, watched him. Surely passion such as theirs was a start. Love would follow.

"I accept," she said softly.

"You won't regret it, Felicia," he said. "I promise you that."

She nodded. There were no words she could say because she could not tell him her hope.

It was late afternoon with dusk rapidly approaching when they pulled into the circular driveway of The Folly. Oswald was still in London, so a footman met them. Felicia soon found herself in her old suite, where she collapsed on to the bed. She felt as though she had come home after a long and perilous journey.

She fell instantly asleep, feeling safe.

Felicia started awake.

Sitting up, she realized she had fallen asleep on top of the bed still in her travelling clothes. There was a fire in the grate that sent tendrils of warmth her way.

Movement caught her eye. Guy.

He had pulled the slipper chair near the bed and sat there watching her. He had changed into his robe.

"I did not mean to wake you," he said. "But it's probably best. You did not look comfortable, just exhausted."

She stood, feeling much less vulnerable on her feet than lying across her bed. "Why are you here?"

He got to his feet and dug a small velvet box from his pocket. "To give you this."

She took the container.

"Open it," he said when all she did was look at it.

"A ring?"

He nodded. "The Chillings engagement ring."

Shivers chased down her spine. With fingers suddenly clumsy, she fumbled open the top. Inside was a magnificent ruby ring.

"This is beautiful," she said softly. "I cannot wear this. What if I lost it?"

"You said you would marry me," he replied. "Or have you changed your mind again?"

She shook her head. "No. Only I would feel uncomfortable wearing something this valuable."

He shrugged and stuffed his hands into the robe's pockets. "All the Chillings's brides wear it. It has not been lost for over a hundred years."

She looked from the ring to him. "You did not give this to Miss Duckworth. I would have seen it if you had."

He turned his back to her and went to the fireplace. "No, I did not. The arrangement between her and me was too impersonal. I might have given it to her later."

"Did Suzanne wear this?"

As soon as the words were out of her mouth, Felicia regretted them. This was none of her business.

"Yes. She loved the ring."

Felicia nodded. "I can see why."

"Put it on," he said harshly.

She stared at the piece of jewellery. Surely he cared for her. Surely he felt more than passion. He had only given this ring to one other woman, and he had loved her.

Slowly, her fingers shaking, she took the ring from the box. She set the box on the table and slid the ring on to her finger. It fitted perfectly. She heard him release his breath.

"For a minute, I thought you would not do it," he said.

She held her hand up so she could admire the ruby. It flashed like blood in the light from the fire. "It is lovely."

"Burmese. A Burmese ruby," he murmured. "They are the finest."

Still looking at the ring, she said, "You loved Suzanne a great deal."

He started. "Where did that come from? We were talking about the ruby."

"Yes, I know," she murmured. "But she was the last to wear it. Putting it on reminded me of her."

He pushed off from the mantel and headed to her. He caught her chin in his hand and lifted it so that she looked at him.

"What Suzanne and I had was different from what you and I share."

She gave a tiny, brittle laugh. "You had love."

His eyes widened before narrowing. "Yes. On my part it was more the love of an older brother for a woman he had watched grow up. Oh, I won't lie to you, Felicia. We obviously consummated our marriage, but what I felt for her was nothing like what rages through me when I am near you—or even when I am not." His lips twisted into a self-derogatory smile.

She watched him, waiting and hoping he would say something about love. Yet knowing he would not. He did not surprise her.

Finally, he released her and stepped away. She did nothing to stop him.

"I am leaving tomorrow," he said. "Oswald and Mrs Drummond should arrive. As will Mary."

"You are leaving?" she managed to say around the lump in her throat. "Why?"

He studied her. "Surely you know."

She shook her head. "No, I don't. You have never fled from me before."

"I was never engaged to marry you before. I was never so afraid of losing control with you before."

His vehemence surprised her. "I don't understand."

He scowled and rubbed his long fingers through his beard. "I don't want to get you pregnant, Felicia. I don't want to lose you like I did Suzanne."

She moved towards him, but he spun on his heel and left. It was as though he truly feared what he might do. She did not understand any of this, and he had not given her an opportunity to talk with him about it.

She could follow him. She knew where his rooms were, but what then?

She did not know. She felt totally helpless when she should feel completely happy.

She hoped more than anything that this marriage would not turn out as badly as her first. Surely not. She loved Guy desperately. He desired her. It was a start. It had to be for it was all she had.

Chapter Eighteen

The Folly, six months later...

Felicia stood dressed in lavender trimmed with Brussels lace. Annabell stood as her bridesmaid. The minister who presided over the small family chapel read the marriage ceremony. At first the minister had hesitated, but his living was given to him by Guy and the Special Licence entitled the possessor to be married anywhere, any time, by anyone.

Guy stood dressed in grey with a heavily embroidered waistcoat and matching satin breeches and silk stockings. Dominic stood as his groomsman.

The four of them, Oswald, Mrs Drummond and Mary were the only ones present. Felicia had not asked her father.

Felicia watched her future husband's face. He looked solemn, not joyful or even glad. For the hundredth time since he had collected her from the mail coach, she wondered if she had done the right thing in accepting his offer. It was too late now.

She turned her attention back to the minister. He

droned on until reaching the part where he asked, "Do you, Felicia Anne Marbury, take this man as your lawfully wedded husband, to have and to hold in sickness and in health until death do you part?"

She looked at Guy who was watching her with a quiet intensity that made her nerves jump. "Yes," she whispered.

The minister said, "Do you, Guy William Chillings, take this woman as your lawfully wedded wife, to have and to hold in sickness and in health until death do you part?"

"I do," Guy said firmly, his voice carrying in the stone interior of the chapel.

"The ring."

Dominic stepped forward with a gold band inlaid with channel-set rubies. Guy took it, never taking his eyes from Felicia. She held her hand out, and he slid the circle over her finger until it lay next to the engagement ring with its flawless ruby.

"I pronounce you man and wife." The minister beamed at them. "You may kiss the bride," he prompted.

Guy looked to her for permission. She managed a tiny smile which he took as welcome.

His mouth moved on hers like a butterfly, then he was gone. Brief as the encounter had been, she felt as though he had ravished her. She tingled everywhere.

It was also the first time he had touched her since he put the engagement ring on her finger six months before. She had decided that not only was theirs to be a marriage of convenience, but that he no longer desired her. It was as though his proposal killed whatever else he might have felt for her. She had spent the last six months living at The Folly with Guy never coming to stay at his own home. Still, rumours had reached her that the ladies of the *ton* shunned him. The members of that elite group would never accept her. Even after she and Guy wed, she would not be acceptable to the sticklers.

She felt Annabell's fingers on the small of her back and realized belatedly that Guy had turned to go, his elbow crooked for her to tuck her hand into. She did so, feeling awkward and gauche. Together, they walked sedately down the aisle to the outside door. They passed through the portal into fresh air.

Even the sun smiled down on them. The daffodils were in full bloom, their butter-yellow and pale white clusters the harbingers of the summer to come.

Neither spoke as they made their way down the paved path to the main house. Behind them Annabell and Dominic conversed in hushed tones. Felicia caught mention of a man named Fitzsimmon, but nothing more.

The servants awaited them at the entrance, lined in order of precedence. Felicia nodded and shook hands with every one, right down to the lowest scullery maid.

Very few people came to the after-wedding breakfast. Not many had been invited.

Dominic rose and lifted his champagne glass. "To the happy couple. May they live long and prosper." Everyone clapped and drank their fine French wine.

Annabell rose. "May they be fruitful." Laughs accompanied this toast. "For Dominic and I are not interested in taking over this elephant," she finished, waving her arm to encompass The Folly. "This is Guy's passion and should go to the heirs of his body."

Felicia blushed at such bold speaking. Fortunately all she had to do was smile at their guests.

Guy stood. "Thank you all for being here. Please enjoy yourselves."

He held out his hand to Felicia, who took it and rose to stand beside him. His fingers were warm and strong around hers. She needed to know that he was here. All through the past months she had wondered why he had really stayed away. Together they left the dining room. In the foyer, he released her.

"Mrs Drummond has arranged for your things to be moved into the suite adjacent to mine. The rooms were my mother's. If there is anything you want changed, by all means tell Mrs Drummond."

She nodded.

He gave her a curt bow and turned away. "Guy," she said hastily, "where are you going?"

Even as she said the words, she regretted them. After he took her off the mail coach and sent her here to live without him, everything had changed between them. And not for the better. Now, he had married her after six months of not even writing to her. Why did she think he would give her an explanation? He had not sent even a note during the last half-year. It had been as though she had ceased to exist for him. Then, suddenly, he was here with Annabell and Dominic, saying it was time to marry.

"Out." His tone brooked no argument. Nor did he bother to look at her.

She watched him go, and blinked rapidly to try and stop the moisture from becoming tears. This was her wedding day, not a funeral.

But it was hard.

* * *

Felicia dismissed Mary. "You may go, Mary. And don't bother tomorrow morning. I intend to sleep late after today."

"Yes, my lady." Mary bobbed a curtsy, her face flaming.

Felicia's mouth twisted. Mary thought her mistress and master were going to make love all night. Nothing could be further from the truth. Much as Felicia might wish it otherwise.

Resigned to a wedding night spent alone while her groom was goodness only knew where, Felicia picked up Jane Austen's latest book and sat by the fire. She huddled under a cashmere blanket and the heavy wool of her robe.

She was well into the story when she heard a soft knock coming from the door that connected with Guy's room. She twisted around in time to see him enter, leaving the door open behind him as though he intended to leave in just a minute.

"Felicia," he said, "may I come in?"

She nodded. "You are the master of the house."

Her words were loaded with bitter irony. He was the master and he had made it abundantly clear that she might be the mistress legally, but any woman could fill her position in his life. He might just as well have wedded Miss Duckworth for all the passion there was in this marriage.

He moved closer so the light from the fire and the brace of candles she had lighted to read by showed him better. He wore the same dressing gown he had worn her first night here, when he had interrogated her mercilessly. A glowing white linen shirt, open at the neck, filled in the V formed by the robe crossing his chest. Black satin trousers showed beneath the robe's hem.

And like that night so long ago, she found her pulse

speeding up. He was not a classically handsome man, but the angle of his jaw, the slant of his nose, the full sensuality of his mouth all combined to make her want him with an unrelenting ache.

Would that he felt the same about her—still.

"I wanted to give you this," he said, holding out a velvet case. "It is traditionally given to the Chillings brides on their wedding night."

"Another gift of jewellery?" she asked, not trying to hide her bitter sarcasm.

"Just open it, Felicia," he said.

She did so. This time her fingers did not shake as they had when she had opened the box with the engagement ring. Inside was a pearl and emerald choker. Nestled in the strands of pearls were matching ear drops.

"Oh," she breathed. "It is even more beautiful than in the picture."

"I was going to give it to you to wear at the wedding," he said, stepping forward and taking it from the box. "But it did not go with the lavender you were wearing."

"No." She finally smiled. "It would not."

"Turn around," he said, "and I will hook it."

She did so without thought. It was such a stunning piece of jewellery and it did not have the same emotional impact as the engagement ring had had for her.

His fingers played along her nape as he fastened the necklace. His breath brushed her sensitive skin. Was she the only one feeling this deep need?

"There," he said finally, his voice a rasp.

When he did not step away from her, she turned, her shoulder touching his chest in the process. Completely facing him, she stopped. Inches separated them, but it could be miles. She did not reach for him, only looked at him.

Guy's jaw hardened. "Don't look at me like that."

She notched her chin up. "Like what?"

His hands clenched at his sides. "Like you want me to make love to you."

She flushed, but did not turn away. "We are married."

His Adam's apple moved as he swallowed. "Convenience."

"Ah, yes," she said, sarcasm dripping from every word. "You do seem to have a fondness for convenience."

"And what do you suggest I do, Felicia?" he said coldly, pointedly. "Make love to you, get you pregnant with my child and then watch you die bearing that child?"

If he had hit her, she could not have been as surprised. "That is a macabre chain of events," she said carefully.

She was beginning to understand his behaviour, or so she hoped. If his real reason for avoiding her these past months was fear she would die birthing his heir, then there was hope for them. He had to care for her.

He smoothed down his beard with one long finger. "It is a very possible scenario."

"Why?" she asked softly. "Because that is how you lost Suzanne?"

He nodded. "It is not uncommon."

"You need an heir."

He shrugged, turned and walked away from her. "Dominic can provide one. Even Bell can if Dominic does not. We Chillings are fortunate in that regard."

"I see," Felicia said, taking a step towards him,

careful not to be too aggressive. "You have no intention of making love to me because you do not want me to die in childbirth."

He tensed. "Yes," he said, his voice full of pain.

She shook her head slowly and took another step toward him. "I have already had two children, Guy. My chances of dying like Suzanne are very slim." Her mouth quirked just a little. "If I were a gambler, I would put odds on my survival."

"What kind of odds?" he asked, watching her with eyes full of hunger.

"Ninety-nine to one," she murmured, drawing closer.

"You exaggerate."

"Perhaps, but none the less they are very good." She paused when there was only a foot separating them. "And you need an heir. Why should you put that burden on Dominic or Annabell, for I would wager they do not want it?"

His mouth twisted. "You know them well."

"Guy," she said softly, coaxing him with her tone, "do not push me away because you are afraid. I am not, and it is my life."

Instead of closing the distance between them, she reached up and undid the bow that held her nightdress closed at the neck. Guy's gaze darted to the hollow at the base of her throat. She could not stop the smile that curved her lips.

Moving slowly, wondering if other women did this sort of thing and not caring one way or the other, she lifted the fine muslin over her head. She wore nothing underneath.

He took a step back, but his gaze roved hungrily up

and down her body. His robe parted where his response to her protruded. Her smile widened.

She pulled out the ribbon holding her hair in a braid and started combing her fingers through the length. "Would you help me?" she asked, knowing how much he liked her hair.

He gulped.

She closed the distance between them. "You might as well, Guy, for I intend to have you. We are married now. You must do your husbandly duties."

His reaction was swift and fierce, as though a dam had broken inside him. He grabbed her to his chest and devoured her lips. The dread of his rejection that she had held at bay slipped away. She wrapped her arms around his neck and held tightly.

The fine silver thread on his robe pricked at the tender flesh of her bosom. It was shockingly arousing while his mouth was on hers and his maleness pressed to the juncture of her thighs. When he lowered his mouth to her bosom, bowing her back so that his loins pressed into hers and his teeth caught her nipple, Felicia exploded.

She gasped with surprise and pleasure.

He released her only to gather her into his arms and carry her to the bed. She lay there watching as he pulled his robe off, then his shirt and then his trousers. He never took his gaze off her, and then he was beside her, stroking her, stoking her desire once more.

She rose to meet him, her mouth grazing over every part of him. Her hands explored him as intimately as was possible. His breathing became ragged.

He was above her, then below her. She straddled his hips, her eyes never leaving his. She saw surprise move over him as she caught him in one hand and slowly guided him inside her. She did not stop her downward movement until he was deeply buried.

She bit her lower lip at the intense pleasure. He remained perfectly still, as though to move would shatter everything. She began the age-old rhythm.

His hands went to her hips and guided her, speeding them up, then slowing them down. It was sheer bliss.

His fingers tightened on her skin and he lifted her up. Suddenly aware of what he intended, she shook her head.

"No."

She gripped his wrists and took him by surprise. She pulled his hands from her and sank down, deeply, irrevocably. She gasped. His moan joined hers as he bucked, taking them both over the edge.

She collapsed on top of him, still holding him tightly inside her body. She never wanted to let him go.

He took the decision away from her. This time when he lifted her, she let him. She sank down on to the bed beside him.

"Why, Felicia?" He lay on his back, one leg bent at the knee, one arm flung over his eyes.

"Because I love you. Because I could not stand to be married to you, to see you every day and not make love with you. It would have killed me more surely than giving you a child."

"It was only once. I can hope that nothing will come of it."

She sat bolt upright and then straddled him. "I intend to pursue you morning, noon and all night."

She rotated her hips, a fleeting sense of embarrassment at her boldness heating her already warm skin. She pushed the hesitation away. She was fighting for her happiness.

She moved again, an invitation so erotic that Guy instantly accepted before he even knew what was happening. She rode him to ground until both of them panted in exhaustion and release.

"You cannot keep away from me forever, Guy," she said.

"You are a determined woman, Felicia."

His chest rose and fell as he took gulping breaths of air. His entire body felt like he had been well used. Satisfaction curved his lips.

She leaned over him, her mouth finding his nipple while her fingers went lower. It was minutes only before, still inside her, he found his pleasure yet again.

"It has now been three times," she said, her lips swollen and her eyes dilated with desire. "Do you think we can make it four?"

He groaned. "Felicia, I am not a stud."

Her smile was seduction itself. "I think we can remedy that, my love."

He gasped as she lifted off him only to take him into her mouth. It was long, agonizingly pleasurable minutes before he was able to think coherently again.

"Enough," he panted.

"Promise me you will never deny me or yourself again, Guy?" Her fingers took the place of her mouth.

"Gads," he moaned. "I don't...know....how much...more I can...take..."

"Promise?"

"I..."

"Guy," she said, "I am not a hothouse flower to be cosseted and left to live a sterile life. I love you. I want to bear your children. I will bear them, will you or nill you."

He looked at the determination written over her face

and knew she spoke the truth. She knew the power she wielded over him and she would not hesitate to use it. His good intentions would be as naught when she began to caress him.

With the little energy he had left, he caught her face in his hands and kissed her. "You are stubborn, my love. Stubborn. I pray to God that you are as strong as you claim, for you have made it abundantly clear that I cannot resist you when you set your mind to having me."

She returned his kiss with ardour. "I love you, Guy William Chillings. Our children will love you."

Epilogue

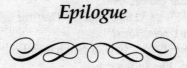

The Folly, nine months later...

"Guy. Guy," Felicia said, pushing her husband in the ribs in an attempt to wake him.

They lay in his large four-poster bed where they had slept every night since their wedding. The fire was dead and the room was freezing.

"Guy," Felicia tried again, poking him harder this time.

"Wha—?" He raised up to one elbow. "Is it...?"

"Yes," she said, joy filling her voice. "I...oh, that was particularly strong."

"Right." Naked as the day he was born, he jumped from the bed and groped in the dark for his robe. He pulled its warmth on and yelled, "Jeffries."

Felicia, both amused and exhausted from the last nine months and knowing the next hours were going to be trying, laughed. "Guy, I have done this twice before. Calm down."

"Jeffries," he yelled again.

Felicia angled herself into a sitting position and

rested. "Guy, please help me up. It will be easier and quicker if I can walk some."

He rushed to her side. "Don't get up, Fel. I need to light a lamp. The doctor did not say anything about walking. Stay there," he said more forcefully when she tried to stand on her own.

"Jeffries," he yelled again. "Drat the man. Where is he when I need him?"

"Sleeping, Guy," Felicia said patiently. "I need Mrs Drummond. Please fetch her."

"I cannot leave you," he said stubbornly. "Jeffries will fetch her."

"Jeffries isn't here to get her, Guy. You are."

He rubbed his beard. "Promise me you won't get up."

"I won't promise you anything, Guy. You need to trust my judgement. I know what I am doing."

He scowled. The yellow glow from the gas lamp he had lit showed him her grimace of pain. "All right. Stay here."

She smiled. "There is nowhere I can go in this condition," she said, humour lacing her words.

He cast one last anxious glance at her and raced from the room. Felicia's smile disappeared as another cramp spasmed through her abdomen. She had never told Guy that her last delivery had been long and difficult. It would have done no good and worried him to the point that he would have been impossible to deal with through the pregnancy. But Mrs Drummond knew and had found a very good midwife.

She struggled to her feet and took slow, deep breaths in an effort to control the pain. Her water broke.

"My lady," Mrs Drummond said, coming through

the door with Guy close behind. "I have sent for Mrs Jones."

"I have sent for the doctor," Guy added.

"Thank you, both of you. *Oh!*" Felicia gasped.

Mrs Drummond turned back to Guy. "It is time you left, my lord. This is women's work."

Guy's mouth tightened.

Felicia waddled over to him and put a hand on his arm. "It is going to be fine, my love. A woman knows these things."

He stared at her, his pupils dilated. "I will be right outside." He grabbed her by the upper arms and pulled her to him, burying his face in the crook of her neck. "I love you so much, Fel. Don't leave me."

She slid her arms around his waist and turned her head so that her lips brushed his cheek. "Never, my love. Everything is going to be fine. I promise."

He took a deep, shuddering breath and released her. With infinite tenderness, he smoothed the loose tangles of hair back from her face and hooked them behind her ears. Just hours before he had lost himself in its luxuriant length.

"I love you," he murmured, kissing her lightly on the lips.

She nodded, tears at his tenderness and concern blurring her vision. She heard the door close behind him. Then Mrs Drummond was at her side.

Guy paced the hallway.

Annabell stuck her head out of the bedroom. "Guy, go to the library. You are not doing any good torturing yourself like this, and you already look awful."

He turned a haggard face to her. His hair was unkempt. He was still in his house robe with nothing on beneath. He was a mess.

"No. I'm not leaving until I see my wife and child safe and healthy."

She shook her head. A moan of pain came from inside. "I must go. This shouldn't be much longer, Guy."

The door slammed shut.

Guy stood still looking at the place where Bell's head had been. This should be going very fast. Mrs Drummond had assured him that Felicia would have no trouble. Felicia had assured him.

He was glad Bell had come to stay with them this last month. She had been a good companion for Felicia and a rock of strength for him. She remembered Suzanne's lying-in and oftentimes understood his fear where no one else could. Felicia had been so positive that everything would be fine. He had learned that about her these last months.

When he first met her, she had been recovering from grief. As their marriage and their bond had strengthened, her naturally positive outlook on life had surfaced. She had brought him great happiness. He could not lose her now. He could not.

He turned to go down the opposite length of the hall. Ten paces later, he heard the door open.

"Guy," Bell said.

He whirled around, dread turning his stomach to mush.

"Guy," Bell said, "you have a healthy son." Her smile broke through. "And an exhausted, but otherwise fine, wife."

His entire body slumped with relief, followed by an energy he had thought long gone in the wake of the last hours. He sprinted to the door and into the room. He sensed Bell and Mrs Drummond leaving, but he did not say anything to them. He couldn't. His entire focus was on his wife.

Felicia lay propped on a mountain of pillows, her hair spread around her like a copper-shot satin skirt. Her face was white from exhaustion and her eyes bruised, but she smiled.

"Guy—my love—" she said softly, "you have an heir."

He closed the ground between them and took her hand and raised it to his lips. "More importantly, I have you safe."

Snuggled into the curve of her arm, his face nuzzled to her breast, was his son. A tuft of dark hair sprouted from the baby's head. Joy and amazement filled Guy.

"He has blue eyes," Felicia said softly. "But that may change. All babies have blue eyes."

He looked at her, not understanding the importance of this. "He is perfect no matter what colour his eyes. He is ours."

She continued to smile, but he could see she needed rest. He circled to the other side of the bed and got in next to his wife and son. Careful not to squash the baby, he gathered mother and child into his arms.

Felicia sighed and laid her head on Guy's shoulder. "You see," she said, her voice drifting. "I told you not to worry, that everything would be fine. I was right."

He stroked her hair, his fascinated gaze on his son's face. "Yes."

"And the next one will be easier still," she murmured, falling into sleep.

Love such as he had never thought possible filled Guy. He looked in wonderment at his family. Miracles did happen.

* * * * *